Twin Spirit Star

A Fantasy Novel

River Horns

Chapter 1

Kauko and Bamei

In the southwestern frontier of the Daze Kingdom, a vast expanse of lakes and towering mountains intertwined to create a grand yet serene natural landscape. The wind gently brushed over the tranquil waters, carrying a thin mist, while the distant peaks seemed draped in a delicate veil. Hidden within this natural tapestry lay a mystical mountain, unknown to most. This mountain, towering into the clouds, appeared isolated from the mortal world, shrouded in an impenetrable fog of immortality—calm, profound, and enigmatic. Those who attempted to approach it inevitably lost their way in the alluring mist, vanishing into the boundless expanse.

Only on certain quiet nights, when the moonlight caressed the lake's surface, faint celestial melodies drifted on the wind, drawing listeners into deep reverie.

On this mountain lived a Taoist priest who called himself "Dapeng" and named the mountain "Tian Mountain" (Heavenly Mountain). Often, he stood at the mountain's summit, on the edge of a cliff, his silver-gray hair flowing over his shoulders as he gazed into the distance, his eyes deep and contemplative, as if observing the myriad changes of the world below. Immersed in his own world, he gently touched the ancient stone steps, each inch etched with the marks of time and history. His age, like the mountains and rivers, was silent yet profound, carrying an unfathomable depth. In this secluded realm, he resembled a solitary painter, quietly crafting his own masterpiece—a canvas that held centuries of waiting and longing...

He had once been the personal guard of Marshal Tianpeng in the Heavenly Court, descending to the mortal world alongside the marshal after their banishment. The marshal reincarnated as the infamous "Zhu Bajie," while he became a reclusive Taoist priest.

Now, Dapeng sat on a stone stool in the corner of an orchard, holding an ancient book—Kauko's textbook. He flipped through the pages, but his gaze occasionally drifted forward. Kauko, his eight-year-old pig-faced disciple, squatted nearby, wide-eyed with curiosity as he examined every leaf and butterfly in the orchard, as if discovering a new treasure. For the little one, the words in the book were far less interesting than the vibrant orchard.

Under the morning sun, the master's gentle gaze followed his unusual disciple as he nimbly ran through the orchard, leaping like a mountain sprite. The sunlight reflected off his peach-colored skin, radiating a natural warmth. His ears, tall and alert, twitched slightly, capturing every subtle sound around him. His bright eyes, filled with intelligence and curiosity, seemed to pierce through every secret before him. His hair, flowing in the wind, shone like golden wheat in autumn, vivid and lively. Though his appearance was unconventional, his deep eyes and innocent smile gave him a unique charm. Kauko stepped on the soil, hopped over to his master, and offered a fresh, crimson peach, saying sweetly, "Master, I picked this for you!"

Dapeng gently patted his head, silent, but his eyes revealed a mix of helplessness and affection. He wanted to teach Kauko more—not just reading, but also martial arts and cultivation—because he knew that one day, this pure little soul would leave this sanctuary to explore the human world. "Master, Songmao is calling me," Kauko pointed to a nearby patch of green grass, where a squirrel's tail stood upright, waving like a tiny flag in the wind.

The master smiled and waved his hand in approval. Kauko quickly caught up to Songmao—his clever squirrel companion—and the two darted through the colorful flowers, disappearing and reappearing.

They had planned to visit the Feilong Canyon on this sunny day, a mysterious place said to be guarded by flying dragons. Bravely, they passed through a waterfall cascading from great heights, listening to the earth-shaking roars of dragons. They then leaped into the clear stream, spreading their limbs and letting the current carry them through various mountain streams. They played in the water, splashing and occasionally swallowing mouthfuls. Their laughter, like a mountain spring, seemed endless.

As they reveled in the natural beauty, a group of colorful dragonflies appeared beside Kauko, their delicate wings dancing in the air, seemingly trying to catch his attention. Captivated by their graceful movements, he reached out to touch them, but they skillfully evaded him.

Suddenly, the dragonflies formed an arrow shape, pointing behind Kauko. Songmao screamed in panic, "Run!" They scrambled ashore, narrowly escaping being swept into the bottomless abyss by the rapid current!

Kauko, catching his breath, suddenly burst into laughter, "Hahaha, why not take this chance to explore the human world?" His laughter echoed through the canyon, filled with the thrill of adventure.

But Songmao sternly stopped him, "This is no joke. The master will punish us." His expression was filled with worry.

The dragonflies seemed to mock their clumsiness, circling above them a few times before gracefully flying back to the grass, disappearing into the lush greenery.

Soon, they forgot everything and climbed an ancient tree. Kauko sat on a curved branch, playing his copper flute. The melodious tune swirled through the trees, and birds gathered around, as if following his melody, their rainbow-colored feathers shimmering in the sunlight.

As lunchtime approached, the two headed back. Along the way, they bent down to pick up colorful pebbles, examining them closely in their hands. When they reached the cliff's edge, they cautiously peered down into the seemingly endless abyss. Kauko tossed a small pebble, watching intently as it arced through the misty air before vanishing.

He took a slight breath and whispered to Songmao, "What would have happened if we had fallen today?" Before he finished, a bold thought emerged: What was the world below the mountain really like?

Filled with curiosity, he entered the study room, lying on a pile of books, his fingers gently brushing over the slightly yellowed pages as he silently read the stories within. The pages depicted a little fairy escaping to the mortal world, dancing in the bustling night market and singing in the peach groves by the abyss. A glimmer of longing flashed in his eyes, and he reached out as if to touch that beautiful world, murmuring, "Wait for me, okay?"

But as he turned to look out the window at the high cliffs, faintly visible through the mist, they seemed to separate Tian Mountain from the mortal world. His small hand rested on the windowsill as he gazed into the distant horizon, searching for a glimmer of hope. The setting sun's glow bathed his face, reflecting a radiant hope. He had often dreamed of flying through the thick clouds like his master, soaring in the human world's sky. He continued to piece together a fantastical human world from the lines of text, as if seeing his own role and the adventures he had yet to experience.

"Kauko, reading can wait. Come eat!" The master's call pulled him from his reverie.

Kauko put down the book and sat at the table, devouring the meal. But even the delicious food could not stop his thoughts. He paused, chopsticks in hand, and asked, "Master..."

Dapeng turned his eyes to Kauko, "What is it? Does the food not taste good today?" His voice carried both kindness and hesitation.

Kauko's bright eyes looked directly at his master, his childish voice filled with curiosity, "Master, why do I have the surname 'Kau' instead of my father's surname 'Zhu'?"

The master took a light breath, plucked a grain of rice from his beard, and replied, "You'll have to ask your father! He didn't even know he had a son, too busy heading west to fetch scriptures, hoping to become an immortal and return to the heavens. In this world, only your mother loved you, sacrificing everything for you. Tell me, whose surname should you take?"

"Then, Master, I'm not a singer. Why do I have a given name as 'Ko' (singing)?"

"That's because you have a loud voice. If it weren't for that unique voice, how could I have heard your cries as a baby from thousands of miles away and rushed to save you from a fire?" The master paused, then pointed his chopsticks at the little squirrel on the peach tree behind Kauko, adding, "If you don't like the name I gave you, I can let you take his surname. From now on, you'll be called 'Songqiu' (Pine Ball)..."

Kauko quickly bowed to his master, "Master, don't be upset. Kauko is fine. You're my master; you can call me whatever you want. I was just curious."

Songmao, perched on a branch, softly asked, "Master Dapeng, do I take my father's or mother's surname?"

The master laughed warmly, "Your father and mother both share the surname 'Song.'"

Songmao, the clever little squirrel, was originally the pet of Zhu Bajie's wife, Sister Kau, living in the quiet bamboo grove of the Kau family's backyard. His fur was light gray, his eyes round and bright, no different from the other small creatures in the forest.

However, on an extraordinary day, his fate took a dramatic turn.

It was the day Zhu Bajie set off on his journey west with Tang Sanzang. Sister Kau, reluctant to part, clung to her husband's sleeve, while Master Tang urged them to hurry. In his haste, Bajie swung his thousand-pound rake, digging up the local land god and demanding, "Do you still have any of those premium immortal mushrooms in your cave? Give me one!"

"I can't, Marshal. Those mushrooms are grown for Mother Wangmu (Queen of goddesses and immortals)," the land god replied.

"I don't have time to argue with you. Watch me collapse your cave with my rake!" Bajie threatened.

The land god quickly tried to calm him, sending someone to fetch a fresh red immortal mushroom.

Bajie handed the mushroom to the little squirrel Songmao, whispering, "Songmao, eat it, roots and all. With this spiritual energy, I hope you'll become clever, at least as smart as a child. Take good care of my wife, and when I return, I'll take you to the heavens."

Songmao swallowed the mushroom, and in moments, his gray fur faded, replaced by a silvery sheen. His eyes gained a spark of intelligence, and he could now speak human language, leaping effortlessly from tree to tree, crossing narrow mountain ravines as if they were flat ground.

Yet, fate was often unpredictable. Though Songmao gained extraordinary abilities, he was powerless to protect Sister Kau. One day, a sudden fire engulfed the Kau family courtyard. Sister Kau bravely shielded Kauko and Songmao from the flames, saving their young lives, but she never emerged from the fire.

As time passed, Kauko grew up knowing little about his parents' past. His companion was the silver-furred squirrel, Songmao, who stayed by his side, offering silent comfort with his sincere eyes and unwavering presence. Even on countless quiet nights, without his mother's embrace, Songmao made him feel warm, as if he were never truly alone.

***

That year, the sounds of war became the lullaby for children. The skies of the Daze Kingdom were shrouded in the smoke of battle, and the once-beautiful landscapes were reduced to ruins under the iron hooves of the Sherkon invaders. The fleeing artists of the Dianshui Opera Troupe, along with other displaced people, trudged through rugged mountain paths, muddy forests, and grasslands. The disorganized crowd followed nearly broken-down carriages, their props rattling inside.

The troupe eventually found temporary refuge in a dilapidated ancient temple on the border. The temple swayed in the wind, its walls cracked like spiderwebs, and the cold northern breeze seeped through, stirring the faded prayer flags.

Inside the temple, a small fire provided meager light, its flames trembling in the cold. The performers huddled around it, their faces etched with worry and exhaustion.

On a stormy night, a woman named Weigu, clutching a young child, stumbled into the temple seeking shelter. Her delicate features were striking, even beneath her tattered clothes and low-brimmed hat.

The troupe's leader, a gaunt man with sharp, eagle-like eyes, examined her under the dim candlelight, a sly smile creeping across his face. He approached her with feigned warmth, offering her and the child a dry corner.

Not long after, the leader married Weigu. The troupe members whispered among themselves, pitying her: "How could someone so ethereal marry such an old man?" Weigu remained silent, never speaking of her past or the child's origins, simply calling herself the child's aunt and naming the girl Bamei.

Weigu had some scattered silver, which she occasionally used to support the troupe. As time passed, her money dwindled, and the leader's initial warmth faded, replaced by cold indifference.

Bamei, just over two years old, was too young to understand the world, but the leader soon forced her to learn opera, harshly declaring, "The troupe doesn't feed freeloaders!" Weigu, furious, retorted, "She's too young and frail for this!"

But the leader coldly replied, "Learning a skill early will keep her from starving later."

Weigu had no choice but to relent. From then on, Bamei trained daily with the older performers, while Weigu took up painting, meticulously crafting opera masks to supplement their meager income. Each mask seemed to carry her unspoken secrets, as if the characters she painted listened to her silent pleas.

Now seven years old, Bamei had become a talented and spirited young performer. Her every move captivated audiences, and her eyes sparkled with charm. Her signature act was "Zhu Bajie Carries His Wife," a comedic skit she performed with her senior, Tichu. She played the tender wife, while Tichu portrayed the clumsy yet endearing Zhu Bajie. The audience often roared with laughter, but behind every smile, Weigu's heart ached.

Bamei knew nothing of her parents or siblings. Her world was the stage and the roles she played. As the troupe traveled, many knew the masked "Bamei" for her performances, but few ever saw her true face—the delicate features hidden beneath the makeup.

On the fifteenth day of the first lunar month, the troupe was bustling with activity. Firecrackers and cheers filled the air as the crowd gathered for the much-anticipated "Zhu Bajie Carries His Wife." As the drums and gongs sounded, Tichu stumbled onto the stage, his portrayal of Zhu Bajie more unsteady than usual. Bamei, wearing an exquisite mask, sang with a voice as clear as a mountain spring, her playful tone captivating the audience:

Atop the Cang Mountain lies my home,
Brother carries Sister back to her family.
The winding path stretches nine thousand and nine,
Sister has a million love songs to sing.
Tigers and wolves line the road,
Brother, don't let your legs tremble.
If bandits come to rob us,
Sister will call you to show your fangs.
The forest spirits call for Brother,
But don't turn your head unless it's Sister.
Beware the vines that tangle your feet,
Lest you drop Sister and lose her forever.

After the song, Bamei gently patted Tichu's shoulder, whispering, "Steady now, don't wobble." But Tichu's steps grew heavier, and as he turned, his arm faltered, causing Bamei to lose her balance and fall heavily onto the stage. Tichu also collapsed, his body crumpling like a broken puppet.

The audience's laughter died, replaced by murmurs of discontent and even angry shouts. Tichu was quickly carried backstage, while Bamei stood up, removed her mask, and burst into tears.

A middle-aged man in a silk robe, holding a feathered fan, approached the stage. He gazed at Bamei for a long moment before softly saying, "What a pitiful child. Don't cry." He stepped onto the stage, picked up the mask, and handed it back to her.

The troupe leader hurried onto the stage, apologizing profusely, "Respected ladies and gentlemen, please forgive us. The child was unwell! We'll perform extra acts to make up for it."

As the crowd dispersed, the man in silk approached the leader, introducing himself, "I am Wang Wu, known as Master Wang. May I have a word?"

The leader, eyeing the wealthy-looking man, nodded eagerly, "Master Wang, please join me in the pavilion."

Seated in the pavilion, Wang Wu asked, "That little girl who cried—who is she to you?"

The leader replied slowly, "She's my wife's child."

Wang Wu nodded, "So she's your stepdaughter?"

"Not exactly. She's a relative's child."

Wang Wu cut to the chase, "Would you be willing to let me take her?"

The leader was taken aback, "Master Wang, why would you want her?"

Wang Wu smiled calmly, "My mother is in seclusion for spiritual practice and needs a companion. The child wouldn't have to do chores—just keep her company and ease her loneliness."

The leader, tempted but cautious, replied, "Though she's not my own, I've raised her with great care. She's clever and obedient, the apple of my wife's eye."

"I admire her intelligence and charm. If my mother is pleased, I won't let you down," Wang Wu said, slipping a sum of money into the leader's hand.

The leader, though tempted, feigned hesitation, "I'll need to discuss this with my wife. She's the troupe's star, and my wife would be heartbroken."

Wang Wu doubled the offer.

The leader smiled, thinking of the younger wife he could now afford. "I'll bring gifts tomorrow. How does that sound?"

"Very well, but let me consult my wife first."

Wang Wu handed over a silver ingot, "This is for today's troubles. The audience doesn't understand a child's mistakes."

After Wang Wu left, the leader returned backstage. Seeing him, Bamei instinctively clung to her senior's sleeve, her face filled with fear. But to her surprise, the leader, unusually gentle, wiped her tears and picked her up, saying cheerfully, "Bamei, no more practice today. Let's go find your aunt."

Bamei, confused but relieved, nestled in his arms, unaware of what was to come.

Weigu was in the backyard, carefully storing the dried masks. She noticed a Zhu Bajie mask hanging on a rack, seemingly smiling at her. She held it to her face, feeling its warmth, and through the eyeholes, she gazed at the pear tree, as if Zhu Bajie himself were there, wagging his large ears.

"Brother Zhu, where are you now? Are you well?" she whispered, her voice tinged with regret. "Forgive me for using your name to earn a living."

These masks were more than props—they were part of her life, each character a companion through countless days and nights. "For the sake of our shared roots, bear with me," Weigu believed the masks could hear her, as if they shared an unspoken bond, silently guarding her unyielding heart.

As she lost herself in thought, Bamei's voice called out, "Aunt, you like Zhu Bajie too!" Weigu looked up to see her husband carrying Bamei. Surprised, she set down the mask and took Bamei, asking, "What are you scheming?"

Her husband glared, "You old hag, I have good news." Weigu sent Bamei to play in the front yard.

She pressed her pale cheeks, trying to hide her weariness. Since falling ill with a cough the previous year, her once-radiant face had dulled, making her look older than her years. She asked, "Are you taking a second wife?"

"Do I need your permission for that? I'm talking about Bamei." He placed a silver ingot on the table. "If you agree to my plan for her, this is yours. There's more later!"

"Where did this silver come from? Are you selling her?" Weigu's face flushed, and she coughed violently.

"It's not selling! She's lucky—I found a wealthy family to adopt her," he explained.

Weigu demanded details, and the two began to argue. Tichu and Bamei, hearing the commotion, crept to the wall to listen.

Weigu protested, "This child has suffered enough. I'm her only family. How can you sell her? If you don't drop this, I'll take Bamei and leave tomorrow."

Her husband retorted, "You can go, but Bamei stays. I've raised her all these years." Bamei burst into tears, rushing to Weigu's arms, crying, "I won't go anywhere! I want to stay with Aunt!"

Seeing her husband's resolve, Weigu stopped arguing and took Bamei inside.

That night, the leader called Tichu, lazily propping his feet up. "Fetch me hot water and scrub my feet." Tichu silently obeyed, gritting his teeth as he washed the calloused feet, disgusted by the rough toes. He thought, "If only I could break these toes and throw them to the dogs!"

After washing the feet, the leader kicked his dirty shoes aside. "Clean these and bring them back tomorrow. I need them to collect money for selling

Bamei."

Tichu picked up the shoes, his heart heavy. As he scrubbed, he muttered, "If only I had Zhu Bajie's power to fly, I'd take Bamei far away, where no one could find us." He sighed, knowing it was just a dream—he couldn't fly, fight, or even stand up to the leader. Without Bamei, the troupe meant nothing to him.

Bamei's sobs gradually faded into the night, her small body trembling with exhaustion as she fell asleep. Weigu gently stroked her tear-stained face, the lone oil lamp casting a faint glow in the room. Outside, the wind whispered through the eaves.

Weigu sat on the edge of the bed, resolved to protect Bamei at all costs. Late into the night, she still hadn't found a solution. Then, a scorpion crawled out of a crack in the wall, tangling with a spider. Forgetting the scorpion's danger, Weigu grabbed it.

It struggled in her hand, its pincers clicking, its venomous tail probing. She wondered if it was male or female. If male, its venom might not be fatal; if female and in heat, it could kill. She didn't want to kill him, just incapacitate him for a while. "What else can I do?" she thought, finally deciding. She crept into her husband's room and dropped the scorpion into his mosquito net. Returning to Bamei's bedside, she knelt, begging heaven for forgiveness, and waited for his scream.

Dawn approached, but the room remained silent. Tichu knocked softly, and Weigu let him in. He entered the leader's room, placing the clean shoes by the bed. "Master, breakfast is ready. Time to rise."

There was no response. He called again, but still nothing. Weigu rushed in, pulling back the net to find the bed empty and cold. As they stood in shock, cries came from the front yard. Weigu ran out to find her husband lying on the stage, bloodied and pale, barely breathing. The crowd murmured that he had been robbed and stabbed by Sherkon soldiers the previous night.

Weigu silently removed her earrings, handing them to a servant. "Pawn these and fetch a doctor." She directed others to carry her husband to the back room.

Tichu followed her, gently waking Bamei and taking her to another room to keep her away. Weigu returned to her husband's room first. She gathered the mosquito net from the bed, carefully hung it on the bed's canopy, and gave the bedding a vigorous shake. Dust and tiny feathers flew all over the room, even dislodging a dried-up dead sparrow that had been hanging on the beam for ages. She looked around carefully, confirming that the poisonous scorpion was no longer there, before instructing others to carry her husband in and place him on the bed.

A cat circled her feet, nearly tripping her. She looked down to see it pawing at a green snake in her husband's shoe. Shocked, she wondered if Tichu had done this. "Such a young boy, yet so ruthless," she thought.

The plan to sell Bamei was abandoned.

Her husband didn't die, but the once-domineering man now sat silently in a corner, his eyes vacant.

Weigu sold her last pieces of jewelry to keep the troupe afloat. Though her heart had been broken repeatedly, she didn't abandon him, often gently stroking his cheek, offering what little comfort she could.

Chapter Two

A Budding Friendship

On the eighth day of the fifth lunar month, it was Kauko's "birthday." However, no one knew for sure if this was truly the day he was born. Master Dapeng had chosen this date for his own reasons.

***

Seven years ago, on this very day, Master Dapeng was meditating in the Wuji Cave of Tian Mountain.

He sat cross-legged, eyes closed, his consciousness immersed in deep introspection. Everything was as still as a calm lake, serene and profound. Suddenly, from the depths of his meditation, he heard the faint cries of a child—"Wah... wah..."—echoing from a great distance, rising and falling, broken and piercing, as if it had traversed the very fabric of the world to reach him. It felt like an invisible hand gripping his heart. He tried to ignore it, focusing on his breath and holding his energy steady, but his spirit seemed to scatter, drawn irresistibly to the unusual cries.

Slowly, he opened his eyes and gazed into the darkness of the cave, a pang of pity stirring within him. "Could it be that I have a connection with this child? Why does this sound unsettle me so?" Master Dapeng pondered. "Perhaps I should go and see what's happening."

He quickly made his way to the edge of the cliff. A small stone dislodged under his foot, tumbling into the abyss and striking the rock face, its echoes reverberating. He took a deep breath, lightly tapped the ground with his toes, and leapt into the clouds.

In an instant, his arms grew large and powerful, his black feathers spreading through the mist, the sound of their friction clear in the silent sky. He transformed into a giant roc, his sharp beak like a black sword cutting through the sea of clouds. Riding the whirlwind, he flapped his wings and flew toward the source of the child's cries.

Soon, the roc was circling above Kau Village. Below, a farmhouse was engulfed in flames, and villagers were running in panic. He recognized it as the home of Zhu Bajie and his wife; he had once attended their wedding banquet. The child's cries grew weaker, and Master Dapeng's anxiety mounted. Without hesitation, he flew to the river west of the village, plunged into the water to douse himself, and then charged into the inferno.

Near the well in the courtyard, he found Sister Kau, who had tragically perished. Her body still shielded the well's opening, a sight too painful to behold. Through the thick smoke, he spotted a basket inside the well, holding a child and a small squirrel, both soaked and covered in soot, their faces unrecognizable. He quickly grabbed the basket, flew out of the flames, and returned to the sky, his body now scorched and wounded. Looking back, he saw Kau Village consumed by fire.

Back at Tian Mountain, Master Dapeng examined the child in the basket and was startled to see that the baby had a human body but a pig's face, strikingly similar to Zhu Bajie.

"He is the son of Marshal Zhu and Sister Kau," the little squirrel piped up, poking its head out of the basket.

"Oh, you can speak? What else do you know?" Master Dapeng asked, touching the burns on his face, unable to laugh.

"He was born after Marshal Zhu left. If Marshal Zhu knew he had a son, he wouldn't have left, and we wouldn't have been set on fire."

"Who set the fire?"

"I didn't see."

Master Dapeng cleaned the child, wrapped him up, and placed him on the bed, unsure how to care for him. He had never raised a child, and there were no women around to help. But he couldn't abandon this child. In the heavens, he had served as Marshal Tianpeng's guard for many years, sharing a life-and-death bond. As he fretted, the child puckered his lips and waved his tiny hands. Master Dapeng picked him up and held him close. The child clung to his neck, pressing against his chest.

He felt the child's warm body and the faint scent of milk in his hair. Burying his nose in the child's hair, he nuzzled him affectionately, a surge of tenderness washing over him. He couldn't bring himself to let go.

***

Now, Kauko was eight years old and likely didn't remember the events of his infancy, focused only on having fun. Every year on this day, Master Dapeng remembered Kauko's birthday. Today, he finished his morning exercises early and called out in the courtyard, "Kauko, where are you?"

"Master, I'm tidying up the brushes and ink," Kauko replied from the study.

Master Dapeng smiled. "Come here. You have the morning off." These words were music to Kauko's ears.

Kauko dashed to his master like a gust of wind, asking excitedly, "Why?"

Noticing ink stains on Kauko's hands and face, Master Dapeng gently wiped them away with his sleeve and said kindly, "Today is your birthday! What would you like to eat?"

"Master, this year I don't want food. I've run out of brushes and ink. Can you go down the mountain to buy some?" Kauko said, glancing at Songmao, who sat in the flower bed, smiling mischievously.

Master Dapeng was puzzled. "Really? I bought so much last time. Have you used it all?"

"Let me show you." Kauko took his master's hand and led him to the study, rummaging through the bookshelves and desk to prove his point.

Convinced, Master Dapeng agreed to go down the mountain after lunch. Unbeknownst to him, Kauko and Songmao had secretly buried the extra brushes and ink deep in the orchard, all to lure the master down the mountain. Following the traditions of the Daze people, Master Dapeng prepared a bowl of birthday noodles for Kauko, handing it to him with the words, "Eat well. I hope you grow up quickly." He also instructed Songmao, perched on his shoulder, "Keep an eye on Kauko. Don't let him near the cliff."

Songmao nodded obediently, brushing his tail against the master's face.

As Master Dapeng prepared to leave, he glanced around and frowned. "Kauko didn't come to see me off?"

Songmao chuckled playfully. "He's secretly enjoying his treats." With that, he hopped to the ground, waiting for the master to depart. Master Dapeng said, "Then I won't wait for him. See you later." With a light leap, his broad, powerful wings spread like sails.

At that moment, Kauko, hidden in the treetops, suddenly jumped, trying to land on the roc's back. He wanted to fly out with his master and see the world beyond. But he only managed to grab a few tail feathers before plummeting into the clouds, screaming in panic. Fortunately, Master Dapeng hadn't flown far. Hearing Kauko's terrified cries, he knew something was wrong and swiftly turned, diving toward the sound. With lightning speed, he caught the falling Kauko in his powerful talons and tossed him onto his back.

"Kauko, you little rascal, you nearly scared me to death!" Master Dapeng's voice was a mix of anger and concern. "I ought to take you back and lock you up."

Kauko cried pitifully, pleading, "No, I want to go down with you! I've begged you a hundred times, but you never let me. Why?"

Hearing Kauko's words, Master Dapeng sighed deeply, his anger dissipating. He let Kauko cling tightly to his back and agreed to take him to experience the world below. As they flew, Master Dapeng gently explained the harsh truth: "Child, you look different. Not everyone is as accepting as I am. Many people down there can't stand those who look different from them. They might do foolish things."

"Would they eat me?" Kauko asked, both curious and nervous.

"Sometimes, hurting you is worse than eating you," Master Dapeng said gravely, his words beyond Kauko's understanding.

Soon, they flew over the outskirts of a small town, where a winding river was lined with bustling crowds. Master Dapeng told Kauko, "We'll play here for a while. Quickly, change your face."

"I'm ready, Master," Kauko said proudly. He was skilled at face-changing, able to switch between a human face and his pig face with a twitch of his ears.

Master Dapeng reminded him, "Keep your human face on. Don't reveal your true form, or it could cause trouble. Do you understand?"

"I understand, Master. Let's go down quickly!" Kauko urged excitedly, his eyes sparkling with anticipation.

"And promise me you'll speak less."

"Got it, Master. I'll act like I'm mute."

Master Dapeng, dressed in a light blue coarse robe, his long hair fluttering in the summer breeze, led the lively Kauko through the bustling crowd by the river. Passersby couldn't help but glance at the handsome child, wondering whose well-dressed little treasure he was. In truth, Kauko looked good in anything, and today he simply wore a new white robe with a black sash and carried an ancient copper flute.

Kauko followed his master closely, his eyes darting curiously through the crowd. The sea of people, the shouts of vendors, and the creaking of carriages on the stone road made his heart race. The laughter and songs drifting from the flower boats on the river were soothing, casting a magical spell.

His gaze then turned to the busy stalls and the children tugging at their parents' sleeves. He saw a boy his age pointing eagerly at a fragrant stall, begging his mother for a treat. Their smiles eased his tension, making him feel part of the lively scene.

As they walked on, Kauko began to crave snacks like the other children. Stopping at a stall, he looked up at his master.

"Alright," Master Dapeng said, buying him a meat bun.

Kauko devoured it in one bite and waited for another.

Master Dapeng chuckled and obliged but warned, "Save some room. There's better ahead."

A few steps later, Kauko's eyes lit up at the sight of candied hawthorn sticks. He reached out, his fingers brushing the glistening, jewel-like fruits. With his master's encouragement, he plucked one off and popped it into his mouth. The cool sweetness made him grin.

Further ahead, a steaming stall caught his eye. A kind-looking old woman was busy flipping golden tofu in a hot pan, the sizzling sounds filling the air. Kauko accepted a portion wrapped in brown paper, the warmth seeping into his fingers. He took a careful bite, the savory, crispy exterior and tender inside making his eyes sparkle.

As they strolled through the bustling market, Kauko and his master sampled various snacks, their laughter blending with the surrounding noise. Following the crowd, they arrived at the lively Village God Temple, where colorful flags fluttered in the breeze.

On the temple stage, Bamei, dressed in a red gown, peered out from behind a vibrant mask, her crystal-clear eyes gazing at the audience. She began to sing, "Atop the Cang Mountain lies my home, Brother carries Sister back to her family..." Her sweet voice, like an invisible hand, gently tugged at the hearts of the listeners. Kauko's eyes were glued to the performance, his candied hawthorn stick slipping from his hand unnoticed. Master Dapeng tugged at his sleeve, but Kauko was too captivated to move. He pointed to the boy beside Bamei and said, "That boy looks like me..."

Master Dapeng quickly covered his mouth, whispering, "Don't say that! He's wearing a mask."

"Oh, who made the mask? It's quite realistic," Kauko replied, glancing at his master with a smile.

"This play isn't worth watching. Let's go somewhere else," Master Dapeng said, wanting to shield Kauko from the spectacle of people mocking his parents.

"Master, this play is fun. I want to keep watching," Kauko insisted, feeling an inexplicable connection to the performance.

Just then, Master Dapeng caught a glimpse of a young woman in a red cloak. She flashed by, revealing only her back before disappearing into the crowd. His heart stirred, reminded of a woman he had once loved. Her figure resembled hers! He quickly lifted Kauko onto a stone lion's back and said, "If you really want to watch, I'll let you finish this play. Stay here and don't move. I'll go find someone and be right back."

"Master, go ahead," Kauko said, his eyes still fixed on the stage. He hummed softly along with Bamei's melody.

Bamei's voice, clear and melodious like a mountain spring, enchanted Kauko, each note resonating deep within him. He longed to see her true face, but Bamei remained hidden behind her mask.

As soon as Bamei and Tichu finished their act, the audience erupted in applause, tossing coins onto the stage. Bamei gracefully retreated backstage, while Tichu crouched to collect the scattered coins.

Kauko looked around and, seeing that his master hadn't returned, slid off the stone lion and sneaked into the room where Bamei had gone.

Bamei was busy preparing for the next performance, adjusting her costume and mask. She had just undone the bun from her role as the young bride, her long black hair cascading over her shoulders. Sunlight streamed through the window, illuminating her beautiful face.

Kauko hid behind a row of hanging costumes, peeking out to watch Bamei's every move. A strong urge welled up in him to step out and befriend her. He even fantasized about performing on stage with her, playing the adorable little pig while she sang on his back. Lost in this happy daydream, he unconsciously reverted to his pig face and giggled softly. Hearing the sound, Bamei turned toward the costumes and saw a little pig face peeking out. Mistaking him for Tichu playing a prank, she called out, "Come out! I don't have time for hide-and-seek. Come help!"

"I'll help," Kauko replied excitedly, pushing aside the costumes and hopping out.

Bamei, surprised to see a boy who wasn't Tichu, asked, "Who are you?"

"I'm Kauko," Kauko answered cheerfully, his eyes shining with childlike innocence.

Bamei pressed, "What are you doing here?"

"I wanted to see you," Kauko admitted shyly.

"You've seen me. Now hurry and leave. If anyone catches you, they'll think you're a thief and break your legs," Bamei urged anxiously.

Just then, she heard footsteps and quickly grabbed Kauko's hand, pulling him to a red chest filled with costumes. She opened the lid and hurriedly pushed Kauko inside.

As soon as the lid closed, Tichu walked in. "I heard you talking to someone. Where are they?"

"No one's here," Bamei said nonchalantly, sitting on the chest. "I was reciting my lines."

"Strange, did I mishear?" Tichu walked up to Bamei. "Bamei, get up for a moment. I need to find something for the senior brother."

"I'm not getting up. Tell me what you're looking for first," Bamei said, crossing her legs on the chest.

"I'm looking for the Sea Dragon King's vest."

"Check the chest next door. I remember putting it there."

"Alright, I'll go look." Tichu left for the other room.

Bamei quickly jumped down, opened the chest, and pulled out a yellow vest from under Kauko, who was curled up inside. Just as Kauko was about to get up, Bamei pushed him back down. "Tichu, come here! The vest is here."

"Thanks, Bamei!" Tichu took the vest and headed out, reminding her before leaving, "Don't forget, we have a performance later."

"I know, go on." Bamei waited until Tichu was gone before letting Kauko out.

Kauko, who had been cramped in the small chest, emerged with flushed cheeks, taking a deep breath. He complained with a hint of grievance, "You're so cruel. I almost suffocated in there."

Bamei rolled her eyes and replied, "Where did you come from, you little monster? You don't understand my kindness. I don't even know why I saved you..."

Hearing the word "monster", Kauko's heart ached, and his eyes dimmed. He interrupted her, saying softly, "I'm not a monster."

Bamei, touched by the boy's vulnerability, quickly softened her tone. "I'm sorry, Kauko. I didn't mean you're really a monster. It's just a figure of speech." Her voice was like a spring breeze brushing over withered branches, brightening the room again. "Take off your mask, and you won't look like one." She reached out her slender hand, trying to touch Kauko's face, but to her surprise, her fingers met his skin. She realized he wasn't wearing a mask at all.

Kauko gently pushed her hand away, his eyes filled with confusion. "This is how I look. I was born this way. Tell me... am I really a monster?"

Bamei stared at Kauko's face, speechless.

Seeing her puzzled gaze, Kauko shrank back, timidly asking, "Am I?"

"No, no, you..." Bamei's mind flashed with an image of someone, but she couldn't quite place it.

Kauko took over, "I know what you're thinking. I look like the one in your play, the one who carries you on his back, Zhu Bajie, right?"

Bamei grinned, "Exactly."

Her smile carried understanding and acceptance. Encouraged, Kauko suddenly confessed, "I'm not him. I'm his son."

Bamei's eyes widened in disbelief. "Is that true?"

Just then, Kauko's ears twitched slightly. He keenly picked up the sound of approaching footsteps. Panicked, he instinctively hid behind Bamei.

Bamei quickly came up with an idea. She took Kauko's hand and led him cautiously to a small room in the backyard.

The room had a kitchen downstairs and a cluttered attic above. The kitchen was empty at the moment, and the two sneaked into the attic like little foxes. They sat together on an old brown wooden box by the window, sharing a smile.

A faint beam of sunlight streamed through the small window, illuminating their youthful faces.

Bamei looked at the nervous Kauko and whispered gently, "It's okay, don't be afraid. No one will come up here." Her voice was comforting and warm. "I've never heard that Zhu Bajie—I mean, the Rake King (honorific title) —had a son."

Kauko said regretfully, "My father didn't know he had a son. He left before I was born."

"So you're from Kau Village?" Bamei continued to ask.

"No, I'm from Tian Mountain," Kauko replied.

"Where's Tian Mountain?" Bamei blinked her bright eyes.

"I don't know. It's my first time coming down the mountain. My master brought me here. I've always lived on Tian Mountain with him," Kauko said, his voice tinged with innocence.

"What about your mother?" Bamei asked.

"She died in a fire when I was one," Kauko replied sadly.

"Oh, you're a poor thing, just like me," Bamei comforted Kauko. "I don't know who my parents are. I only have my aunt."

Their similar circumstances brought Bamei and Kauko closer. They asked and shared their stories with each other.

Meanwhile, Master Dapeng chased after the woman in the red cloak, his sharp eyes scanning the area. After searching for half a mile, he found no trace of her. He wondered if he had imagined her or if it was some kind of spell. Not daring to delay further, he hurried back to find Kauko. When he returned to the bustling stage area, Kauko was no longer on the stone lion's back. Frantic, he asked the people around, and someone pointed toward the river, saying the child might have gone there. Without hesitation, Master Dapeng rushed to the river.

Back in the attic, Bamei and Kauko had become fast friends. Kauko declared himself Bamei's "Pig-Head Brother" and began showing off his skills, confidently claiming he could play the mountain song Bamei had sung on stage. He pulled out his flute from his waist.

Bamei quickly stopped him. "No, the flute will attract too much attention." Kauko put the flute away and then came up with a new idea. He asked Bamei to close her eyes, then twitched his ears and transformed his pig face into a handsome human face. When Bamei opened her eyes, she was stunned to see a gentle, youthful boy before her. Kauko, pleased with her reaction, grinned and said, "Don't recognize me? I'm still your Pig-Head Brother." With another twitch of his ears, he reverted to his pig face. Bamei gently tugged his ear, smiling brightly. "Stop messing around. I still prefer your pig face. It reminds me of a friend."

"You mean the boy who acts with you?" Kauko asked curiously.

"Not him. A friend from my dreams," Bamei admitted, sharing her little secret.

"Could that be me?" Kauko asked hopefully.

The question made Bamei thoughtful. She had often dreamed of a pig-faced boy carrying her as they flew to unknown places. She trusted this boy more than even Tichu. She had once asked her aunt, "Do you think there's really a boy like that in the world?" Her aunt shook her head, "No." Bamei then asked, "What about in the heavens?" Her aunt laughed. "You're too immersed in the play. You've brought Tichu into your dreams!" Sometimes, when she sang "Cang Mountain Sister" on stage, she felt as if she could hear the boy from her dreams harmonizing with her, making her voice even more beautiful. Other times, when she was upset and didn't want to confide in her aunt, she would tell her troubles to the boy in her dreams, even asking him to take her to a world without worries.

Thinking of this, Bamei felt a little dazed. Kauko and the boy from her dreams seemed to overlap. She studied Kauko's face, comparing it to the image in her dreams, but the dream figure gradually blurred. She couldn't help but make a request: "Can I touch your nose?"

Kauko instinctively covered his upturned nose. Songmao often sneaked touches, and the light tickle was unbearable. But how could he refuse her? After a moment's thought, he nodded. "Alright, but be gentle." He tilted his head toward Bamei, striking a pose.

Bamei's fingers lightly touched the tip of his nose, then slid down the bridge. The warm touch felt like a gentle breeze, giving Kauko a sensation beyond the usual tickle.

Seizing the opportunity, Kauko caught Bamei's hand and made a request of his own. "Since you touched my nose, you have to promise me something."

Bamei asked curiously, "What is it?"

Kauko looked at her earnestly. "I want to stay and perform with you. Will you help me?"

Bamei's face first showed surprise, then hesitation. She sighed helplessly. "It's hard. The troupe can barely feed itself. Some of the older performers were just let go."

Kauko was clearly dissatisfied with this answer. He frowned and said, "Then you can't touch my nose anymore."

Bamei couldn't help but laugh. She reached out unexpectedly and tickled his nose again, then said playfully, "Alright, I'll do my best! Wait here for me. I'll take you to see my aunt after the performance."

After Bamei left, Kauko's stomach growled like a little beast. He peeked downstairs, confirming the kitchen was empty, then crept down like a cautious cat. His keen nose caught a tempting aroma. Following the scent, he found a few golden steamed buns on the stove.

Kauko hesitated, a struggle visible in his eyes, but he couldn't resist. He quickly grabbed a bun and stuffed it into his mouth. He felt a bit ashamed; if his master were here, he'd surely punish him with a ruler. He turned to go back to the attic, but his stomach and feet were at odds. In the end, his stomach won, and he couldn't move. His hands, obeying his stomach, grabbed the remaining buns and devoured them.

Still, his stomach wasn't satisfied and continued to growl. Kauko's eyes wandered around the kitchen and landed on an ancient clay jar. He opened the lid, and a rich aroma of rice wine wafted out. Unable to resist, he took a small sip, then another.

In less than half an hour, the entire jar of rice wine was empty.

He wondered how he had finished it so quickly, then worried about how to explain it to Bamei. The alcohol made him dizzy, his eyelids heavy, and his body unsteady. Finally, he collapsed onto a pile of firewood and fell into a deep, sweet sleep, snoring softly. In his drowsiness, he felt a stick poking his foot and suddenly woke up. The person holding the stick, terrified, dropped it and fled. Outside, a crowd had gathered, and at the sight of the "monster" waking up, they backed away in fear.

Kauko, panicked, rushed into the courtyard. All around him, he heard piercing shouts: "Monster!" "Freak!" "Kill him!" The harsh words felt like sharp arrows, piercing his heart. Remembering his master's warnings, he suddenly understood their meaning. He took off running, trying to change his face as he went, but his panic made the transformation erratic, leaving his face a twisted pig mask. This only confirmed the crowd's belief, and they hurled stones and debris at him like a storm.

He stumbled toward the stage area, drawing even more onlookers and putting himself in greater danger. He hid in the shadow of a willow tree, dodging left and right. His once-pristine white robe was now stained and tattered, resembling the belly of a spotted pig—a birthday gift from his master. Just then, Bamei and Tichu arrived. Bamei pushed through the crowd and ran to the willow tree. She spread her slender arms like a brave little eagle, shielding Kauko. Her clear, childlike voice was firm and strong: "He's not a monster!" Though small, she showed extraordinary courage.

Tichu, hiding behind the crowd, urged Bamei to come back and leave the monster. A shirtless man, seeing Tichu holding a spear from the performance, snatched it and aimed it at Kauko. Tichu, worried the man might hurt Bamei, held onto the spear tightly.

Bamei bit her trembling lip, standing firmly between Kauko and the enraged crowd. A stone flew silently toward her, striking her forehead. She swayed slightly but stood even firmer, shielding Kauko. Blood trickled down her temple, blurring her vision, but she didn't retreat, her eyes wide and unyielding.

Kauko, heartbroken for Bamei, let out a sharp cry, startling the crowd into retreating. He seized the moment to climb the tree, scaling it to the top. He clung to the slender branches, swaying precariously in the air.

The shirtless man, having pushed Tichu aside, raised the gleaming spear and hurled it at Kauko.

At that critical moment, a massive black shadow swooped down from the sky—it was the roc. Master Dapeng swiftly grabbed Kauko, dodging the spear. The roc flipped in the air, stirring up a black whirlwind that engulfed the shirtless man, vanishing him from the crowd's sight.

Chapter 3

The Master's Beloved

Ten years passed in the blink of an eye, and Kauko had grown into a handsome young man. In the eyes of his master, whether in his pig form or human form, this disciple was three times more handsome than his father, clearly benefiting from his mother's beauty. His pig face was that of a domestic pig from Cang Mountain, still retaining the shape of a pig's snout and mouth, but without the ferocious tusks of a wild boar. He was just larger than an average person, with a touch of foolishness, charm, and a hint of exotic features. These were the master's impressions, though outsiders might not see it the same way.

As for his human form, there was no need for exaggeration. Beneath his thick brows, a pair of deep, piercing eyes shone with vitality. His facial features were sharp and well-defined, with an innate intelligence radiating from his brow, giving him the demeanor of a prince. If Marshal Tianpeng had possessed such looks back in the day, perhaps Chang'e's gaze wouldn't have been so cold, and she wouldn't have watched indifferently as he was condemned by the Jade Emperor and banished to the mortal world.

Over the years, Kauko had never left the mountain. Standing atop the peak, he gazed at the land shrouded in clouds and mist below, his heart filled with silence. The mountain breeze brushed his face, but it couldn't dispel the chill buried deep in his memories. He had experienced the cruelty and filth of human hearts and had long since lost any desire to step back into that tainted world.

In his heart, two names remained etched like scars, no matter how time passed. One was his mother, the most beautiful woman within a thousand miles and the warmest, most pitiable mother in the world. The other was Bamei, the girl who had never looked down on him for being different and who had risked her life to save him in times of danger. Whenever he thought of them, his chest felt as if it had been hollowed out by the mountain wind, leaving no place for his worldly attachments to hide.

In truth, Kauko had often wondered: if his father was truly as powerful as the rumors claimed, how could he not sense that he had a son? How could he let him suffer alone in this world, enduring scornful glances? If his father ever appeared, Kauko would follow him down the mountain, facing even the most wicked people without flinching. But in the end, this was just a fantasy. His father had never shown up, as if, as Master Dapeng had said, he was too busy walking his own path to immortality, enjoying himself somewhere unknown.

Lately, Kauko had taken to solitude, sometimes hiding in places even Songmao couldn't find.

One day, he lay on a large boulder, holding a banana leaf to shield his eyes from the glaring sun. His disheveled, sandy-brown hair framed his large, floppy ears. He felt idle, lazily lounging as a gentle breeze swayed the treetops nearby. He imagined himself rising and falling with the branches, and he seemed to hear Bamei's mournful cry beneath the tree.

He thought of Bamei, wondering if she still bore any scars on her head, what she looked like now that she had grown up, whether she was still as warm-hearted, and if she still remembered her pig-headed brother.

He asked himself, "If I could fly, should I go find her?" "Why would I go find her? She's from another world," he muttered to himself. "Just to let her touch my nose and call me 'pig-headed brother'!"

As he indulged in these thoughts, Songmao finally found him, sneaking under a pine tree and picking up a pinecone to hurl at Kauko's forehead. Kauko sat up, dodging another pinecone with a tilt of his head.

"Take this!" Songmao shouted, using both hands and feet to send a flurry of pinecones flying toward Kauko.

Kauko dodged left and right, pulling out the copper flute from his waist and using it to smash the incoming pinecones into dust, sending a cloud of ash into the air. For some reason, the ash instantly spread across the sky. The sun disappeared, and dark clouds rolled in from behind the treetops. A deafening thunderclap echoed from the depths of the sky. Kauko stood on the rock, looking up to find the source of the thunder.

The churning clouds split open as if cleaved by a sword. A purple light flickered in the gap, and Kauko felt as though someone was peering at Tian Mountain from there. A deep red hue seeped out, intertwining with the dark clouds.

This strange celestial phenomenon had never occurred on Tian Mountain before, and Kauko felt a surge of fear. He jumped off the boulder, eager to inform his master.

Songmao stood atop the tallest tree, calling out to Kauko, "Look! Smoke is rising in the east! Something's wrong!"

Hearing this, Kauko quickly said, "Lead the way! Let's go see what's happening!"

The two of them made their way through the dense forest, and in the distance, they saw columns of black smoke rising from the valley, as if foretelling some impending disaster.

They pressed on, crossing a wide meadow and arriving at a damp marshland. A thin mist hung over the swamp, and the sky, heavy with dark clouds, felt oppressively gloomy. Kauko picked up a mud-covered stick and cautiously followed Songmao, who scouted ahead.

As they ventured deeper into the marsh, the atmosphere grew increasingly eerie. The once-calm water surface began to ripple, and sharp sizzling sounds filled the air, like water droplets hitting hot oil. Kauko nervously watched the ground as small bubbles began to form and grow, as if something beneath was pushing them upward.

Suddenly, the bubbles burst into roaring flames, illuminating the dim swamp. Kauko was terrified out of his wits. His stick fell into the water, and he stumbled around like a startled deer. Songmao, knowing Kauko's fear of fire stemmed from a childhood trauma, shouted, "Kauko, don't run!" But Kauko seemed not to hear, continuing to panic and crash about.

Songmao quickly caught up, jumping onto Kauko's shoulders and trying to calm him. "Don't be afraid! The fire hasn't reached us yet! You're the son of the Rake King—show some of your father's courage!" These words seemed to have some effect, as Kauko struggled to calm himself. His legs were still weak, but he managed to stand steady.

Songmao looked around, searching for an escape route. An idea struck him, and he tore off a piece of Kauko's clothing, quickly tying it over his eyes. "Don't look at the fire. Just follow my lead." Blindfolded, Kauko could only rely on Songmao's voice to guide him. Though he stumbled along, he eventually made it back to safety.

Kauko took a deep breath of fresh air and removed the blindfold. Looking back, he saw the flames of the marsh intertwining with the smoke from the valley, like black flowers blooming across the sky, sending chills down his spine.

They hurried home, eager to tell their master about the strange phenomena they had witnessed. Before they reached home, they heard the sound of drums from the Moon-Watching Pavilion—their master summoning them.

Master Dapeng sat calmly in the pavilion, his hands resting lightly on his cane, as if he had already understood everything and remained unperturbed.

"Master, something strange happened in the sky just now, and in the valley..." Kauko began urgently, his voice still tinged with fear.

The master raised his hand slightly, cutting him off. "I already know. Let's eat first."

Kauko suddenly remembered, "Oh, Master, I forgot to cook!" He looked apologetic.

The master smiled gently; his eyes filled with affection. "I've already prepared the meal."

Kauko grinned. "Master, you've worked hard. Let me carry you inside." Without waiting for permission, he hoisted the master onto his back and trotted off.

The master chuckled as he was jostled, accidentally sucking a strand of his white beard into his mouth and nearly choking himself.

At the dinner table, Kauko brought up the earlier events and asked the master what they meant. The master sighed. "That was a celestial sign. It likely means my time is near. Child, you've grown up, and I have no more worries."

"Master, aren't you cultivating the art of immortality? How can something like 'time' apply to you?"

The master smiled. "No matter how much you cultivate, you can't defy heaven and earth."

"I see. Is it because you've neglected your training? You've been pushing me to practice, but I haven't seen you train in a long time."

"Ah, my disciple, are you saying I've been lazy?"

"Not at all, not at all!" Kauko shook his head, his pig head transforming into a youthful human face. He blinked and asked, "Then what's the reason?"

"It's because I've come to accept my fate. Do you remember how I found you?"

"You've told me many times. I remember. What does that have to do with it?"

"Just as I was reaching the most critical stage of my cultivation, your cries reached me from a thousand miles away, disturbing my spirit so much that I couldn't continue. Saving you, little rabbit, cost me a thousand years of ascension." The master spoke calmly, as if recounting someone else's story, without a trace of resentment.

"So, it was my fault that your cultivation was disrupted." Kauko looked at the master's weathered face and realized that he had truly aged. His white hair was tied in a bun atop his head, his long, snow-white eyebrows drooped like a squirrel's tail, and his silver-gray beard stretched down to his chest. Perhaps one day, the master really would leave him.

Kauko asked worriedly, "Is there any way to achieve immortality?"

The master joked, "By eating elixirs. Unfortunately, the ones I've refined aren't quite there yet. I should have brought a few from the heavens!"

The next morning, Kauko was surprised to find that the master hadn't gotten up yet. He peeked into the bedroom and saw the master still sound asleep, with a book lying on the floor. He picked it up and saw that it was a manual on alchemy and immortality.

As Kauko flipped through the pages, a passage caught his eye: "In Daze, there is a miraculous herb called immortal grass (an herb). Brewed as tea or used in medicine, it can extend one's life by at least a hundred years, or even allow one to become a spirit."

"Wow!" Kauko couldn't help but exclaim, waking the master.

The master rubbed his eyes, half-asleep, and grumbled, "Kauko, what are you doing, disturbing my dream of cultivating the secret of immortality?"

Kauko excitedly held up the book. "Master, is immortal grass real? Let's go find it!"

The master took the old book, gently touching its yellowed pages, and sighed. "Immortal grass is mentioned in many ancient texts, but I've searched Daze for most of my life and never found it."

Kauko's heart stirred. He grabbed the master's hand. "Then let's go, Master! Take me down the mountain. I'm fast—I'm sure we can find it!"

The master shook his head, smiling wryly as he put the book down. "Ah, how can I take you? I can barely fly myself. I don't have the strength to carry you."

Kauko refused to give up. "Then teach me how to fly. I'll go down the mountain and search on my own."

The master was silent for a moment before slowly standing up. "In truth, with your current abilities, you should be able to fly. But I don't encourage you to do so. The world beyond the mountain is dangerous and complicated. You'll need to wait a little longer."

A flicker of disappointment crossed Kauko's eyes. "Then, Master, when will you let me go out on my own?"

The master replied, "You don't need to ask me that. When you're ready to stand on your own, you'll naturally spread your wings and soar."

Kauko, puzzled, asked, "Master, you're not hiding any advanced techniques from me, are you?"

"You mischievous child, you really know how to annoy me! I've taught you everything I can. What I can't teach, I don't know myself. Do you think I'm really some great celestial bird? True rocs possess incredible magic, far surpassing your father's thirty-six transformations. Let me tell you, I'm just a guard who served your father, Marshal Tianpeng. My name happens to include 'Peng (roc),' but all I know are a few tricks. Claiming to be a roc is just me putting on airs." Master Dapeng's expression darkened, as if he were truly upset—otherwise, he wouldn't have revealed his true background.

Kauko chuckled. "Don't be angry, Master. I was just teasing you."

The master smiled. "If I got angry at you, I'd have died of rage long ago." Noticing a tear in Kauko's robe, he told him to take it off so he could mend it later.

Once back in his room, Kauko sat on the edge of his bed, lost in thought.

"The master said I can fly. I need to train harder." He pulled out a few books on flying techniques and began reviewing them, trying to practice. He felt the flow of energy within him, but his feet seemed glued to the ground, refusing to lift off. Eventually, he collapsed onto the bed in frustration, feeling as though he truly lacked the spark of genius. Just then, Songmao quietly slipped into the room looking for food, accidentally making some noise. Kauko pretended to be annoyed. "Stealing food again, knowing it drains spiritual energy!"

Songmao put on a pitiful face. "Just a little, even one piece will do."

Kauko tossed him a single peanut. Songmao deftly caught it and began nibbling, complaining, "I've never met a brother as stingy as you!"

But Kauko didn't respond as he usually would. Noticing his distraction, Songmao asked curiously, "Why so glum?"

Kauko sighed. "I want to go down the mountain to find immortal grass, but I can't fly."

Songmao teased, "In such a hurry to fly—is it really just for immortal grass?"

"What else would it be for?" Kauko retorted.

"Care to bet there's no thought of finding Bamei in there?" Songmao prodded.

"Fine, fine. I want to see her too, okay?" Kauko finally admitted.

"I didn't say you couldn't. I just don't like hearing insincere words." Songmao wiped his mouth and added, "Finding Bamei is up to you, but as for immortal grass, I can give you a hint. Think about it—immortal grass likes to grow on cliffs, right? So where would be the best place for it to grow?"

"You mean Tian Mountain?" Kauko blurted out, his eyes lighting up.

***

Early the next morning, Kauko entered the forest and climbed to the top of the tallest tree. The birds and small animals in the forest, thinking he was going to play his flute, gathered around. Kauko waved them away, signaling not to disturb him. He muttered some incantations, feeling the energy flow within him, then closed his eyes and leaped, hoping to float. Instead, he crashed to the ground. Fortunately, his thick skin saved him, and aside from a yelp, he was unharmed. The small animals, seeing this, rushed to tell Songmao that Kauko had gone mad.

Songmao arrived to find Kauko practicing his flying techniques again. He didn't interrupt but instead wandered around, trying to catch Kauko's attention. But Kauko was too focused to notice, completely absorbed in his training.

Finding it dull, Songmao headed to the Wuji Cave to see what Master Dapeng was up to. The cave was not only the master's training ground but also where he refined his elixirs. The master was opening the alchemy furnace, and a colorful light drifted out. He called to Songmao, "Go to the beam and fetch my gourd."

Songmao retrieved the gourd and placed it on the table. The master held a pea-sized, multicolored elixir in his palm, beaming with joy.

"Master, you've been refining elixirs your whole life. Why is this one making you so happy?"

"Come and smell it."

Songmao leaned in and caught a whiff of a fragrant aroma. "Ah, it smells like a young lady's perfume."

The master mused, "Indeed. Songmao, hang the gourd back up." Instead of placing the new elixir inside, he carefully wrapped it in a silk cloth and tucked it into his robe.

He softly said to Songmao, "Go play with Kauko. I have a wish to fulfill down the mountain."

"Master, are you going to find that celestial sister you often mention? She's already ignored you. Why bother?" Songmao's voice carried a hint of concern and curiosity.

The master smiled faintly. "How did you know I was going to find her?"

"Well, you're carrying such a fragrant treasure. Who else would you give it to?" Songmao teased.

The master sighed, a complex emotion flickering in his eyes. "Songmao, you little rascal, sometimes you understand me better than Kauko. Yes, this is something I've kept to myself for a lifetime. Just this once, and then I'll have no more regrets."

Songmao noticed that the master's expression was eerily similar to Kauko's when he talked about Bamei. A sense of unease crept into his heart, worried that the master's deep feelings might lead to self-harm. He quickly said, "Master, why don't I come with you? I can broaden my horizons too. I promise not to get in your way."

The master thought for a moment. Though it was inconvenient to bring a little one along, considering his limited time and the fact that he had never taken Songmao down the mountain, he reluctantly agreed.

And so, the master and Songmao flew toward Sien City. They didn't enter the city but stopped on a high slope not far from it. From there, they could see lush green grass and a tapestry of flowers, with the faint outline of the town on the horizon. Behind and around them stretched an uninhabited old forest. The wind rustled through the pines, carrying a refreshing scent. With a wave of his hand, the master conjured a large stone and sat on it, as if settling in for a long wait.

28

Songmao couldn't help but ask, "Are you just going to wait here for her?" The master didn't answer, closing his eyes. Songmao thought it was pitiful for the master to wait without an appointment. He decided to let the master enjoy his solitude while he went into the forest to find something to eat.

Master Dapeng's thoughts drifted back to many years ago, as memories of the past unfolded like a faded ancient painting.

***

In his memory, that day, he transformed into a majestic roc, its wings as vast as clouds, soaring freely through the valleys on the wind. Sunlight filtered through the clouds, casting dappled shadows on his gleaming feathers. From the distant woods came the sound of hunting horns and the shouts of knights. Curiosity drove him to lower his altitude and peer into the bustling forest.

He witnessed, deep within the lush trees, a group of knights relentlessly pursuing a target—a fiery fox, the very one he had fallen for. Her radiant red fur, like a leaping flame, darted through the forest, so breathtakingly beautiful that even the roc soaring high above was dazzled. An irresistible urge surged within him, compelling him to swoop down and rescue her from danger. Yet, he knew the fox was proud and aloof; if he acted rashly, she might scorn him. So, he chose to hide behind the clouds, waiting for the decisive moment to intervene.

The fox darted swiftly through the woods, her figure as quick as lightning. After easily shaking off the knights, she stood at the edge of the forest, wagging her tail triumphantly, a proud smirk on her face. Just then, an ambush party suddenly appeared, raining arrows down on her. But the fox nimbly dodged, not a single arrow touching her. She tried charging in several directions, only to realize she was trapped in a snare.

Her only way out was the open ground behind her. If there were hunters there, she would truly have no escape. But at this moment, she had no choice but to take the risk.

She turned and dashed like an arrow toward the exposed slope. However, her steps came to an abrupt halt, as if nailed to the spot. On both sides of the slope, dozens of riders stood in formation, their bows drawn and aimed squarely at her. A few yards ahead, a tall warhorse stood steadily, its rider a man of imposing presence, his gaze firm and deep, his bow fully drawn, as if ready to release a fatal arrow at any moment.

The knights' shouts shattered the tranquility of the slope. "Long live the king!" Their voices thundered, echoing to the heavens. Their armor gleamed in the setting sun, like countless sharp blades. High above, the roc's eyes burned with intensity as it gazed downward, its wings slightly folded, ready to strike. It looked down confidently, as if it could summon a whirlwind at any moment, fast enough to shield the fox from even the swiftest arrow.

The king and the fox locked eyes, time seeming to freeze in that moment. The fox stared intently at the king, her lively eyes filled with wariness and curiosity, as if she had forgotten to struggle, simply standing still, her gaze intertwined with the king's.

The king stared at the beautiful fox, her fiery red fur shimmering brilliantly in the sunlight. A sense of admiration welled up in his heart. He hesitated, then loosened the bowstring, letting the arrow gently fall to the grass.

A guard, seeing this, hurried forward to pick up the arrow and hand it back to the king, but the king waved him off. He took one last deep look at the fox, then gestured for his men to lower their bows and retreat.

The king's procession slowly departed, while the fox remained standing, watching their figures fade into the distance. After walking a mile, the king seemed unable to let go of his lingering attachment to the fox. He turned back for one final glance. Though separated by a great distance, their souls seemed to share a strange resonance.

This fox had a legendary tale, one intricately connected to Master Dapeng. She had once been Chang'e's personal maid, known as Fire Maiden. She possessed fiery red hair that seemed to burn like flames, and her eyes sparkled with wit and cunning.

***

One night long ago, the Heavenly Palace was ablaze with lights, bustling with activity. The Jade Emperor hosted a grand banquet, inviting all the celestial heroes to gather. Marshal Tianpeng, having indulged too much in wine, grew unsteady on his feet. Fortunately, his loyal guard, Dapeng, was by his side to support him, leading him away from the hall to sober up in the garden. The Marshal stumbled, trampling a patch of orchids, and even attempted to bathe in the Heavenly Pool. Dapeng exerted great effort to stop his reckless behavior.

At that moment, Chang'e and her maid, Fire Maiden, strolled gracefully into the garden. The air was filled with the scent of flowers, and the moonlight was pure and bright. Their figures shimmered in the moonlight, dreamlike and ethereal.

At the sight of Chang'e, Marshal Tianpeng's hazy eyes instantly lit up, a mix of awe and desire flashing across his face. He shot Dapeng a meaningful glance, as if saying, "Brother, keep Fire Maiden occupied for me."

But Fire Maiden had already developed feelings for Marshal Tianpeng. She stood nearby, her eyes filled with longing, unwilling to leave. However, the Marshal had no interest in her. He resorted to casting a sleep-inducing spell on her, causing her to grow drowsy.

Dapeng obeyed his master's orders, gently picking her up and carrying her to a secluded pavilion deep within the garden.

On that magical night, Dapeng sat beside Fire Maiden, gazing at her peaceful sleeping face. Unknowingly, a deep affection welled up in his heart. When Fire Maiden awoke, she realized she had missed her chance with Marshal Tianpeng. In a fit of anger, she slapped Dapeng across the face. Seeing Chang'e and the Marshal laughing and chatting in the distance, she was consumed by jealousy and resolved to make the blind marshal and his delusional guard pay.

Fire Maiden stormed off, her red robes billowing like flames, stirring ripples in the Jade Pool. With a furious expression, she approached Mother Wangmu to complain: "Your Majesty, Chang'e has been wronged!" Her words, though brief, were like sparks, instantly igniting Mother Wangmu's anger. Mother Wangmu promptly reported the matter to the Jade Emperor. Seated on his cloud throne, the Jade Emperor remained calm, merely waving his hand.

That very night, Marshal Tianpeng was brought before the grand hall. Kneeling on the pristine jade steps, he tried to explain: "Your Majesty, this is all a misunderstanding! I merely expressed some concern for Sister Chang'e. I meant no offense."

The Jade Emperor saw Chang'e hiding behind Mother Wangmu, her white robes flowing like autumn water, making her appear even more pitiable. He motioned for her to step forward and speak. Chang'e took a few steps but remained silent, her head bowed, tears glistening in her eyes, her shoulders trembling slightly, evoking sympathy from the entire Heavenly Court. Mother Wangmu urged the Jade Emperor: "Your Majesty, don't frighten the child. How can your general, relying on his military achievements, bully the women of your household? What are you waiting for?"

The Jade Emperor spoke: "Tianpeng, this matter concerns the dignity of the Heavenly Court. It cannot be overlooked. Do you understand?" With that, he took Mother Wangmu's hand and left.

Marshal Tianpeng was imprisoned in the Heavenly Prison for three months before being banished to the mortal world along with Dapeng and Fire Maiden.

When Tianpeng was reincarnated, he was sabotaged by his colleagues and reborn as a half-human, half-pig creature. Fortunately, he retained his past-life skills and gained some renown in the martial world. Dapeng became a poor Taoist priest, and through relentless effort, he mastered the art of transforming into a roc. Fire Maiden, the accuser, suffered the most. Though proud and aloof, she failed to become human and instead became a homeless red fox.

***

The fox stood on the high slope, watching the king's entourage disappear into the dust until the last shadow vanished. She took a deep breath, turned, and strode into the dense forest, her steps light yet resolute. Dapeng had been waiting there, his bearded face filled with anticipation and anxiety. Yet, as the fox passed by, she didn't even glance at him.

"Fire Maiden, marry me! Come with me to Tian Mountain. No one will ever bully you again," Dapeng pleaded, his voice filled with longing and urgency.

"Go away. I hate you, I hate the marshal, I hate Chang'e!" The fox didn't look back, her head held high, exuding an air of determination.

"If you marry me, I can turn you into a human," Dapeng persisted, desperate to convince her.

The fox suddenly stopped and turned, her eyes flashing with defiance. "If you truly love me, turn me into a human right now."

Dapeng felt a glimmer of hope. "If I do this, will you marry me?"

The fox sneered and turned away. "Don't dream. Can't you see my heart belongs to someone else? That man just now, he's the one I dream of."

"He's the king of Daze Kingdom, with a harem of wives and concubines," Dapeng tried to dissuade her.

"I don't care. He's the only one for me in this life," the fox declared without hesitation, her gaze firm, her tone commanding. "Give me your treasure now. Don't delay my plans."

Dapeng's heart was broken, but he couldn't resist the command of the one he loved. He took off the small gourd hanging from his neck and placed it around hers.

The fox didn't thank him. Instead, she coldly said, "Leave. I don't want to see you again in this life."

Dapeng hesitated, calling out to her retreating figure, "Wait, this elixir—once you take it and become human, you can never turn back into a fox."

The fox turned her head, scoffing, "Nonsense! Who would want a fox's body when I can be a beauty?"

Dapeng continued, "Also, after taking it, you'll only have one transformation. Whoever you think of in your heart, you'll take their form and won't be able to change into anyone else. You must use it wisely..."

The fox impatiently cut him off, "Is there more? Say it all at once!"

"When you become human, you'll only have a rough human form. You'll need to refine yourself through cultivation. Absorb the energy of heaven and earth at dawn, but don't cultivate at night, or the yin energy will invade your body, with dire consequences..."

The fox looked at him in surprise, "You don't hate me? Why are you telling me all this?"

Dapeng gazed at her, his eyes complex, "Loving someone makes you helpless." His voice was filled with resignation and pain.

***

Master Dapeng reminisced about the past, now admiring Fire Maiden's coldness as a rare form of pride in a woman. He no longer cared that they could never be together, as long as she could chase her dreams and as long as he held a warmth in his heart.

Master Dapeng sat on the stone for a long time. Songmao, growing worried, returned to his side. At the foot of the mountain, a figure appeared, staggering directly toward them.

Songmao gently tapped the master, saying, "A beggar is coming, not a beauty."

The master still didn't open his eyes, replying, "Be quiet, go play somewhere else."

The figure drew closer, cloaked in black robes, her head and face hidden under a hood, a cane in her hand, exuding an aura of coldness. She approached the master, tapped the stone with her cane, and said, "Old Taoist, make some room. Let me rest."

Only then did the master slowly open his eyes, his gaze shifting slightly as he scrutinized the newcomer. He sighed softly, moving over slightly to let her sit beside him. Though he couldn't see her face, hidden beneath the hood, he could clearly sense the chilling yin energy radiating from her and the stark contrast between her imposing appearance and her pitiable state. He said with deep disappointment, "Fire Maiden, you still didn't listen to me, did you? Look at what you've become. It breaks my heart." His words were filled with reproach and sorrow.

"Benefactor, I'm not here for advice! If you have anything to give, hand it over quickly," Fire Maiden rasped.

"You're still as domineering as ever. What do I have left to give you? If you want this old bone, take it," the master said pityingly, though he had secretly changed his mind. The elixir he had brought was originally for her—an enhanced version that would grant her eternal beauty without the need for daily cultivation. But now, Fire Maiden was saturated with yin energy. If it clashed with the elixir's essence, it would destroy her internal organs.

"You look pale too, not much better off than me," Fire Maiden suddenly reached out and grasped his hand. "Let me read your palm." Her grip tightened, and sparks began to fly between their arms.

The master's body trembled slightly, but he remained upright, silently enduring the pain. At that moment, Songmao suddenly leaped out, landing on the beggar's shoulder and letting out a loud fart right in her face. Before Fire Maiden could react, Songmao had already darted into the woods.

She quickly withdrew her hand, her face twisted in disgust, waving her arms frantically to dispel the smell. "That little brat, such a troublemaker!" she exclaimed. Then, she suddenly burst into laughter, her voice filled with mockery, "Old Taoist, I was just playing with you. Did you really think I cared about your old bones? But you haven't changed—still so passive."

The master gently patted his chest, sighing softly, "Ah, you..."

Fire Maiden suddenly stood up and gave an exaggerated bow. "Thank you, benefactor. I'll take my leave now!" With a turn, her black robes instantly transformed into a vibrant red cloak, and a colorful mask appeared on her face, her eyes burning like fire.

She let out a sharp whistle, and a brown deer emerged from the woods. She nimbly leaped onto its back and vanished down the mountain in an instant.

Songmao, seeing this, couldn't help but run to the master's side, his face filled with confusion. "Master, how could you let a beggar bully you like that?"

The master smiled and shook his head, "She is the person I came down the mountain to see."

"Her?" Songmao's eyes widened in surprise, then he hesitated, "Master, when I saw her leaving, she reminded me of someone. If I tell you, please don't scold me."

The master chuckled softly, "What are you talking about? As if I scold you all the time. I promise, no scolding."

"I think... her red figure looked a lot like the person who burned down Kauko's house."

The master's expression darkened slightly but quickly returned to calm. "She wouldn't do something like that."

"But it really looked like her."

"It couldn't be her," Master Dapeng frowned.

Songmao wanted to argue further, but the master's firm gaze silenced him, and he eventually lowered his head in silence.

The master suddenly realized that the elixir he had hidden in his chest was gone. He guessed the fox must have stolen it. "Songmao, the little treasure I brought could kill her. What should we do?"

Songmao's eyes gleamed with satisfaction as he pulled an elixir from his ear and handed it to the master. "Master, don't worry. She stole a fake. The real one is still with me!"

"How did this happen?" The wise master was puzzled.

"Master, I saw she was a troublemaker, not worthy of your sincerity, so I swapped the elixir beforehand," Songmao said, his eyes twinkling with cunning.

The master smiled warmly and patted Songmao's head. "You clever little thing, you saved her life. Keep this elixir safe for me."

Songmao nodded, secretly delighted, and began to dance with joy.

Chapter 4

The Scent of Violet

Fire Maiden had long since transformed, no longer the slightly capricious woman in Master Dapeng's memories. Now, she was the embodiment of flame in the Kingdom of Sherkon, commanding over two hundred thousand Sherkon occupation troops and revered as Governor Fire. She occupied the palace of Daze, serving as the stalwart backbone of Sherkon's hold over the region.

Her past was like smoke scattered by the wind, her true face locked in an unsolvable mystery. She was like a ghost, appearing and disappearing at will, her face concealed behind a mask, hidden in the shadows of her hood, untouched by the mortal world, and gifted with extraordinary abilities. To her generals, she was a divine presence. Only in the presence of Golden Mother (a Goddess) did she reveal her true self, becoming Fire Maiden once more—a woman burdened with too many scars and utterly exhausted.

After obtaining Dapeng's elixir, Fire Maiden did not return to the Daze palace but instead went to Chinmi Garden. Once a bustling nunnery, it had now become her place of cultivation, with no one else allowed to enter.

The gates of Chinmi Garden remained tightly shut, with only a squad of Sherkon soldiers stationed in the guardhouse outside. They had never dared to step foot inside the garden, only peeking in from the outside. They had never seen Governor Fire enter or exit through the gates, nor had they caught a glimpse of her within the garden.

At times, faint sounds of wooden fish and chimes could be heard from within. Peering through the cracks in the gate, they saw the garden as empty as ever, with no trace of anyone. Yet, as night fell and midnight approached, Chinmi Garden would be enveloped in thick black clouds, with bone-chilling winds howling from every corner. If one listened closely, the swirling wind carried faint, mournful wails. This eerie scene would only dissipate as dawn broke.

Chinmi Garden held Fire Maiden's greatest secret. Rumors in Daze claimed that their king had perished during the Sherkon invasion. In truth, he was not dead but had fallen into a deep coma. No one could have guessed that Fire Maiden had saved him and hidden him in the underground chambers of

Chinmi Garden, kissing his lips daily to sustain his life.

She dreamed of the day the king would awaken, and they would walk hand in hand, becoming the most envied couple in the world. Recently, she noticed that the king's eyes often grew moist. Were those tears shed in response to her whispered confessions of love and loneliness? This filled her with mixed emotions—joy tinged with unease. Her years of unwavering devotion seemed to have elicited a response, but if her face, which she dared not reveal, had not fully recovered, would the beauty-loving king even glance her way?

Every night, in the stillness, Fire Maiden divided her accumulated energy into two halves: one half she gifted to the king as a life-sustaining kiss, while the other half she used to restore her own beauty and enhance her magical powers. She had long abstained from participating in Sherkon's campaigns, not out of indifference, but to conserve that precious energy, hoping to once again radiate brilliance.

Fire Maiden's heart pounded as she gazed at the "elixir" in her hand. Though it emitted only a faint glow in the candlelight, to her, it was a star of hope. She had initially planned to share the joy with the king, consuming it in his presence. But she changed her mind. "Ah, a woman should keep some secrets," she thought with a sly smile, secretly swallowing the elixir. "When he wakes, he'll be stunned by my transformation!"

She then approached the king's bedside, her voice softer than a spring breeze, pouring out the heartfelt words she had long kept hidden, like strings of pearls. The king still slept, but she believed her words could pierce his dreams and touch his soul.

Next, Fire Maiden gracefully entered the Bodhisattva Hall of Chinmi Garden, smiling playfully at the golden statue and singing her heart's desire: "I thank Golden Mother for your guidance. I have obtained such a precious treasure. If I wake tomorrow radiant and beautiful, I will build you a true golden statue!"

Golden Mother sighed heavily and spoke slowly, "Benefactor, I was about to tell you that your fate is fraught with hardship. The elixir you retrieved is a counterfeit."

"What?" Fire Maiden was shocked. "Did that old Taoist deceive me?"

"No, it is not the Taoist's fault. It is because the negative energy within you is too great, and you cannot bear the true elixir. I fear you will face even greater trials in the future."

"I refuse to accept this!" Fire Maiden rose angrily and walked away, turning back to say, "If your words prove false, I will tear down your temple."

Golden Mother was unmoved, having long grown accustomed to such threats.

Night deepened, and Fire Maiden could neither cultivate nor sleep. Unwilling to believe Golden Mother's words, she hoped the dawn would reveal her reborn self. She decided to go to the palace, climbing onto the king's bed where they had once lain together. She rolled up a tiger skin and curled up inside, finding the same comfort she had as a fox. She couldn't help but wonder why she had met him, embarking on a path of bloodshed and no return. Back then, she had been so naive, falling in love at first sight with a man who had pointed an arrow at her, willing to risk her life just to gaze at him a little longer.

***

After her encounter with the King of Daze on the grassy slope, the fox hid in the bushes near the city gates every day, longing to see the handsome king again. Finally, one day, the king and his queen rode out of the city on magnificently adorned horses, escorted by their guards, heading to the distant Chinmi Garden. The fox followed them all the way, watching as the king gently helped the queen dismount and led her into the garden. The queen's beauty filled the fox with envy. She imagined herself as the queen, holding the king's warm hand, her white dress trailing behind her, her veil fluttering in the wind, her ornaments gleaming in the sunlight.

One day, the abbess of Chinmi Garden heard moans from behind the Bodhisattva statue and went to investigate. She found a frail woman lying on the cold ground, wrapped in black cloth, with a faint smell of blood. She instructed the nuns to bathe the stranger. They discovered that her body seemed to have shed a layer of skin, and her face was in horrible look, as if burned.

This young woman was the fox, who called herself Fire Maiden. The abbess took her in. In her daily life, she covered her face with a veil, busying herself with chores, tending to flowers and vegetables, and following Dapeng's teachings, cultivating at dawn to absorb the essence of the morning dew. Gradually, her complexion showed subtle improvements.

The king and queen visited occasionally. The queen often came to pray, while the king enjoyed strolling in the garden. Fire Maiden hid among the flowers, her gaze fixed on his every move. She could hardly contain herself, her longing burning like a flame, almost impulsively rushing into his arms. She lamented silently, why was the path of cultivation so slow, like a snail's crawl? Would she have to wait until the end of time?

One dark and windy midnight, the garden was silent except for the soft sounds of insects and the rustling of the wind. Fire Maiden, filled with anxiety, secretly began to cultivate. She sat cross-legged, soon enveloped in a mysterious purple aura. A chilling cold crept in from all sides, piercing her bones, causing her body to gradually lose warmth. But with sheer willpower, she clenched her teeth until her body became as stiff as an ice sculpture in winter.

The next morning, when she looked in the mirror, she was delighted to find her face had become more beautiful. From then on, she threw caution to the wind, disregarding Dapeng's warnings, cultivating diligently every midnight.

Another night, as Fire Maiden bathed in the moonlight in the garden, immersed in her cultivation, a young nun holding a lantern approached her, her face filled with anger. "Are you a demon? Every time you cultivate, this nunnery becomes filled with a chilling wind, like the underworld!" Fire Maiden slowly raised her eyes, which seemed to flicker with flames, glaring fiercely at the nun. In an instant, a fire burst from her eyes, striking the nun. The nun was instantly engulfed in flames and turned to ash. Fire Maiden felt no remorse; instead, she was secretly pleased with her newfound power. "How dare you speak to me like that! I am, after all, from the heavens," she murmured with pride.

She remained seated cross-legged, an invisible force surging within her, once again enveloped in a purple aura, adding an air of mystery and an indescribable allure.

Soon, her face was as radiant as a peach blossom, needing only a touch of feminine softness in her brow. Gazing at her reflection, she imagined the king's infatuation, a smug smile playing on her lips.

Yet, from a thousand miles away, a discordant flute sound suddenly pierced the air, strange and shrill, audible only to her. Whenever this sound reached her, her heart felt as if it had been slashed by a sharp blade. Dizziness and ringing in her ears followed, and dark spots appeared on her face. She desperately covered her ears, trying to block out the maddening sound, but it was futile.

Thus, Fire Maiden took a half-month leave, donning a bright red robe and hiding her beautiful face under an exquisite hood. She silently boarded a bamboo raft, letting the clear river carry her downstream, following the faint sound of the flute until she arrived at Kau Village.

At the village entrance, under the shade of a lush old tree, a young mother played with her toddling child on the green grass. The child's face bore some pig-like features, and in his hand, he clutched an ancient copper flute, occasionally bringing it to his lips to produce sharp, piercing notes that seemed to pierce Fire Maiden's very soul. Realizing this was Kau Village, Fire Maiden understood that this child was the descendant of Marshal Tianpeng. She approached slowly, a faint sneer on her lips, and said to the mother, "What a delightful child. He looks a bit like an old flame of mine."

The mother smiled warmly, "You had such a lover too!" Her voice carried the warmth and kindness unique to mothers.

Fire Maiden's gaze fixed on the flute in the child's hand. Casually, she asked, "Where did this flute come from?"

The mother's face beamed with pride. "It was left by his father."

Fire Maiden feigned surprise. "Oh? A divine flute, then. May I see it?" Before the words left her mouth, her hand reached for the child.

The child's eyes flashed with fear, and he burst into tears, forcing Fire Maiden to withdraw her hand. The mother quickly hugged the child, soothing him with gentle pats until he calmed down. Yet, Fire Maiden was surprised to find herself entranced by the child's cries. To her, they were the most moving melody, like the sacred chants echoing in a temple at night, infusing her with strange energy.

An evil thought arose in her mind, and she reached for the child again. The child wailed heart-wrenchingly, and the mother hurriedly carried him away, trying to distance herself from this strange woman, unaware that Fire Maiden had secretly implanted a silver needle into the child's head.

Fire Maiden hid in a forgotten, dilapidated kiln outside Kau Village. The surrounding vegetation was lush, and the entrance was cleverly concealed by several large rocks. She curled up in the deep corner of the kiln, like a lurking thief, silently listening to every cry of pain and fear from the distant child. These sounds, filled with agony and terror, continuously fed her with a sinister, dark energy.

Days later, Fire Maiden stood by the stagnant water in the kiln, silently gazing at her reflection. She was shocked to find that her appearance and body had undergone astonishing changes. Her skin had become as smooth as silk, tinged with a faint blush. Her waist had become more slender and graceful, rivaling the beauty of the Queen of Daze. Her eyes grew sharper, deep enough to swallow endless darkness, yet bright as burning flames. Her arms seemed to contain boundless power; with a mere thought, she could summon a fireball the size of a bowl, blazing with the heat of the earth's core. Even when she plunged her hand into water, the fireball's heat remained undiminished.

Fire Maiden leaped lightly onto the roof of the earthen kiln. The summer breeze gently brushed past, carrying the fresh fragrance of the fields, softly caressing her long hair and flowing robes. She gazed into the distance, where the village appeared like a hazy ink painting, slowly unfolding before her eyes. Her heart raced wildly, as if it might burst from her chest. She knew that after the life-and-death ordeal of exchanging her fox form for a human one, she had been reborn like a phoenix from the ashes. From that moment on, she was no longer a weak woman to be manipulated but a heroine who could control her own destiny.

Just as she was about to return to Chinmi Garden, a sharp and familiar flute sound pierced the tranquility of the countryside, like a sharp blade stabbing into her heart once more.

Filled with rage, she let out a long cry of "Ah—" and followed the sound to find the seemingly innocent and fragile pig-child. Soon, she arrived at Kau's estate, hiding quietly in the bamboo grove at the back of the courtyard. Through the gaps in the bamboo leaves, she observed everything in the yard.

In the courtyard, she saw a mother and son enjoying a game of hide-and-seek. The son laughed and ran while playing the flute, the melody brimming with joy. The mother slowly paced around him, as if searching for the lively figure. Their laughter and the flute's notes intertwined, floating in the air, creating an atmosphere of happiness and warmth.

Fire Maiden stared at the child in astonishment, marveling at his tenacious little life. She thought to herself, if the flute's sound continued day after day, wouldn't it push her into an abyss of despair? She had hoped the child would suffer alongside the silver needle, but now it seemed hopeless. If that was the case, it would be better to let him reincarnate early, lest he become a source of great calamity. Suddenly, she raised her hand and shot a massive fireball into the courtyard, screaming hysterically, "Farewell, pig-child!"

In an instant, flames spread, threatening to engulf the entire courtyard. Fire Maiden stared at the roaring fire, a strange sense of pleasure filling her with excitement. She couldn't help but let out a fox's screech.

However, just as she was immersed in this twisted delight, the sound of a roc's wings tearing through the sky reached her ears. She looked up and saw a giant bird descending from the heaven, its wings blotting out the sun. A nameless fear surged in her heart, afraid that her despicable actions would be exposed by the roc. Without a moment's hesitation, she turned and fled the scene.

***

The king once again visited Chinmi Garden with his queen. He seemed preoccupied with his own thoughts, leaving the queen in the temple while he wandered into the tranquil garden, losing himself in the sights of spring.

Unintentionally, his gaze was captivated by Fire Maiden's graceful figure. Her every movement exuded an indescribable charm. He slowed his steps, tiptoeing closer, afraid that the slightest carelessness might disturb the poetic tranquility.

Fire Maiden, as if she had eyes on the back of her head, sensed the king's approach. A sweet sensation welled up in her heart; the moment she had long awaited had finally arrived. She remained calm, focusing on tending to the flowers in her hands, pretending not to notice the king's approach. She didn't know how the man she had admired for so long would treat her, but deep down, she hoped he would gently embrace her slender waist from behind. So, she maintained her composure and elegance, leaving him with a trembling, flower-like figure in the breeze.

The king quietly stood behind Fire Maiden, examining her closely. He noticed the translucent white veil covering her face, like a morning mist, adding an air of mystery. He couldn't help but be enchanted, a smile curling on his lips as he softly asked, "This flower is extraordinary. What is its name?"

Fire Maiden turned around, facing the king, and gracefully bowed her head in a deep curtsy. Then, she looked up and replied in a gentle, delicate voice, "Your Majesty, this flower is called violet, originating from the distant land of Persia."

The king listened to her explanation, his interest growing. He gazed into her crescent-shaped eyebrows, bright and deep, as if they could see through people's hearts. A wave of curiosity washed over him, and he couldn't help but ask, "Your bright eyes... I feel as if I've seen them somewhere before."

She was momentarily stunned, secretly pleased that he still remembered her. But she didn't want to reveal that she had once been a fox, so she cleverly avoided the question and replied with a soft laugh, "Your Majesty, it must have been in a past life."

"I smell a rich fragrance. Is it the scent of violets... or yours?" the king asked with a smile.

Fire Maiden responded with a hint of flirtation, "Your Majesty, surely you can tell, can't you?"

The king teased, "Hey, lady, why not remove your veil and let me take a sniff? Let's see if my guess is right."

Fire Maiden lightly removed her veil, revealing a stunning face that left the king speechless. As she handed him the veil, he sincerely praised, "Fair lady, are you truly an immortal descended to the mortal world?" Before his words could fade, a servant hurriedly reported, "Your Majesty, the queen has arrived." The king gave Fire Maiden a subtle glance, quickly hid the veil in his sleeve, and turned to greet the queen.

When night fell, the king secretly sent a trusted aide to bring Fire Maiden into the palace, discreetly hiding her in an unknown place.

***

The king spent many joyful moments with her in the hidden chamber, within the gentle embrace of the dragon-and-phoenix bed. At some point, Fire Maiden quietly fell into a deep sleep, her dreams filled with sweet fragments. When she awoke, the morning light had already filled the room. She gently touched her cheeks with her hands, knowing that the scars still remained. She dared not face her reflection in the mirror, for it would only deepen her sorrow and despair. At this moment, she felt as fragile as an autumn leaf. Her wishes were unattainable in the heavens, and she was powerless in the mortal world, all because she was trapped by the word "love."

***

Fire Maiden had been hiding in the depths of the palace for a long time when she suddenly had an idea. She cooed to the king, "Your Majesty, take me to see the queen, won't you?"

The king warned her, "Do you want to be whipped by her? You should be avoiding her, not seeking her out."

Fire Maiden's eyes sparkled as she softly said, "My king, think of a way. Don't you want to experience the feeling of having two beauties by your side?"

The king laughed, "Ah, let me think... I've got it! Little imp, I'll have to ask you to endure a bit."

The king invited the queen to admire the flowers in the back mountain. He cleverly arranged for Fire Maiden to disguise herself as a maid, blending in with the entourage. Though Fire Maiden possessed breathtaking beauty, dressed in servant's attire, the queen paid her little attention. The king, like a mischievous child, stopped before a cluster of blooming violets and turned to the queen, "My love, these flowers are so fragrant and beautiful. Where do they come from?"

The queen thought for a moment and guessed, "They must be native to our Daze Kingdom, since ancient times."

The king laughed heartily, "Is my queen testing me? It's precisely because I don't know that I'm asking." He then turned to the maids and asked, "You chattering little girls, if any of you know, speak up."

Fire Maiden seized the opportunity to step forward, almost standing shoulder-to-shoulder with the queen. She deliberately created a chance for the king to compare the two of them, then softly said, "In this humble maid's opinion, this flower is delicate and charming, with a unique fragrance. It must be an exotic imported treasure."

The king smiled, "What you say makes sense. Once I verify it, if it's as you say, I'll reward you with a gold ingot."

Only then did the queen begin to carefully examine the maid beside her, asking curiously, "What is your name?"

Fire Maiden respectfully replied, "Your Majesty, this humble maid is named Fire Maiden."

The queen's brow furrowed slightly as she turned to the king, a hint of suspicion in her voice, "When did Your Majesty acquire such a beauty by your side? How come I didn't know?"

The king replied casually, "My love, don't you remember? A few months ago, when the King of Annan visited, he gifted me several betel nut girls."

The queen's voice carried a tinge of jealousy, "Betel nut girls should be tending to betel nuts, not Your Majesty."

The king chuckled, "Am I not more precious than betel nuts?" He then took the queen's hand and continued walking, his other hand hidden behind his back, making a subtle gesture only Fire Maiden could see. She understood and secretly smiled. Fire Maiden was overjoyed, thinking that next time she would play an even more thrilling game.

After returning to the palace, the queen ordered the eunuchs to close the gates. She picked up a vase and smashed it on the floor, glaring fiercely at her trusted maid, Weigu. Weigu, just twenty years old, was deeply trusted by the queen. Knowing something was amiss, she immediately knelt, and the other maids followed suit, prostrating themselves on the ground.

The queen's sharp eyes fixed on Weigu, "You've been sneaking around, trying to keep secrets from me. Speak! Where did Fire Maiden come from?"

Weigu knew the truth could no longer be hidden, but she feared disobeying the king's orders. "His Majesty commanded us not to speak of it, or else..." Her voice was low, filled with fear.

The queen's expression grew colder, her tone severe, "If you don't speak now, you may not live to see His Majesty's 'or else.'"

Cornered, Weigu gritted her teeth and revealed the truth, "Fire Maiden was originally a nun at Chinmi Garden. His Majesty met her there some time ago. Somehow, she used sorcery to bewitch His Majesty and sneak into the palace, staying by his side ever since."

The queen's voice was laced with anger, "Why didn't His Majesty tell me?"

Weigu whispered, "He was afraid Your Majesty wouldn't accept her and might harm Fire Maiden."

The queen sneered, her voice tinged with helplessness and sarcasm, "Harm her? If His Majesty has taken a liking to her, how could I stop him?" She waved her hand, signaling Weigu to rise.

Later, the queen went to see the king, saying she had consulted the ancient texts and confirmed that violets were indeed exotic flowers from Persia. She brought a pair of jade bracelets as a reward for the clever Fire Maiden. The king was delighted and sent someone to fetch Fire Maiden from the cellar where she had been hidden.

The queen took Fire Maiden's hand and praised, "What a slender waist, what a captivating face. Why didn't you come to see me earlier, little sister? You must be the reincarnation of the dragon princess from Annan's great lake. I adore you and look forward to your good fortune!"

The king was overjoyed. He rose from his dragon throne, taking the queen's hand in his left and Fire Maiden's in his right.

The queen chose an auspicious day to make Fire Maiden the king's concubine. She asked the king to wait quietly in the Tengge Hall while Fire Maiden went to Chinmi Garden to bathe and purify herself.

The maids removed Fire Maiden's robes and helped her into a large sandalwood bathtub. When she emerged, she was fragrant and radiant, as delicate as a willow branch. The queen ordered her to be wrapped in a red carpet and carried in a palanquin by eight men, heading straight for a mountain twenty miles away. Fire Maiden realized this was not the way to the palace but to a volcanic crater at the mountain's peak.

"Why, why..." she thought, unable to understand. She wanted to jump out of the palanquin, but her body felt as if it were under a spell, her limbs weak and unresponsive.

Next, she felt herself being thrown into a bottomless pit. As she fell, her skin was scorched by waves of heat. The searing pain forced her eyes open, and she saw the fiery magma beckoning to her. She closed her eyes again, almost all her senses shutting down. There was no more fear, no more pain, only a faint glow in her mind, like the peach blossom petals in the bathtub.

***

Despite the fierce winds still carrying heavy snow across the highlands of Sherkon, the ice beneath the snow began to loosen. Cool droplets fell from the roof of a cave, landing on the head of a solitary old brown bear.

He awoke from his long hibernation, starving. He pushed aside the snow at the cave entrance and cautiously peered out, afraid to venture out for food, lest he freeze to death before finding any. He still had a deep-seated grudge to settle.

The old bear retreated, building a snow wall to block the entrance, planning to sleep a few more days. Just then, a whirlwind swept through, tearing open the cave entrance. A black object was carried in by the wind and landed at the cave's mouth.

After the fierce wind subsided, the old bear cautiously approached to investigate. To his surprise, the black object was a charred human. He felt a surge of delight, thinking this was a gift from the heavens. He dragged the charred figure into the cave and extended his thick, powerful tongue to lick it.

However, the charred figure suddenly opened its eyes, flames shooting from them. The old bear shrank back in fear, quickly pleading, "Immortal, do not harm me. I am willing to help you."

The charred figure retracted the flames and closed its eyes, falling into a deep sleep. This charred figure was none other than Fire Maiden. When she had fallen into the depths of the volcano, a current of hot air had lifted her into the clouds, where a northern whirlwind had carried her to the land of Sherkon.

Although the old bear did not know who Fire Maiden was, he understood that she had descended from the heavens and was no ordinary being. Day after day, he licked her wounds, and under his care, she recovered quickly, her injuries scabbing over.

When Fire Maiden awoke, she was horrified to find her once-proud face now covered in scars. Her heart ached as if pierced by a knife, and she felt unbearable pain. The old bear, witnessing her distress, was heartbroken. Silently, he fetched her clothes, a headscarf, and an exquisitely crafted mask, hoping to conceal her scars and offer her some comfort. Fire Maiden dressed herself, and though much of her face was hidden, her shining eyes and slender figure still exuded a captivating charm. The old bear, filled with admiration and respect, said affectionately, "Lady, your presence now is like a dazzling star in the night sky, your figure like the snow lotus swaying in the wind on our Sherkon Mountain. I am certain you were once a beauty who could topple kingdoms."

A faint smile appeared on Fire Maiden's face, tinged with bitterness. Her voice was soft but carried endless sorrow, "Once, I was peerless in beauty and grace. But fate was unkind, and I was betrayed, reduced to this state."

The old bear's eyes sparkled with empathy. He sighed deeply, his voice laced with self-mockery, "I share a similar fate, sister. I was once the king of Sherkon, but a cunning demon framed me, turning me into this form and stripping me of all I had."

Hearing this, a glimmer of hope ignited in Fire Maiden's eyes, as if her inner flame had been rekindled. "So, Your Majesty, we have both been toyed with by fate. I, Fire Maiden, was once the beloved of the King of Daze. But after crossing the queen, I ended up like this. If you promise to help me conquer Daze, I will immediately assist you in reclaiming your throne."

The old bear's face lit up with anticipation as he listened to Fire Maiden's words. "Fire Maiden, meeting you is truly an honor. Once our plan succeeds, my army will follow you down the mountain to fulfill your dreams. In truth, I have long coveted Daze, but my strength was insufficient. I could only cause trouble at the borders, never daring to venture deeper. If we can truly occupy the warm and fertile lands of Daze, plundering its wealth and capturing its beauties, wouldn't that be wonderful?"

"Then, Your Majesty, could you tell me about the demon who took your throne? What are his characteristics? What does he desire?"

The old bear pondered for a moment. "He is skilled in dark arts and can transform people into bears. He is particularly fond of beautiful women. My queen and palace maids were all taken by him."

Fire Maiden raised an eyebrow. "With such desires, he likely lacks great cultivation! This will be easy. I'll just eliminate him."

The old bear quickly waved his hand. "Wait! I fear that if he dies too quickly, before releasing his hold, I will remain a bear. You must first strip him of all his powers, restore my human form, and then deal with him as you wish."

Fire Maiden narrowed her eyes. "Then how do I get close to him?"

The old bear sighed. "He is extremely cautious and allows no one near him. Unless... you become his woman."

Fire Maiden couldn't help but laugh bitterly. "In this state, would he even look at me?"

The old bear shook his head, but then an idea struck him. He took out a token and handed it to Fire Maiden, instructing her to take it to someone—his own brother, Prince Duan.

Fire Maiden cleverly disguised herself as a beggar, her head wrapped and face covered. Her sharp, vigilant eyes watched quietly as she crouched by the side of Prince Duan's mansion gate.

After the court session, Prince Duan's carriage slowly approached the mansion gate. The prince stepped out, followed closely by his guards. One of the guards noticed the "beggar" and quickly moved to shoo her away. But Fire Maiden reacted swiftly, leaping up and blocking the prince's path, holding out her begging bowl. The prince's gaze fixed on the token inside the bowl, and he immediately realized the gravity of the situation. He stopped his guards and personally led Fire Maiden into the mansion.

Prince Duan was relieved to learn that the King of Sherkon was still alive and that his whereabouts were known. He carefully followed the king's instructions and devised a plan. He ordered Fire Maiden to be dressed in royal attire and summoned the king's youngest daughter, Princess Hongmian, to stand beside her. Seeing that their figures and bearing were nearly identical, a satisfied smile spread across his face.

Princess Hongmian had been spared from the disaster because she had been playing at Prince Duan's mansion when the king was attacked. Now, for the sake of her father and the people of Sherkon, she was willing to step forward as bait.

Prince Duan then ordered his men, "Quickly summon a skilled painter. I need a portrait of Princess Hongmian."

Fire Maiden, hearing this, immediately asked, "Prince, is this portrait meant for the demon in the palace?"

Prince Duan nodded. "Exactly. This painting must bewitch him for our plan to proceed."

Fire Maiden smiled behind her mask. "This is not difficult. Please place the canvas on the table, and I will handle it."

She stood quietly before the table, her hands not touching any tools, nor did she need brushes or paint. She murmured incantations, as if conversing with herself, and the image of Princess Hongmian gradually appeared: "The Princess Hongmian I envision, I want her beauty to become a trap for the demon. Add a dazzling feather fan in her hand, as if she is waving it, saying, 'Come, chase me!' Her eyes must be filled with temptation, as if challenging, 'Do you think you can catch me? Try it!' Her dress must be colorful, as if casting a spell to dazzle and unsettle the demon. I must make this painting full of life, so the demon feels it is not just a painting but a game of challenge and adventure. Prince, do you think the demon can resist such temptation?"

Prince Duan was delighted and praised, "With this magical painting, I am filled with confidence."

He took the portrait of Princess Hongmian into the palace and presented it to the demon, telling him that his young daughter had come of age and was ready for marriage. He asked the demon to act as a matchmaker and recommend a worthy suitor. The demon, who had a human form but behaved like a beast, was captivated by the image of the woman, so different from the three thousand beauties in his palace. His heart stirred with excitement, and he eagerly agreed, asking the prince to bring her for a meeting.

The next day, Princess Hongmian followed slowly behind Prince Duan as they entered the demon's palace. The morning light filtered through the tall palace windows, casting dappled shadows. Her long skirt brushed lightly against the marble floor, leaving a faint fragrance in the air. Her eyes betrayed a hint of unease, but she maintained a dignified posture.

Deep within the palace, the massive, green-skinned demon sat on his throne. His eyes burned like embers, and when the princess appeared, he was immediately captivated by her beauty. He leapt to his feet and strode toward her, roughly pulling her into his arms. In a deep, domineering voice, he said, "Such a beauty should be my queen, not married off to someone else. Stay, stay!"

Prince Duan remained calm and composed. "Your Majesty, becoming your queen is indeed an excellent choice. But we must follow royal etiquette, perform the rituals to heaven and earth, and inform the people. We cannot do without the grand procession and ceremonial cannons."

The demon grew impatient, unwilling to wait. "All of that, all of that, but we can do it tomorrow. I cannot bear to let this delicate beauty leave my side!"

Prince Duan chuckled softly and said leisurely, "Your Majesty, if I told you that good things come in pairs, would you be willing to wait one more day?"

"Tell me more," the demon asked curiously. "Do you have another daughter?"

Prince Duan replied cleverly, "Your Majesty is wise. My daughter is a twin. The two look exactly alike. If one becomes your queen and the other does not, it would be unfair. If you are willing to wait until tomorrow, I will present both daughters to you."

The demon laughed heartily, releasing the princess and clapping his hands in satisfaction. He ordered his servants to prepare for a grand wedding the next day. The princess and prince hurriedly left the palace, leaving the demon alone in his excitement, eagerly awaiting the next day. In less than half a day, the entire city knew that the demon was taking another queen.

The next day, at the break of dawn, Prince Duan's mansion was already bustling with activity.

Eight burly men, dressed in festive attire, waited beside a magnificent sedan chair. The two brides, dressed in red and veiled, entered the same sedan chair. The sedan chair was slowly lifted and carried toward the sacred altar. Despite the sunny day, the faces of the people lining the streets were clouded with worry. They silently prayed that the gods would protect these two unfortunate brides.

On the altar, the demon stood in resplendent wedding attire, his face filled with excitement and desire. When he saw the two identical brides, he could not contain his joy and eagerly reached to lift their red veils. However, Prince Duan stepped between the brides and the demon, emphasizing the solemnity and propriety of the ceremony. The ritual proceeded swiftly and solemnly, after which the two brides were escorted to a lavish bridal chamber.

The demon, unable to contain his excitement, reached out to pull Princess Hongmian into his arms. At that moment, Fire Maiden suddenly grabbed his hand, firmly gripping his wrist, a sly smile playing on her lips. "Wait, you must embrace me first!" Her eyes gleamed with an unusual light, and the strength in her hand gradually increased.

The demon's face twisted in pain as he struggled to break free from Fire Maiden's grip. One of his hands accidentally knocked off her mask. He screamed in terror, "You... you..."

"Haha, I am also a demon!" Fire Maiden laughed triumphantly, quickly draining the demon's essence.

He collapsed weakly to the ground, transforming into an ordinary spotted lynx.

Fire Maiden exhaled softly, a satisfied smile spreading across her face. She looked at the small lynx before her, pondering how to tame it and put it to use. Just then, a deep, slightly hoarse male voice echoed in her ears, "Master, your powers are truly extraordinary. Why not let me serve you as your servant?"

Fire Maiden stood in the center of the bridal chamber, her eyes scanning the room, her voice filled with confusion and wariness. "Who are you?"

The voice spoke again, "I am Wu Long, a sorcerer from the realm of witches."

Fire Maiden frowned, her voice tinged with displeasure. "If you are a sorcerer, why not reveal your true form? Why lurk in the shadows like a ghost?"

Wu Long seemed to be enduring some inner pain as he replied softly, "Master, to be honest, my skills are still shallow, and I cannot manifest my true form."

Fire Maiden sneered, "It seems you've done many wicked deeds, and this is your retribution, isn't it?"

Wu Long's voice carried a hint of self-reproach. "Master, you are wise. I have indeed done some wicked deeds to ease my master's worries and bring him fortune. I have my flaws, and I hope you can forgive me."

Fire Maiden asked directly, "Then what can you do for me?"

Wu Long's voice exuded confidence. "I am skilled in transformation. Just say the word, and I can turn anyone you dislike into whatever form you desire."

Fire Maiden pointed at the small lynx on the ground. "Really? Then turn this little creature into Zhu Bajie for my amusement."

Wu Long then made a serious request. "But can you promise me one thing? When you ascend to immortality, do not forget to take me with you."

Fire Maiden laughed. "Ah, why does everyone want to go to the heavens? Life there is not as glorious as you imagine."

Wu Long's voice carried a hint of sorrow. "I heard that my beloved has gone there, and I wish to reunite with her."

Hearing this, a wave of tenderness washed over Fire Maiden. "Very well, another hopeless romantic. I agree. Begin." She gazed expectantly at the small lynx.

In an instant, the lynx transformed into the figure of Zhu Bajie, clumsily spinning before her, looking utterly bewildered. Fire Maiden couldn't help but praise, "Wu Long, you truly have skill. Now, quickly restore my beauty!"

"Apologies, Master, I can only turn humans into beasts, not create beauties."

"You've given me false hope!" she roared in anger, her eyes flashing with pain and despair.

The King of Sherkon regained his human form and returned to his splendid palace. He joyfully reunited with his queen and concubines, his heart filled with long-awaited satisfaction and happiness.

But he did not forget his promise to Fire Maiden. He generously allocated an army of over two hundred thousand soldiers, appointing Fire Maiden as their Governor and Prince Duan as the military counsellor. Fire Maiden led this vast army, riding the howling winds of the highlands, descending upon Daze like an avalanche.

Chapter 5

The Star of Hope

Fire Maiden led her fierce army, augmented by her dazzling fire dances and the deceptive illusions of the fake Zhu Bajie, and they swept through the land like a storm. Soon, they reached the capital of Daze, Sien City. She left Prince Duan in charge of the main forces while she selected a few dozen elite soldiers and quietly infiltrated Chinmi Garden.

Chinmi Garden, once a peaceful sanctuary, was now in ruins. Fire Maiden stopped and asked a hurried villager, "Why has this place become like this?" The villager whispered, "The queen did it. She killed the abbess and drove away the nuns."

Fire Maiden adjusted her mask and pulled her scarf lower, leading her team through a secret passage known only to a few trusted confidants of the King of Daze, not even the queen. It was through this passage that Fire Maiden had been smuggled into the palace.

They entered the palace without incident. Fire Maiden's figure flitted through the halls like a ghost, elusive and unpredictable. Behind her, Sherkon warriors clashed fiercely with the palace guards, but Fire Maiden's eyes were fixed on one target—the cold-blooded queen.

Fire Maiden stormed into the queen's chamber like a whirlwind. There, she saw the King of Daze holding a sword, protecting the terrified and disheveled queen as they retreated to the rear courtyard. Following closely behind them was Weigu, clutching a small bundle—no, a baby! Fire Maiden's rage burned like a volcano on the verge of eruption, ready to unleash a fireball as a "surprise" for the queen. Just then, the King of Daze looked up, his eyes filled with shock. "Fire Maiden!" His call froze her in place.

At that moment, a poisoned arrow flew silently toward the king. The arrow struck its target, and the king's body swayed unsteadily.

Fire Maiden dashed forward like lightning, catching him in her arms. The king's hand gently touched Fire Maiden; his voice weak but filled with affection. "I have missed you every day..." These words struck a chord in Fire Maiden's heart. She thought to herself: My poor king, even through the mask, you recognized me. If I had turned to ashes in the volcano that day, you would have known it was me! The heart that had been consumed by rage and vengeance suddenly overflowed with warm tears, falling onto the king's face, as if releasing a mix of love, hatred, sorrow, and anger.

Fire Maiden turned and sent the Sherkon soldier who had fired the poisoned arrow to his grave. Then, she gently carried the king to Chinmi Garden, her once peaceful sanctuary.

***

Years after the fall of Daze, on a quiet night, Midd, the royal advisor of Daze, gripped the cloth wrapped around his head and pulled it off, his cold gaze returning to the worn sheepskin map spread on the table.

After the generals left, only he remained in the tent. The lingering smoke of tobacco swirled around his bald head under the dim oil lamp, as if gathering all the gloom to form a floating veil that stretched to the top of the tent, pressing down on him alone. In the tent, only the five "burn scars" left from his tonsure were clearly visible, like a few animated white ants crawling on his skull.

The sheepskin map on the table, its edges curled like withered leaves, showed faint yellowing in the worn areas, as if time had left its own weathered texture. The position of Daze stood out prominently, its center covered by a rough, irregular dark brown ink stain, a testament to the land's suffering. Symbols of smoke signals were scattered like fallen leaves across the once-prosperous land. Each mark appeared chaotic and hurried, like the despair and helplessness of a lost people. The strokes seemed to narrate a history of conquest, each line a scar of humiliation, each mark a memory too painful to speak.

What the map did not depict were the despairing eyes of women taken in fear, the cries of orphans over cold corpses. These scenes, impossible to illustrate, were etched deeply into every inch of the land—the wind-eroded ruins, the desolate graves illuminated by moonlight.

Midd's rough hand brushed over the map a few times, as if he could wipe away the past like dust. His eyes dimmed as he recalled a conversation with the king. That day, sunlight streamed through the palace's ornate windows, illuminating the young king's smiling face.

***

"Advisor, look at this vast land. The three kingdoms are like three brothers standing shoulder to shoulder," the king said with a childlike metaphor, his voice filled with pride. "Our Daze, rich and fertile, is like the brightest star among them."

Midd knew the fragility and risks hidden behind this map. He looked up, his eyes betraying a hint of hesitation. He understood the dangers of words but also the cost of silence. With trepidation, he advised, "Your Majesty, the times are unpredictable. Please proceed with caution."

The king waved his hand dismissively. "The sun is shining today. Let's not speak of ominous things."

Midd's finger traced the northern part of the map, where Sherkon lay in the cold winds, wrapped in silver snow. The barley and yaks at the foot of the snow-capped mountains were the lifelines of the Sherkon people's struggle for survival. Their resilient nature seemed to embody the spirit of ice and snow. Midd couldn't hide his worry, his voice growing somber. "The Sherkon people's desires do not stop at border raids. Their gaze is fixed on lands beyond..."

The king interrupted him. "Are you saying they harbor ill intentions?"

A bitter taste filled Midd's throat. He knew that once these words were spoken, they might sever the bonds of kinship. "I dare not say so, for blood is thicker than water."

The king's voice carried displeasure. "Advisor, let us speak no more of such things, lest they become a curse."

***

Midd pulled himself back from his thoughts and lowered his gaze. The wick of the lamp in the tent flickered faintly, as if tied to the last glimmer of hope in his heart. Finally, the oil ran out, and the flame died in silence. He took a deep breath, the hesitation of the past now an eternal regret.

He sat quietly in the dim corner, his eyes gazing through the window as if they could pierce the endless night and see the three ancient trees that bore the weight of an old alliance. Those shadows, though separated by thousands of mountains and rivers, still carried the earnest hopes and solemn promises of the previous king. Once, their branches were lush, their leaves whispering in the wind, witnessing the unyielding vows of three brothers. Now, only bare branches remained, rustling mournfully in the wind, like an elegy for the promises of the past, withering in the river of time.

The Sherkon cavalry had swept across Daze, leaving only the border mountains and forests as a sliver of hope for Midd and his resistance. Yet, Midd's heart, loyal to the King of Daze unto death, remained as steadfast as a rock. His responsibility weighed as heavily as the mountains, and even in the face of peril, he never wavered. But where was the dawn of restoration? He could not see it clearly, his heart filled with unease.

As the first light of dawn broke, a soft glow seeped through the cracks of the tent, like a gentle veil unfurling. Midd slowly rose, pushed open the tent door, and a fresh breeze swept through the treetops, shaking the leaves and scattering dew like pearls onto his body. He tilted his head back, closed his eyes, and caught a few drops of heavenly nectar on his tongue. The cool, refreshing moisture was like nature's comfort, bringing a rare softness to his weathered face.

Through the shadows of the leaves, he saw an unusual light in the sky. The moon had long set—what could it be? He walked to an open area and saw a lone star flickering in the southeastern sky, like a bright gem embedded there by the Queen of Daze. It flickered, as if about to break through the heavy fog and reveal the secrets of fate.

As the sun burst forth, the star, like a silent messenger, quietly faded away. Midd quickly returned to the tent, his hands dancing lightly over his astrolabe, as if playing an ancient melody. Mysterious characters appeared on the astrolabe, as if the secrets of heaven and earth were being unraveled. Suddenly, the words "Twin Spirit Star" appeared clearly. Midd's eyes sparkled with clarity, and a faint smile curled on his lips. That smile held a firm belief in the future and a hidden joy. Though Daze was currently in turmoil, the auspicious star had given a hint.

Midd walked to the tent entrance and gazed eastward. He knew the road ahead was long and arduous, but as long as he held onto the undying flame of hope, it would light the way forward and dispel the deepest darkness. What he did not foresee was that this beam of hope, as two children—Kauko and Bamei—grew, would gradually illuminate the skies of Daze. He bowed deeply, as if paying homage to the lone star that had vanished in the morning light.

***

In a corner of Chinmi Garden, Fire Maiden's fingertips lightly touched the cold bronze mirror. She gazed at the trembling mask reflected in the mirror and asked, "When can I remove it and restore my beauty?" Was she asking the mirror or herself? The reflection seemed to sigh, stirring the helplessness and sorrow deep within her.

She turned resolutely, suppressing the turmoil in her heart. Her arm traced a magical arc in the air, as if casting a spell unique to her. An indescribable force stirred within her. She was determined to reclaim her lost beauty before the King of Daze awoke.

When she first took control of Daze, she allowed the Sherkon army to run rampant, plunging the people into misery. At the time, she believed such methods would fill the land with endless cold and darkness. Every night, she wielded her staff like a sorcerer summoning evil spirits, drawing fear and pain from all directions to enhance her own power. However, as time passed, unease grew in her heart. The people's fear was no longer as overwhelming as before. Instead, the flames of resistance quietly spread across the land, forming an invisible force that silently countered her dark power. Faced with this, she had to change her strategy.

She spoke to Prince Duan and the generals in a lecturing tone. "Stop mindlessly killing. We'll collapse before we finish off the people. We need to play a smarter game—how about psychological warfare?"

Thus, she tasked Wu Long with selecting an innocent Daze citizen each day and turning them into a pig-headed person. At the same time, she spread rumors that these pig-headed people were evil monsters who would sneak into homes at night to abduct children and harass women. The strategy worked, spreading fear and unrest, concentrating the people's terror on the innocent pig-headed individuals. Fire Maiden secretly rejoiced. "This works well! But we can speed it up and make the show even more thrilling!"

She summoned Wu Long and asked in a probing tone, "Wu Long, can't you improve your magic? One pig-headed person a day is too slow! Increase the pace—three or five a day, how about that?"

Wu Long's heart tightened, and he cautiously replied, "Master, forgive my bluntness, but forbidden acts are no small matter. Overuse will bring disaster."

Fire Maiden, however, dismissed his concerns with a hint of threat. "Disaster? Have you forgotten that if I'm unhappy, your reunion with your beloved will be difficult?"

Wu Long fell silent, knowing Fire Maiden was not exaggerating. After an internal struggle, he finally nodded. "Master, forgive my hesitation. I will try."

Yet, as days passed, Wu Long vanished without a trace. Fire Maiden waited anxiously, a sense of unease growing within her. She began to suspect he had betrayed her. "Time waits for no one!" she sighed inwardly. She knew she couldn't rely solely on Wu Long and had to find another way. Thus, she decided to seek Golden Mother's guidance.

In the temple, the golden Bodhisattva sat solemnly on a lotus throne, illuminated by flickering candlelight, exuding an air of mystery. Fire Maiden approached with reverence and caution. She carefully placed fresh, colorful fruits on the altar, then lit three incense sticks. With a tone of apology, she said, "Golden Mother, I spoke out of turn before and offended you. I hope you can overlook my past words and guide me to a quicker path of cultivation."

The voice of Golden Mother seemed to echo from a distant horizon, resonating softly within the temple: "Benefactor, there are no shortcuts in cultivation. One must take each step carefully, accumulating progress day by day."

Fire Maiden interrupted her, "Mother, I don't need your lectures. There are rumors that Marshal Tianpeng's son is still alive. Is it true? If so, I fear my luck has turned. Please help me find him. I think he can assist me."

Golden Mother warned, "Unless you have attained enlightenment, do not approach him. He is a fusion of immortal and mortal. You should avoid him."

But Fire Maiden insisted, "If the world says he still lives, I must meet him!"

Golden Mother sighed, "Ah, benefactor, if something happens to you, who will build my golden statue?" Yet, in the end, she reluctantly told her, "Go southeast and find the old Taoist. The child is with him."

Fire Maiden immediately set off, disguised as a beggar, riding the thousand-mile deer gifted by the King of Sherkon, to search for the old Taoist she despised.

As Fire Maiden walked away, Golden Mother let out a long sigh. She had always appreciated Fire Maiden's sincere offerings and wished to help her attain enlightenment sooner, so she could reunite with her beloved king and live a life of passion. But her own powers were limited. She could only provide guidance and advice; she was powerless to intervene directly.

Golden Mother had originally been a large rat in Chinmi Garden, stealing incense offerings for years until she gradually gained spiritual energy, enabling her to hear and see far and wide. After the queen destroyed the temple and the nuns scattered, the original Bodhisattva also left. The rat saw an opportunity and stayed, possessing the clay statue in the temple and calling herself Golden Mother. One day, she gained her first client—Fire Maiden.

Fire Maiden knelt before the dust-covered clay statue, tears streaming down her face, praying for a way to save her beloved, the King of Daze. Desperate, she had turned to the statue without expecting it to speak. The statue told her, "Benefactor, the poison in the king's body is too severe. There is no immediate cure. He can only slowly expel the toxin himself."

Fire Maiden pleaded, "Bodhisattva, can the king's life be extended until tomorrow? And how can he slowly expel the poison?"

"That depends entirely on you. Every day, kiss his lips and transfer a portion of your spiritual energy to him—not too much, not too little. In time, a miracle will occur."

***

At the break of dawn, Kauko woke from a dream, feeling uneasy. He put on the robe his master had mended and went to see him. Songmao sat on a small wooden stool by the door, signaling Kauko to be quiet and step outside. In the courtyard, Kauko whispered, "What's going on?"

"Master has been coughing all night and only fell asleep in the early hours. Don't disturb him."

"Is that so?" Kauko said worriedly. "I wanted to master the art of flying and then search for the immortal grass herb on the cliffs. But it seems I can't wait. I must go now."

"The cliffs are dangerous. Let's go together," Songmao said with concern.

"No, stay here and take care of Master. Stay by his side at all times. Remember, don't tell him where I've gone." With that, Kauko patted Songmao, grabbed a bamboo basket, and left.

The master woke late and scolded Songmao for not waking him, though he didn't ask about Kauko. After a simple breakfast, he headed to the Wuji Cave.

After a few steps, he turned back and called, "Little spirit, come with me."

Inside the cave, the master pointed to the beam. Songmao understood and nimbly climbed up to retrieve the small gourd. Meanwhile, the master placed a seal on the alchemy furnace, murmuring incantations.

When the master turned around, Songmao asked, puzzled, "Master, are we done with alchemy?"

The master took the gourd from Songmao and shook it in front of his chest. "Everything we need is here. Ah, where's Kauko?"

Songmao smiled. The master had finally remembered Kauko. He casually replied, "He's probably in the woods practicing his flying techniques."

The master beckoned Songmao to sit on the table and asked, "Where is the elixir you're responsible for keeping?"

Songmao pulled the colorful elixir from his ear and handed it to the master. The master then poured out a golden elixir from the gourd. He held both elixirs in his trembling hands, examining them carefully in silence for a long time. Then, he carefully placed them back into the gourd, sealed it tightly, and said to Songmao, "Take it! I entrust both elixirs to you. The golden one is for Kauko. The boy faces great dangers ahead. Without it, he may not survive until his father returns. The colorful one is for you. When you find your beloved, give it to her."

"Thank you, Master," Songmao said. "Why don't you give it to Kauko directly?"

The master sighed, his voice filled with deep concern and helplessness. "Kauko is honest but fragile. I don't want to burden him too much. I offended some immortal by refining these elixirs, and the reaper is likely already on his way. The celestial phenomenon last time was a warning."

Tears welled up in Songmao's eyes. "Master, we can give up the elixirs and plead for mercy. Your life is what matters most."

The master spoke slowly, "Foolish words. Immortals do not understand human emotions." His tone seemed to transcend all worldly concerns. "Tell Kauko that the flute his father left has a life of its own. He must not play it carelessly. Use it only when facing demons and monsters."

Every word the master spoke felt like a last testament, weighing heavily on Songmao's heart.

While the master meditated, Songmao hurried to the cliffs to find Kauko, hoping to devise a plan to save the master.

"Kauko, where are you?" Songmao called out when he couldn't find Kauko immediately.

At that moment, Kauko was clinging to the steep cliff face, his hands gripping the sharp edges of the rocks. Sweat dripped from his forehead like broken beads. He focused intently, searching for the next foothold. The faint sound of Songmao's intermittent calls reached his ears, and he turned to listen. Suddenly, a fierce mountain gust swept through, causing Kauko's body to sway unsteadily. The rocks beneath his feet began to loosen. Before he could react, his footing gave way, and with a sharp cry, his body plummeted like a broken kite into the abyss below.

Songmao caught sight of Kauko's falling figure and panicked. Just as he was about to jump down to rescue him, the master suddenly appeared. He grabbed Songmao's tail and urgently asked, "Where is Kauko?"

Tears streamed down Songmao's face as he pointed a trembling finger toward the bottomless cliff. Without hesitation, the master leapt into the misty abyss, transforming into a giant roc.

The roc's figure flickered in and out of view, its massive wings brushing against the rocks, creating a howling wind. Through the mist, the master's sharp eyes caught sight of Kauko struggling in mid-air. But the roc's wings gradually lost control, like tattered sails, unable to harness the wind's power. Still, the master pushed on, using momentum to chase Kauko's falling form. At the critical moment before Kauko hit the ground, the master managed to grab him. His wings were completely numb, devoid of any strength to struggle. They had no choice but to crash into the jagged rocks below.

Kauko woke from a brief unconsciousness, feeling suffocated under the heavy, lifeless wings wrapped tightly around him. He called out with all his strength, "Master! Master!" Hearing his cries, the master slowly loosened the roc's wings enveloping Kauko. Kauko struggled to his feet, and the roc transformed back into human form.

Kauko knelt on the ground, gently lifting the master, who lay in a pool of blood, and cradled him in his arms. Despair and fear surged like a tidal wave, causing him to break down in tears. The master struggled to open his eyes, his lips trembling as if he had countless words to say. Kauko leaned in close, straining to catch the faint, fading whispers, but only silence followed.

At that moment, the master's finger weakly pointed toward the hem of Kauko's robe, signaling something. But Kauko couldn't understand the gesture. He clutched the master's hand, his confusion and despair deepening.

A faint smile crossed the master's face, as if comforting Kauko. Then, his breath gradually faded. Seeing the master's smile, Kauko's tears slowly stopped. He clung to a sliver of hope, thinking the master had merely fallen into a deep sleep. He carefully wiped the blood from the master's lips and held him quietly. Time seemed to stand still until the master in his arms vanished, replaced by a small gray sparrow fluttering above Kauko's head, chirping loudly. It circled a few times before disappearing into the treetops.

Kauko sat on the desolate rocky slope, rubbing his tear-filled eyes, unable to shake the lingering doubt in his heart. He firmly believed the master had not truly left. Perhaps this was just a game of hide-and-seek from their childhood. Had the master returned to the mountain? Was he testing Kauko's flying skills?

He suddenly stood up and, following the techniques in the manual, attempted to soar into the sky. Again and again, he tried, only to crash onto the cold, hard rocks each time. His body was covered in wounds, the pain a cruel reminder that this was no dream. Finally, exhausted, he leaned against a cold stone, gazing at the sky above as silent tears fell.

At that moment, Fire Maiden sensed a distant sorrow, like a shark catching the scent of blood. A strange excitement stirred within her. She remembered the little "pig-child" who had once evoked a similar feeling in her. Could it be him again? She focused, listening to the faint sobs coming from the direction she was heading.

Fire Maiden laughed maniacally like a madwoman, following her intuition. She soon arrived at the foot of Tian Mountain. She hid behind a massive rock and peered through a crevice, spotting a young man curled up in despair. His sobs were intermittent, his words incoherent. His face shifted between human and pig, as if he had lost his mind.

She was certain this was Marshal Tianpeng's son. The boy's human form had inherited all the charm of his father, reminding her why she had been so infatuated with Tianpeng back then. His pig-like face might surpass his father's in some ways—still ugly, but it evokes a certain pity. "Ugh!" Fire Maiden interrupted her own thoughts, reminding herself, "I'm not his mother." She marveled that the pig-child had survived the flames. There must be something extraordinary about him. Perhaps heaven had spared him for a reason, and she could use him to her advantage.

Fire Maiden adjusted her tattered beggar's disguise and limped toward Kauko, her voice hoarse. "Young master, benefactor, do you have any food to spare? If not, some pennies will do."

Kauko looked up and, seeing a stranger, immediately shifted to his human face. He sighed heavily, his voice weak. "Take my life instead."

Fire Maiden feigned surprise. "Oh, young master, why so pessimistic?"

Kauko hung his head in despair. "It's my fault. I killed my master."

Her eyes flickered with astonishment. "You mean Master Dapeng?"

He looked up, confusion in his eyes. "Yes, him. Do you know my master?"

Fire Maiden continued her act, feigning sentimentality. "I received some alms from him once. Did he leave anything behind?"

Kauko shook his head, his voice filled with sorrow. "No, he left no words."

She sighed. "He was a proud man, to leave like this. Child, what will you do now?"

He pointed to the sky. "I want to return to the mountain, but... I can't find the way back."

Fire Maiden was stunned for a moment. She saw nothing but emptiness where Kauko pointed. Had the boy truly lost his mind from the shock? She couldn't help but think that her attempt to kill him earlier had been unnecessary. She probed further, "Do you still have that copper flute?"

Kauko replied bitterly, "I lost it on the mountain."

A glint of cunning flashed in Fire Maiden's eyes. She slowly pulled a copper flute from her sleeve and handed it to Kauko. "Poor child, I found this a few days ago. Let me give it to you."

Kauko took the flute and found it nearly identical to his own. He pressed it to his chest, as if drawing some comfort from it. He asked, "How can I thank you?"

Fire Maiden smiled. "Just play more tunes with it, and I'll be satisfied."

Kauko nodded. "Alright."

Fire Maiden gazed at him and suddenly suggested, "Young master, why not travel the world with me?"

Kauko shook his head. "No, I must stay here to mourn my master."

"Very well, until we meet again." With that, Fire Maiden turned and walked into the rocky terrain, her figure soon disappearing into the depths of the forest.

Kauko stayed at the foot of the mountain for seven days, convinced that his master had passed away and that returning to the mountain was no longer an option. A thought began to form in his mind—he wanted to see Bamei. He vaguely remembered that the place where he had last seen her was somewhere to the southwest, near the border. He knelt before Tian Mountain, bowing repeatedly, grateful for the master and the mountain that had given him a beautiful childhood.

Learning from his past mistakes, he decided not to reveal his true appearance easily. Disguised as a beggar, he covered his head and face with a cloth, leaving only his deep eyes visible. He set off on foot, walking along the endless path, his clothes fluttering in the wind, kicking up dust with each step.

While passing through a lonely mountain village, he encountered a group of men drinking openly at the village entrance, the enticing aroma of food wafting from a nearby fire. Unable to resist the smell, he approached. Before he could speak, an elder tossed him a wine gourd and warmly said, "A guest has arrived. Come, sit with us."

He sat on a stone bench nearby and handed the wine gourd back to the elder. "Uncle, I don't drink."

The elder examined Kauko and realized that despite his tall and sturdy build, he was still a child. He signaled to one of his men, who immediately ladled a bowl of spicy and sour tripe from the steaming pot and handed it to Kauko.

Kauko devoured three bowls in quick succession, his face flushing and his eyes sparkling with satisfaction. "This tripe is truly a delicacy!" He curiously asked the elder for the recipe.

The elder chuckled. "You're a clever one. I'll tell you. It's not hard to make, but the ingredients are rare. First, you need a good cow. After slaughtering it, clean the tripe thoroughly, mix it with seasonings and cilantro, then simmer it over low heat for an hour."

Kauko nodded in gratitude. "Thank you, Uncle. I'll remember that." He patted his chest. "I can't eat for free. Is there any work I can do for you?"

The elder smiled approvingly. "Sure. Later, we're heading into the mountains. You can come with us."

Kauko followed the group into a thicket, helping them dig pits and set traps for wild boars. They sharpened bamboo stakes and covered the traps with branches. After finishing, he bid them farewell and continued on his journey.

Just as he reached the path, a young boy came running toward him, followed closely by the sound of approaching hoofbeats. Kauko quickly hid behind a large tree. As the boy passed by, Kauko's hand shot out like an eagle's talon, firmly grabbing the boy's arm.

"Come with me!" he whispered, dragging the boy into the dense bushes. He urgently asked, "Who's chasing you?"

"Sherkon soldiers!" the boy gasped.

Soon, two cavalrymen rode into the bushes, brandishing long sabers, rapidly closing in on Kauko and the boy. Seeing no way to escape on foot, Kauko remembered the traps. He quickly pulled the boy toward the boar traps, skillfully avoiding them, then slowed down to wait for the pursuers.

The boy cleverly pulled out a small copper mirror from his pocket, expertly reflecting sunlight into the cavalrymen's eyes, blinding them and causing both men and horses to fall into the traps.

Kauko turned to examine the boy closely, noticing that his face bore some resemblance to his own, though the boy had a monkey-like appearance. He asked curiously, "Little one, what's your name?"

The boy raised his head. "I'm Monkey Three. Don't treat me like a kid. I'm just short."

"Brother Monkey Three," Kauko said with an awkward smile, "where are you headed?"

"I'm fleeing for my life! There's no place for me in Daze anymore! The Sherkon people are inciting others to hunt down freaks like me just because we look different. They want to wipe us out. I've decided to go to Annan. I heard that even someone like me can live in peace there."

"Is there really such a paradise in this world?" Kauko asked skeptically.

"My ancestor saw it with his own eyes. He never lied to me," Monkey Three said with conviction.

A glimmer of hope sparked in Kauko's heart. He flicked his ears, revealing his pig face, and joked, "Look at this pig face of mine. People either think I'm a demon or a monster."

Monkey Three leaned in curiously and teased, "You're not the reincarnation of Marshal Tianpeng, are you?"

Kauko smiled bitterly and self-deprecatingly said, "Believe it or not, I'm his son. Unfortunately, he's never seen me, leaving me to wander the world alone."

Monkey Three patted Kauko's shoulder. "I believe you. With a face like that, how could it be fake? My king and your father were sworn brothers."

Kauko asked curiously, "Who is your king?"

"The Great Sage Equal to Heaven (Sun Wukong)!" Monkey Three said proudly.

Kauko suddenly understood. "Then why did you come to Daze, this land of trouble?"

Monkey Three sighed. "It's a long story. After the king left, our home was destroyed. We've been wandering ever since, ending up here."

Kauko couldn't help but sigh. "I wonder when those great heroes will return from the West. Perhaps they've already ascended to heaven and forgotten about us."

Monkey Three was silent for a moment, then said, "I've long given up hope. We have to find our own way." Suddenly, his eyes lit up. "How about we travel together to Annan?"

Kauko looked deeply at Monkey Three, a grateful smile on his face, but he shook his head. "I still have unfinished business. I can't go with you."

before parting, Monkey Three took out his small copper mirror and handed it to Kauko. "This is a token of my gratitude. Please take it."

Kauko examined the antique mirror and said, "You should keep it to give to a girl."

"It's fine," Monkey Three replied. "I've been making mirrors since I was a child. If I meet someone I like, I'll make one for her."

"Then thank you," Kauko said with a smile. "Actually, I really like this little mirror, but I don't know how to use it. If I give it to someone someday, you won't mind, will you?"

"Of course not. Brother Kau must have someone in mind, right?"

Kauko just smiled, but a subtle emotion flickered in his eyes.

Chapter 6

Trembling Heart

Under the scorching sun in the wheat field, Kauko was so exhausted that he couldn't keep his eyes open. He leaned against a pile of wheat and dozed off. The landlord's young son, about eleven or twelve years old, led a group of village kids, sneaked up to Kauko with mischievous smiles, lifted the cloth covering his face, and gently tickled his nose with a wheat stalk.

"Ah-choo!" Kauko sneezed violently, and with that sound, his true face was fully exposed to the sunlight—a completely unexpected pig-like appearance. The children froze in shock, their eyes wide with fear, and then erupted into screams: "Monster! Monster!"

Filled with a mix of fear and excitement, the children picked up clods of dirt and stones, hurling them at Kauko. Panicked, Kauko covered his face with his hands, as memories of his unbearable childhood came flooding back. He stumbled to his feet and ran desperately into the depths of the forest, kicking up a cloud of dust. As he ran, he berated himself, "I've made the same mistake as when I was a child. Now, without my master to save me, what should I do?"

Kauko ran wildly, his heart pounding like a drum. Ahead was the edge of the forest, where a rushing river blocked his path. Summoning his courage, he leaped across, barely making it to the other side, but the steep and treacherous riverbank cut off his escape route. Helpless, he turned to face the pursuing children, his eyes filled with panic and pleading, as if begging them to let him go.

The landlord's son climbed onto a rock by the water, holding a stone in his hand, and sneered as he took aim at Kauko. Faced with the threat, Kauko instinctively hunched over, baring his tusks like a cornered beast, letting out a low growl. The intimidating aura made the landlord's son freeze, his legs trembling. Before he could scream, he slipped into the river and was swept away by the swift current.

The remaining children, seeing their companion disappear into the water, were struck with terror. They screamed and scattered in all directions.

As night fell, torches illuminated the riverbank. The landlord, on horseback, led a group of villagers armed with shovels and machetes to the downstream area, where they found the drowned child. The child, dripping wet, pointed into the darkness and said with a hint of gratitude, "Father, it was the monster who saved me. He's not as scary as we thought."

The landlord immediately scolded his son, "If that's the case, how can he be a monster? Keep your mouth shut!" He then called out into the darkness, "Benefactor, come out. I want to thank you."

Kauko, forgetting to change back to his human face, timidly stepped forward. The villagers gasped and backed away. The landlord, however, took Kauko's cold hand and said, "Child, you may be ugly, but you have the heart of a Bodhisattva. I'll give you this horse. Leave quickly. It won't be long before the Sherkon soldiers come for you. And take your wages..."

Kauko mounted the fast horse and rode along the dusty ancient road, eventually arriving in the area frequented by the Dianshui Opera Troupe. He hurried past a small inn, hesitating whether to stop.

At that moment, a soft, melodious song drifted through the half-open window of the inn. Kauko suddenly stopped, his heart leaping into his throat. The tune was unmistakably the mountain song Bamei used to sing. Every word, every note, was deeply etched in his memory—"At the top of Cang Mountain is my hometown, my brother carries his sister back to her mother's house..."

Through the dimly lit window, Kauko caught sight of a young woman sitting in a dark corner, her head slightly bowed as she sang. Her voice was soft and clear, like a flowing spring. His heart skipped a beat, and a glimmer of joy flashed in his eyes. The familiar melody made him think of Bamei. Without a second thought, he dismounted and hurried into the inn.

Holding his breath, he approached the singer step by step, his heart filled with anticipation. However, when she turned her face, he was disappointed to find that she was a stranger, not the person he had been longing for.

He pulled out a worn copper coin from his pocket and carefully placed it in front of the singer, his voice low, trying to hide his eagerness. "This song... where did you learn it?"

The singer stopped plucking her pipa and looked up with a gentle smile. "Brother, this is a song from the Dianshui Opera Troupe. I learned it there."

Kauko pressed further, "Then, is the singer named Bamei?"

The singer nodded. "Yes, it's Bamei."

Hearing this, Kauko's heart leaped with joy. His eyes instinctively scanned the inn, as if Bamei might magically appear before him at any moment. He turned urgently to the waiter. "How can I find the Dianshui Opera Troupe?"

The waiter, a young man about Kauko's age with a clever look in his eyes, smiled and said, "Sir, you may not know this, but the Dianshui Opera Troupe travels all over. It's hard to say where they are. But it just so happens that in two

64

days, we'll have our Torch Festival here. They come every year to perform. If you're not in a hurry, wait two days, and they might show up on their own."

Kauko's eyes lit up, and the heaviness in his heart lifted as if he had seen a ray of light. He nodded firmly and decided to stay.

Two days passed in the blink of an eye. At the first light of dawn, Kauko was already sitting in the inn's main hall, his eyes repeatedly scanning the doorway as waves of cheerful passersby walked by.

The waiter came out from the backyard with a bowl of hot noodle soup and greeted him with a smile. "Sir, can't wait any longer? Have this bowl of noodles, and then we'll go."

Kauko quickly finished the noodles and immediately dragged the waiter out the door. They wound through narrow alleys, avoiding the bustling crowds, and headed straight for the open-air theater on the outskirts. The noise along the way gradually gave way to the sounds of gongs, drums, and suonas. Kauko's steps quickened, wishing he could leap to the stage in one stride. When they finally arrived at the theater, they were too late. The play "Zhu Bajie Carries His Wife" was nearing its end.

Kauko pushed through the crowd, his eyes fixed on the stage. In his haste, he accidentally stepped on a girl's foot. The girl gasped in pain and turned around, ready to slap him, but froze when she saw his face.

"It's you?" she exclaimed softly. It was the pipa-playing singer from the inn.

Kauko quickly bowed his head and apologized, "I'm sorry, I'm sorry." He stepped back and stood behind her, glancing up at the stage. The girl tilted her body and pointed to a graceful figure on stage, her voice tinged with envy. "See that? The one wearing the mask is Bamei! Her singing is amazing. If only I had half her talent..."

Her voice continued, but Kauko's mind was no longer on her. He quietly pulled the waiter behind the singer and silently retreated to the back of the crowd. Though he stood far away, his height allowed him to see the stage by standing on his tiptoes.

His gaze followed the masked female lead on stage, the familiarity like a melody buried deep in his memory, now suddenly awakened. He was certain that even if the singer hadn't pointed her out, he would have recognized her as Bamei.

On stage, Bamei wore the costume of a young bride, her movements graceful and captivating. Though a mask hid her face, it couldn't conceal the sparkle in her eyes. As she bowed slightly to thank the audience, it felt as if the entire world had fallen silent.

Bamei and Tichu disappeared behind the curtain, leaving behind a joyful dream that lingered in the audience's hearts. The fans were reluctant to leave, their cheers rising like a tide: "Encore! Encore!"

Kauko stood at the back of the crowd, staring eagerly at the stage, but the curtain did not rise again, and Bamei did not reappear. Suddenly, he remembered a mischievous trick from his childhood and quietly slipped around the stage, sneaking into the dimly lit dressing room.

There, he saw Bamei standing in front of Weigu, her face unhappy, her words filled with resentment. "I won't perform anymore! I'm tired of playing this young bride!"

Weigu crossed her arms, her brow furrowed, and asked coldly, "Then what do you want to do?"

Bamei pouted. "I want to play a princess! Why can't I play a princess?"

Weigu glanced at the door, waved Tichu away, and fixed Bamei with a sharp gaze. "Anyone can play a princess, except you."

Bamei was stunned, her eyes glistening with tears, her voice tinged with bitterness. "Is it because I'm ugly? Or because I come from a lowly background?"

Weigu shook her head lightly, her tone as faint as a wisp of smoke. "Neither. It's just not your destiny."

Bamei pressed her lips together, silent for a moment, then finally let her emotions spill over. "I'm grown up now. I'm tired of always being carried on Tichu's back as a young bride!"

Weigu was silent for a long time, then reached out to stroke Bamei's soft hair, sighing deeply. "Fine, one last time. Let's give them a proper farewell. The crowd outside is getting restless."

"One last time," Bamei murmured, wiping the tears from the corners of her eyes and putting on her mask. Weigu nodded, called out "Tichu," and walked toward the backyard.

Tichu entered the dressing room and, seeing Bamei with her head down, gently took her hand. "Come on."

The curtain rose again, and Tichu carried Bamei onto the stage, the audience cheering wildly.

This time, Tichu seemed to put more effort into his performance than ever before. He carried Bamei on his back, sometimes straight, sometimes sideways, and even lifted her over his shoulder at one point. Bamei, initially in low spirits, gradually cheered up as Tichu's antics grew more playful. Her singing became even more radiant.

Tichu subtly slipped a flute from his sleeve and played half a tune with her. The melody flowed like a clear mountain stream, blending seamlessly with Bamei's crisp singing, creating a beautiful harmony. Bamei couldn't help but wonder, since when could Tichu play the flute so well? It matched her performance perfectly! She tried to catch Tichu's eyes, but he kept his head turned away, not giving her the chance.

When he lifted her onto his shoulder, Bamei deliberately tilted her body, breaking her balance and slipping into his arms. He caught her steadily, their eyes meeting briefly behind the mask. In that instant, she realized that the person who made her laugh and cry had returned like a mystery, staging another grand performance! She wanted to laugh out loud but managed to hold it in.

Amid the bustling crowd, a pair of sharp eyes glimmered under the shadow of a hat. It was Fire Maiden, hidden behind her mask! She had been patrolling a hundred miles away when she heard Kauko's enchanting flute music and came to see the spectacle, wanting to witness how the boy played the "magic flute" she had given him and created so much dark energy.

When the play finally ended, Bamei could no longer contain herself and burst into laughter backstage. She grabbed a bunch of dried flowers and playfully hit "Tichu" on the head, her voice filled with coquettish excitement. "Tell me! Are you really him?"

"Tichu" dodged and chuckled, not giving a direct answer.

Bamei persisted, her laughter brimming with joy. "Still playing dumb? Do you think you can fool me?"

The other troupe members, drawn by the sudden commotion, crowded around, their eyes sparkling with curiosity. In the midst of the noise, Kauko gently took Bamei's wrist and steadily removed his mask. Bamei's laughter stopped abruptly as she stared at Kauko. The handsome young man before her was beyond her imagination of Kauko. "Tell me, who are you really?" she whispered.

The troupe members exchanged glances, murmuring, "Who is this handsome young man? Some kind of deity?"

Kauko, however, was in no hurry to reveal himself. He smiled slyly, like a magician, and shed his costume. Then, from his sleeve, he pulled out a scarf, covered his face, and mysteriously shook his ears. With a quick tug, he revealed his familiar, comical pig face!

Everyone burst into laughter. It was the mischievous little pig brother from back then! Bamei's eyes sparkled with excitement. She jumped up and, catching Kauko off guard, playfully tugged on his big ears. "It really is you! Did you come for the rice wine?"

Kauko smiled modestly, touching his big ears. "I wouldn't dare. My master punished me for that! This time, I came specifically to see you, Bamei, and everyone else. After this, I'll leave."

His innocent, lively words brushed past Bamei's ears like a morning breeze, stirring ripples deep in her heart. Her smile softened, and a faint blush spread across her cheeks, like the first bloom of spring flowers, tinged with shyness.

The senior sister seemed to sense Bamei's feelings and said to the group, "Alright, everyone, get back to work. Let Kauko and Bamei talk." The others chuckled and dispersed.

Bamei had a thousand things she wanted to say. She wanted to ask, "Did you think of me all these years? Will you stay this time?" But these words couldn't be spoken, as a few sisters were eavesdropping outside the window. She could only say something trivial. "Kauko, Tian Mountain is a place of immortals. Why didn't you stay there?"

Kauko smiled and asked, "Bamei, from the way you say it, it sounds like you're not very welcoming."

"Welcoming? You showed up and caused trouble on stage. You're lucky I'm not punishing you!" Bamei said loudly, while giving Kauko a playful look and secretly grabbing his hand, pulling him toward the back door.

Tichu, holding a spiked club, suddenly blocked their path, glaring at Kauko. "Stop! So, it was you who tricked me and made me pass out! Take this..."

Bamei quickly stepped in front of Kauko, pleading, "Tichu, Kauko rarely visits. He was just joking. Don't take it seriously, okay?"

Tichu, seeing Bamei protecting Kauko, grew even angrier. But how could he swing his club at Bamei?

Suddenly, a commotion erupted in the courtyard. A group of Sherkon soldiers stormed into the theater, quickly surrounding the troupe. A cold, thunderous voice shouted, "All performers, gather in front of the stage!"

Kauko had already changed back to his human face, but Bamei was still worried. She quickly handed him a painted mask and whispered, "Put this on. Be careful."

The troupe members guessed that Kauko might be in trouble again. Many of them also put on masks, hoping to confuse the soldiers.

The soldiers herded everyone to the front courtyard and ordered, "Remove your masks!"

Kauko's heart tightened. He slowly took off his mask and clutched it in his hand, reminding himself not to reveal even a hint of his pig face to avoid implicating the troupe. However, the soldiers' eyes merely swept over him without suspicion. They roughly separated the male performers and scrutinized the female performers one by one, their gazes lecherous, as if selecting flowers or birds. Bamei and a few other sisters were unfortunately chosen. The soldiers grinned. "Don't be afraid. You're just going to the barracks to perform."

Weigu's eyes flashed with anger as she shielded Bamei with one arm and pointed at the soldiers with the other, scolding, "They're not going anywhere!"

Before her words could fully land, a soldier shoved her to the ground. Bamei hurried forward to help Weigu up, whispering, "Auntie, leave this to us. You should rest." She handed Weigu over to someone behind her, then turned coldly toward the soldier who had pushed her aunt. Suddenly, she channeled her inner energy and struck out with both palms, hitting the soldier's chest with thunderous force. The soldier let out a cry, clutching his chest as he fell to the ground. Tichu and the other male performers, seeing this, erupted in fury, charging at the soldiers. In an instant, fists, clubs, and blades flew, and the air was filled with shouts and the clash of weapons.

Tichu was like a tiger descending the mountain, his long staff whirling with such force that soldiers fell or fled wherever he went. Meanwhile, Kauko, holding his copper flute, looked somewhat panicked. Though he had trained in martial arts for years, he had never engaged in real combat, let alone a life-and-death struggle. Reluctant to harm anyone, he nervously waved his flute from time to time, trying to deter soldiers from attacking Bamei.

Fire Maiden watched coldly from the crowd, a hint of mockery in her eyes. She observed the self-important Sherkon soldiers, who, under the provocation of the troupe, behaved like startled birds. To her, the scene was like a farcical comedy. Her gaze lingered on Kauko, the pig-child with whom she had formed an inexplicable bond over a flute. Recently, whenever he played the copper flute she had given him, it seemed to send waves of dark energy her way, and she found herself growing fond of this naive boy. Watching his clumsy attempts at fighting, she thought to herself, "He doesn't have a trace of his father's skill. Perhaps it's because of the needle I planted in his forehead."

At this critical moment, Kauko whispered to Bamei, "Be careful. I'm going out." With that, he quickly disappeared from sight. Tichu, witnessing this, asked Bamei in confusion, "What do you even see in a coward like him?"

Suddenly, Kauko returned, riding a majestic horse and leading another. He charged into the crowd like a storm, knocking several soldiers to the ground. His horse came to a halt in front of Bamei, who, with a sparkle in her eyes, nimbly leaped onto the saddle.

A soldier swung his sword at Kauko, but Fire Maiden, quick as lightning, threw a stone that struck the soldier's wrist, causing him to drop his weapon. "Don't hurt my treasure!" she muttered to herself.

After breaking through the encirclement, Kauko reined in his horse and turned around, revealing a fierce, green-faced pig visage. He let out a thunderous roar that shook the heavens, causing the soldiers to tremble and retreat in fear.

The captain of the soldiers, after a moment of stunned silence, suddenly flashed a greedy look in his eyes and shouted, "What are you afraid of? Capture that monster, and the reward will be doubled!" He mounted his horse, brandished his spear, and urged his men to follow. Though still fearful, the soldiers' greed was ignited, and they quickly remounted their horses.

Kauko subtly signaled to Bamei, and the two galloped away, quickly disappearing into the forest and leaving the soldiers half a mile behind.

Seeing the pursuers fall behind, Weigu ordered the able-bodied members of the troupe to tend to the wounded while she went inside to fetch money, intending to distribute it so everyone could flee. As she entered the room, she froze—a woman in a red robe, wearing a skull mask, sat in her chair. The woman's cold eyes glowed like ghostly flames from behind the mask. She stirred the tea on the table with her fingertip, creating eerie ripples on the surface.

Weigu's gaze fell to the floor, where her husband lay slumped under the table, clutching a broken bowl, his face pale and lifeless. In that instant, she understood who had come. The day she had feared had finally arrived. It wasn't for herself that she worried, but for Bamei.

"Weigu, you've made me search for so long," Fire Maiden said with a cold smile.

Weigu slowly sat down across from Fire Maiden and replied calmly, "I know you hate me, thinking I betrayed you. But think about it—without me, your fate would have been the same. The palace was always a life-and-death stage."

Fire Maiden narrowed her eyes. "Let's not talk about me. That girl—she's the princess, isn't she?"

Weigu's heart turned cold. "No, no, she's my—"

Fire Maiden interrupted with a mocking laugh. "Haha, you were going to say she's yours and the king's? I see the king in her, but she resembles the queen more. Where's your trace in her?"

Weigu's knees buckled, and she fell to the ground. She had promised the queen, who had died during their escape, that she would protect the princess and raise her to adulthood. Her voice trembled with pleading. "Spare this child. She doesn't know she's the princess, and I've never told her anything. She's had a hard life, growing up performing in operas, enduring so much suffering. She's kind-hearted and has never harmed anyone. She won't be a threat to you. She doesn't even have a real name, just the stage name 'Bamei.' She has no connection to the royal family."

Fire Maiden sneered. "Do you think I'm some merciful Bodhisattva? I've harmed people who never wronged me, people who had nothing to do with me."

Weigu's voice grew more desperate. "But how could you? You loved the king. If you harm his bloodline, how will he rest in peace?"

Fire Maiden's eyes flickered, as if struck by Weigu's words. "Ah! You have a point. You've touched a soft spot in my heart. What a loyal servant! Why not join me?"

Weigu's breathing quickened. "No, the queen treated me well. Let me join her today." She stood up, and under Fire Maiden's gaze, picked up the bowl from the table and drank its contents in one gulp. She collapsed beside her husband, like a teardrop falling into the dust, silent and unnoticed.

***

Bamei and Kauko galloped across streams and through forests, covering a hundred miles in one breath until they reached a hill, where they finally felt safe, believing they had shaken off the relentless Sherkon soldiers. Bamei slowed her horse and rode alongside Kauko, her gaze lingering on his handsome face. She studied him as if she didn't recognize him and asked with a smile, "Are you really Pig-Head Brother?"

Kauko pretended to be offended. "You just tugged on my big ears, and you still doubt me? Fine." With a shake of his head, he transformed back into his pig face and added, "Do you want to tug on the other one?"

Bamei laughed. "Of course I want to tug on your ears, Pig-Head Brother. But I mean, how dare you lead all those enemies here?" She gave him a thumb-up.

Kauko's face lit up with a childlike, triumphant smile. "With you here, Bamei, I have nothing to fear. But from here on, it's up to you."

"I know this area well. I'll take you somewhere safe," Bamei replied confidently.

Suddenly, Kauko's ears perked up, and his expression grew tense. Through the faint rustling of leaves, he caught the sound of pursuing soldiers' hoofbeats.

Bamei dismounted and deftly tied a bundle of leafy branches to her horse's tail. With a gentle pat, the horse bolted down the forest path, kicking up a cloud of dust. Meanwhile, she and Kauko hid behind the hill, watching as the soldiers appeared, then disappeared into the dust and trees.

Bamei and Kauko rode together on one horse, moving through the fading light of the sunset, away from the soldiers' direction. Kauko sat behind Bamei, the breeze gently lifting her hair, which occasionally brushed against his face, carrying a faint, sweet fragrance that tickled his cheeks. His hands hovered, wanting to wrap around her slender waist as it swayed with the horse's movements, but an inexplicable timidity held him back. The jostling of the horse caused them to bump into each other from time to time, each touch bringing an unprecedented joy.

Bamei was also waiting, longing for Kauko's arms to encircle her waist. Yet, she too felt a hint of unease, unsure if her desire was too much to hope for. But Kauko's hands never settled, and after each accidental touch, he would murmur an apology: "I'm really sorry," or "I didn't mean to. Don't mind me."

Tired of his half-hearted apologies, Bamei suddenly spurred the horse into a gallop, leaping over several obstacles in quick succession. Caught off guard, Kauko instinctively wrapped his arms tightly around her. Bamei, held firmly by him, felt a ripple of emotion in her heart. She deliberately raised her voice, teasing, "Still not letting go? Aren't you afraid I'll call for help?"

Kauko no longer wanted to let go. Instead, he playfully flapped his big ears against Bamei's neck, making her burst into laughter. It was as if they had returned to their childhood, to the little attic where the world consisted only of their warm friendship.

In the last rays of the setting sun, they came upon a dilapidated Buddhist temple. Its walls were mostly collapsed, and the glazed tiles on the spire glimmered in the fading light.

Above the temple gate hung a weathered wooden plaque with the bold characters "Jingxin Temple." As they stepped inside, a few startled birds flapped out from above their heads, disappearing into the darkening sky.

"How will we spend the night here?" Kauko asked curiously.

"Since I brought you here, I have a plan," Bamei replied confidently. She found a bowl of candles in a corner and deftly lit one.

In the flickering candlelight, Kauko's shadow stretched long and monstrous. Worried it might frighten Bamei, he quietly shifted back to his handsome face and followed her to the backyard.

Bamei gestured for Kauko to lift a stone slab hidden in the grass. They carefully descended into an underground chamber, then covered the entrance. The chamber was the size of two or three rooms, dry and quiet, furnished with simple tables, chairs, bedding, and even a small stove.

"Bamei, have you been here before?"

"I came here with Aunt Wei when I was little," Bamei replied, pointing to some jars on a wooden shelf along the wall. "Do you want to know what's inside?"

Kauko squinted and joked, "It's not gold and silver, is it?" He stepped forward and gently opened one jar, revealing white flour. He opened a few more, finding dried sweet potato strips, bamboo shoots, and mushrooms. He couldn't help but ask, "Are you hungry?"

"Starving!"

"Princess, take a seat. I'll make you a three-delicacy noodle soup."

Bamei, hearing Kauko call her "princess," couldn't help but ask, "What did you call me?"

"Princess!" Kauko replied casually as he worked by the stove. "In my eyes, you're a princess."

As Kauko busied himself, Bamei fell into deep thought. A few days ago, she had overheard a stranger talking to Aunt Wei.

***

It was dusk, and the golden light of the setting sun draped the ruined courtyard like a delicate veil. A man with a grave expression stood before Aunt Wei, seemingly delivering a command. He whispered to her that the people of Daze were stirring in secret and needed a banner to rally behind—the legendary Princess Wenxi. The man emphasized, "On the day the princess turns seventeen, you must bring her to Jingxin Temple. The rest is not your concern."

Aunt Wei's face changed, and she waved her hands in agitation, her voice filled with reproach and anger. "Where were you self-proclaimed heroes when the princess needed you? Now you want to place the burden of saving the nation on the shoulders of a young girl!"

The man had no response and silently turned to leave.

When night fell, enveloping the courtyard in a heavy black shroud, Bamei quietly approached Aunt Wei, her innocent eyes wide. "Auntie, am I the legendary princess?"

Aunt Wei took a deep breath, her tone tinged with helplessness. "What nonsense are you thinking? It's not you; it's someone else. But remember, if you ever hear of someone named Fire Maiden, you must stay away from her."

Bamei asked in confusion, "How will I recognize her? How can I avoid her?"

Aunt Wei sighed softly, her gaze distant, as if seeing through time to those buried memories. She said she knew a little and couldn't help but open up.

"What does the palace have to do with me? Go tell Princess Wenxi," Bamei said, blinking her eyes. Despite the turmoil in her heart, she pretended not to care.

Aunt Wei looked at her, a trace of sorrow in her eyes. She knew the child's fate had already been woven, and she could only silently pray for Bamei.

***

Since that deep conversation with Aunt Wei, Bamei, though she hadn't received a definitive answer about her royal identity, had grown increasingly certain in her heart. A sense of mission had quietly emerged within her. Recently, whenever the senior sister performed "Princess Changting" on stage, Bamei couldn't help but hold her breath, completely immersed in the story. The princess in the play, who donned armor and marched to the battlefield after her husband's death, seemed like a mirror, reflecting Bamei's own heart with greater clarity. She often felt as if she were that princess, walking a thorny path to save the people.

However, Kauko's sudden appearance disrupted her heroic aspirations. Over the years, during quiet nights, she would often sit by the window alone, gazing at the distant stars, inevitably thinking of him. Their childhood friendship was like a soft beam of moonlight, traversing the long years to bring solace to her lonely nights. Their reunion was more real and more sudden than she had imagined. Beyond the irrepressible joy, a strange and sweet sensation stirred deep within her, leaving her both confused and flustered. Every word Kauko spoke felt like a warm current, flowing straight into her heart.

Having acted in many emotional plays, she had guessed her own feelings but dared not face the obvious truth. "Auntie, what should I do?" she cried out in her heart. "I don't want to be a banner for thousands of soldiers. I just want Kauko by my side!"

But she knew this wish was self-deception. Aunt Wei couldn't change her fate, and the princess in the play had never had a choice. Bamei slowly lowered her head, hiding the complex emotions in her eyes. She knew that ahead of her lay the heavy responsibility of protecting her country, a path fraught with thorns and storms. And Kauko should not be dragged into this turmoil.

"Before affection can sprout, it must be severed," she thought, biting her lip and forcing herself to look away from Kauko's innocent smile. In that moment, her heart felt as if it had been cut by a knife, but she chose silence, knowing it was the best way to protect him.

Kauko, full of joy, brought over a bowl of steaming noodle soup and gently handed it to the frowning Bamei.

She took the bowl, her face lighting up instantly. Carefully holding it, she walked to the small table and sat down. She savored the taste, which seemed to carry a warmth of home, deeply touching her heart. Kauko, seeing the satisfaction and happiness on Bamei's face, smiled proudly and said, "My cooking isn't bad, is it? My master always praised me."

Mentioning his master, Bamei asked with concern, "How is Master Dapeng? Why did you come down the mountain alone?"

Kauko's smile faded. He set down his chopsticks, a deep longing flashing in his eyes. He began to slowly recount his memories with his master—sweet, bitter, and joyful moments unfolding like a scroll of paintings. Bamei listened quietly, her expression changing with Kauko's narration, as if her heart too was carried away to that mysterious, sunlit place.

At the end of the cavern, a beam of moonlight spilled in. Beneath that silver glow, a resilient red rose stood, listening to their wondrous tale. Rooted in the rock, clinging to a broken wooden barrel gifted by a kind soul, she had weathered a century of storms and sun, transforming the harsh elements into a single, radiant bloom. Her beauty was so captivating that no one had ever dared to pluck her, allowing her to survive and thrive. She had once dreamed of cultivating herself for another century or two, transforming into a rose fairy, surpassing all other flowers in elegance and never withering. But upon witnessing the two youths and their heartwarming story, she couldn't help but fantasize about becoming a princess herself, falling in love with a boy who could cook and change his face.

That night, Bamei was weighed down by her thoughts, like clouds gathering in her heart, until she finally succumbed to exhaustion and fell asleep. Kauko carefully tucked her in and then quietly lay down on the adjacent bed, closing his eyes. He wondered to himself, if he could fly, would Bamei be willing to join him and soar to the clouds above the Tian Mountain? To a dream that belonged only to them?

In the early morning, the first gentle rays of sunlight filtered through the narrow cracks of the cave, silently illuminating the dark corners. Kauko awoke to the melodious chirping of birds, filled with hope and joy for the new day. He turned to look at Bamei, who was still lost in a sweet dream. Her serene face resembled a sleeping lotus, filling Kauko's heart with an indescribable warmth. But then he remembered his master's words: "If the sun is up and someone is still lazing in bed, the day will be filled with misfortune." He had always lived by this teaching since childhood.

He tiptoed to Bamei's bedside, leaned down, and whispered softly by her ear, "Bamei, the sun is up. Do you remember our plans for today?" Bamei's eyes slowly opened, and she managed a faint smile, though her sorrow seemed to deepen. She replied softly, "It's not 'our' plans, but yours. You should go. I... I have my own mission." In truth, she had spent the entire night torn between her affection for Kauko and her sense of duty.

Kauko was taken aback by her words, unsure why she was being so resolute. He didn't press her, but instead maintained his composure, forcing a bittersweet smile as he said gently, "Then, may I cook you one last meal, as a farewell?"

Hearing this, Bamei's defenses seemed to crumble under the weight of his kindness. She sighed, "Very well, let's stay one more day. But sooner or later, we must part."

Kauko looked at her carefully and asked, "Is it because we look different?"

Bamei shook her head gently, motioning for him to sit down. She took a deep breath, as if gathering all her courage, and said, "No, it's not that, Kauko. I must tell you... I am already betrothed."

Kauko's smile froze, the news hitting him like a sudden storm. But he quickly composed himself. Their bond had always been pure, like that of friends, and he didn't want his feelings to become a burden to her. With the weight lifted from his heart, he smiled again and teased, "Let me guess, is it to Tichu? He's always carried you on his back since we were kids, looking after you so well."

Bamei didn't confirm or deny, but her voice trembled as she said, "You won't blame me, will you? Perhaps, between us, there was just a little less fate."

Kauko replied sincerely, "Bamei, meeting you has been the greatest joy of my life. How could I blame you? I truly envy Tichu's good fortune."

At this, Bamei could no longer hold back her tears, which fell like shattered pearls. Seeing her tear-filled eyes, Kauko's heart grew heavy. He reached out to wipe her tears, but his hand hesitated mid-air and eventually dropped. He said firmly, "Bamei, don't be troubled. I'll leave tomorrow, and we may never meet again. I'm going to Annan to find a friend."

Bamei looked up and asked, "What kind of friend?"

"A good friend, you could say."

"That sounds nice!" Bamei's mood lightened slightly. She wiped her tears with her sleeve, stood up, and straightened her clothes, as if shaking off her worries and sorrows. She said with a hint of cheer, "Alright, let's go play in the woods, shall we?"

She handed Kauko a basket and led him through the ancient forest behind the temple. After an hour or so, they had gathered a basket full of fresh bamboo shoots, wild mushrooms, and tender fern fronds. Then, they crouched by the stream, carefully washing the gifts of nature.

Tiptoeing on the stones in the stream, they crossed like two playful deer, bounding lightly to the grassy slope on the other side. In the open meadow dotted with wildflowers, they chased each other, their laughter echoing through the valley.

Kauko picked a cluster of vibrant flowers and deftly wove them into a crown, gently placing it on Bamei's hair. The crown swayed with her movements, attracting a flurry of butterflies that danced around her. Inspired by the scene, Bamei began to dance the skirt-swaying dance beloved by the girls of Daze, her steps light and full of life. Kauko took out his flute and played a melodious tune, accompanying her graceful movements. Every twist and turn of her dance seemed to harmonize with the blooming flowers of spring.

Kauko felt as if a small sun had risen in his heart, warming him with its glow. But just as he was basking in the moment, he suddenly felt as if struck by a wave of heat. His vision blurred, and he swayed uncontrollably before collapsing at Bamei's feet. At first, she thought he was joking, but when she reached out to pull him up, she was shocked to find blood trickling from his nose. She hurriedly helped him up, letting him lean against her as she carefully wiped the blood with her handkerchief, asking anxiously, "What's wrong with you?"

Kauko forced a weak smile, trying to downplay the situation. "It's nothing, just a bit dizzy."

"Dizzy? Has this happened before?"

"No, not before. It started after I left Tian Mountain. But usually, it's just a slight dizziness, not like today where I blacked out."

Bamei grew more concerned. "Then why did it happen today?"

Kauko grinned mischievously, "Maybe I was enchanted by your dance."

Seeing his playful mood return, Bamei gave him a gentle push, and Kauko fell back onto the grass. This time, Bamei lay down beside him, and together they gazed at the azure sky, letting the tranquil sounds of nature envelop them, as if they had become one with the earth.

The sunlight fell like golden threads, gently warming their bodies. The white clouds above painted poetic strokes across the sky, creating a dreamlike tapestry. The wildflowers in the meadow bloomed in a riot of colors, smiling in the breeze like joyful hearts.

Nearby, a flock of cranes glided gracefully past, like mystical messengers carrying an otherworldly aura, imparting a sense of peace and harmony to those who watched them.

Young hearts beat in this serene setting, filled with dreams and hopes. The once distant dreams now seemed within reach, tangible in this beautiful moment.

Unconsciously, Bamei reached out to find Kauko's hand. Her fingers moved inch by inch through the grass, her heart in turmoil. Suddenly, her hand touched something cold and snake-like, startling her into pulling back. She turned her head and saw that it wasn't a snake, but Kauko's flute!

The flute glinted in the sunlight.

Bamei quickly sat up and asked Kauko, "What kind of flute is this?"

Kauko replied, "It was given to me by a female beggar. I lost my own flute back in Tian Mountain."

"A beggar? Was she wearing a mask?" Bamei recalled Auntie Wei's description of Fire Maiden.

"How did you know?"

"Auntie Wei mentioned her." Bamei didn't elaborate further, but asked, "Kauko, how is this flute different from yours?"

"If I play it for too long, my hands and feet go cold."

Bamei stared intently at the flute. Though it looked ordinary, it seemed to hold some mysterious power. She decided to test it again, cautiously reaching out to touch it. The moment her fingers made contact, the terrifying image of a brownish-yellow snake appeared again, startling her and deepening her unease. She couldn't understand why Fire Maiden would set such a cruel trap for an innocent like Kauko. Was it because of her that Kauko had become entangled in this complex web of intrigue?

She quickly grabbed Kauko's hand and pulled him to his feet, hurrying back the way they came. The mysterious flute lingered in her mind. She suspected it was a dangerous object, and now that it had attached itself to Kauko, it wouldn't be as simple as discarding an old possession. As long as it remained with him, he would be in danger, his fate uncertain. What could she do? In the past, she would have turned to Auntie Wei for advice, but now, who could she turn to?

As they entered the temple gate, Bamei thought she saw the great Buddha blink at her. She stared intently, but the statue remained still, as if it had been her imagination. She shook her head, chiding herself for being overly suspicious. However, she noticed the thick layer of dust and cobwebs covering the Buddha, making it look unusually desolate. Filled with compassion, she decided to do something for the statue. She found a broom and, together with Kauko, gently swept away the dust and cobwebs, restoring the Buddha's majestic and sacred appearance. After cleaning, Bamei lit a stick of incense and reverently placed it in the incense burner. Instantly, the temple was filled with a serene and peaceful fragrance, soothing their hearts.

At that moment, though the Buddha remained silent, they heard a voice: "Kind souls, why not complete your good deed by offering something precious to this Buddha?"

Bamei was both startled and delighted. She silently prayed, "Merciful Bodhisattva, my friend here has a flute. Though it is not a worldly treasure, it is unique. Would you accept it?"

The Buddha's voice echoed softly, "It is fitting. Place it on the altar."

Bamei turned to Kauko and whispered, "Take it out."

Kauko looked puzzled. "Take what out?"

Bamei explained, "The Buddha wants your flute. Are you willing to offer it?"

Kauko smiled. "Why wouldn't I? It's been making me uncomfortable, and I was about to throw it away. If the Buddha can use it, that's the best outcome." With that, he handed the flute to Bamei. But she didn't dare take it, motioning for him to place it directly on the altar.

Kauko respectfully placed the flute on the altar. Suddenly, a flash of lightning lit up the temple, accompanied by the cry of a beast, and the flute vanished in an instant. Kauko stared at Bamei in astonishment, murmuring, "The moment the flute disappeared, I felt so much lighter. Isn't that strange?"

Chapter 7

The Distant Land

In the deep caverns of Jingxin Temple, Kauko was busy preparing dinner. Meanwhile, Bamei wandered like a lost fawn, her gaze occasionally lingering on Kauko before drifting off into the unknown distance. In her heart, she was silently planning how to bid her final farewell to him.

She stopped at the end of the cavern, where a ray of sunset filtered through a crack above, illuminating a few blooming red roses. The sight instantly brought life to the otherwise monotonous cave. Bamei's eyes were captivated by the unexpected beauty, and her steps involuntarily halted. The flowers seemed to beckon her, calling out to her. Overjoyed, she reached out and gently touched the most striking red bloom.

At that moment, the branch trembled, and a thorn pricked her fingertip. She let out a soft cry, "Ah!" A tiny drop of blood rolled down her finger, landing on the petal. Bamei pinched her finger, a slight frown crossing her face as a flicker of pain passed through her.

Hearing her cry, Kauko hurried over, concerned. He examined her wound, seemingly wanting to suck away the pain, but Bamei waved him off with a smile, indicating it was just a minor prick. Kauko returned to his cooking, while Bamei said she would lie down for a while.

When dinner was ready, Kauko quietly approached Bamei's bedside, only to find her already asleep. He gazed at her peaceful face, reluctant to wake her, and silently sat by the dim oil lamp, keeping watch.

Late into the night, Bamei's murmurs broke the silence. Her voice was weak, tinged with pain, "Kauko, my head hurts..." Kauko quickly leaned in, touching her forehead to find it burning like a furnace, and her fingers swollen like small buns. His heart tightened with worry, but he remained calm, whispering softly, "It's okay, I'm here." Remembering how his master had cared for him when he was once pricked by a thorn, he decided to follow the same method.

He fetched a cool, damp cloth and gently placed it on Bamei's forehead, quietly watching over her as she drifted back to sleep under its soothing comfort.

Before dawn, Kauko set out with a basket. He returned with it full of dandelions and wild chrysanthemums, glistening with dew. He brewed a pot of medicinal soup, its fragrance filling the air. With Kauko's help, Bamei drank the steaming soup, feeling some relief from her discomfort. He then applied an herbal paste to her swollen hand, wrapping it gently with a cloth. Seeing that Bamei had no appetite, he brought her some homemade chrysanthemum jelly, sweet as honey.

Bamei, who was usually not one to act delicate, suddenly felt a wave of vulnerability. She looked up at Kauko with tearful eyes and whispered, "Thank you, Kauko."

By the next day, Bamei woke up feeling much better. Her fingers were no longer swollen, and her fever had subsided. Seeing the medicinal soup Kauko handed her, she wrinkled her nose and said, "I'm already full of bitter water." She gently took Kauko's hand, staring at his upturned nose with a mischievous glint in her eyes, "Can I touch it?"

Kauko raised an eyebrow playfully, "What will you call me then?"

"Pig-headed brother, may I touch your nose?" she asked softly.

Kauko smiled and leaned his nose closer to her. She reached out cautiously, feeling the unique shape, and couldn't resist giving it a gentle pinch. Then, she looked at him seriously, her eyes warm and firm, "Remember, Pig-headed brother, you're not a monster. I think you're a gifted immortal!"

"Are immortals human too?" Kauko's large eyes sparkled with innocence.

"Of course, immortals are human too, but they possess abilities ordinary people don't have," Bamei explained.

"Then am I the same as you?" Kauko pressed further.

"Ah, I don't have any special powers," Bamei shook her head.

"In my eyes, you do. You have wisdom and courage that others lack," Kauko affirmed.

"Ha, since you say so, I'll consider myself an immortal too, thanks to you."

Kauko laughed, and the two of them shared a moment of joy.

Bamei then asked curiously, "Besides changing faces, you must know many other spells, right? Why don't you try them?"

"I have," Kauko said, somewhat dejected. "But besides changing faces, nothing else works. My master said I could fly and even left me a mantra, but I've never understood how to use it. Let me show you!" He opened his robe, revealing the words his master had sewn into it before passing away. It was a riddle waiting to be solved, with a stream of only one word "长" (grow or long).

Bamei pondered for a moment but couldn't make sense of it. "Let me think about it slowly. Let's go out for some fresh air."

The morning mist clung to the earth like a shy bride, reluctant to leave, while the orange hues of dawn slowly painted the sky. As they stepped out of the ancient gates of Jingxin Temple, their figures seemed to blend into a painting.

Admiring the scenery, Kauko couldn't help but exclaim, "What day is today? It feels like a piece of Tian Mountain has been brought to the mortal world."

"Ah, today!" Bamei gasped, covering her mouth with her hand, stunned.

"Bamei, what's wrong? Did I say something wrong?" Kauko asked with concern.

"Nothing! It's just that my legs feel so weak," she said, extending a hand to Kauko, much like a cue from a stage play. His heart leapt with joy—Bamei wanted him to carry her. He immediately bent down, letting her climb onto his back, and set off with light steps, his heart soaring like in the plays, heading straight for the woods behind the temple.

But Bamei knew this was her feigned vulnerability, a ploy for this moment of closeness. Today was her seventeenth birthday, and she was about to embark on a new journey dictated by fate. The carefree days with Kauko might never return. On this fresh morning, she just wanted to borrow his back, to play the delicate maiden, and leave herself a beautiful memory. Nestled against his sturdy back, a sweet warmth spread through her heart. She asked softly, with a hint of elusive sorrow, "If I never get better, will you always carry me?"

Kauko answered without hesitation, his voice firm and tender, "If you're willing, I'll carry you through every season." He paused, then teased, "But I'm afraid Tichu might not be happy."

Bamei couldn't help but laugh, having nearly forgotten the fictional fiancé she had concocted. "Yes, Tichu... well, I wouldn't want you two to fight."

As their laughter faded, Bamei fell into a long silence. Kauko felt a twinge of unease and asked softly, "Why are you so quiet?"

Bamei shook her head, tears welling up in her eyes. "It's nothing. I just thought, if we never meet again, you must remember me—a girl named Bamei, who once laughed like the radiant spring on your back."

Kauko stopped and turned as if to look at her face, solemnly promising, "Bamei, no matter what happens, I will never forget you, just as I will never forget my own name."

Bamei closed her eyes, tears silently falling. In that wordless moment, she poured all her unspoken emotions into a soft sigh.

They walked through the woods and across the stream, arriving at the spot where they had danced the day before. Sitting among the flowers, they watched butterflies flit by and listened to the birds sing. The stream below sparkled as it flowed south, and the nearby Bodhi tree swayed its branches as if recounting tales of past lives. A gentle breeze carried a morning glory vine to Bamei's feet, as if beckoning her. Its delicate beauty reminded her of a small purple parasol held by a lady on an outing. Inspired, she exclaimed excitedly, "I remember a nursery rhyme I learned as a child. Let me sing it for you—it might help you!"

She hummed softly:

Zhǎng cháng zhǎng cháng zhǎng cháng,
Cháng zhǎng cháng zhǎng cháng zhǎng.
Morning glories climb the wall,
Red in May, fragrant in June.
Flowers lush, vines grow long,
Morning glories pair in twos.
Not for butterflies, not for immortals,
Morning glories seek the cowherd.
Autumn winds rise, leaves turn yellow,
Good times fade, but love lingers.
Winter nights, stars grow cold,
Life and death part, hearts grow numb.
If I don't see the cowherd in this life,
Next year I'll be a morning glory again.
Zhǎng cháng zhǎng cháng zhǎng cháng,
Cháng zhǎng cháng zhǎng cháng zhǎng.

As her song faded, Bamei turned to Kauko, her eyes glimmering with meaning. "The word '长' changes its pronunciation, each carrying a different significance. Perhaps this is the revelation your master left for you."

Kauko's eyes lit up. He eagerly recited the nursery rhyme's mantra: "Zhǎng cháng zhǎng cháng zhǎng cháng cháng..." Suddenly, he felt an ethereal energy awaken within him, and his feet lifted off the ground in rhythm with the mantra.

However, his flight was like that of an untrained fledgling. Just as he rose a foot off the ground, a sharp pain shot through his head, causing him to lose control and crash to the ground. Despite this, he scrambled up with childlike excitement, "Bamei, I really flew!"

Relieved to see he wasn't hurt, Bamei asked with concern, "What happened?"

Kauko rubbed his head, puzzled. "A headache. This always happens when I use my inner energy. It's been like this since I was a child."

Bamei comforted him, "How strange. Don't rush it. Besides, if you fly away, how will I ever catch up?" Her words, though playful, carried a deep sense of attachment.

Kauko looked at Bamei and smiled warmly.

Bamei glanced up through the gaps in the trees, her gaze fixed on the high noon sun. Though the scene was ordinary, it left an indelible mark on her heart. Yes, the time for farewell had quietly arrived.

Their steps were heavy as they made their way back to the temple. Though the sun was scorching and the sky vast and blue, Bamei's heart was clouded with an unspoken gloom. Confusion and reluctance made each heartbeat feel as heavy as her steps. She longed to confide in Kauko, to tell him that she was about to embark on an unknown path, one from which there might be no return. But the words stuck in her throat.

"Let's make a wish before the Buddha," Bamei broke the silence. Perhaps, deep down, she still held a sliver of hope that their wishes before the Buddha might bring them a miracle.

As soon as they stepped into the temple, they were struck by the sight before them. The weathered Buddha statue lay in pieces, fragments scattered across the floor. Bamei immediately suspected the Sherkon people were behind it. She was about to warn Kauko when the temple's tranquility was shattered. Sherkon soldiers, like hungry wolves, pounced on them, their cold armor glinting as their blades pointed menacingly.

Kauko instinctively shielded Bamei, using his body as a barrier. But the Sherkon soldiers didn't engage in combat. Instead, they threw a hunting net over him, trapping him. Kauko stumbled and fell heavily, the thud resonating like a mournful drum in Bamei's heart. He struggled, but chains quickly bound him, leaving him immobilized on the ground.

Bamei was seized by two strong soldiers. A flash of fear shot through her, but she quickly composed herself, a newfound strength and determination rising within her. This was the responsibility of a princess—she couldn't afford to show any sign of weakness or fear. For Kauko, for the people of Daze who awaited her, she had to be fearless!

The soldier in charge pointed at Kauko and barked, "Don't be fooled by his human appearance. I'm certain he's the pig-headed monster. Guard him closely. We'll take him to the capital, parade him through the streets, and then send him to the camp." Then, he gently stroked Bamei's cheek and ordered, "Make sure not to harm this beauty. We'll present her to Prince Duan. He'll reward us handsomely."

The soldiers tied Bamei's hands and slung her over a horse like a sack. Kauko was tethered to another horse with a long rope.

The soldiers, smug with their victory, mounted their horses and prepared to return to Sien City. Just as they were basking in their triumph, Tichu and the underground forces of Daze closed in like ghosts. In an instant, arrows rained down, catching the Sherkon soldiers off guard. They fell from their horses one by one.

Tichu, agile and swift, rushed to Bamei, deftly freeing her from the horse and untying her bonds. He took her hand and led her proudly to General

Langkun, announcing, "General, the princess you seek is here!"

General Langkun quickly produced a portrait and compared it to Bamei. Confirming her identity, he knelt and performed a deep bow. "Princess Wenxi, Langkun has been sent by the royal advisor to escort you and discuss our plans."

Everyone knelt in reverence, except for Kauko, who stood frozen until Tichu gave him a meaningful look. Only then did he kneel as well.

Though Bamei had never experienced such a scene before, she mimicked the etiquette she had seen in operas, clasping her hands and replying, "Thank you all for saving me. I am willing to join you in serving our homeland."

General Langkun stood up, his gaze solemn as he looked out over the land. "Princess, this place is not safe. We must depart quickly."

Bamei nodded gently, her bright eyes shining with unwavering resolve. "Lead the way, General."

Kauko stood up, his eyes filled with confusion. The Bamei who had once stood shoulder-to-shoulder with him was now surrounded by the reverence of the crowd, as if an invisible barrier had risen between them, leaving him feeling more distant than ever. He tried to approach her, but Tichu stood like a wall in front of him, blocking his path no matter how he tried to maneuver. Kauko's chains clinked as he struggled, his eyes filled with helplessness and despair. An older soldier, seeing his plight, tried to help him break free but couldn't find the key.

Amidst the chaos and anxiety, Kauko's spirits sank further. He had dreamed of facing the future alongside Bamei, but fate had cruelly pushed them onto separate paths. He felt superfluous in that moment, overwhelmed by a sense of powerlessness and defeat.

Meanwhile, though Bamei was the center of attention, admired like the moon among stars, her heart was troubled by the unbridgeable distance between her and Kauko. This was the heavy burden fate had placed on her, a pain she kept hidden deep within. At this critical juncture, she had to face her destiny, even if it meant parting ways with Kauko. She smiled under the gaze of the crowd, but the turmoil in her heart was hers alone to bear.

Despite his despair, Kauko refused to give up. He shouted loudly, "Bamei, no, Princess, I am willing to fight alongside you against the invaders..."

Before he could finish, Tichu coldly interrupted him, announcing to the crowd, "He is not one of us. It's best to keep him away from the princess."

Kauko's gaze fell on Bamei, hoping for her response. She silently observed him for a moment before speaking indifferently, "This matter has nothing to do with you. You don't need to be involved."

The group began to move slowly along the narrow forest path. Tichu stayed behind, whispering to Kauko, "You freak, stay away from the princess. You're nothing but a curse. When you came ten years ago, the princess got a scar on her head. This time, because of you, our troupe is gone, Auntie Wei is dead, and Bamei almost got into trouble." With that, he coldly tossed the key he had just picked up onto the ground.

On horseback, the princess dared not look back at Kauko's lonely figure. Bitterness and sorrow welled up in her heart. She fought back tears, her heart as bitter as a lotus seed.

Tichu's harsh words pierced Kauko's heart like needles, and doubt began to spread within him. He had once dreamed of finding his place in this world, but now he couldn't help but wonder if he truly was a harbinger of misfortune. He thought to himself that if fate had destined him to be this way, he would rather wander alone, bearing all the misfortune himself.

Having made up his mind, he decided to leave the land that had once given him fleeting joy, to go far away, out of Bamei's sight. Once, her presence had been like a ray of sunlight breaking through the clouds, warming his world and lighting up his life with sincerity and trust. But now, without her by his side, even the vastness of Daze Kingdom could no longer offer him a place to belong.

He was filled with resentment. Why did people judge by appearances, without understanding the purity of his heart? This skin, given to him by his parents, could not be easily changed. He wearily shook his large ears, his heavy heart feeling as if it were bound by invisible chains.

He followed the princess's entourage from a distance for several miles before finally stopping, watching them go with his eyes. Afterward, he aimlessly wandered along the winding forest path, not caring where it led or if it had an end. No matter how beautiful the streams or flowers he passed, they failed to catch his attention.

Unconsciously, he began to encounter more travelers on the road, most of them ragged and exhausted. Kauko asked them who they were. Those with children said they were homeless, while those hiding their faces said they were "monsters" being hunted. Why were they all heading in the same direction? An old woman looked up, her eyes filled with hope, "They say if you keep going south, to the edge of the world, there's a country called Annan, where everyone is a Bodhisattva. If we can make it to Annan, we'll be saved."

This reminded Kauko of what Monkey Three had said about Annan. He decided to follow these desperate souls southward.

After what felt like an eternity of traversing mountains and rivers, they finally arrived at the small town of Luding. The words "Annan Kingdom" emblazoned in red on the city gate stood like a promise, offering a glimmer of solace to every soul who reached it. Above the gate, a tricolor flag fluttered proudly, and soldiers patrolled the walls with authority.

Kauko looked up in awe at the tricolor flag, which seemed to wave at him invitingly. His steps followed the crowd as they slowly moved toward the city gate.

"You, stop!" A spear suddenly blocked Kauko's path. He followed the spear to see a guard addressing him.

"Officer, why are you stopping me?" Kauko asked, puzzled.

The guard's gaze was sharp, as if trying to pierce through Kauko's disguise and uncover his intentions.

"I have my reasons! Who are you?" the guard demanded loudly.

Kauko spread his hands and replied honestly, "I heard you take in refugees, so I came."

The guard's eyes narrowed, "Are you homeless, or are you being persecuted?"

"I'm a blacklisted person in Daze Kingdom. My mother was murdered by villains, and my father abandoned me, so I have no home. My appearance is different from others, so the authorities hunt me, and even children bully me. I am among the persecuted," Kauko's voice carried a hint of bitterness.

The guard signaled him to wait, "Let me report this." He walked over to an officer in military attire, pointing at Kauko, "Look at that guy. He's strong, decent-looking, and articulate. He claims to be a refugee, but I think he's more like a spy from Sherkon."

The officer approached Kauko, squinting as he scanned his figure, "I hear you claim to be a wanderer. Why are you alone, yet show no signs of panic?"

"I was born in turbulent times. I've seen storms and tempests. Why would I panic over being displaced?" Kauko replied calmly.

The officer pressed further, "Even if you're a wanderer, why would children dare to bully you?"

Kauko lowered his voice, "I'm different. My appearance is not like others."

The officer persisted, "How are you different? Explain clearly."

Kauko sighed and whispered, "Do you want to see?"

"Yes!" the officer said firmly.

"Alright, don't blame me if it scares you." Kauko shook his ears, and his face instantly transformed into that of a pig. He forced an exaggerated smile to avoid frightening anyone. However, the soldiers and onlookers around him showed no surprise. Instead, they laughed warmly.

Kauko felt a pang of confusion. He reached up to touch his face, confirming it was indeed the pig face that the world shunned. He couldn't help but think, "Are they just ignoring me?" He curled his lips, revealing sharp tusks, and let out a soft snort, a hint of challenge in his tone. Yet, the crowd continued to laugh, finding him utterly amusing. It seemed that in Annan, such peculiarities were commonplace.

The officer waved his hand to quiet the crowd, "Alright, you must be a descendant of Rake King, right?"

"Yes, Sir," Kauko replied succinctly. He sensed a hint of respect in the officer's tone and instinctively straightened his back, a sense of pride in his lineage.

The officer smiled, "Interesting. Not long ago, the family of the Great Sage Equal to Heaven arrived. Now, the descendants of Rake King are here. In a few days, perhaps even the descendants of Tang Sanzang will come. This is a sign of Annan's prosperity."

Kauko's eyes sparkled with anticipation, "Can I enter the city now?"

"Of course, this is your home now," the officer said, waving his hand to let him pass.

Kauko asked the officer, "Where does the Great Sage's family live now?"

"Go to the eastern part of the city. Most newcomers live there," the officer pointed in the direction.

As Kauko entered the eastern part of the city, he was amazed by the diversity of the people there: horse-faced, cat-faced, and even fox-faced individuals, all going about their business without hiding or disguising themselves. The streets were like a stage for a grand variety show, with each person playing a unique role.At first, Kauko kept his human face, but gradually, he was infected by the atmosphere of freedom and decided to let go. He gently shook his ears, revealing his true form. He even began to feel a sense of pride, realizing that in this colorful world, he too was unique.

He strolled through the bustling streets, his eyes wandering. Suddenly, he spotted a monkey-faced woman wearing a bamboo hat, selling flowers on a street corner. Kauko approached her and asked kindly, "Miss, excuse me, do you know Monkey Three? You look a bit like him."

The flower seller looked up, her blue eyes and golden brows instantly captivating Kauko. She smiled and replied, "You must be Brother Kau, right?"

Kauko was surprised, "Have you met me before?"

She laughed and explained, "Brother Monkey Three often talks about you. His description matches you perfectly. He even told me to keep an eye out for you on the streets, sure that you'd come eventually."

"Is that so! Miss, what else did Monkey Three say?"

"Brother said that you're a great hero."

These words warmed Kauko's heart. His first day in Annan had already brought him joy. Though he inwardly scoffed at the idea of being a hero, the praise stirred a small sense of pride in him. "Ah, miss, don't say that. What if a real hero comes to challenge me? Quick, take me to see your brother."

The flower seller told him that Monkey Three had gone to work and would come to pick her up later. He helped others pick fruits from trees—durians, coconuts, mangoes—the taller the tree, the better he was at it. Kauko stayed with her, chatting and watching her sell flowers.

Passersby preferred to sit at the nearby street food stalls, spending money on snacks and drinks. As for the flowers, they would pick them up, sniff them, and since they couldn't eat them, put them back in the basket.

The flower seller's name was Monkey Shang. A few months ago, she had been sold to Annan by human traffickers to perform street tricks for her master. Monkey Three, feeling sorry for her, had bought her freedom and taken her in as his cousin.

Monkey Three and Monkey Shang lived in the eastern district—a gathering place for new immigrants. The area was filled with simple thatched huts, available for rent or resale to newcomers. For a small fee, newcomers could live in these huts, and once they saved enough money, they could buy them. When their livelihoods stabilized, they would move to the upscale districts to purchase proper houses and rent out the huts. Monkey Three was still in the renting phase, but Monkey Shang praised his hard work, confident that he would eventually rise in status.

Monkey Three appeared at the intersection, a bamboo basket swaying on his back. When he saw Kauko, his lips curled into a crescent smile, and he greeted him warmly, "Brother Kau, I've been waiting for you!"

Kauko glanced at the basket on his back and reached out to take it. The basket was filled to the brim with colorful, fresh fruits. He teased, "Have you switched to selling fruits now?"

Monkey Three scratched his messy hair, his smile tinged with bitterness, "Ah, don't mention it. Today, I went to work, but the family couldn't pay me. All I got was this basket of fruits as 'wages.' Thankfully, I have these, or I wouldn't know how to entertain you, my hero."

Kauko picked up a plump peach, tossing it lightly in his hand, his tone carrying a hint of probing, "Actually, I wanted to ask if I could stay with you tonight? Don't call me a hero. I really need a place to stay."

Monkey Three immediately became serious, "Brother Kau, don't say that! Your coming here is an honor. Not just for tonight, if you're willing, consider this your home!"

Kauko was taken aback. He tightened his grip on the peach, a long-lost warmth surging in his heart. He said softly, "Then I'll stay."

"Great!" Monkey Three's eyes lit up, and he excitedly pulled Monkey Shang along.

The three of them exchanged smiles, chatting and laughing as they headed home.

For the first few days, Kauko followed Monkey Three, helping him with heavy labor and assisting Monkey Shang in selling flowers. Though it was a novel experience, he realized how hard it was to earn money and began brainstorming ideas. He pulled out the small bronze mirror Monkey Three had given him and asked, "You have such good skills. Why don't you make mirrors to sell?"

Monkey Three spread his hands, with bitter smile, "Materials and tools all require capital. I don't have the means."

Kauko continued to ponder.

One day, as he lay in bed, an idea struck him. He eagerly woke Monkey Three and Monkey Shang, his eyes sparkling with excitement, and shared his experience of making jelly from wild flowers back in Tian Mountain. "Here, it's spring all year round, and flowers are everywhere. The materials are abundant and cheap. With just some simple kitchen tools, we can make something amazing!" Kauko described enthusiastically. Monkey Three and Monkey Shang were stunned, then thrilled, immediately supporting the idea.

Kauko busied himself by the stove, creating a variety of delicious, aromatic jellies. Rose jelly was fragrant and beautiful, osmanthus jelly was delicate and sweet, lotus jelly was refreshing, and mango jelly was smooth and sweet.

Monkey Three and Monkey Shang were the first to taste them, praising them endlessly. Then, they invited neighbors, both adults and children, to share the treats. Soon, Kauko's jellies became the talk of the town. Curious crowds flocked to try them.

As the business boomed, Kauko had a bigger plan—to rent a shop on the main street, allowing more people to enjoy the sweetness. Their new shop was named "Ge San Shang," taking one word from each of their names, symbolizing their partnership and dreams.

Customers were curious about the poetic name. While Kauko worked in the kitchen and Monkey Three sourced ingredients, Monkey Shang, who handled the front desk, always explained warmly, "When you're hungry, we have sweet jellies and flower pastries; when you're thirsty, we have fragrant spring tea; and when you're tired, we offer soothing flower sachets as gifts."

"Ge San Shang" quickly became synonymous with taste and elegance. The delicious treats, unique name, attractive service, and thoughtful hospitality drew a steady stream of customers. However, as the business flourished, they began to feel short-handed. Monkey Three sent word to his younger brother in Daze, inviting him to join their venture. He told his brother that he was now working with the son of the Rake King and had established a foothold, hoping his brother would come and help build this new world together.

Chapter 8

Ge San Shang

Fire Maiden was deeply troubled. The enchanting melody of Kauko's demonic flute, which had always been the source of her dark power, had suddenly ceased. It was as if the music had been swept away by the fierce northern wind of the previous night. Without delay, she mounted her agile stag and rode across the fields and forests, arriving at the place where the flute's melody had last been heard—the ancient and weathered Jingxin Temple.

The temple was deserted, both inside and out. Only a shattered Buddha statue remained, its single cold eye staring at her. She summoned the demonic flute, but there was no response. Closing her eyes, she allowed her senses to ripple outward like waves, and soon she detected movement in the cavern beneath the temple's rear courtyard.

Sliding through a crevice in the stone, Fire Maiden entered the cavern. She looked around and saw a lush rose trembling in the breeze, its enchanting petals gathered together to form the outline of a young girl. The figure flickered in and out of view until it finally revealed a face Fire Maiden recognized—"Bamei" from the opera troupe. Instinctively wary, she suspected a trap and considered destroying it. But then a faint, urgent plea emerged from the rose: "Master, help me!"

Fire Maiden asked, "What kind of little demon are you?"

The rose spirit began to tell her story. She explained that a single drop of a princess's blood had nearly allowed her to fulfill her dream of becoming a princess herself. All she needed now was the final touch of guidance from a powerful master. "If you help me, Master, I will serve you for the rest of my life."

Fire Maiden saw a reflection of her younger self in the rose spirit—innocent, beautiful, and romantic. She couldn't help but feel fondness for her. "Very well," she said, "I will take you as my disciple. You must obey me for eternity."

"Thank you, Master, for your kindness. Your disciple will serve you wholeheartedly."

With a wave of her hand, Fire Maiden tucked the rose spirit into her sleeve and returned to the capital. She brought the aspiring rose spirit back to the

Chinmi Garden, planting it next to the violets in a corner she cherished. It was the same spot where the King of Daze had once touched her cheek.

Fire Maiden admired the rose spirit's delicate beauty and envisioned shaping her into a younger version of herself, a reminder of how captivating she had once been. However, she also placed dozens of tiny beetles, no larger than ants, at the base of the rose tree. She had enchanted them to remain dormant, but with a single incantation, they would awaken and gnaw at the tree's heart.

During her nightly rituals, Fire Maiden would send a chilling breeze toward the rose. The rose spirit struggled under its influence, yearning to become a pure and virtuous princess but finding her heart growing increasingly clouded.

Dissatisfied with herself yet powerless to change, the rose spirit remained deeply grateful to Fire Maiden. She believed that she would soon descend from the rose tree and experience the joys and sorrows of being human.

Many days later, Fire Maiden approached the rose tree and gently blew on it. "Fire Rose," she said, "you may descend now."

The rose spirit awoke from her dream and asked, "Master, is Fire Rose my name?"

"Yes," Fire Maiden replied. "You are now a rare beauty. Why linger there? Come out and serve your Master."

Fire Rose appeared before Fire Maiden, her figure captivating to all who saw her. Fire Maiden removed her red cloak and draped it over Fire Rose. As she studied Fire Rose's face, she could hardly distinguish her from Princess Wenxi.

***

Shocking news arrived from the border: the resistance army of the Kingdom of Daze had clashed head-on with the Sherkon Army and achieved a decisive victory. Behind this news, one name was being celebrated—Princess Wenxi.

Prince Duan, the military counsellor of the occupying forces, hurried to see Governor Fire. Standing before her curtain, his face filled with anxiety, he pleaded, "Governor, Princess Wenxi's influence is growing. I fear we cannot hold out much longer. Shouldn't you take the field yourself?"

Fire Maiden merely raised an eyebrow. "She's just a girl leading some remnants of the former dynasty in the mountains. You overestimate her, Prince."

Duan urgently countered, "Governor, you don't understand. She has become a symbol of hope for the people of Daze. If she is not dealt with, our foundation here may crumble."

Though initially dismissive, Fire Maiden could not ignore Duan's grave concern. However, her magical cultivation and the King of Daze's recovery consumed all her energy, and she was reluctant to waste her hard-earned power on the battlefield. After a moment's thought, a sly smile crossed her face. She had a plan to deal with the princess while sparing her life. She needed to seek guidance from Golden Mother once more.

Bringing fresh fruits as an offering, she placed them on the altar and whispered earnestly, "Golden Mother, I beg you to use your divine power to help me find a missing person."

Golden Mother's voice emerged from the swirling incense smoke, tinged with reproach. "You seek Wulong, do you not? Your cleverness led him to violate the taboos of the witch realm, and now he is imprisoned. Yet you, his master, have shown no concern."

Fire Maiden defended herself, "Goddess, you know how busy I am."

Golden Mother instructed, "Burn some paper money for him. He may be able to buy his way out of trouble and return sooner."

Returning to the Chinmi Garden, Fire Maiden ordered Fire Rose to imprint copper coins onto spirit paper and burn them in the backyard. Within an hour, Wulong's low voice echoed in her ear: "Master, thank you for saving my life. But I have only one transformation left. After that, I will be useless. Please, do not abandon me again."

Fire Maiden frowned. "How did you lose all your skills?"

"I have been exiled from the witch realm. The last transformation is all I have secretly kept."

Fire Maiden narrowed her eyes, calming herself. "Then keep it hidden. I will need it for a special purpose. Stay close and await my orders." She turned her gaze to Fire Rose, her tone challenging. "Fire Rose, do you wish to become a true princess?"

Fire Rose's eyes sparkled with excitement. "Master, it has always been my dream."

Fire Maiden smiled mysteriously. "If you truly wish to become a princess, you must serve me well. When I am satisfied, I will make you a princess."

Fire Rose eagerly nodded; her eyes filled with longing. "I am willing to work hard."

"Good. First, you will impersonate Princess Wenxi and experience the life of a true princess."

Fire Rose frowned slightly, confused. "Impersonate her?"

"Exactly," Fire Maiden said leisurely. "It's like a game. You will go to the border between Daze and Annan, secretly observe Princess Wenxi's movements, find an opportunity to approach her, mark her with your rose perfume, and then report back to me."

Fire Rose hesitated. "You want me to replace her? Who would believe I am the princess?"

Fire Maiden's smile widened. "That's not difficult. Fate has made you strikingly similar in appearance. You only need to learn a bit of her demeanor."

Fire Rose said innocently, "Princess Wenxi is someone I admire. Isn't this harming her?"

Fire Maiden's expression darkened. "Set aside your concerns. There is no right or wrong here."

Fire Rose immediately felt the weight of Fire Maiden's authority pressing down on her like a mountain. She knelt and pleaded, "Master, I fear I am not the best choice. Please select someone more capable. Let me do something else, please."

Fire Maiden snorted coldly. "You don't understand the rules!" Her voice carried an unyielding resolve. She began to chant an incantation, her voice swirling in the air, filled with mysterious power.

Fire Rose's body trembled uncontrollably. She felt countless tiny insects scratching at her heart, causing both itchiness and pain. She collapsed to the ground, writhing and struggling, crying out, "Master, have mercy!"

Only after Fire Rose had rolled from one corner to another did Fire Maiden slowly cease her chant. She calmly observed Fire Rose, as if examining a freshly molded piece of clay. "Listen carefully. This is a small reminder from your master. What I ask of you and how I ask it are not up for negotiation."

Fire Rose wiped her tears and sobbed, "I understand. Master, that nearly killed me."

Fire Maiden said indifferently, "Good. Both rewards and punishments are at my discretion."

As Fire Rose staggered away, Fire Maiden felt an inexplicable sense of satisfaction. Perhaps this was how the Queen had felt when she had thrown her into the volcano all those years ago.

***

In the quiet morning light of early summer, the ancient temple stood serene and solemn. Advisor Midd, the former advisor to the King of Daze, sat quietly before the Buddha. Though he now wore the robes of a monk, his mind was far from the ascetic life.

When the Kingdom of Daze fell into crisis and the king disappeared, Midd had chosen to hide among the monks, secretly building a network of resistance. After years of effort, he had found the king's daughter—Princess Wenxi. He had waited patiently until the princess turned seventeen. Now, she was not only the last surviving member of the Daze royal family but also a symbol of hope and resistance.

In the dimly lit side room of the temple, Advisor Midd had once pored over a sheepskin map and secret documents, planning each move. Since the princess had joined the resistance, he was no longer alone. Though young, she had already shown remarkable courage and wisdom, earning the admiration of her soldiers.

Now, Advisor Midd excitedly made his way to the rear chamber of the temple, a hidden and peaceful place seemingly untouched by the world's chaos. Tichu, the princess's personal guard, led him into her quarters. The room was simple yet warm, with vines swaying gently outside the window, casting delicate shadows. Everything felt tranquil.

The morning light filtered through the window, illuminating the yellowed pages of the book in Princess Wenxi's hands. When she looked up and saw Advisor Midd approaching with a smile, she felt a surge of joy. She stood gracefully and greeted him, sensing that today would bring good news.

Advisor Midd bowed to the princess, his eyes sparkling with excitement. "Princess, I bring joyous tidings."

The princess asked expectantly, "Advisor, is it news of victory from the front?"

"Even better," Advisor Midd replied.

The princess smiled. "Advisor, you rarely show such joy. Please, tell me more."

Advisor Midd spoke mysteriously, "From the astral charts, I have glimpsed a sign. It seems a young man has appeared in our land, as if a demon-slaying envoy has been reincarnated. With his help, the Governor Fire's sorcery will be no match for us."

The princess pressed, "Can you tell me more, Advisor?"

Advisor Midd shook his head gently. "Princess, the young man's image flashed through my mind like a shooting star across the night sky. But I saw his heroic aura and the magical flute in his hand."

The princess's heart stirred, and a familiar figure came to mind. She smiled faintly. "I know of a young man with a magical flute. His name is Kauko, an old friend of mine. He possesses a remarkable bronze flute."

Advisor Midd's expression turned to surprise. "Is that so?"

The princess nodded. "He has an extraordinary background. Born in Kau Village, he is the son of Zhu Bajie, and the daughter of Squire Kau. He is a year older than I am. That magical flute belonged to his father."

Advisor Midd nodded thoughtfully. "I see. This Kauko must indeed be remarkable."

The princess chuckled. "Though he is unique, with a face resembling Zhu Bajie's and the ability to change his appearance, he is otherwise no different from any other young man."

Advisor Midd asked, "Has he trained in martial arts?"

The princess replied, "He has a divine master named Dapeng, once a guard of the Heavenly Marshal Tianpeng, who descended to the mortal realm. Kauko was raised by him, and they live together in Tian Mountain southeast of Daze."

Advisor Midd was astonished. "Tian Mountain? I have never heard of such a place. It must be a mountain of endless mysteries."

The princess shook her head gently. "Advisor, you overestimate him. I once asked about his training, and he admitted to having difficulties. Moreover, when we were captured by the Sherkon soldiers, he showed no extraordinary abilities."

Advisor Midd sighed. "Yet, aside from his lack of displayed power, he fits all the criteria. A remarkable birth, a magical flute, and a divine master. "

Princess Wenxi smiled faintly at Advisor's words. "Advisor, it seems you still hold high hopes for him?"

Advisor's eyes sparkled with anticipation. "Indeed! He might be one of those late bloomers. I wish to meet him personally. Princess, could you arrange an introduction?"

The princess's expression darkened, and she spoke slowly, "He... has been gone from Daze for quite some time now."

"Why is that?" Advisor pressed.

The princess sighed, "I was the one who sent him away. He wanted to follow me, but his heart is too pure. I feared he would only find danger by my side."

Advisor shook his head in regret and asked, "Where is he now?"

The princess replied, "I sent people to inquire, and they found out he went to Annan."

A glimmer of joy flashed in Advisor's eyes. "This is truly fate! I was just about to suggest that you personally visit Annan to strengthen our alliance. Now, you can also retrieve our treasure."

The princess's face grew serious, her brows furrowed, and a complex mix of emotions flickered in her eyes, as if recalling the moment she bid farewell to Kauko. She stood up and answered, "Annan is a journey I must make. As for Kauko..."

"Surely Princess won't refuse this old minister, will you?" he prodded, fearing her hesitation.

"I... will personally investigate," the princess reluctantly agreed.

The Advisor bowed deeply. "Princess is wise. Though Fire Maiden is powerful, the will of heaven is unpredictable. Kauko might just be our turning point."

The princess turned to gaze at the distant green mountains outside the window, as if searching for an unknown answer. "Kauko, you are full of mysteries!" she murmured. She truly hoped he possessed hidden strength, something that could aid her. Yet, this wish seemed too extravagant. As she lost herself in thought, the advisor had already summoned General Langkun. Seeing the serious expressions of the princess and the advisor, the general assumed they were discussing military matters and immediately asked, "Princess, when will you give me the military token?"

The princess motioned for the general to sit and personally poured him a cup of tea. She then spoke slowly, "General, you've come at the right time. I plan to visit Annan to meet with the King of Annan. Would you be willing to leave your troops and accompany me?"

The general was slightly surprised and asked, "Is Princess going to borrow troops? Forgive my bluntness, but our forces are sufficient. All we need is your command."

The princess smiled and turned to the advisor. "Please explain."

The advisor spoke slowly, "What we face is not just the Sherkon army but also Fire Maiden behind the scenes. For years, she has been cultivating the Great Demonic Arts, and we have overlooked her presence. Judging by the unpredictable weather above the capital, it seems she has mastered seventy percent of this magic. Once she reaches ninety percent, no one in Daze will be able to stop her."

"Advisor, you must already have a plan, don't you?" the general asked, confident in the advisor's wisdom.

"Perhaps there is one person who can deal with Fire Maiden. You must escort the princess to Annan and bring back that treasure."

The general stood up. "Princess, what are we waiting for? Let's set off at once!"

The general personally selected a dozen guards, including Tichu, and disguised them as tea merchants. Princess Wenxi also dressed as a man, blending into the group. They packed tea leaves into large, moisture-proof baskets, loaded them onto horses, and set off along the ancient trade route through the dense forests toward Luding, a small town in Annan.

Along the way, Tichu's brows remained tightly knit. In his heart, he had always believed the princess possessed unparalleled wisdom, yet this decision of hers left him puzzled. Seizing a moment alone with the princess, he asked, "Princess, you don't really believe Kauko has the power to defeat demons, do you?"

The princess thought for a moment and said, "I can't say for sure, but I trust Advisor."

"Perhaps not? The princess is willing to travel thousands of miles just to see Kauko."

"Tichu, do you dislike him so much?" the princess continued. "We've performed many ancient plays together. In those plays, the wise ones who appear foolish—doesn't Kauko resemble them? Enduring hardship, treating others with kindness, enduring bullying without fighting back, intelligent yet never deceitful. Such people are born for the world, nurtured for the people. Given time, they will surely achieve greatness."

"Princess, if he is so good and so powerful, why not send me alone to find him? Why must you go?"

"Am I not also going to borrow troops from the King of Annan?"

"I don't understand. If Kauko is so powerful, why do we need to borrow troops?"

The princess gently patted Tichu's back and spoke earnestly, "People are different. Extraordinary people can do extraordinary things, but some matters still require collective effort. I don't think you're confused; I think you're just feeling emotional." She advised Tichu to focus on his own tasks, as the road ahead was fraught with danger.

Tichu remained stubborn in his views. He harbored resentment toward the princess's favoritism toward Kauko, believing it to be utterly unreasonable. Last time, they had finally managed to send Kauko away, and now the princess was going out of her way to find him again. He believed Kauko would only bring trouble to the princess and saw no other value in him.

After a long journey, the princess and her entourage finally arrived at the ancient city of Luding on the border of Annan. Despite numerous dangers along the way, they had relied on their wisdom and courage to overcome each one.

General Langkun presented the official letter, and the city's commander quickly skimmed through it before sending a messenger pigeon to the King of Annan. The princess and her party were temporarily housed in a military post station, awaiting the king's reply. Inside the station, the princess gazed out at the ancient city bathed in the setting sun, her heart filled with both anticipation and worry. She knew the importance of this mission—it was not only about the alliance between the two nations but also about Kauko. Was he truly the key figure Advisor believed could counter Fire Maiden?

General Langkun came to inspect the princess's quarters and specifically instructed Tichu, "This city is bustling with all sorts of people. We can't rule out the possibility of demons hiding among them. You must remain extremely vigilant."

Tichu nodded with a stern expression and immediately issued orders to the guards: "If anyone with a strange appearance approaches the princess, kill them on sight."

The princess, overhearing this from the window, quickly stepped out of her room and signaled to Tichu. When he entered, she spoke with a hint of reproach, "Tichu, we must not judge people by their appearances, nor should we harm the innocent. Now that we are in this land, we should embrace its culture with an open mind." She paused briefly before continuing, "You don't need to stay by my side at all times. The guards of Annan are more than capable of ensuring my safety. I have another important task for you."

She pulled Tichu closer and whispered, "I find this city quite peculiar. Go to the market and see if you can gather any information about Kauko."

Tichu nodded, his stern expression softening slightly. "Princess, rest assured. I will do my best."

As night fell, Tichu strolled through the dimly lit streets. He repeatedly asked passersby if they had seen someone with a face resembling Zhu Bajie. Soon, a friendly local pointed him to a small shop called "Ge San Shang," informing him that the chef there was the person he was looking for.

Tichu stepped into the shop, greeted by a warm and cozy atmosphere. Soft candlelight cast gentle shadows in every corner. He chose a seat by the inner window, where he could clearly see into the kitchen.

There, Kauko was busy at work, wearing a light blue chef's uniform, neat and tidy. Under his half-spherical hat, a few strands of brown hair swayed gently with his movements. In the candlelight, his prominent ears seemed even more lively, twitching occasionally. Around his waist was a white apron stained with colorful jelly spots, adding a unique charm to his chef's persona.

Tichu watched him intently, a smile involuntarily forming on his lips.

He had never imagined that such a robust, pig-faced man could be so adept in the kitchen. The stark contrast was both amusing and heartwarming. He couldn't help but chuckle softly, the sound carrying clearly in the quiet shop.

"Sir, you seem to be enjoying yourself. What would you like to order?" A sweet voice interrupted Tichu's thoughts. He looked up to see a monkey-faced beauty standing by his table, placing a pot of tea in front of him. She wore a red pleated skirt, her figure graceful, and her face adorned with a gentle smile. She was the second one with extra-ordinary look he had ever seen, yet he felt no discomfort.

"Little Miss, why don't you recommend a snack?" Tichu said with a smile.

"Of course! We have freshly made osmanthus jelly, sweet but not cloying, fragrant and delicious. I'm sure you'll love it!" Monkey Shang recommended with a bright smile.

"Then I'll have a plate of that, and another to take away," Tichu replied without hesitation.

Monkey Shang turned gracefully and soon returned with a plate of translucent osmanthus jelly. Tichu picked up a piece, the coolness melting on his tongue, the subtle sweetness carrying a hint of floral fragrance, refreshing and delightful.

His gaze drifted back to the kitchen. Kauko was bent over his work, the blade in his hand flashing across the cutting board like a spring stream flowing over rocks, silent yet powerful. His movements were effortless, yet carried an innate elegance. Occasionally, he would glance up at the bronze mirror hanging on a wooden pillar, a faint smile curling his lips. That smile was like a warm breeze, brushing past the kitchen's steam, exuding a carefree ease and boundless confidence in his craft.

At that moment, Tichu saw Kauko in a new light, feeling a sense of kinship. He was about to call out to Kauko when he heard him humming a familiar tune: "The road is full of tigers and wolves, but brother, don't let your legs tremble..."

The song struck a chord in Tichu's heart, and a pang of jealousy arose: You're living a comfortable life here, yet you still can't forget the princess? Don't you know you're nothing but a curse to her?

Tichu's heart was in turmoil, and he ultimately changed his original plan. Perhaps Kauko should stay in this little shop and continue his culinary career. Otherwise, if he returned and got involved with the princess again, he would only bring her endless trouble and worry. Unconsciously, Tichu picked up the jelly he had originally prepared for the princess and devoured it in a few bites. He pulled out a few copper coins, quietly placed them on the table, and then took one last deep look at Kauko before turning and disappearing into the night.

His steps were hesitant, his heart uneasy. He felt he had betrayed the princess's trust, but at the same time, he thought, wasn't this for her own good?

***

Seated on his dragon throne, the King of Annan twirled his gray beard, his eyes lingering on the small piece of paper in his hand. The message on it sparked a glimmer of excitement in his eyes. He flicked the paper lightly, as if the words could transport him back to the old days when he shared drinks and laughter with the King of Daze.

He waved to his ministers. "Quickly, send word to invite Princess Wenxi to the capital. Daze has asked for our help, and I cannot stand idly by."

The prime minister hurried forward, holding a fan to partially conceal his face, as if hiding his doubts. He leaned close to the king's ear and whispered, "Your Majesty, the Sherkon army is practically at our doorstep. And then there's Fire Maiden—she's a formidable figure. If we provoke her, won't she turn her wrath upon us?" He paused, then continued cautiously, "Besides, Daze has been in turmoil for so many years without any resolution. If we get involved, will it really make a difference?" He circled around and added in a low voice, "Moreover, Daze and we haven't had much interaction. Suddenly, a princess appears. Is she really worth our attention?"

The King of Annan stroked his beard and pondered for a moment before speaking. "What you say makes sense, Prime Minister. However, I vaguely recall an agreement with the King of Daze that when Princess Wenxi came of age, she would marry my son, Qin. I wonder how she has grown up in the wild. If a marriage alliance is possible, wouldn't Daze also belong to Qin in part?"

The prime minister immediately understood the king's intentions—he was likely eyeing Daze's fertile lands. He quickly added: "If that's the case, Your Majesty, why not send Prince Qin with some silver to Luding? If he and the princess have a connection, we can help her. If not, we can simply give her some silver and be done with it."

***

Sunlight sparkled on the vast surface of Daqian Lake, where Prince Qin of Annan and the prince of Tianluo were engaged in a fierce dragon boat race. Prince Qin, just twenty years old, was in the prime of his youth. Tall and handsome, his skin glowed with a healthy tan under the sun. The prince of Tianluo had brought thirty stunning beauties with him, skilled in song and dance, and with lively, outgoing personalities. Prince Qin had been spending his days in their company.

On the water, two dragon boats surged forward like leaping dragons, their oars cutting through the waves and sending sprays of crystal water into the air. On each boat, ten women rowed with focused determination, their long hair flying in the wind like battle flags.

Prince Qin stood at the bow of the dragon boat; a waist drum slung diagonally across his shoulder. The sunlight glinted off his golden mandarin jacket, making it shine brilliantly. His white long skirt fluttered gently in the breeze, while the red and blue ribbons and scarves added a touch of heroism to his appearance. The rhythm of the waist drum in his hands was precise and powerful, each beat not only guiding the tempo but also serving as a rallying cry.

On the lakeshore, the cheers of the spectators rose and fell like waves, their intensity ebbing and flowing with the speed of the dragon boats.

The women from Tianluo were physically strong, and in the final sprint, they displayed astonishing power, quickly taking the lead. However, Prince Qin had anticipated this and had arranged for underwater ambushers in advance. With a secret signal, his underwater troops cleverly attached a large stone beneath the Tianluo dragon boat, instantly slowing it down. In the end, Prince Qin's dragon boat broke through the finish line, winning the intense race.

The joy of victory was evident on Prince Qin's face. He was about to select one of the Tianluo beauties as his prize when a messenger from the king summoned him to the palace. He said to the Tianluo prince, "Wait for me to return, and I'll definitely pick one!"

Upon learning that he was to go to Luding City to meet a homeless princess he knew nothing about—and who might potentially become his wife—Prince Qin felt no enthusiasm. He said to the prime minister, "You go in my place. If the princess is beautiful, bring her back. If not, let her find another match."

The prime minister looked anxious and reminded him, "Your Highness, this matter concerns national affairs and will influence our decision to send troops to Daze. We cannot take it lightly."

Reluctantly, the prince agreed to go. Before departing, he asked the prime minister, "Will that Tianluo fellow still be here when I return?"

The prime minister smiled and replied, "I've arranged for him to stay a few more days. Your Highness need not worry."

Upon arriving in Luding, Prince Qin immediately heard rumors that the Princess of Daze was a beauty capable of toppling cities and kingdoms. Unable to contain his curiosity, he quickly changed into commoner's attire and decided to personally investigate the post station. Just as he was about to leave, the prime minister stopped him. "Your Highness, wait. I must accompany you."

Prince Qin was dismissive. "Is she really so extraordinary that we need to make such a fuss?"

The prime minister replied, "Not exactly, but with me present, I can help convey your intentions."

The prince nodded and accepted the prime minister's suggestion. They brought a few attendants and quietly arrived at the post station. The station's leader, a weathered old man, greeted them with caution and respect. Under his guidance, they made their way to the backyard. The old man pointed to a figure under a cherry blossom tree and whispered, "That is Princess Wenxi."

Prince Qin and the prime minister carefully hid behind an old locust tree, secretly observing. Under the blooming cherry blossoms, Princess Wenxi stood gracefully, like a fairy from a painting. She wore a light, flowing dress that swayed gently in the breeze, dancing in harmony with the cherry blossoms. Beside her stood a burly man, her personal guard, Tichu. The prince's eyes sparkled with admiration, and he couldn't help but exclaim, "Is she the legendary Peacock Princess?"

The prime minister chuckled softly beside him. "Your Highness, she is Princess Wenxi."

The prince asked again, "And Tichu? What is his relationship with the princess?"

The prime minister whispered, "Tichu is the princess's guard."

At that moment, the princess and Tichu began practicing martial arts under the tree, as if performing an exciting fight scene. Every smile and movement of the princess captivated the prince's attention. He was eager to step forward, but the prime minister quickly held him back.

The prime minister whispered a reminder, "Your Highness, in your current attire, appearing now would be improper. Let us return and change into more suitable clothing, then formally invite the princess to the palace as our guest."

The prince agreed and immediately returned to the palace to fetch the princess and her entourage, arranging for them to stay in an elegant residence. He then meticulously planned a warm banquet to welcome them.

At the banquet, the princess sipped a few drinks and then rose with high spirits to perform a solo dance called "Strolling on the Path." She portrayed a graceful maiden wandering through a twilight field, dancing with the flowers as the spring breeze encircled her. She sang and danced, her steps hesitant yet charming, as if meeting her beloved at dusk.

The princess's enchanting dance and radiant smile captivated the prince. As the music ended, he walked up to her without hesitation and praised her sincerely, "Your dance was like a dream, as if a celestial maiden had descended to the mortal world."

She smiled softly, her beauty natural and effortless. Her eyes sparkled like a deep lake. Prince Qin mustered his courage and invited her, "Would you honor me with a dance to 'The Ballad of the Shang River Maiden'?"

After the dance, the prime minister of Annan quietly pulled the prince aside and asked softly, "Your Highness, you and the princess danced so harmoniously. Do you have feelings for her?"

Prince Qin chuckled and countered, "Did my father really say that I was betrothed to her as a child?"

The prime minister's face lit up with joy. "Indeed. From the looks of it, you seem quite taken with her?"

Prince Qin laughed; his gaze still fixed on the princess's profile.

Later, the prime minister approached General Langkun and explained the marriage alliance between Daze and Annan, hoping the general would discuss it with the princess.

Upon hearing this, the princess's face showed a flicker of surprise, and she shook her head slightly. "Prince Qin is indeed charming, but we know so little about each other. How can we hastily commit to a lifelong bond? Even if I were inclined toward him, I would need to wait until Daze's turmoil has subsided."

The general said with concern, "Princess, I understand your feelings, but the prime minister hinted that only through marriage will Annan offer its assistance."

The princess sighed softly, "Why does fate always push people into corners?" She leaned against the desk, tears welling up in her eyes.

Standing nearby, the general said with emotion, "Princess, do not worry. As long as I am here, no one can force you. I will convey your true intentions to the prime minister."

The prime minister relayed the princess's hesitation to Prince Qin. Instead of showing displeasure, the prince expressed genuine admiration for her pride. "The princess's integrity only deepens my respect for her. Please give me some time. I will surely make her see me in a new light."

The next day, Prince Qin personally visited the princess's residence. With sincere humility, he apologized, "Princess, please do not worry about the marriage alliance. Even if we are not destined to be together, my admiration for you will never change. I assure you; I will do everything in my power to persuade my father to support Daze's cause."

The princess looked up at the prince, her eyes glistening with tears. She nodded gently, the weight in her heart seemingly lightened by the prince's sincerity.

In the days that followed, the two shared countless thrilling and joyful moments. Galloping across the vast grasslands, the princess's worries seemed to dissipate with the dust kicked up by their horses. At bonfire gatherings, the folk songs and dances allowed her to momentarily forget the burdens of her nation and revel in the present joy. During mountain hunts, the princess displayed her bravery and decisiveness, her agile movements like a leopard's, further winning the prince's admiration.

As night fell, they stood side by side in the palace's rear garden, releasing sky lanterns together. The lanterns flickered in the night sky like stars of hope, tracing beautiful trajectories. Suddenly, Prince Qin reached out and gently wrapped his arm around the princess's waist. Startled by the sudden intimacy, the princess was about to speak when the prince's low, magnetic voice interrupted her. He whispered in her ear, "Please don't move, my noble princess. Every gesture of ours is being watched by the prime minister and the general. I assure you; my father will soon decide to send reinforcements."

The princess felt the warmth of the prince's hand and the sincerity in his words. Her tense body gradually relaxed, and a faint smile unconsciously appeared on her lips. She nodded slightly, as if acknowledging the prince's goodwill and showing her trust in him.

"It seems our prince is both charming and cunning," the princess murmured, her tone a mix of teasing and admiration, her fondness for him growing.

Hearing her words, the prince smiled. "Whether you're praising or mocking me, your smile is enough." He continued, "I admit, deceiving my father to help you was for the greater good, but my feelings for you are genuine. I have requested to lead troops to Daze. Perhaps we can fight side by side."

The princess, concerned, replied softly, "You shouldn't make such reckless decisions. Daze is fraught with danger."

The prince laughed. "Princess, don't scare me with tales of the battlefield. Are you afraid I'll cling to you?"

The princess glared at him. "I'm being serious."

The prince's smile faded, but his humor remained. "My princess, even your glare is enchanting. Let's not argue. Everything depends on my father's decision. How about I take you downtown tomorrow?"

The princess hesitated slightly. "But I don't want to draw too much attention."

"That's simple. We can dress as commoners and wear masks, enjoying a day of leisure."

Finally, the princess smiled, her heart filled with a sense of anticipation for this prince who was about to become her comrade-in-arms.

Chapter 9

The Prince's Gift

The prince and princess, wearing bat masks, quietly blended into the bustling crowd of Luding City. Dappled sunlight filtered through the dense canopy of phoenix trees, casting golden spots on the cobblestone streets that danced with their footsteps. As they passed by Ge San Shang, the princess's gaze was drawn to the colorful fruit jellies displayed in the window. The vibrant, translucent desserts, resembling works of art, made her slow her pace involuntarily, her eyes sparkling with childlike wonder.

Noticing her expression, the prince smiled slightly and took her hand, leading her into the shop. The shop was filled with customers, and the air was thick with the sweet aroma of fruits. Monkey Shang, dressed in colorful attire, greeted them warmly and handed them a delicate menu.

The princess's eyes lingered on the fruit jellies.

"These are our signature dishes, each with its unique flavor," Monkey Shang introduced sweetly.

The princess, filled with curiosity, gazed at the exquisite desserts and asked softly, "Who is the master behind these delightful creations?"

Monkey Shang's face lit up with pride. "These are the works of my brother Kau."

The princess's eyes brightened instantly, as if she had caught onto something. "Brother Kau? Could it be Kauko?"

Monkey Shang was surprised. This mysterious guest knew Kauko? She nodded happily. "Yes, it is. How do you know him?"

The princess smiled faintly, trying to mask her excitement. "I've only heard of him. His reputation precedes him. Is he here now?"

Monkey Shang shook her head regretfully. "He had some business to attend to today and might not be back until later."

A flicker of disappointment crossed the princess's eyes, but she was grateful for the mask hiding her emotions. Countless questions flooded her mind: How was he doing? Did he possess the legendary martial arts skills? Would he be willing to stand by her side and fight for the people? Did he still resent her for leaving him in the forest?

Monkey Shang interrupted her thoughts, smiling as she asked, "What would you like to try, miss?"

The princess, unable to contain her emotions, suddenly stood up, her voice trembling slightly. "I'm sorry, I'll come back another day." With that, she hurried out the door. The prince followed closely, his face filled with confusion and concern.

Back at the palace, the princess sat by the window, unable to hold back her tears any longer. She didn't know why she was crying—was it from surprise or worry? Every time she thought of Kauko's pure and warm presence, her heart felt like it was breaking.

She half-reclined on the bed, her fingers brushing against the pillow as she reached for the book *A Glimpse of Huaxia* on the bedside table. She flipped through the pages hurriedly, as if trying to calm the turmoil in her chest through the touch of the paper. The pages stopped at the chapter on Annan, filled with praises of the country's prosperity and peace. Her gaze lingered for a moment before she took a deep breath, trying to find the section on Daze. But there was no trace of it. Disappointment pierced her chest like a cold wind.

She frowned and flipped further, stopping at the section on Sherkon. She had only intended to see how this devil-ruled nation was portrayed, but as she read, her eyes narrowed—Daze was listed as a mere province of Sherkon. The cold words on the page stabbed at her heart.

At that moment, her thoughts were forcibly pulled back to reality. She remembered Advisor's instructions: she had to face Kauko herself and confirm whether he was the demon-slaying hero who could save Daze.

During dinner, the table was filled with an array of fruit jellies, as if the entire menu of Ge San Shang had been brought over. The princess's eyes lit up, and under the prince's gaze, she picked up a piece of jelly and took a bite. The familiar taste was exactly like the ones Kauko used to make. She looked at the prince curiously. "Who made these?"

The prince smiled mysteriously. "Follow me." He led her through the palace's intricate corridors to a half-open kitchen door.

The princess peeked inside and recognized the familiar figure—Kauko, though his face was blurred by the steam. He was busy at the stove, with iron chains wrapped around his waist and wrists, his back looked so pitiful it stirred compassion in anyone who saw it. Just as Kauko turned his head, the princess quickly retreated, her heart filled with anger and sorrow. She turned and walked away heavily. In a dim corridor, she suddenly drew her dagger, its tip pointing at the prince's throat. "Why are you treating Kauko like this?" Her voice was cold, her eyes sharp as a blade.

The prince looked shocked and quickly explained, "I only wanted to invite him to the palace to make fruit jellies, but he refused, so I..."

Before he could finish, the princess's eyes were already filled with tears. She said resolutely, "Release him immediately, or I will consider you my enemy."

The prince, like a child caught in a mistake, stammered apologies. "Princess, please forgive me. I only wanted to make you smile..."

He quickly ordered his men to release Kauko and gave him a few silver ingots as compensation.

The princess secretly watched as Kauko limped out of the courtyard, his figure disappearing behind the red glow of the sunset. Her heart was filled with endless sorrow. Tichu had once said that Kauko was a curse, that anyone who got close to him would suffer misfortune. But the princess felt the opposite was true—every time she met Kauko, it was he who suffered.

This incident only strengthened her belief that Kauko was not the demon-slaying hero the advisor was looking for. The true hero must be someone else. As for Kauko, he must stay away from Daze's conflicts.

Under the soft light, the amber wine in the prince's cup swayed slightly, as if reflecting the mischief in his eyes. His gaze occasionally drifted to the princess across from him, but her eyes were fixed on the window, her brow slightly furrowed, her fingers gently tracing the rim of her cup, seemingly oblivious to everything around her.

The prince deliberately coughed lightly, drawing everyone's attention. He smiled and said, "Since tonight is so lively, let me tell you an interesting story!" He put down his cup, leaned forward, and began gesturing animatedly, his expression playful as he recounted the fierce dragon boat race with the prince of Tianluo. He described how he had secretly attached a heavy stone to the bottom of the opponent's boat, ultimately securing victory.

The listeners were stunned at first, then burst into laughter. Even the maids in the distance couldn't help covering their mouths to stifle their giggles.

Laughter filled the hall, and someone slapped the table, exclaiming, "So that's how it was! No wonder they looked so confused when they lost!"

The princess sat quietly at first, seemingly unmoved by the story. But as it reached its climax, she finally looked up, her eyes meeting the prince's in a silent exchange that seemed to convey a hint of forgiveness.

The prince felt a warmth in his heart. Though the princess didn't smile, that brief moment of eye contact gave him an indescribable sense of relief. She had forgiven him.

Another beautiful morning arrived, and the sun streamed through the embroidered window as the princess sat by the window, doing her makeup. The prince sent someone to inquire if she would like to watch a play to lift her spirits. The princess replied that she felt too lazy today and would not make any arrangements.

At noon, the princess asked Tichu to guard her courtyard, ensuring no one would disturb her. Dressed in plain clothes, she went to the backyard to admire the flowers. Seizing the opportunity, she climbed over the wall and left the palace, wearing her mask as she made her way to Ge San Shang.

Monkey Shang recognized her from the day before and warmly invited her to sit, handing her the menu. The guest removed her mask, revealing a rare beauty.

The princess handed the menu back to Monkey Shang and said softly, "I'd like a bowl of three-delicacy noodle soup."

Monkey Shang looked apologetic. "Miss, we don't have that on the menu."

The princess smiled gently. "Then could you ask the chef if he'd be willing to make it?"

"Of course, I'll go ask right away," Monkey Shang replied, turning and hurrying to the kitchen.

A moment later, she returned with good news. "The chef said to please wait a moment. I'll need to go across the street to buy some ingredients."

While waiting, the princess quietly stood up and peered through the inner window, catching a glimpse of Kauko busy in the kitchen. He was fully immersed in his cooking, his face filled with satisfaction and pride. This sight filled the princess with joy—this was the life she had hoped for him! He had once shared his passion for cooking with her, and now it seemed he had truly realized his dream. Yet, amidst her happiness, a faint jealousy stirred within her. Why couldn't she pursue her own dreams as freely as he did? What were her dreams? To act, to break free from the constraints of being a princess, to play the role of Zhu Bajie's companion; to gallop on horseback with Kauko through dense forests; or perhaps more, though those dreams were too extravagant to ever be realized.

Monkey Shang soon returned with the ingredients. The princess sat back down, secretly wondering if Kauko had guessed that the noodle soup was for her.

"Miss, Brother Kau says the soup will be ready once the broth boils a bit more," Monkey Shang said with a smile.

The princess smiled in return. "I can already smell the delicious aroma. By the way, little sister, what's your name?"

"My name is Monkey Shang."

"That's a lovely name, as charming as you are," the princess complimented.

Monkey Shang blushed slightly, feeling shy from the praise.

"I must be the first to try this noodle soup, right?" the princess asked curiously.

"Yes, I didn't expect Brother Kau to agree so readily," Monkey Shang replied. "Didn't he ask who ordered it?"

"He was too busy to ask," Monkey Shang explained before attending to other customers.

A moment later, the three-delicacy noodle soup was ready. Kauko said to Monkey Shang, "Shang, I'll deliver this bowl myself. I want to see who ordered it."

Monkey Shang pointed. "It's the lady sitting at the fifth table on the right."

Kauko eagerly carried the bowl of soup to the table, only to find the guest had already left. He placed the bowl on the table, looking around in confusion. He called Monkey Shang over to ask, but she was equally puzzled.

"What did she look like?" Kauko asked, a hint of curiosity in his voice.

"She was a young woman, very beautiful," Monkey Shang replied, her voice filled with admiration.

Kauko shook his head slightly, a look of regret on his face. "Let's wait a bit longer. If she doesn't return, Shang, you can try it. If you like it, we'll add it to the menu and create a new series."

Monkey Shang couldn't help but praise him. "Brother Kau, how do you know so much?"

"Shang, you don't know this, but I love the kitchen. Maybe it's because I love eating," Kauko laughed.

The princess hadn't come for the soup. She only wanted to see him and find out if he still remembered her. She had hoped that the little episode with the three-delicacy noodle soup would give Kauko a clue, allowing him to sense her blessings and prayers. She didn't dare wait for the soup to be served, nor did she have the courage to taste it and leave the shop calmly. She noticed a teahouse across the street and walked over.

She sat down quietly and ordered a pot of tea. She brought the cup to her lips occasionally, but her gaze remained fixed on Ge San Shang through the window, lingering on everyone who entered and exited. Whenever Kauko appeared in her line of sight, her heart raced, but she quickly looked away, as if afraid he might see her watching.

Time passed slowly as she waited. The princess's teacup was refilled and emptied repeatedly as she silently rose and made several trips to the restroom. The sunlight streaming through the window fell on her, but it couldn't dispel the melancholy in her heart.

As the sky gradually darkened, the teahouse was left with only the princess as its final customer. The owner reminded her that they were about to close. She handed him a silver coin, asking him to wait a little longer and refill her tea.

The lights at Ge San Shang went out, and the shop closed. Kauko, holding

Monkey Three and Monkey Shang's hands, walked along the star-lit street. The princess followed them, wishing she could join them, holding hands and living an ordinary life. At that moment, they began singing the song "Cangshan Sister", its joyful and familiar melody almost captivating her soul.

***

During the prince's absence from the capital, the beauties from Tianluo felt unusually lonely. The prince of Tianluo came to see the King of Annan to bid farewell, planning to take the women back to their homeland early. The old king asked for the reason and learned that the women had been neglected. He chuckled. "It seems I haven't been attentive enough. Stay a while longer, and let me treat you properly."

In the grand hall, the king sat on his ornate throne, his gaze wandering among the dancers in the ballroom. They wore thin silk garments, their movements agile and alluring. As they twirled, their long hair drew graceful arcs in the air, and the silver ornaments around their slender waists swayed, the tinkling of bells bringing whispers from distant lands.

Just as the king's eyes sparkled with appreciation and joy, a servant quietly approached the throne, holding an urgent report.

The king reluctantly shifted his gaze from the dancers and took the report. The news on it brought an unmistakable excitement to his face: Prince Qin and Princess Wenxi were getting along splendidly in the palace, as if destined for each other.

The king smiled slightly, his plans already forming. He decided to send fifty thousand cavalries to Daze, supporting the prince's ambition to expand their territory. More importantly, he agreed to the prince's request to appoint him as the commander, joining forces with Princess Wenxi to bring a new dawn to Daze and add a glorious chapter to the prince's future.

***

Under the dim afterglow, the princess and Prince Qin strolled along the garden path, discussing their future plans. The princess would return to Daze first, while the prince needed a few days to gather troops and prepare supplies.

After the prince left, General Langkun quietly reminded the princess, "Princess, it seems you haven't paid much attention to Advisor's request to find Kauko."

The princess sighed softly. "Actually, Kauko is in Luding. The other day, he was even captured by the prince and brought here to make fruit jellies. He doesn't possess the legendary divine powers—he can't even protect himself!"

General Langkun frowned uneasily. "What you say makes sense, Princess, but I fear the advisor will be disappointed."

The princess replied firmly, "We depart for Daze tonight. I will explain everything to the advisor myself."

General Langkun had no choice but to set aside the matter of Kauko and turn to prepare for their departure. Unexpectedly, Prince Qin was waiting for him ahead.

"General, there's something I don't understand. May I ask for your guidance?" Prince Qin gestured for General Langkun to join him in a nearby pavilion. Once seated, he recounted the incident where the princess had pointed a sword at him, his words filled with confusion.

General Langkun chuckled. "The princess once faced danger among the common folk, and it was Kauko who saved her. Though he lacks martial skills, his courage forged a deep bond between him and the princess."

The prince's eyes flickered with curiosity. "I never expected someone so gentle-looking to have such bravery! But between him and the princess, there isn't anything...?" A hint of doubt crept into his tone.

General Langkun laughed lightly and waved his hand. "Your Highness, you overthink it. They are merely close friends. Besides, the people of Daze are not as accepting as those in your kingdom. Our citizens struggle to accept those who look different, let alone when it involves the royal family."

The prince nodded. "I only hope the princess will become mine."

The general continued to reassure him. "Your Highness and the princess are destined by fate. Your union is profound and not something others can interfere with."

The prince smiled happily. "Your words are comforting, General, but the princess hasn't agreed yet. By the way, what's the story behind Kauko's pig-like appearance?"

General Langkun explained, "I've only heard that he resembles his father, but I've never seen it for myself."

The prince looked surprised. "So he was born that way? It's not some curse cast by Fire Maiden?"

The general confirmed, "That's correct."

The prince asked further, "Is he the son of Zhu Bajie?"

"Your Highness is right."

The prince exclaimed excitedly, "If he has the blood of an immortal, he must possess extraordinary abilities! How could you let him work as a cook in our kingdom? Hurry and bring him back with you!"

The general smiled wryly. "The Advisor did instruct us to bring him back. But the princess is deeply attached to him and fears he might be harmed in the war."

The prince said, "General, I understand the princess's feelings, but you mustn't let them cloud your judgment. Perhaps you should discuss this further with her."

The general shook his head. "The princess has made up her mind. My words won't change it. However, if Your Highness could persuade her personally, it might make a difference."

The prince joked, "I'd rather not have the princess pointing a sword at me again."

***

Kauko was busy in the steamy kitchen when Prince Qin arrived with a guard, startling him so much that the porcelain bowl in his hands fell and shattered.

Prince Qin quickly raised his hand to calm Kauko. "Don't be nervous. I'm here to discuss something important. Princess Wenxi needs you."

Kauko asked in surprise, "What's wrong with the princess? Where is she?"

"Actually, she's in the city," the prince said, glancing at the jellies on the kitchen table. "The jellies you made last time were specially prepared for her."

Kauko was puzzled. "If the princess is here, why didn't she come to see me directly?"

The prince explained, "She did come, but she cares for you and doesn't want you to be dragged into the war because of her. If you consider yourself a part of Daze, then stepping forward is your duty."

Recalling the woman who had ordered the noodle soup but never ate it, Kauko suddenly understood. He took a deep breath. "I thought the princess feared the misfortune I bring and wanted me to stay away. Since the princess wishes it, how can I stand by and do nothing?"

Prince Qin grasped Kauko's hand firmly. "The princess is leaving Luding tonight. If you decide to join her, you must come to my palace before dark."

Kauko nodded. "I'll be there."

As the prince disappeared into the night, Kauko returned to the shop and sat down with Monkey Three and Monkey Shang around their familiar round table. The warm light from the kitchen illuminated their serious faces. Kauko spoke from his heart, "I've made up my mind. I'm going back to Daze with the princess."

Monkey Three was silent for a moment, his expression complex. "Brother, I understand you and your bond with the princess. But Shang and I... we fear the cold stares of the people in Daze. We can't follow you."

Monkey Shang's voice was as soft as a mosquito's. "Yes, in Daze, we're outsiders."

Kauko looked at them with deep affection. "I'll always be grateful for everything you've done for me. I won't force you to come with me, but I hope you won't resent me for leaving halfway."

Monkey Three gripped Kauko's hand tightly. "Though we won't go with you, take the shop's savings. Use them to support your cause with the princess."

Kauko packed a small bag and hurried to the palace. Prince Qin had already ordered guards to wait at the gate, and they led him directly to the prince. The prince treated him to a good meal and tea, then had him change into a black outfit worn by caravan traders.

The prince smiled. "Since you're a good friend of the princess and mine, I owe you an apology for how I treated you before. Today, I want to give you something to make up for it. Tell me, what would you like?"

Kauko looked around at the items on the prince's table and walls but found nothing that caught his eye. "I'm a cook. How about some noodles?"

The prince laughed and had a small bag prepared for him.

At that moment, General Langkun arrived to discuss departure plans with the prince. He suddenly noticed the pig-faced man standing nearby and froze, his hand instinctively reaching for the sword at his waist. "Who is this?" he asked in a low voice, his eyes flashing with caution.

Prince Qin laughed heartily and waved his hand. "General, don't be alarmed. This is Kauko."

General Langkun was stunned for a moment, staring at Kauko's pig-like face. Then, as if realizing something, he forced a smile to ease the awkwardness. "I should have guessed! So this is Brother Kau!"

Kauko smiled openly. "General, don't worry. I'll change back." With a slight shake of his ears, he transformed into his handsome human form, exuding a heroic aura that even the prince couldn't help but admire.

General Langkun's eyes widened in amazement, and he slapped his thigh. "So that's how it is! I remember now! I saw you when I picked up the princess. You were wearing this face back then. You truly have some divine power. I'll take you with me." The general smiled but added a warning, "But don't show your pig face again. It scares me in the dark."

Prince Qin said to the general, "General, I'll take him to the city gates to wait. When you leave the city, he'll follow you. He's my gift to the princess. But don't tell her until tomorrow, or she'll send him back."

As night fell, the princess's convoy quietly left the city, carrying baskets of tobacco leaves. The princess, still disguised as a man, bid farewell to the prince at the city gates. The prince, without hesitation, wrapped his arm around the princess's shoulder, his eyes filled with reluctance but his tone playful. "Little brother, you go ahead first!"

The princess thanked the prince, mounted her horse, and followed the convoy.

The prince called after her retreating figure, "I've sent you a gift. I hope you like it!"

The princess turned to General Langkun beside her and asked, "What gift did the prince send?"

The general deliberately played coy. "We'll know tomorrow when we take inventory. There are too many gifts—silver, jewels, gunpowder."

***

On Tian Mountain, on the day Master Dapeng and Kauko failed to return, the summer sun was suddenly obscured by thick clouds, and soon snow covered the entire mountain range. Snowflakes danced in the air like sky spirits, and a biting cold wind swept through, cutting like knives.

Amid the endless snow and cold, a small figure stood defiantly against the wind at the mountain's peak. It was Songmao, his eyes fixed ahead with anticipation, occasionally looking up, hoping to see Master Dapeng and Kauko descending from the sky. He had absolute faith in his master's abilities.

Day after day, Songmao sat on the same rock. Every bird call made him hope they would bring news of his companions. Every gust of wind made him imagine it carried messages from them, though the mountain wind seemed to mock him, whispering past his ears.

Gradually, his confidence waned, replaced by endless doubt and worry.

He imagined all the dangers Master Depeng and Kauko might have encountered—perhaps they had met powerful enemies and were trapped in peril. Perhaps Master Dapeng, due to his age, no longer had the strength to soar through the skies. Or maybe they had simply forgotten about him, each pursuing their own paths.

One night, Songmao had a dream. Kauko was captured by a red-clad demon and locked in an iron cage, being dragged toward the capital. His desperate eyes met Songmao's before he vanished.

The dream weighed heavily on Songmao's heart, leaving him feeling as if he had lost his soul. He decided he could wait no longer. He would go find them, no matter the challenges. Songmao had never traveled alone before, and the thought of facing the unknown filled him with fear, but he would not turn back.

As he prepared his belongings, he hopped around Kauko's bronze flute, his small eyes filled with hesitation. The flute was too large for his tiny frame. He scratched his head and muttered, "If only it could shrink."

As soon as he spoke, the flute emitted a soft glow and shrank to a size he could easily carry. Songmao's eyes widened in amazement. "It really is a magical item!" He carefully placed the flute in a small pouch, a satisfied grin spreading across his face.

Before leaving, he visited all the places he and Kauko had played together, saying goodbye to each and marking them with a sprinkle of urine.

Songmao trudged through the thick snow to a lone banana tree standing in the icy wilderness. He looked up at its large leaves fluttering in the wind, then climbed up and tore off one of the massive leaves. Its surface was smooth as a mirror, reflecting the blue sky. He skillfully bent the leaf into the shape of a parachute and stood at the edge of a cliff. The wind seemed to pause, as if waiting for his next move.

He took a deep breath, gripped the end of the leaf, and leaped into the air. His small figure, carried by the large leaf, floated like a lone seed in the cold wind. Sunlight pierced through the mist, casting dappled shadows on him as he danced through the sky with the leaf.

Gradually, Songmao found his momentum, gliding swiftly through the air, crossing endless mountains and rivers. The wind's roar faded, and the parachute began to descend slowly, revealing a glittering silver expanse—a wide river shimmering in the sunlight.

Knowing he was a poor swimmer, a chill ran through his body like an icy snake. His heart clenched, and fear gripped his breath. The water's surface glimmered coldly, deep and unfathomable. He screamed, closed his eyes, and braced for the moment he would plunge into the endless abyss.

But he didn't fall. Instead, he was caught by something. Songmao opened his eyes in surprise to find himself resting on a furry hand. His gaze followed the arm upward to a monkey-faced man standing on a bamboo raft, grinning broadly with a row of white teeth.

"Well, little brother," the monkey-faced man said cheerfully, "you're quite bold, trying to hitch a ride without paying!"

Songmao was stunned for a moment, then jumped onto the raft, stammering, "I... I don't have any money. Please don't eat me! My nephew will reward you handsomely!"

The monkey-faced man laughed even harder at Songmao's nervousness. "Don't worry, little brother. Monkey Four never bullies the weak. What's your name?"

Songmao relaxed slightly, his shoulders loosening. "I'm Songmao, from Kau Village."

Monkey Four's eyes lit up. "Kau Village in Daze? Then do you know Rake King?"

Songmao's eyes sparkled with pride, and he straightened his back. "Of course! He's my nephew's father."

Monkey Four burst into laughter. He crouched down and patted Songmao's shoulder gently but with brotherly affection. "I see! We're practically family! My former king was the Great Sage Equal to Heaven, and he and Rake King were sworn brothers."

Songmao's eyes widened with excitement, and he jumped onto Monkey Four's shoulder. "Brother Monkey Four, we're destined to meet! Where are you headed?"

Monkey Four gazed at the distant water and said calmly, "I'm going to Annan to find my third brother. He's made a name for himself there and asked me to join him." He turned to look at Songmao. "What about you? How did you end up here?"

At the mention of his journey, Songmao's smile faded, replaced by anxiety. "I got separated from my nephew. I'm out here looking for him."

Monkey Four's expression turned serious, and he asked in a low voice, "Is your nephew named Kauko?"

Songmao looked up sharply. "You know him?"

Monkey Four nodded slightly, a mysterious smile on his face. "You don't need to look anymore. I know where he is."

Songmao's eyes widened. "Really?"

Monkey Four smiled confidently. "Of course! He's with my third brother. Just follow me."

Monkey Four and Songmao, covered in dust, arrived in Luding City and pushed open the door of Ge San Shang. They were greeted only by Monkey Three and Monkey Shang. Songmao asked timidly, "Where's Kauko?"

"Brother Kau left. He went back to Daze with the princess's convoy," Monkey Three told him.

Songmao's shoulders slumped, his excitement instantly replaced by disappointment. Monkey Four stood still, his cold gaze fixed on Monkey Three. "If Kauko is off to do great things, why didn't you go with him?"

Monkey Three was stunned for a moment, then raised his head. "Fourth Brother, I barely escaped Daze. How could I go back and risk my life again?"

"Risk your life?" Monkey Four took a step forward, his eyes sharp. "Have you forgotten so quickly how Big Brother and Second Brother died at the hands of the Sherkon people?"

Monkey Three's face showed guilt, and his voice lowered. "I... haven't forgotten."

"Haven't forgotten?" Monkey Four pressed closer, his eyes icy. "And what about you? If it weren't for Kauko, you'd be a pile of bones by now!"

Monkey Three lowered his head, his brow furrowed as if wrestling with his conscience. His voice was barely audible, filled with inner turmoil. "Fourth Brother, it's not that I don't understand righteousness, nor am I afraid of death. But... look at us. Would the Daze army accept us? Not to mention Shang is here. I can't leave her behind."

Monkey Four stared directly at Monkey Three, his gaze as sharp as a blade. "Who said we have to join the army? Remember the old days? Sleeping in treetops, making caves our homes, taking shelter in broken temples. Anywhere can be home. We don't need to show ourselves. We can follow Kauko in secret and help him from the shadows."

Monkey Three seemed convinced but remained silent.

Then, a clear voice came from the shadows. "I miss Brother Kau too. I want to go with you." Monkey Shang stepped out, her eyes shining like stars.

Songmao, unable to contain himself any longer, jumped onto the table, his cheer nearly knocking over the items on it. "Since everyone agrees, what are we waiting for? Let's go!"

Monkey Three looked up, his tone still subdued. "But even if we've decided, how can we catch up to them?"

The question left everyone momentarily speechless, and the atmosphere grew heavy. Songmao looked around, then his eyes lit up. "I know! We came south from Daze, so they must be heading north."

Monkey Three's expression softened, and he nodded slowly. "That makes sense. The ancient road north from Luding is rugged, but we're agile. We should be able to catch up."

Monkey Four gave Songmao a thumbs-up. "Good, it's settled then! No more delays. Let's go!"

Without another word, the group quickly packed their belongings and set off.

Chapter 10

Rose in the Sleeve

The moon hung high, its silver light cascading like water over the mountains and forests. Under the swaying shadows of the trees, the princess and her party moved cautiously by the moonlight.

When they reached a deep valley, General Langkun raised his hand. Torches were lit one by one, their flickering flames like strings of pearls stretching along the winding procession, dispelling the darkness of the night.

Tichu walked in the middle of the group, his eyes constantly scanning the surroundings. A sudden night breeze carried a subtle, unfamiliar scent, instantly putting him on edge. He leaned closer to the princess and whispered, "There's an extra person."

The princess, focused on the path ahead, chuckled lightly, her tone casual. "Before we left the city, the general counted everyone."

Tichu's frown deepened, his eyes darting through the shifting shadows of the torchlight. He replied in a low voice, "Something still feels off. I'll go talk to the general."

He stopped by the roadside, waiting for the general, who was at the rear of the group, to approach. He vaguely noticed a tall, shadowy figure beside the general, its form indistinct. As he stepped forward to ask, the general quietly pressed the scabbard of his sword against Tichu's shoulder, whispering a warning, "Stay quiet."

At that moment, Kauko pulled the torch in his hand closer to his face and made a playful grimace at Tichu. Tichu froze for a moment, then his brow furrowed. He cursed inwardly, "It's him again!" A surge of frustration rose in his chest, as if he couldn't shake off a persistent nuisance.

He returned to the princess's side, trying to read her expression for any clues. But the princess remained calm, showing no signs of concern.

Seeing his sullen expression, the princess couldn't help but ask, "Did you find anything?"

Tichu replied nonchalantly, "The headcount matches, Princess."

By midnight, the general called for the group to stop and set up camp in the woods.

Kauko shared a tent with a cook, the air inside heavy with the smell of oil and smoke. Sitting on his bedding, he squinted at the cook, who was busy organizing pots and spoons, and asked, "What are we making for the princess tomorrow morning?"

The cook didn't stop working but glanced at him sideways. "The princess eats what everyone else eats."

Kauko straightened up. "That won't do. I'll prepare the princess's meals."

The cook paused and asked, "Who are you?"

"I'm the princess's personal chef!" Kauko declared confidently, stepping past the cook to rummage through the baskets and sacks in the corner.

The cook tried to stop him. "Don't make a mess!" But curiosity got the better of him. "What are you looking for?"

Kauko brushed the dust off his hands. "Do you have any fresh ingredients?"

The cook shook his head. "We're on a long journey. There's no fresh food."

"Fine, I'll manage," Kauko said, undeterred. He grabbed a small shovel and a bag from the corner and slipped out of the tent like a shadow.

The night was thick, and the moonlight faded, but Kauko was accustomed to the darkness. The forest was as clear to him as daylight. He moved nimbly, like an agile cat, weaving through the trees. His footsteps were so light they didn't even disturb the fallen leaves, and his eyes scanned every corner for fresh mushrooms and ferns. Soon, his bag was full, exuding a fresh, earthy scent.

Suddenly, a strange sound came from the distance, like something scraping against a cliff. Curious, he followed the sound, pushing aside the bushes to see two figures climbing up the rocky cliff. Their movements were steady and powerful, and the large knives strapped to their backs glinted coldly, exuding a faint aura of menace.

Kauko was certain these two were up to no good, and he grew worried for the princess's safety. He picked up a dry branch, crouched down, and hid in the dense vegetation, ready to act.

The two men reached the top of the cliff, panting heavily, and were about to sit down for a rest when Kauko let out a terrifying wolf howl, startling them so much that their knives trembled in their hands.

"Is that a wolf? Or a ghost?" one of them stammered in a low voice.

"Shut up!" the other snapped, trying to sound calm. "Are you even a Sherkon warrior?"

"So, they are indeed up to no good!" Kauko thought to himself. He wasn't panicked. With his night vision, he was confident he could handle anyone in the pitch-black night.

Taking advantage of their fear, Kauko extended the dry branch from the shadows, accurately striking their wrists. "Clang! Clang!" The two knives fell to the ground. Then, he leaped out from the shadows, his tall figure startling the two men, who stumbled backward and fell off the cliff. After confirming there was no movement below, Kauko shook his head and sighed, "It wasn't me who took your lives. Heaven wouldn't let you continue your evil deeds." He continued searching for ingredients.

The next morning, Kauko prepared a delicious bowl of noodle soup and carried it to the princess's tent. Tichu, who had been watching his every move, stopped him at the entrance. "Take that away. The princess isn't someone you can just see whenever you want!"

Kauko tried to step forward, but Tichu's hand moved to his sword. Reluctantly, Kauko gave up and was about to leave when he remembered the two men who had fallen to their deaths last night. He turned to Tichu and said, "Please tell the princess to be careful. Last night, I almost caught two Sherkon spies."

"Were you dreaming last night?" Tichu rolled his eyes, his tone dismissive.

"Fine, don't believe me," Kauko muttered, returning to the open-air stove.

When the princess woke up, she rolled up the small curtain of her tent and saw it was a clear morning. The smoke from the cooking fires wafted through the dawn light, and the cooks bustled around the stoves. One of the figures reminded her of someone she cared deeply about. If he were here, she could have a bowl of three-delicacy noodle soup. She turned away, darkening her face with makeup and dressing as a man.

Kauko was busy by the stove, stirring a mysterious stew. The cooks gathered around him, laughing frequently. It seemed he was quite popular here. General Langkun watched him from a distance, squinting.

Could this guy really defeat demons? Watching him stir that pot, he seemed more like a cook! Regardless, he was a gift from Prince Qin, and the general had to deliver this "prize" to the princess.

The general approached Kauko and asked, "Haven't you seen the princess yet?"

"He won't let me," Kauko replied, glancing at Tichu, who stood guard at the tent entrance like a stern sentinel.

"Don't worry, follow me," the general said, waving for Kauko to follow.

Kauko didn't forget the three-delicacy noodle soup and carried it as he followed the general. When Tichu saw the general, he quickly announced, "The general is here!"

"Please come in," a voice replied from inside the tent.

The general gestured for Kauko to enter first. Kauko didn't recognize the disguised princess and assumed the young "man" before him was one of her attendants. He asked, "Little brother, where's the princess?"

The princess, delighted to see Kauko, almost forgot her disguise and wanted to tug his ears. But she changed her mind, deciding to tease "Pig-headed Brother" a bit.

She lowered her voice, imitating a man's tone, and said, "Who are you to the princess?"

Kauko, unsuspecting, set down the bowl and chopsticks and replied proudly, "I'm Kauko. Are you new? Hasn't the princess mentioned me?"

The princess pretended to be serious and pressed further, "Why are you looking for the princess?"

Kauko looked around and said earnestly, "Of course, to help her."

The princess frowned, feigning seriousness. "Help with what?"

"That's up to the princess," he said casually, as if everything depended on her.

The princess sniffed the aroma of the noodle soup on the table. "I heard the princess is in need of a cook. How about it? Interested?"

Kauko's eyes lit up. "A cook? Perfect! That way, I can stay by the princess's side."

The princess smiled faintly. "A cook is busy. There's no time to stick by the princess."

Kauko looked dejected. "Then can I be a guard like Tichu, standing outside her door?"

The princess pretended to think. "Tichu knows martial arts and is clever. Can you do that?"

Kauko mimed pulling a flute from his waist and gestured with it. "See? I know a thing or two. And my heart to protect the princess is no less than Tichu's."

The general, standing nearby, could barely contain his laughter. The princess decided not to tease him further and asked tentatively, "Do I look like the princess?"

Kauko turned his head away dismissively. "Don't joke around. The princess doesn't have any brothers."

The princess laughed, unwrapped her headscarf, and let her long hair fall. "Kauko, take another look!"

Only then did Kauko realize the "young man" before him was the princess. He exclaimed in concern, "Princess, it's only been a few days, but you've gotten so thin and dark!" He stepped forward, about to touch her face.

The general stopped him. "Kauko, don't be rude."

The princess waved her hand. "It's fine. There's no one else here."

The general stopped laughing and said to the princess, "Kauko is yours now. He's a gift from Prince Qin, who believes this young man can be of great help to you."

"Prince Qin is very thoughtful," the princess said, taking Kauko's hand affectionately. "I didn't want you to come, but fate brought you here anyway. I don't have Master Dapeng's magical powers. How can I protect you?"

"Princess, don't worry. I may not have my father's abilities, but I'm no worse than Tichu," Kauko said. To prove his point, he offered to take the princess and the general to the cliff behind the woods, where he had driven off two Sherkon spies the previous night.

The general was skeptical but advised the princess to stay behind while he took a few soldiers to follow Kauko. Sure enough, two knives lay at the edge of the cliff, glinting in the rising sun like evidence. Following Kauko's direction, they looked down and saw two figures lying at the bottom, one still weakly struggling. The general ordered a soldier to investigate.

The soldier returned and reported that Fire Maiden had sent out over a dozen pairs of scouts to search for the princess. These two unfortunate men were one of those pairs.

The general's expression turned grave. He looked at Kauko with newfound respect. "Kauko, they were indeed Sherkon spies. I'll report this to the princess and recommend you for a reward."

Kauko smiled and returned to help with the cooking.

***

After Kauko and the general left, the princess placed the noodle soup on the small table and gently stirred the noodles with her chopsticks. The aroma of the soup filled the air, as if opening a door to the past.

She recalled her younger self, arguing fiercely with Auntie Wei over who would play the princess in their plays. She remembered the comedic skits she performed with Kauko on stage, as if it were just yesterday. The princess vividly recalled the cozy cavern in Jingxin Temple and the thorny, poisonous yet beautiful roses. She fondly remembered the days when she had playfully clung to Pig-headed Brother's back.

After finishing the soup, she picked up the bronze mirror on the table and saw her face covered in charcoal powder, as if wearing a theatrical mask. She touched her cheek, feeling as if she were touching someone else, and scolded herself, "No wonder Kauko didn't recognize me. I don't even recognize myself!" A mischievous thought popped into her head: why not remove the disguise and show Kauko her true face, giving him a surprise?

But she quickly dismissed the idea, realizing it was just a childish whim popping up at the wrong time. She knew the general would think her too young and impulsive. Sighing, the princess decided to save the surprise for a more appropriate moment.

As she lost herself in thought, the mirror reflected a beautiful woman's face. Her eyes were like clear spring water, transparent yet deep, her willow-leaf eyebrows gently curved, as if a breeze had rippled across a lake, bringing a sense of calm. Her lips were a soft pink, like morning peaches glistening with dew, moist and full. Her skin was as white as jade, glowing with a fresh radiance, like osmanthus flowers blooming quietly under the moonlight.

The delicate, gentle face leaned closer, pressing against the princess's. A strong scent of roses filled the air, and the princess felt dizzy, suddenly forgetting who she was. She turned to see a familiar-looking young woman in a rose-red dress standing before her. Dazed, she asked, "Who are you?"

The woman in red countered, "Do you know who you are?"

The princess's mind went blank. She stared at the mirror in her hand, unable to recall her identity. The reflection showed a grotesque pig's face, its tangled hair like twisted vines. Suddenly, the mirror slipped from her hand and shattered with a sharp "crack." Outside, Tichu's voice called, "Princess, what happened?"

The woman in red calmly replied, "Nothing, just a broken mirror." She turned to the princess and whispered, "This isn't where you belong. Go, as far as you can." She lifted a corner of the tent and watched as the princess fled into the deep forest.

The woman in red was Fire Rose. She activated a secret method to contact Fire Maiden, reporting that she had successfully replaced the princess and informing her of the princess's escape route. Fire Maiden ordered her to continue playing the role of the princess and enjoy all the glory that came with it.

The princess ran through the forest, her mind in chaos, unsure of where to go. The woman's words echoed in her head: "This isn't where you belong. Go, as far as you can."

She felt as if her world had collapsed in an instant. Her identity, memories, and trust had all become blurred.

***

Princess Wenxi had been replaced without anyone noticing. When Fire Rose interacted with Tichu and the general, a faint rose scent always lingered, as if carrying a mysterious magic that softened their sharp gazes, leaving them relaxed as if hypnotized.

As for Kauko, his clear, lake-like eyes were always filled with trust. Even when the "princess" occasionally said strange things, he never doubted her. In his heart, the "princess" was always worthy of his faith.

The general's subordinates grew fond of the new "princess." She was carefree, and her occasional mischief always brought laughter, making her seem like a familiar girl next door, approachable and natural.

In the depths of the palace, Fire Maiden lit a purple candle, its smoke curling upward as her low voice echoed softly, "Fire Rose, next, you must make Kauko fall madly in love with you, then break his heart. Only then will he release the energy I crave."

Fire Rose gently touched her charming face, confident that this would be an easy task.

One evening, she called Kauko into her tent, pacing beside him before leaning in close, her eyes sparkling with a coquettish and mysterious light. She exhaled softly, expecting him to be enchanted by the mist-like fragrance and fall under her spell. She planned to coldly reject him at the height of his infatuation, leaving him heartbroken.

But when she gazed into Kauko's eyes, she was startled. His eyes were like a tranquil lake, calm and bright, seemingly unaffected by her bewitching scent. He smiled at her, polite and kind, as if nothing were amiss.

Fire Rose's confident eyes flickered with unease. She had believed her soul fragrance was invincible, yet it had no effect on Kauko. Worried she might fail her mission, she called out to Fire Maiden, describing Kauko's state and pleading for help, "Master, I... I think I need your guidance."

Fire Maiden's eyes flashed with surprise, finding it hard to believe Kauko's resilience. After a moment of contemplation, she said, "It seems Kauko is different. The fragrance alone won't work. You'll need to put in more effort— use your emotions!"

Fire Rose naively asked, "Use my emotions? If I fall in love, will you let me keep him?"

Fire Maiden immediately cut her off. "You can use your emotions, but don't let yourself truly fall in love. Understand?"

"Master, I don't understand."

"Sigh, your emotions are a blank slate. It's hard to explain all at once. In short, find a way to captivate him."

"Alright, I understand."

Fire Rose lay on her bed, pondering the word "emotions." Since her master had told her to use her emotions, she realized there might already be genuine feelings for Kauko in her heart.

One day, the group camped near a hidden waterfall, the faint sound of flowing water echoing in the distance. Fire Rose told the general she wanted to take Kauko to the waterfall to bathe and instructed him to keep the others from peeking.

On the forest path, Fire Rose asked Kauko, "Not long ago, in that cavern, you and I were so close," she described the scene between Kauko and Bamei.

"Now, even though you're kind to me, there's a distance between us. What are you afraid of?"

"You said you were engaged to Tichu. How could we be close? Unless it's in another lifetime."

"Now I'm the princess. Why should I be tied to him?" As she spoke, she reached out her hand to Kauko. "Hold my hand so I don't trip on the rocks."

He took her hand and replied, "If you don't marry Tichu, there's still Prince Qin waiting."

"What if I said I have feelings for you?" Fire Rose stopped Kauko, her large, watery eyes fixed on him, her hair fluttering in the wind, her chest rising and falling like the wild grass by the roadside. Her words were not an act; they came from her heart, the reason she had signed a contract with Fire Maiden.

"Princess, don't tease me. I once had childish thoughts of being with you—or rather, with Bamei—forever. But when you left me in the forest, I finally understood I come from another world, one that people can't accept. How could I force you to love me?"

"You really are a bit slow. I just said I like you, and you're still rambling!" Fire Rose, taking him by surprise, kissed him on the cheek, then let go and ran toward the waterfall, stripping off her clothes as she went, tossing them into the air.

Kauko was stunned by her sudden kiss and didn't dare look at her retreating figure. Only after she disappeared into the waterfall did he begin to gather the scattered clothes, hiding behind a large rock with them. Thinking of the princess's affectionate gesture, he couldn't help but feel a sweet warmth.

The water cascaded from the cliff, gently splashing into a clear pool. The rocks beside the waterfall were covered in thick moss, and clusters of water plants grew in the shallow water, dotted with faint wildflowers swaying in the mist. The sunlight slanted onto the waterfall, forming a faint rainbow.

"Kauko, I'm done. Bring me my clothes!" Fire Rose's voice came through the mist.

Kauko stood up but didn't dare turn around. He called out, "Princess, you're naked. How can I bring them to you?"

"You're holding my clothes. Do you expect me to come get them?"

"Then I'm coming over!" Kauko closed his eyes and fumbled toward the water, following the sound of the princess's laughter. But he soon tripped over a rock, and when he opened his eyes, the princess was right in front of him, though she was crouching in the water, only her head and shoulders visible, giving Kauko a false scare.

Seeing Kauko's shyness, Fire Rose felt a surge of affection and said, "Don't hold the clothes anymore. Put them by the water, and you go wait up there."

Kauko set down the clothes and retreated behind the rock, keeping his head down. Suddenly, he heard the princess call out, "Kauko!" Thinking something had happened, he quickly stood up, only to see the princess running along the water's edge, her clothes fluttering in the wind. She seemed to be pulled by the golden sunlight, running lightly, her sleeves releasing countless rose petals that fluttered in the wind, forming a ribbon of flowers that soared into the sky.

Kauko quickened his pace, catching up to her in a few strides. He reached out and grabbed a few petals, bringing them to his nose to savor their faint fragrance. He then grabbed her arm, peeking into her sleeve, but found no petals. He asked in confusion, "Where are you hiding them?"

Fire Rose chuckled. "In my sleeves!"

Kauko pleaded, "Can you teach me?"

"I can't teach you even if I wanted to," she said, quickly pulling her sleeves back, regretting her momentary impulse.

The general's group continued north. The "princess" rode on horseback while the others, including the general, led their horses on foot. Along the way, Fire Rose suddenly called the general over, complaining loudly, "General, you need to do something. This mountain road is too bumpy. My bottom hurts!" Everyone laughed, momentarily forgetting their own sore feet.

The general stopped the group and said, "Princess, how about I carry you for a while?"

Fire Rose pointed her whip at the general's back. "That's a good idea, but your old back is harder than the horse's. How about Kauko carries me instead?"

"Fine," the general called out. "Kauko, come carry the princess!"

Kauko jogged over and easily lifted the princess onto his back, walking in the middle of the group. Fire Rose enjoyed being carried by the man she liked, her body swaying gently with his steps, her heart floating in bliss.

"Kauko, will you carry me all the way back?" she asked.

"As long as the princess wishes."

After a few miles, Tichu couldn't stand it anymore and approached them. "Kauko, you look tired. Let me carry the princess."

"Ask Kauko," Fire Rose replied.

"I'm not tired," Kauko said, feeling full of energy. Since the princess had said she might not marry Tichu, why should he give way?

After several hours, the princess on his back grew heavier. Kauko remembered the play where he and the princess acted out carrying a bride. He chuckled and asked Fire Rose, "Are you still the princess?"

"Of course I am. Why do you ask?" Fire Rose found his question strange.

"I was thinking of my father. He carried his bride, and as he walked, she grew heavier and heavier. In the end, he was carrying the Great Sage Equal to

Heaven," Kauko murmured. "I'm afraid if I keep carrying you, I'll end up carrying Mother Wangmu."

"Haha, you're killing me!" Fire Rose had Kauko put her down. "I think you're done, aren't you?"

Kauko sat down on a large rock, panting. "Princess, I can do it. I just need a break."

The group stopped to rest. Fire Rose sat across from Kauko, brushing her hair. Kauko suddenly asked, "Are you really the princess?"

This startled Fire Rose, but she quickly composed herself. "Of course I am. Did you really think I was Mother Wangmu?" Fire Maiden had told her to play the princess with authority.

"Then where's the scar on your head?"

"What scar?" Fire Rose was confused.

"The scar from when you were hit by a rock as a child," Kauko explained.

Fire Rose laughed. "Haven't you heard that girls change a lot as they grow up? The scar's gone."

Kauko sighed in relief. "Good, it's best that it's gone! I've always felt guilty about that scar. But princess, you're a bit heavy. Just now, I really felt like my father, carrying a deity."

Fire Rose raised an eyebrow and smiled. "Then will you keep carrying me? Or should I ask Tichu?"

He stood up and jumped a few times. "I can do it! What's so hard about being a porter?"

Kauko had an unusual day, carrying the princess on his back for hours. He ate a quick dinner and then collapsed in his tent.

Fire Rose returned to her tent, recalling Kauko's tired yet adorable appearance, feeling a warmth in her heart. For her, this day had been the happiest. She had experienced his sincerity and tenderness. Though her mission remained, the softness in her heart had subtly shifted her feelings.

At that moment, Fire Maiden's voice echoed in her ears. "Fire Rose, did you two have fun?"

Fire Rose reported happily, "We did, Master."

"And what about my task? Where's the pain I wanted?" Fire Maiden's last words suddenly thundered like a storm.

Fire Rose shrank in fear, hiding in a corner of the tent, trembling as she replied, "Master, I haven't forgotten. But he's naturally optimistic, carefree. It's hard to make him suffer."

"It seems you're having too much fun, too engrossed. Listen, make him suffer for love, now!" Fire Maiden left no room for hesitation.

"Yes, right away!" Fire Rose replied hastily, filled with deep fear, but she couldn't think of a good plan.

"I'll be waiting in Chinmi Garden!"

Under immense pressure, Fire Rose called out to Fire Maiden, "Master, teach me a new trick. What should I do this time?"

"Listen, I'll give you one more method, and I won't repeat it. Don't be half-hearted. I want results..." Fire Maiden explained her plan.

"Master, I understand. I'll try it now." Fire Rose struggled internally, knowing that following through would likely destroy the bond she had just formed with Kauko. But not doing it would have even worse consequences.

Kauko had just closed his eyes when he heard the princess summon him. He hurried to her tent, learning to announce himself first. "Princess, I'm here."

Fire Rose called out brightly, "Come in." He lifted the tent flap, and the scene before him stunned him. In the warm candlelight, the "princess" was gently kissing Tichu's cheek. The tender, lingering kiss was just like the one she had given him the other day.

A complex emotion flashed through Kauko's heart. He was about to leave quietly when the princess's voice stopped him. "Kauko, tonight I want to reminisce with Tichu. Go prepare a pot of fragrant tea and some fruit jellies. Bring them at midnight."

Kauko suppressed his disappointment and replied, "Princess, it might take two hours. I need to gather ingredients in the forest."

"Go ahead, but stay away from the cliff. Don't get distracted and fall," Fire Rose said casually, though there was a hint of concern in her voice.

Kauko didn't understand the princess's behavior, linking it to Bamei's mood swings at Jingxin Temple. He quickly let it go. After all, Tichu had grown up with the princess. He shouldn't compare himself. He soon calmed his emotions, focusing on his task, determined to make a midnight snack that would satisfy the princess and never disappoint her.

By midnight, the snacks and tea were ready. Kauko carried the tray back to the princess's tent, only to find Fire Rose alone. As he set down the tray, Fire Rose gestured for him to sit with her.

Kauko, noticing her distracted expression, asked, "Princess, where's Tichu? Did he upset you?"

Fire Rose replied with anger, "It's you who upset me!"

Kauko was stunned, his heart filled with confusion. "Me? What did I do?"

***

After Fire Maiden imparted the secret of the "love triangle," she waited quietly in Chinmi Garden. Soon, she felt a fleeting sensation of pain, like a flash of lightning, but it passed quickly, leaving no trace. After waiting impatiently for over an hour, she began to suspect that Fire Rose had not faithfully carried out her orders. Her anger flared.

"Fire Rose!" Her voice was as cold as a winter wind. "You'd better explain why Kauko is still carefree and not in pain!"

Fire Rose replied nervously, "Master, I'm doing my best, not slacking at all. But Kauko's nature is strange. He seems unaffected."

Fire Maiden questioned, "You didn't mix in your own feelings of pity, did you?"

"Master, I wouldn't dare!" Fire Rose hurriedly defended herself.

"Ah, so he's immune to our feminine charms?" Fire Maiden's temper cooled slightly. "I'll give you one or two more days. Find a way to deal with him, or I'll have to step in myself. Don't forget, I have no pity for that pig-headed boy."

Fire Rose quickly added, pleading, "Master, just two days! Please don't trouble him yet."

Fire Maiden sneered, "Have you really fallen for him?"

Fire Rose's heart trembled. Had she truly developed feelings? But she tried to hide her inner turmoil and said firmly, "Master, I just want to complete the task without causing him too much suffering."

***

Fire Rose stood before Kauko, her breathing rapid as she struggled to suppress her inner turmoil. "You say you like me, but when you see Tichu close to me, why are you so indifferent? You don't interfere, nor do you show a hint of jealousy!"

Kauko's gaze was calm, like a still lake, as he replied honestly, "Princess, I do admire you. But I respect your choices even more."

Fire Rose frowned slightly and sneered, "Are you trying to show off your so-called masculinity?"

Kauko's expression remained gentle. "Yes, precisely because I am a man, I understand my actions. I must never let the princess feel even a hint of discomfort."

Fire Rose nearly growled, "If you truly care for me, you should feel pain, anger, and sorrow, just like I do!"

Kauko took a deep breath. "Princess, my world has become beautiful because of you. How could I let such negative emotions arise because of you?"

Fire Rose suddenly closed the distance between them, hooking her finger under Kauko's chin and forcing him to meet her gaze. "Tell me, what will it take to truly make you suffer?"

Kauko was startled, as if overwhelmed by her intense emotions. A deep apology flashed across his face, followed by a hint of mischief in his eyes. "Princess, what I fear most is being called ugly or a monster. If someone were to insult me like that, I would be utterly heartbroken. Do you remember? When we first met as children, you called me a monster, and I was truly devastated at that moment."

Fire Rose stared at the seemingly innocent Kauko before her, momentarily at a loss for how to respond. She could only sigh and say, "I hope what you say is true. Otherwise, someone will teach you a lesson."

The next day, the general gathered the troops, waiting for the "princess" to be ready before setting off. That day, Fire Rose shed her male disguise and donned a dazzling red dress. Tichu helped her onto her horse.

The "princess" addressed the group, "In two more days, we'll reach the base camp. Let's take it easy today. Last night, I had a dream. I dreamed that there was an ugly monster in our group who tried to kiss me, and I slapped him so hard he fell into Erhai Lake. Do you want to know who that monster was?"

The crowd erupted in excitement. "Princess, tell us who it was!"

The "princess" drew her sword, her gaze sharp. "When I say his name, he will be punished." Fire Rose's sword traced an arc in front of the crowd, and everyone lowered their heads, afraid they might be the unlucky one. After a moment of silence, Fire Rose pointed her sword directly at Kauko, who was in his human form, and shouted, "It's him! The ugly monster, the big ugly monster! Everyone, isn't he ugly?"

The crowd exchanged puzzled glances, unsure what the "princess" was up to. When it came to ugliness, Kauko, with his handsome features, was the last person anyone would think of. Tichu wanted to respond, but the general stopped him. The general had already warned Tichu not to discuss Kauko's identity.

The general took over Fire Rose's words. "Princess, are you perhaps comparing Kauko to Prince Qin? In my humble opinion, Kauko is indeed inferior to Prince Qin. Don't you all agree?"

Someone in the group replied dismissively, "If Kauko were dressed in the prince's clothes, he might even surpass Prince Qin."

Kauko walked up to the "princess's" horse with a smile. "Princess, since I'm the ugly monster, how do you plan to punish me?"

She pressed her sword against his shoulder and turned to the crowd. "Should I cut off an ear or an arm?"

An elderly soldier with a wrinkled face, feeling pity for Kauko, pleaded, "Princess, please have mercy. Don't harm this boy. If you don't fancy him, why not let him be my son-in-law?"

Fire Rose showed a faint smile. "Since you've pleaded for him, I'll spare him. But this future son-in-law of yours must serve as my beast of burden today and carry me on his back all day!"

Laughter spread through the group. A burly man with a scarred face shouted, "I'm probably the ugliest one here, Princess. If you're going to punish someone, punish me!"

Then, the soldiers chimed in one after another, "Princess, I'm uglier! Punish me instead!"

Chapter 11

The Pig Demon

Princess Wenxi ran wildly through the ancient dense forest until her legs felt like lead, each step a struggle. The forest seemed endless, and fear, like creeping vines, grew wildly in her heart, entangling her mind. Her pants were torn by thorns, stained with patches of blood.

She was plunged into unprecedented confusion and bewilderment. The unfamiliar, ferocious face haunted her like a nightmare, making it impossible for her to recognize herself. Memories of the past seemed shrouded in thick fog, becoming blurred and distant, like fragments from another world.

A piercing cry split the sky. The princess looked up and saw a vulture circling above the treetops, as if waiting for its prey to collapse. She struggled to pick up a stick, trying to drive away the ominous bird, but the vulture only screeched more fiercely, ignoring her resistance.

Her world began to sway. The trees seemed to be falling, and the surrounding forest twisted into a blur of green shadows. She swung the stick in her hand, proving her resilience and determination, until her arms grew too heavy to lift. Suddenly, her knees gave way, and she fell heavily to the ground. The scent of earth mixed with the smell of blood, clouding her thoughts.

She clenched her teeth, her mind focused on one thought: "Get up!" She knew that if she fell now, she would never rise again. The vulture had landed on a branch, cawing excitedly, flapping its wings.

The princess reached out, her fingers brushing against a thorny cactus. She gripped it tightly, the sharp pain shooting through her body like a bolt of lightning, cutting through her confusion. She opened her eyes, grabbed the stick, and with its support, staggered to her feet. She looked up at the vulture. The tree shadows swayed, and a ray of sunlight fell into her eyes, refracting a golden light that shot toward the vulture like a sword. The bird fled in terror.

The princess slowly moved to the edge of a stream, its waters shimmering faintly in the sunlight. She dipped her blood-stained hands into the water, the icy coldness washing over her skin, the chill penetrating her bones. She stared at the unfamiliar reflection in the water, her disheveled hair and blood-streaked face blurred.

She lowered her head and submerged her entire face in the cold stream. The water gently flowed over her face, like a silent comfort, washing away the dirt and tears. The cold seeped into her body, and her thoughts gradually cleared in the icy sensation.

When she lifted her head, her gaze fell on a cave not far away. The entrance was dark and deep, as if nature had prepared a refuge for her. She swayed as she slowly walked toward the cave. However, as she reached the entrance, two golden panda cubs jumped out, blocking her path. Their eyes were firm, their tails raised, and they issued a warning in their tiny voices: "You can't come in, this is our home!" Though their voices were small, they carried an undeniable authority.

The princess was stunned, a wave of helplessness washing over her. She thought, these seemingly cute little creatures were treating a person in distress so harshly. Her legs gave out their last bit of strength, and she slowly sat down by the cave entrance, tears slipping down her cheeks unnoticed.

More panda cubs gathered around, curiously examining the unexpected guest while calling out, "Mommy, mommy!" The mother panda put down what she was doing and came over to investigate. Seeing that the princess didn't seem like a threat and had the face of a beast, she took pity and helped her into the cave.

The princess had just sat down on the soft grass bed when she fainted. When she woke up, she was greeted by the smiling faces of the panda cubs and a pile of fragrant wild fruits. She thought, "Well, it seems this is my new home."

In the days that followed, the princess became inseparable from the little ones. In the morning mist, she explored the forest with them, traversing overgrown paths and crossing clear streams. The panda cubs nimbly climbed trees, searching for food, while she waited below, catching the fruits they tossed down, occasionally bursting into laughter. As the sun set, they returned to the cave, tired but happy, with their bounty. At night, she learned to weave small beds from soft leaves and told the cubs stories. They lay beside her, ears twitching, eyes focused, not wanting to miss a single word.

But this peace did not last long. One evening, as they returned to the cave laden with their harvest, a sharp, cold presence greeted them. Before she could react, several rough hands reached out from the shadows, pinning her and the panda cubs to the ground. She struggled, even using the "bear paw techniques" she had recently learned, but it was futile. The attackers were too many, and her resistance was insignificant.

The panda cubs twisted their small bodies, letting out pitiful cries, calling for their "mommy," their tiny voices echoing in the cave. Their mother lay in a pool of blood, her eyes open but lifeless.

It turned out that a group of Sherkon soldiers had been lying in wait for the princess. They tied up the panda cubs, stringing them together and tethering them to a tree root in the cave. Then they dragged the princess out, bound her hands and feet, and threw a torch into the cave. Flames instantly engulfed the entire cave. The princess was roughly thrown onto a horse, her body swaying weakly. She desperately turned her head, looking at the rising smoke, the firelight reflecting in her eyes, her heart filled with endless despair and anger.

Days later, she was brought to Sien City in the Daze Kingdom. Her appearance was no longer what it once was. A black prisoner's robe covered her emaciated body, her head and hands locked in a wooden cangue, the heavy iron shackles on her feet clanging with every step. Her large ears swayed in the wind, a red silk tightly gagging her mouth to prevent her from uttering "ominous" words.

The prisoner's cart slowly moved along the stone-paved street, three horses plodding heavily with each step. The streets were lined with onlookers, their laughter and noise making it seem like a festival. Suddenly, a shout came from a corner, igniting the crowd's fury. Rotten eggs and tomatoes rained down on her like a storm, covering her face and prisoner's robe. The stench of filth and the crowd's sneers were like sharp blades, cutting into her dignity.

She closed her eyes, trembling as she endured it all. Every jeer, every piece of filth seemed to awaken a long-buried memory. A small, blurry figure gradually emerged—pig faced Kauko. He had been surrounded and beaten just like this, as if everyone wanted him dead. She remembered how she had been humiliated while trying to protect him. For days, she had been confused about who she was, but now she realized—she was Bamei.

Though she still couldn't fully recall how she had ended up in this situation, she remembered leaving Kauko in a remote ancient temple deep in the forest. Her lowered head slightly lifted, a glint of determination flashing in her eyes. She silently vowed to break free from these chains, to shatter the curse upon her, to find her true self, and to reunite with her dear friend Kauko.

A woman standing on a balcony overlooking the street poured a basin of overnight foot-washing water onto the princess as the prisoner's cart passed by.

The dirty water drenched the princess and splashed onto a Sherkon soldier. Enraged, the soldier shot an arrow. The woman tumbled from the balcony.

At that moment, as if the heavens were mourning for the princess, a fierce wind swept up, carrying yellow sand from a hundred miles away into Sien City, making it impossible to keep one's eyes open. The onlookers scattered in fear, and the street doors quickly closed. The public display was abruptly cut short, and she was taken to a pig demon concentration camp. A scar-faced guard took the princess from the soldiers, and the heavy iron door slammed shut behind her with a loud "boom."

The massive camp was located in a dust-filled valley, where thousands of pig-faced laborers toiled, sweating as they wielded tools, chiseling marble into the building materials needed for the Heavenly Altar. This altar was meticulously designed for Fire Maiden to cultivate her mysterious Heavenly Demon Magic, each stone seemingly imbued with extraordinary spiritual significance.

The guard, holding an iron rod, expressionlessly drove the princess to meet the warden. The heavy iron shackles on her feet clanged with each step, like a mournful elegy. The dust kicked up by her steps swirled behind her, as if quietly proclaiming her royal status. The pig-faced laborers around her stopped their work, watching her pass with a mix of awe and reverence, sensing her unique aura.

The princess's toe lightly kicked a small stone, pretending to slip, and she tumbled into a deep pit, raising a cloud of dust.

"Get up!" the guard barked, his iron rod striking the ground heavily. His gaze lingered in the pit for a moment, seeing the princess curled up, unresponsive. He cursed under his breath and jumped into the pit, trying to pull up the "unconscious" prisoner.

Just as he reached out, the princess suddenly flipped over, the iron chains in her hands swiftly wrapping around his neck like a venomous snake. Her movements were sharp and decisive, her hands gripping the chains tightly, her breath held, muscles tense, her eyes cold and fierce.

The guard's eyes widened as he struggled desperately, but gradually, his flailing arms weakened like broken branches in the wind, finally falling limp.

The princess released the chains, and the guard's body slumped to the ground. She searched his body, hoping to find the key to unlock her chains, but found nothing.

She looked up, her gaze fixed on a nearby pond, a wide expanse of murky water. Not far from the pond, a guard sat on a large rock, leisurely smoking a water pipe. His line of sight covered her escape route. She crouched, like a startled leopard, waiting in the pit for the right moment.

The laborers around her noticed the commotion. They exchanged knowing glances and then deliberately made a loud noise, drawing the guard's attention.

Seizing the opportunity, the princess slipped into the pond, hiding in the reeds, nervously watching the outside.

Moments later, a pig-faced laborer pushed a cart full of dirt toward the pit. He pretended to casually dump the dirt into the pit, completely covering the guard's body.

The warden sat behind his desk; his brow furrowed. The new pig-faced laborer had not arrived, making him uneasy, as reports suggested she might be the princess of Daze.

He stood up and walked to the window, squinting at the worksite outside. Under the scorching sun, the laborers worked with mechanical heaviness, everything seeming normal.

"Someone!" he called, "Go check the gate. Has the Daze princess arrived?"

Soon, a subordinate rushed back, panting, "Warden, she's gone missing!"

The warden's face darkened; his heart heavy. He barked, "Search immediately!"

The guards sprang into action, their shouts and footsteps echoing throughout the camp. They scoured every corner, even the woodpiles and ditches. Time passed, and the guards returned empty-handed. The warden listened to the report, his face clouded. "Increase the guards at the gates and walls. No matter where she's hiding, she must not escape!"

Meanwhile, Fire Maiden, resting in Chinmi Garden, had received word: the princess had been sent to the pig demon concentration camp. A glint of excitement flashed in her eyes, and she decided to personally meet this somewhat legendary wild girl.

She donned a black gown, draped a dazzling red cloak over it, and intricately braided her hair into a magpie's nest shape. She then put on a mysterious skull mask. She examined her reflection in the bronze mirror, satisfied with her sinister and imposing appearance. Fire Maiden was confident that this attire would strike fear into the girl, making her kneel in submission. Then, she could smoothly guide the girl, take her as a disciple.

She swiftly arrived at the highest watchtower of the concentration camp and ordered the warden, "Bring the princess to me."

The warden feigned confusion, "Governor, there is no princess here."

Fire Maiden impatiently snapped, "The one brought in this morning, isn't that her?"

The warden's heart skipped a beat. The governor was so concerned about this pig demon! He pretended to be casual, "Oh, you mean her? She's just a lowly princess from Daze."

"I'm talking about her! Where is she?" Fire Maiden pressed.

The warden tried to bluff, "I heard reports that she might have died of illness."

Fire Maiden's eyes instantly flared with anger, her voice sharp, "What did you say? The Daze princess is dead?"

The warden knew things had taken a bad turn and quickly knelt, "Governor, no, I'm not sure. Is she important?"

"Your question only infuriates me more! I tasked you with building the

Heavenly Altar, and you keep delaying. I told you to guard the princess, and you lost her the moment she arrived. You've ruined such an important matter, and you don't even know your crime!" Fire Maiden was utterly disappointed with the warden's incompetence. She had been eager to take the princess as her disciple, and now her plans were ruined!

She paced back and forth a few times in the watchtower, waving the magic wand in her hand, then suddenly turned and grabbed the warden by the throat, draining his life force in an instant. She pointed at the lifeless body on the ground and coldly said, "Take him out and feed him to the wolves."

She took a moment to calm herself, then called out, "Wulong, are you there? Turn the princess back into a human immediately!"

Wulong's voice, low and hoarse, echoed beside her, "Master, you know I can't turn her back. My magic is depleted, unless..."

Fire Maiden pressed, "Unless what?"

Wulong hesitated. He wanted to say, "Unless I die, the things I transformed can revert to their original form." But he feared that saying this might cost him his life. "Unless you master the Heavenly Demon Magic, then you'll have the power to transform her yourself," he quickly amended.

Fire Maiden's face darkened, her eyes scanning the area as if trying to hook Wulong with her gaze. Terrified, he hid under her skirt, fearing she might force him to reveal himself. She slammed the table and barked, "Excuses! Another freeloader!"

Wulong broke into a cold sweat, his lips twitching, "Master, I... I can still be useful! I can be the warden, definitely ten times better than the one who just died. Give me a chance!"

Fire Maiden pondered for a moment, weighing his loyalty, then said, "Fine, considering your years of loyalty, I'll give you one more chance. But remember, the Heavenly Altar construction must speed up. Any mistakes, and you'll answer to me!"

Wulong nodded repeatedly, "Yes, yes, Master, I won't slack off!"

Fire Maiden commanded, "Move to the Heavenly Altar construction site and keep a close eye on that architect. He's from Kau Village, so don't let him cause any trouble."

Wulong cautiously probed, "That Kau Lame, since he's unreliable, why not just eliminate him?"

Fire Maiden's eyes turned icy as she rebuked, "Do you have Kau Lame's skills? If anything happens to him, it'll be your life on the line!" She continued, "Keep searching for the princess. If she's still alive, report to me immediately."

Fire Maiden turned and left. Wulong wiped the cold sweat from his brow and muttered to himself, "In my next life, I need to find a better master." He arrived at the construction site and entered a side room of the Heavenly Altar, shouting, "Kau Lame, get out here! Did you hear? I'm the warden now!"

The cellar door creaked open slowly, and a dim light spilled into the cold underground space, illuminating an elderly man with a deeply lined face. He hunched over, his steps unsteady, as if each one carried the weight of years. He lifted his eyelids and glanced at the doorway, guessing Wulong was there. "Oh, it's the great Wulong... oh, I mean, Warden."

"That's right, call me Warden! From now on, when you speak to me, you must say, 'Your Honor, your humble servant awaits your command,'" Wulong said smugly.

Kau Lame immediately adopted a respectful posture and replied, "Your Honor, your humble servant awaits your command. Would you like me to steal a jug of osmanthus wine for you?"

Wulong's tone carried a hint of disdain, "Ha, I'm here to stay! Do you know why? To keep an eye on you and make sure the project doesn't fall behind. As for wine... well, now that I'm in power, why should I skulk around like before?"

Though his words were bold, there was a trace of bitterness in his voice. Since his magic had dried up, he had fallen from grace, becoming a nobody, terrified that Fire Maiden would abandon him, cutting him off from his beloved in heaven. Every night, he dragged his despondent body to Kau Lame's place, using strong liquor to numb himself. The alcohol offered a brief escape from his cold reality, allowing him to touch the edges of that distant paradise and find a sliver of solace.

Kau Lame sneered inwardly, "You're so arrogant now, but let's see if you can still remember who you are after a few jugs." As he thought this, he picked up a jug of osmanthus wine and tossed it toward the door.

Wulong caught the jug and, without a second's delay, downed it in one go.

Still unsatisfied, he ordered Kau Lame to take him to the wine cellar. "I want to stay there. It'll be easier to drink."

Kau Lame quickly waved his hands, "Your Honor, the wine cellar is the domain of the wine god. We must not disturb it. If the wine turns bad, I can't bear Fire Maiden's wrath."

At the mention of Fire Maiden, Wulong's drunkenness faded slightly. He knew all too well how volatile and ruthless his mistress could be. He grumbled, "Fine, then give me another jug."

Kau Lame, wanting to keep Wulong as far away as possible, said, "Your Honor, let me get you settled first. There will be plenty of wine. Follow me. There's a room upstairs, much more comfortable than the wine cellar. You'll like it."

After settling Wulong, Kau Lame took a bucket and headed to the nearby pond while there was still some light. He knelt on a bamboo platform extending into the water and dipped the bucket in. Unexpectedly, he saw a pig-faced head peeking out from under the platform, looking at him timidly. Kau Lame pretended nothing was amiss, though he recalled the mysterious pig-faced person who had escaped earlier. He pulled up the bucket, stood, and as he left, said, "Look at the Heavenly Altar. After dark, you'll see a light flicker in the window. Come find me then."

***

The night was deep, and Chinmi Garden was as quiet as a dream, with only the distant chirping of insects, like the gentle plucking of a zither. In the dimly lit temple, Fire Maiden's red dress flickered in the candlelight, like a ghostly flame. Her arms moved through the darkness, leaving faint traces, as if summoning some mysterious power.

Yet, things did not go as she wished. No matter how she tried to channel her magic, she couldn't capture even a trace of Kauko's energy. Disappointed, she sighed from behind her mask, "Fire Rose is too inexperienced to control that boy Kauko!"

She had a new plan and no longer wanted to let Kauko roam free. She needed to capture him quickly. She softly chanted a secret incantation, sending her thoughts to Fire Rose: "I will make him suffer the pains of the mortal world, becoming a source of power for me, hahaha." The candlelight flickered, and her figure gradually disappeared into the darkness.

***

The general's troops wound their way along the riverbank, the water shimmering in the sunlight like a silver thread cutting through the vast wilderness. In the distance, towering mountains stood like slumbering giants, silent and still. At a fork in the road, the troops halted for a brief rest.

The general unfolded a map and said cheerfully to Fire Rose, "Princess, look. If we take the left path, we'll reach the base in a day."

However, Fire Rose did not respond immediately. She gazed at the left horizon, where dark clouds gathered like ink over the mountaintops, brewing an impending storm. She worriedly murmured, "General, the left path is under heavy clouds. A tornado might be coming. Perhaps we should take the right path."

The general followed her gaze. The clouds on both the left and right were equally thick! He replied, "Princess, if a tornado really comes, I'm afraid neither path will be safe."

Fire Rose raised her hand, signaling the general to come closer. Her movements were graceful and deliberate, carrying an invisible authority. The general obediently leaned in, and a faint fragrance wafted over, slightly stirring his heart. When he looked up at the sky again, he couldn't help but feel she was right, and his hesitation vanished.

Kauko stepped forward, a hint of concern in his voice, "Princess, the mountain path is rough. Do you want me to carry you?"

Fire Rose shook her head slightly, saying nothing, but raised her hand to signal him to stay close. Her gaze pierced through the mist between the trees, fixed on a distant peak, as if searching for something.

Kauko noticed her furrowed brow and felt a pang of unease. He moved closer and asked in a low voice, "Are you worried about the tornado?"

Fire Rose continued to gaze into the distance, her eyes deep and complex, as if seeing through the clouds to a place beyond reach. After a moment, she sighed softly, her voice low but carrying an indescribable weight, "It's not just the tornado. The real danger is often harder to guard against than a storm."

Her thoughts returned to the moment before they set out. Fire Maiden's command still rang clearly in her ears: "Enter through the left mountain path. I will have men ambush Kauko deep inside." Yet, standing at this crossroads, Fire Rose felt a silent rebellion rising within her.

Without hesitation, she took a firm step onto the right mountain path. In that moment, all weighing and hesitation were cast aside, as if she had finally broken free from an invisible chain, no longer caring about the consequences that might follow.

Kauko followed behind her, vaguely sensing that her steps were more resolute than before. He didn't ask, but quietly quickened his pace, staying by her side, ready to face any unknown dangers on the mountain path.

As they reached the mountainside, an eerie wind sound reached their ears, starting as a low hum but quickly turning into a roar. The sky above the left mountains seemed to tear apart as dark clouds swirled rapidly, like a giant beast devouring the heavens. Someone screamed, "Tornado!"

"Quick, take cover under that cliff!" the general urgently ordered.

They moved in panic but with order, rushing toward the cliff.

The tornado was like a massive gray pillar, uprooting tall pine trees and hurling them into the swirling vortex. The ground shook, rocks split, and dust and debris flew wildly with the storm. Seeing the tornado closing in, and with the cliff still a hundred yards away, the general decisively ordered, "Abandon the horses! Everyone, move quickly!"

However, Kauko, who was at the back of the group, looked at the tornado and noticed something unusual. He shouted, "General, the tornado isn't coming for us! Look!"

Everyone stopped and watched. They saw that whenever the tornado tried to sweep toward them, it seemed to be blocked by some mysterious force and quickly veered back to the left. This miraculous sight left them in awe. Kauko faintly felt that the force blocking the tornado was like the gentle sweep of a giant bird's tail.

The group began to chatter, "Then there's no need to hide. Let's just keep going."

Fire Rose felt a weight lift from her heart, relieved that Kauko was safe, but she began to worry about Fire Maiden's punishment. Her legs felt weak, barely able to move. Luckily, Kauko was by her side and supported her, asking with concern, "Princess, did the tornado scare you?"

She gave a faint smile, "Can I just make an excuse for you to carry me for a while?"

Kauko happily hoisted the princess onto his back, chuckling, "Princess, you don't need an excuse next time you want a ride."

The group continued on, ignoring the raging tornado, and soon left it far behind.

By evening, they reached the mountaintop. The sunset's afterglow dispelled the dark clouds, and each beam of light seemed imbued with magical warmth, casting a golden-orange hue over everything. Wild grass swayed gently in the breeze, rustling softly, as if nature were whispering.

In the distance, a few birds returning to their nests flew across the sky, chirping as if singing, searching for their warm homes. After the long journey, the group basked in the gentle sunset, their faces filled with the peace and satisfaction of having escaped danger.

Fire Rose gently smoothed her wind-tousled hair, her smile mysterious yet tinged with an indescribable sorrow. Her voice carried a hint of exhaustion as she said, "I'll rest in the tent."

With that, she turned gracefully, her skirt swaying like a summer lotus. Tichu remained loyally on guard, while Kauko busied himself at the stove, preparing dinner.

As night fell and a gentle breeze blew, Kauko carefully lifted the tent flap, holding a plate of fragrant food. But the tent was silent, with no sign of the princess. He set the plate down and called softly, "Princess?" Still silence. A sense of foreboding rose in his heart, and he shouted, "Tichu!"

Tichu rushed over. The two exchanged anxious glances in the dim light and hurried to the general's tent, reporting in a panic, "General, the princess is gone!"

The general stood before the tent, hands behind his back, gazing into the distance with a knowing smile, as if everything was under control. "Don't panic. We're no longer in Sherkon force territory. The princess... she always likes to find a quiet place on nights like these to enjoy some rare peace."

He turned to the anxious Kauko and Tichu, a glint of wisdom in his eyes. "Kauko, go check the palm grove to the east. The moonlight there is like water, and the shadows are beautiful. The princess might be there enjoying the moon. Tichu, you go west. The princess loves the sound of waves, calling it nature's symphony."

Following the general's instructions, they hurried off in their respective directions.

Kauko's eyes were sharp in the darkness, and he soon spotted Fire Rose. She emerged from a grove, her steps slow and heavy, each one carrying an inexplicable weight. Kauko quickly approached and steadied her swaying body, helping her sit by a palm tree.

Fire Rose's eyes were vacant, like a lost fawn. She leaned silently against Kauko, her head resting gently on his chest, her hair cascading like a waterfall, completely hiding her face.

Kauko was at a loss, urgently whispering, "Princess, what's wrong?"

Fire Rose didn't respond, only shook her head slightly, tears silently streaming down her cheeks.

The surroundings were silent, save for the gentle whispers of the wind through the trees. Kauko could only silently accompany her, feeling the deep, unspoken sorrow in her heart.

***

Fire Maiden had stationed a group of loyal followers on the left mountainside, hidden in the dense forest. Their eyes were sharp as eagles, locked onto the winding path leading to the peak. They waited in silence, eagerly anticipating the arrival of Kauko and his group. However, their long wait was in vain, as a sudden tornado swept through, mercilessly swallowing them. When Fire Maiden heard the news, her rage turned toward Fire Rose. She awakened the beetles sleeping beneath the rose tree's roots, driving them to sink their sharp teeth into the tree's vital points.

Fire Rose writhed in agony on the ground, never uttering a word of plea to her master. She felt this might be the end of her life. Yet, Fire Maiden suddenly stopped the spell and demanded harshly, "Do you admit your mistake?"

Fire Rose, still weeping, remained silent. Fire Maiden waited for a long time, fearing Fire Rose might take her own life, and softened her tone, "It pains me to punish you. After all, who hasn't made mistakes in their youth? I'll spare you this once, but don't let it happen again!"

Fire Maiden spared Fire Rose, but not out of mercy. She had a new task for Fire Rose to complete.

***

Fire Rose gradually regained her senses and looked up at Kauko, who was holding her. She asked softly, "I called you ugly and humiliated you in public. Why aren't you angry?"

Kauko smiled gently and said sincerely, "Princess, when it comes from you, I don't mind at all. If it were someone else, it'd be different."

Seeing Kauko's unconditional trust, Fire Rose felt a pang of sorrow. She wished she had died earlier, sparing herself the burden of this heavy mission. Thinking of the task ahead and how Kauko would be dragged into it again, her heart trembled.

She whispered, "You should leave here. I'm afraid... I might do something to hurt you."

Kauko smiled calmly, "You wouldn't."

Fire Rose avoided his gaze, her brow furrowed, "Sometimes, I have no choice."

"I know you have big plans. If I can help, I'm willing to give my life," Kauko's voice was resolute.

Fire Rose's heart quivered, and she nestled closer, "How many lives do you have to give?"

Kauko gently patted her back and said softly, "As many as I have. Princess, let me carry you back. Everyone's looking for you." He carefully hoisted Fire Rose onto his back and walked slowly toward the camp. To comfort her, he hummed a tune called "Cangshan Sister", his voice warm in the night. Fire Rose listened to the soothing melody, her heart rippling, and asked softly, "What song is this?"

Kauko was slightly surprised and asked, "Princess, this is the song Bamei used to sing since she was little. Have you forgotten?" He didn't dwell on the detail, convinced she was the princess, and whatever she did was right.

***

As night quietly fell, the temple was enveloped in tranquility. Under the dim glow of an oil lamp, Master Midd, the royal advisor, lowered his gaze, his fingers slowly tracing over an ancient Bagua (Eight Trigrams) diagram. Each symbol seemed to come alive under his touch, as if silently communicating with him. However, at that very moment, his fingers suddenly paused—a faint tremor had reached him from afar, disrupting his precise rhythm.

The advisor frowned slightly, a hint of confusion flashing in his eyes. "Is this thunder on a clear day?" he murmured. He rose slowly and walked lightly into the courtyard, gazing up at the star-filled sky. The night was clear, with no sign of thunder or lightning.

Thinking he might be overworked and hallucinating, the advisor closed his eyes and began to circulate his energy, performing a set of Daoist exercises to refresh his spirit. But just as he was finishing, he sensed dark clouds gathering over the capital of Daze, accompanied by rolling thunder and flashes of lightning, within which he faintly glimpsed the figure of Fire Maiden.

The advisor inhaled sharply and sighed, "She can actually command the power of thunder and lightning!" It seemed her strength had grown significantly, and he wondered what sinister plot she was brewing. After a moment of silence, he turned solemnly to his assistant and whispered, "Send a skilled scout to infiltrate the capital of Daze and investigate Fire Maiden's movements. But be cautious and operate in complete secrecy." The assistant bowed and left, while the advisor remained in the courtyard, his eyes reflecting the starry sky, as if searching for the hidden mysteries of the universe.

A few days later, an urgent report quietly appeared on the advisor's desk. The scout's findings confirmed his suspicions: Fire Maiden had begun her move. She had mobilized tens of thousands of elite troops, silently crossing the Red River and hiding on the western flank of the rebel forces, ready to strike.

The advisor's eyes swept over the map like a hawk.

His fingers lightly tapped the location of the Red River, his brow furrowed in deep thought, as if wrestling with his own mind. Suddenly, his hand stopped at a specific point.

"So that's it... Fire Maiden, this is your decoy!" the advisor murmured softly, a glint of cunning in his eyes. He had seen through her strategy and recognized a perfect opportunity.

He pushed open the curtains in front of his desk, his gaze piercing through the mist as he looked into the distance, gradually forming a grand counterplan in his mind. If Fire Maiden's army was indeed a decoy, why not turn the tables? He would stage a massive feint on the eastern front, forcing the Sherkon army to divert their main forces there. Meanwhile, he would concentrate his troops on the western front and launch a sudden, decisive attack, annihilating Fire Maiden's isolated forces. This would be the largest counterattack by the Daze rebels.

The candlelight flickered behind the advisor, like restless eyes. He slowly turned, his gaze returning to the Bagua diagram before him. Yet, his eyes now carried a trace of unease and anxiety. The name of Fire Maiden loomed like a shadow over his heart. Her hidden cultivation was like an unfathomable abyss, not to be underestimated.

He decided to patiently wait for General Langkun and the princess to return. Once they were all together, they would discuss their strategy. After all, this was a matter of life and death.

The next morning, the first warm rays of sunlight gently bathed the temple. Magpies hopped joyfully among the treetops, their chirping as if announcing the joy of a new day. In the distant valley, auspicious clouds drifted like silk threads, a sign of heavenly favor.

The advisor sat quietly in his room, his fingers lightly pinching as if calculating something. As time passed, his brow gradually relaxed, and a bright, joyful light shone in his eyes. He was convinced that today was an auspicious day, and the princess and the general might soon arrive.

He sent out a welcoming party, then closed his door and began to meditate. Inside the room, the rhythmic sound of a wooden fish echoed, clear and melodious. The advisor's spirit gradually sank into a deep, meditative state, as if transcending time and space, where he once again saw the pig-faced youth: holding a divine flute, his face brimming with confidence, as if awaiting his sacred mission.

Just then, the advisor's meditation was interrupted by the voice of a servant. He slowly opened his eyes to see General Langkun standing before him, a pleased smile on his face.

The advisor asked warmly, "General, after traversing countless mountains and rivers, how is it that you show no sign of fatigue?"

The general replied excitedly, "As you hoped, Annan has provided us with fifty thousand armored cavalry. We await only the princess's and your command to march."

Hearing this, the advisor felt greatly reassured. He stepped forward and embraced Langkun, then asked, "And what of the divine flute youth I mentioned? Have you brought him back?"

The general smiled slightly, a playful glint in his eyes, and replied, "Indeed, we have brought back a youth. He is quite clever, though I did not see him holding a divine flute."

The advisor was about to inquire further about the youth's whereabouts when he suddenly sensed a powerful surge of energy. His face lit up with even greater joy, and he exclaimed, "General, you and the princess have indeed accomplished something extraordinary. This youth is the very person I have been searching for!"

Fearing that the advisor might place too much hope in Kauko, the general quickly tempered his expectations: "Advisor, Kauko is indeed likable and possesses some unique minor abilities, such as face-changing and night vision. However, while these skills are rare, they may not be enough to contend with Fire Maiden."

The advisor, however, showed no disappointment. A gentle smile spread across his face as he replied, "General, you need not worry. I trust my intuition. Though young, this boy's talent is extraordinary."

Seeing the advisor's unwavering confidence, the general chose not to argue further but made a suggestion: "I, too, hope he is the one we seek, capable of living up to our expectations. But I would like to witness his abilities firsthand. I propose a sparring match between him and my men to see if he is truly as remarkable as you say."

The advisor shook his head lightly, "I do not intend for him to engage in combat. His abilities lie elsewhere."

The general was puzzled and asked, "If he cannot fight, how can he defeat the formidable Fire Maiden? After all, what we need is a warrior."

The advisor smiled, "Rest assured, he has his own way. However, if you insist on testing him, I have no objection. Select a few of your best soldiers and let them spar with him."

The general carefully chose ten skilled and valiant soldiers and sent a guard to fetch Kauko from the kitchen.

Shortly after, Kauko followed the guard to the general. The general took Kauko's hand and was about to lead him to the advisor, who was seated in a corner of the viewing platform. However, the advisor gently waved his hands, smiling to indicate that no formalities were necessary. The general turned to Kauko, "I hear you are trained by a renowned master and possess extraordinary martial skills. Today, we would like to spar with you."

Kauko's gaze swept over the line of soldiers in front of him. They were strong and vigorous, their eyes sharp—clearly elite soldiers trained to perfection. He smiled slightly, "General, you want me to spar with them?"

"Indeed, young man. What do you say?" The general's eyes sparkled with anticipation.

Kauko nodded, a look of excitement spreading across his face. He thought to himself that since childhood, he had only practiced with Songmao as his sparring partner. Today, he finally had the chance to test his skills against real masters. If he won, he would request to become the princess's personal guard!

He walked up to the line of soldiers, examining each one carefully, silently assessing their martial prowess. His master, Master Dapeng, had taught him how to discern an opponent's skill level and style from their eyes, gestures, stance, and movements. After his assessment, Kauko gently removed his chef's apron and looked around for a place to put it. At that moment, he noticed the advisor sitting not far away, smiling as he watched him. Kauko casually rolled up the apron and tossed it toward the advisor, "Sir, would you mind holding onto this apron for me? Let's not let it get dirty."

The advisor caught it with a smile, his eyes filled with amusement. He looked at Kauko's tall, handsome figure, sensing the natural aura radiating from him, exactly as he had appeared in his meditation. A sense of inexplicable relief washed over him.

The general stepped forward, offering his sword to Kauko. But Kauko shook his head gently, declining, "General, I need no weapon. I wouldn't want to hurt anyone." He turned and picked up a wooden stick from the side of the field, twirling it lightly in his hand before nodding to the general, signaling he was ready. Instantly, the atmosphere grew tense, and the crowd held their breath.

The general took a deep breath and issued the command: "Soldiers, step forward one by one and spar with Kauko. Show him your best skills."

Kauko moved through the field like a graceful dancer, his figure agile and light, deftly dodging the soldiers' fierce attacks. Whenever an opportunity arose, he would glide past like a breeze, his short stick lightly tapping his opponent's arm, instantly numbing it and rendering them unable to continue. The general watched Kauko intently, his heart filled with admiration.

To test Kauko's limits, the general ordered all ten soldiers to attack at once.

They moved in perfect coordination, their attacks fierce and relentless, surrounding Kauko. Yet, Kauko remained unshaken by the sudden onslaught. He had his own strategy. He narrowed his eyes, spread his feet slightly, and took a deep breath, trying to gather his inner energy to break free from the encirclement. But just then, a sharp pain shot through his head, as if countless needles were piercing him. He collapsed to the ground in agony.

The soldiers, thinking he was feigning injury, moved in to deliver a beating. But the advisor suddenly raised his hand and shouted, "Stop!" The soldiers immediately halted and stepped back.

The advisor turned to the general with a firm look and said, "Take him to the secret chamber!"

The general quickly stepped forward, lifting Kauko and shielding him in his arms. The two hurriedly left the training ground.

Once the three were seated, the advisor first returned the apron to Kauko and asked with concern, "You were doing so well earlier. What happened?"

Seeing the old man's masterful demeanor, Kauko answered truthfully, "Master, I've had headaches since I was a child."

The general interjected, correcting Kauko to address him as "Advisor." But the advisor smiled and replied, "Calling me 'master' is just fine. With you as my disciple, the world will surely envy me."

"Master, please accept my bow," Kauko said, then respectfully kowtowed to the advisor.

The advisor, filled with joy, helped him up. "Kauko, give me your hand. Let me check your pulse." He carefully felt the pulse, but his brow gradually furrowed. "Do you feel a headache when you use your inner energy?" he asked.

Kauko nodded slightly, "Yes, Master."

The advisor sighed regretfully, "Your Baihui acupoint has been sealed by dark magic, blocking the flow of energy throughout your body. Your inner energy cannot be released freely and instead harms you." He realized the gravity of the situation—it seemed they could not yet rely on Kauko.

Kauko asked earnestly, "Master, thank you for the diagnosis. Is there a way to undo this?"

The advisor sighed deeply and said slowly, "The one who cast this spell is immensely powerful. There is likely only one person in the world who can break it."

"Master, please tell me, who is it?"

"That person is you," the advisor explained further. "Your Baihui acupoint is locked by a mystical needle, fused with your body. If we try to remove it by force, it may harm you. But if you can learn to calm your mind, gather your spirit, and channel your inner energy, in time, you may expel the needle yourself. However, it is hard to say when you will reach that level."

Kauko smiled, "Master, don't be disappointed! Give me a few days, and I'll show you a new me."

The general interjected, "Kauko, this is no time for jokes. We're discussing serious matters."

But the advisor smiled encouragingly, "Go on, what are you thinking?"

Kauko said, "Now that you've pointed me in the right direction, I understand why I am trapped. As for the solution, I've actually learned it before, but I was too lazy to practice it properly."

"How do you practice it? You wouldn't keep it a secret from your master, would you?" the advisor asked curiously.

Kauko replied, "Of course not! My master Dapeng, taught me a secret technique to open the body's and soul's energy gates, connecting them to the energy of the universe. Once mastered, the mind and body are no longer susceptible to dark magic. Don't you think this practice is perfect for my condition?"

Upon hearing this, the advisor slapped his thigh in excitement. "Excellent! Focus on your training. I have full confidence in you."

The general then reminded Kauko to temporarily set aside his kitchen duties.

Although Kauko still didn't know who had cast the dark magic on him or why, he felt a sense of pride. A wise man like Master Midd had placed such high hopes in him, and he began to believe wholeheartedly that he could succeed.

After settling Kauko, the advisor and the general went to meet the "princess." Fire Rose was already waiting in the hall. As the advisor approached the princess's door, he felt a wave of demonic energy rushing toward him. He couldn't help but mutter, "Where is this demonic aura coming from..." Before he could finish, Fire Rose stood before him, blowing a thick, intoxicating rose-scented mist into his face. He immediately changed his tone, "It's been a while, Princess. You've grown even more graceful."

"Thank you, Advisor," the "princess" replied with a smile.

The advisor couldn't take his eyes off the "princess". She was dressed in a red robe, delicate and smooth, draping elegantly over her slender figure. The crown on her head shimmered faintly, like a crescent moon resting on her hairline. Her dark hair cascaded over her shoulders like a waterfall, with soft curls at the ends resembling velvet. Her eyes, large and bright, sparkled like autumn water, and her long lashes fluttered gently, like the wings of a celestial maiden.

The "princess" gently took the advisor's hand, which was lost in thought, and guided him to sit down.

The advisor unfolded the map, his fingers tracing the Red River region as he slowly laid out his plan of feinting east while attacking west. He explained every step, every ambush, trying to gauge any differing opinions from the princess and the general. To his surprise, they nodded along enthusiastically, as if listening to a thrilling story. Seeing their relaxed demeanor, the advisor was momentarily stunned and said, "The only thing that worries me is if Fire Maiden herself takes to the field, and Kauko isn't fully prepared. We might find ourselves in a difficult position."

Fire Rose raised an eyebrow, a playful smile on her lips. "What's the harm in that? Why not spread the word that our army has a new divine flute youth, specifically here to challenge Fire Maiden, eagerly awaiting her arrival. She might think twice before stepping out of Sien City."

The advisor laughed heartily, "A brilliant strategy, Princess! Deception is the essence of warfare!" Immersed in the rich fragrance of roses, the weight on his heart seemed to dissipate.

The general immediately began making arrangements. His troops would advance from the center, while a small detachment would destroy the iron-chain bridge across the Red River, cutting off enemy reinforcements and retreat routes.

The battlefield was chosen in the vast forests of the mountainous region, ideal for covert troop movements.

The general sent a message via carrier pigeon to Prince Qin, instructing him to lead his forces to the lower reaches of the Red River in Daze.

Fire Rose volunteered to personally go to the southwestern border to meet Prince Qin's forces. The advisor selected a cavalry unit to escort her, but Fire Rose waved her hand dismissively, "What do I need an escort for? Just prepare a fast horse for me. I'll go alone."

The advisor frowned, insisting, "Princess, at least let Tichu and a few others accompany you for part of the journey. The road is dangerous; you mustn't take it lightly."

Fire Rose hesitated slightly, then nodded in compromise. "Fine, let Tichu come with me, but once we arrive, he must return immediately. You'll need more hands here."

Under the starry night, Tichu prepared the horses early and waited quietly outside the tent. Meanwhile, Fire Rose instructed Kauko inside the tent, "While I'm away, stay in the camp and focus on your training. Don't slack off."

Kauko asked, confused, "Princess, why can't I come with you?"

Fire Rose smiled softly, her tone gentle, "This journey doesn't require a chef."

Kauko argued, "Then I can hold your horse, fetch water, set up tents..."

Fire Rose shook her head, patting his shoulder lightly, her eyes carrying a hint of something hidden. "Tichu can handle all that. I don't need more helpers."

Kauko couldn't hide his disappointment. "Princess, am I really that useless?"

"If you want to be useful, train your skills. Running around with me won't make you stronger!" With those words, she turned and rode off swiftly toward the southwest with Tichu and the others, leaving Kauko standing alone in the camp.

Chapter 12

Falling Stars

The advisor, draped in a dark robe and holding a short staff, rode alongside General Langkun on a majestic steed, leading the troops forward. As night fell, they arrived at a dense forest and set up camp. The advisor chose a quiet corner, where his attendants pitched a black tent for him.

After a brief rest, the advisor intended to enter a meditative state to sense the celestial signs. However, a surge of intense energy struck his back, unsettling his mind and preventing him from focusing. He couldn't help but wonder—had Kauko followed them? The princess had explicitly ordered him to stay behind and focus on his training.

The advisor stood up and walked around several tents, eventually spotting a figure in black behind a cluster of trees. The person sat cross-legged, his head tightly wrapped in a hood, his body hovering a foot above the ground, perfectly still. Who else could it be but Kauko?

The advisor threw his staff at the figure, hitting its backside. However, when the black robe fell to the ground, it was empty, leaving the advisor stunned. At that moment, Kauko appeared behind him, smiling and calling out, "Master, I'm here!"

"You little rascal, playing tricks on your master!" the advisor said, though his eyes sparkled with delight. "Your ability to shed your shell like a cicada shows real progress. Does your head still hurt?"

Kauko seized the opportunity to complain, "This headache is really hard to shake. If it weren't for you, Master, I wouldn't bother with such painful training."

The advisor couldn't help but laugh. "Ah, my boy, this isn't just for me. It's for the sake of all living beings."

Kauko quickly reminded him, "Master, please don't tell the princess."

The advisor nodded. "You weren't supposed to come, but since you're here, stay by my side."

Kauko picked up the advisor's staff and asked with concern, "Master, let me carry you for a while?" The advisor gently poked Kauko's shoulder with the staff and chuckled, "It's too early for that. My legs are still strong."

***

As dusk deepened, Prince Qin's camp stood quietly in an open area at the foot of Mount Yi. The tents were neatly arranged, and the fading sunlight cast a solemn glow on the military flags, adding a touch of solemnity.

Inside the central command tent, Prince Qin idly twirled a jade cup in his hand, his gaze fixed on the message from General Langkun. Though his face maintained its usual composure, the occasional tapping of his fingers on the table betrayed his inner unease. The news that Princess Wenxi had not yet arrived left him restless.

As night enveloped the land, bright bonfires sprang up in the camp. The flames licked at the darkness, and laughter and songs rose and fell, carried by the wind and swallowed by the distant mountains.

Fire Rose and her group had quietly approached the camp and captured one of Prince Qin's patrolmen. Fire Rose blew a faint mist of intoxicating fragrance into the soldier's face, and he obediently revealed the camp's layout and Prince Qin's location. Learning that the prince was drinking with his generals around a bonfire, Fire Rose's eyes gleamed with confidence.

"Princess, should I go ahead and make contact?" Tichu asked in a low voice.

Fire Rose smiled faintly. "Prince Qin is carefree and unconventional. It's better if I surprise him myself."

Tichu asked again, "Should we wait here for your signal?"

Fire Rose waved her hand. "Tichu, your task is complete. Take your men and return. The prince will treat me well. Your presence here would only hinder me."

Though reluctant, Tichu obeyed Fire Rose's wishes and led his men away quietly.

Fire Rose changed into a soldier's uniform and slipped past several sentry posts, her figure moving like a shadow as she approached Prince Qin's tent.

By the bonfire in front of the tent, several officers were drinking and laughing, the firelight illuminating their faces and the cups in their hands. Fire Rose identified the young man with an imposing presence, who was clearly held in high regard by the others, as Prince Qin. She steadied herself, took a wine jug from a guard, and boldly sat down beside the prince.

Prince Qin was slightly taken aback and asked with curiosity, "Who are you?"

Fire Rose smiled, already dispersing the rose-scented mist. She raised her cup and said, "An old acquaintance. Do you remember me, Prince?" Her eyes held a hint of deeper meaning as she lightly clinked her cup against his, her demeanor calm and composed.

Prince Qin squinted for a moment, then burst into laughter. Half-drunk, he slung an arm around her shoulders and said casually, "Whether old friend or new, come, let's drink."

Fire Rose smiled and proposed, "How about a little game? Whoever wins tonight will be the prince of this gathering. What do you say?"

The officers exchanged glances, and one of them frowned, saying sternly, "Don't be ridiculous! The prince is here. How can we allow such nonsense?"

But Prince Qin was intrigued. He waved away their concerns and said, "A splendid idea! Let's see who will be the prince of the cups tonight!"

After several rounds of drinking games, the generals, now thoroughly drunk, collapsed onto the grass. Prince Qin, his vision blurry, grasped Fire Rose's hand and said, "Little brother, if you can beat me tonight, you'll be the prince."

Fire Rose playfully retorted, "And if I become the prince, what do I get?"

The prince, his eyes already glazed, replied, "You can sleep in my soft bed."

"Then it's settled," Fire Rose said, raising her cup again. Her gaze met Prince Qin's in the flickering firelight.

He couldn't help but ask, "Little brother, do you have any sisters at home?"

Fire Rose feigned confusion. "Why do you ask, Prince?"

Prince Qin shook his head and murmured, "You remind me of Princess Wenxi of Daze." His body began to sway, and Fire Rose quickly steadied him, smiling. "It seems I've won. Tonight, I am the prince."

In his drunken state, Prince Qin remembered his earlier promise and called out to the guards, "Take the prince to my bed. I'll sleep on the floor."

Fire Rose had only intended to tease Prince Qin, never expecting to actually sleep in his luxurious silk bed. It seemed Prince Qin, like Kauko, was a man of passion, and she felt a warmth in her heart. However, she couldn't bear to let the prince sleep on the floor, so she helped him onto the bed. They slept peacefully, one at the head and the other at the foot, sharing the night without incident.

The next morning, Prince Qin woke first and saw a long-haired woman sleeping at the foot of his bed. He leaned closer and realized it was the stunning "Princess Wenxi". Surprised and delighted, he couldn't remember what had happened the night before. He hurried out of the tent to question the guards, feeling both guilty and amused that the princess had spent the night near his feet. Yet, he couldn't help but feel a sense of joy at her playful mischief.

Outside the tent, Prince Qin ordered a red carpet to be rolled out, and the guards formed a straight line. A military band played thunderous music on either side of the formation. Inside the tent, Fire Rose was awakened by the commotion. Rubbing her sleepy eyes, she peeked through the tent flap and saw the guards shouting in unison, "Welcome, Princess! Welcome, Princess!" She quickly pulled her head back, smoothed her disheveled hair, and lightly touched her eyebrows. However, her soldier's uniform made her hesitate, and she nervously tugged at the hem of her clothes.

After waiting for a while with no response, Prince Qin had no choice but to enter the tent himself. He smiled warmly and said, "Princess, I apologize for last night's impropriety. Please join me in reviewing the troops and witnessing their loyalty."

Fire Rose glanced down at her clothes and said with some embarrassment, "Prince, perhaps it's better to dismiss them. I'm not exactly dressed for the occasion."

Prince Qin studied her for a moment, then a clever idea struck him. He quickly removed his golden silk quilt and deftly wrapped it around Fire Rose. The fabric, under his skilled hands, transformed into an elegant Annamese-style butterfly dress, the fine silk accentuating her graceful figure. Admiring the newly transformed "princess," he proudly placed his jade-encrusted silver crown on her head.

He then donned a cavalry helmet, his expression bright and spirited. With a slight bow, he extended his arm, inviting Fire Rose to take it. The two stepped out of the tent together, and the military band immediately struck up a triumphant tune. The soldiers' cheers rose and fell like waves.

After breakfast, they rode side by side along a winding path toward the Red River region. Fire Rose gazed ahead, her face calm, but her heart was tightly focused on Fire Maiden's mission: she had to lead this army silently into the secret ambush deep in the forest.

Two days later, Prince Qin's fifty thousand troops and General Langkun's hundred thousand elite soldiers had been moved to the designated area. Meanwhile, the Sherkon army of fifty thousand had quietly withdrawn to the north bank of the Red River. The scouts sent by General Langkun had been ambushed and slaughtered, their bodies sinking into the Red River.

That night, Fire Rose lay in bed, her heart churning like turbulent waves. Now, there was another person complicating her thoughts. On one hand, she hoped Kauko would stay far away from the impending war; on the other, she had to plan an escape route for Prince Qin.

***

Songmao and the three monkey siblings set foot on the ancient caravan trail, a path steeped in countless stories and secrets.

The old trail wound its way through dense forests and rugged mountains, branching off like a meandering stream. It wasn't as easy to navigate as one might think. Along the way, Songmao focused intently, occasionally bending down to touch the hoofprints on the trail or pick up fresh broken branches and leaves, examining them carefully. "This way! I can smell Kauko's scent," Songmao said mysteriously, playing the role of guide.

However, the weather turned against them. Days of relentless rain washed away the hoofprints and footmarks, turning the trail into a muddy quagmire. Songmao's small frame struggled through the mire, each step sinking deep into the mud. His ankles were tightly gripped by the thick sludge, and every time he pulled his feet free, mud splattered onto his face. Yet, he remained undeterred, focused on finding the way.

The three monkey siblings followed behind, laughing at his comical appearance but soon feeling a pang of sympathy.

"Songmao, climb onto my shoulders. You'll collapse if you keep going like this," Monkey Four said with concern.

"No, I need to stay close to the ground to sense Kauko's presence," Songmao insisted, continuing to trudge through the mud.

For several days, they stumbled along the slippery, muddy path. No matter where they went, the sky seemed to pour down cold rain, obscuring their direction and turning the road into a swamp. One evening, they took shelter in a dilapidated wooden shed. As they sat down, Monkey Shang looked around and suddenly exclaimed, "We've... been here before!"

Monkey Four frowned and shook his head. "Shang, these sheds all look the same. You must be mistaken."

"No, I'm sure!" Monkey Shang bent down and picked up a bunch of dried flowers from the corner. "Look, I left these here a few days ago!"

Monkey Three suddenly realized what had happened and slapped his thigh. "We've been going in circles! All this time, we've been wandering aimlessly!"

Songmao listened to their conversation, his expression changing, but he remained silent. He crouched down and sniffed the damp earth.

"Songmao," Monkey Three said coldly, "are we lost?"

Songmao panicked and quickly said, "Let me climb a tree and see if I can find the way."

Monkey Three snorted. "You? Climb a tree? Do you expect to see Kauko from up there? I've always thought your 'intuition' was unreliable!"

"Brother," Monkey Four interjected, his tone soothing, "even if Songmao is wrong, we've only lost a few days. There's no need to be angry."

Monkey Three retorted, "But don't you think he's too confident?"

"Enough!" Monkey Four suddenly said, his voice firm. "Right now, we need to support each other, not blame one another."

Though the two fell silent, the tension remained. Suddenly, the sky darkened, and dark clouds blotted out the sun. A fierce wind howled, threatening to tear the shed apart. Monkey Shang quickly grabbed her brothers' hands and scolded, "If brothers can't get along, even the heavens are unhappy. Do you want the wind to blow me away before you stop arguing?"

Monkey Three and Monkey Four, amused by their sister's words, hugged her tightly, afraid she might really be swept away by the wind. At that moment, the roof of the shed was torn off, and hailstones the size of goose eggs began to pelt down, leaving them scrambling for cover. In the chaos, Songmao leaped down from a tree and shouted, "Follow me!" He led them into a nearby dark and spacious cave.

The cave walls were carved with images of celestial soldiers and generals, each so lifelike they seemed ready to step out of the stone. Monkey Three and Monkey Four were captivated, their earlier argument forgotten as they pointed and marveled at the intricate carvings. Who could have created such a masterpiece in this desolate place?

Suddenly, Songmao gently tugged on Monkey Three's sleeve and whispered, "Where's Shang?"

Monkey Three looked around and realized Monkey Shang was missing. His face paled, and he called out in panic, "Shang! Shang!" His voice echoed in the cave, followed by an eerie silence.

"How could you be so careless? You're usually the most alert!" Monkey Four scolded, his voice tinged with anxiety.

"She was right beside me!" Monkey Three said defensively, rushing to leave the cave.

Monkey Four grabbed him. "Calm down! The hailstones outside are like rocks. Going out now would be suicide!"

Songmao seemed to sense something and suddenly walked to one side, stopping in front of a statue seated on a stone chair. His face lit up, and he called out, "Come and see!"

The others quickly gathered around. Songmao pointed at the statue. "Look!"

Monkey Three stared at the statue in disappointment. "I thought you'd found Shang."

Monkey Four asked, puzzled, "Is this statue some kind of general?"

Songmao corrected, "No, this is Marshal Tianpeng, Kauko's father as he appeared in the heavens."

Monkey Four was even more puzzled. "What does that have to do with Shang's disappearance?"

A mysterious smile appeared on Songmao's face. "It must be related! Do as I say, and you'll see Shang soon."

"Stop being cryptic and tell us!" Monkey Three urged.

"Listen carefully," Songmao said, enunciating each word. "We need to silently recite a secret phrase: 'My love, I have come.' On the count of three, we'll start."

Monkey Three squinted at him. "Is it 'my love' or 'Shang'?"

"My love!" Songmao emphasized, slapping Marshal Tianpeng's large foot.

Monkey Three was skeptical. "We're looking for Shang, so why are we calling out 'my love'? What kind of trick are you playing? Are you trying to make a fool of me?" He crouched down, staring directly into Songmao's eyes, half-jokingly threatening, "Should I pluck one of your whiskers?"

Songmao jumped onto Monkey Four's shoulder and said urgently, "Monkey Four, Shang is waiting for us."

Monkey Four urged Monkey Three, "Come on, let's do as Songmao says!"

The three of them huddled together, closed their eyes, and silently recited the phrase. Instantly, a warm current of air enveloped them, and the sound of wind whistled in their ears. When they opened their eyes again, they found themselves in a sunlit forest. Not far ahead, Monkey Shang stood waving at them, tears glistening in her eyes.

Monkey Three, overcome with emotion, tightly grasped Shang's hand, afraid of losing her again. "Shang, how did you end up here alone?"

Shang shook her head. "I don't know. It was like a gust of wind brought me here."

Songmao interjected, "Shang, what did you do before the wind came?"

"I touched the immortal in the stone chair," Shang replied.

"And then?" Songmao pressed.

"I saw some words carved on the immortal's arm and silently recited them."

"Do you remember what they were?" Songmao asked eagerly.

"They were, 'My love, I have come,'" Shang answered.

"That's it! You recited the secret phrase," Songmao said excitedly.

He turned to the bewildered Monkey Three and asked, "Are you even more confused now? Let me explain. First, I must announce that we are now within the borders of Daze! That strange encounter just saved us five or six days of travel."

"Tell us, what's going on?" everyone gathered around Songmao.

Songmao gestured for them to sit on the grass and began to explain, "Do you know why I brought you to that cave? Actually, I've been tracking Kauko's scent. But in the end, I realized I was wrong! That scent was actually from Kauko's father."

Everyone looked at him curiously. "How so?"

Songmao continued, "Kauko's father once told me that when he first descended to the mortal world, he was from Annan and lived in a cave. To ease his loneliness, he carved these celestial soldiers and generals to keep him company. Later, he traveled to Daze and met Kauko's mother, the daughter of a wealthy family. However, because of his appearance, he wasn't accepted by her father. But he didn't give up. Every day, he traveled between Kauko's village and the cave, doing heavy labor for the family. To save time, he built a secret passage—the one we just took."

At this point, Monkey Shang interjected, "If it's a secret passage, why was the phrase written out?"

Songmao wagged his tail. "According to Kauko's father, he wanted to benefit future generations, so he made the phrase public. After he moved to Kauko's village, he no longer needed the cave or the passage."

Monkey Three apologized to Songmao, "I shouldn't have doubted you." He then gently patted Monkey Shang's head and added, "But Shang, you're even more intuitive than Songmao! You found the shortcut first."

Songmao chuckled, acknowledging Monkey Three's humor.

In the following days, they continued north through the vast forest.

A newly trodden path appeared before them, winding forward, with trampled grass on either side, as if telling the story of those who had hurried past. Fresh horse droppings emitted a pungent smell, a reminder that life was not far away.

Songmao crouched down, his fingers lightly brushing the trampled grass, as if listening to the footsteps that had passed. His eyes lit up with excitement. "Look at these tracks. The group ahead can't be far. But..." He paused, a hint of worry in his eyes. "I don't know if Kauko is among them."

Monkey Four looked up at the darkening sky and frowned. "Songmao, it's almost nightfall. This is great news, but we can't rush after them. What if it's the Sherkon army? We should find a place to rest, gather our strength, and set out tomorrow."

Songmao nodded. "Alright, we'll do as you say."

The four soon found a hidden cave entrance, cleverly concealed by dense vegetation. Stepping inside, they were greeted by a spacious, dry interior, filled with a fresh and tranquil atmosphere. The cave walls were rugged, each part showcasing the raw beauty of nature. Stalactites hung from the ceiling, their shapes varied and translucent, emitting a soft glow in the dim light.

They lit a fire, and the flames danced in the cave like spirits, illuminating their tired but hopeful faces.

Monkey Three found a flat stone and placed it over the fire. He then took out the pine nuts they had collected along the way and carefully poured them onto the stone. The nuts gradually released a tantalizing aroma as they roasted, making everyone's mouths water.

They sat around the fire, enjoying the delicious treat while listening to

Songmao recount his adventures with Kauko in the Tian Mountain. The stories of friendship, courage, and the breathtaking beauty of the mountains captivated them, as if they had truly been transported to that magical world.

Before long, the three monkey siblings drifted into a warm sleep. Songmao quietly slipped out of the cave and, with his agile movements, leaped onto an ancient pine tree. He nimbly moved through the forest, his figure like a ghostly wisp in the night wind, elusive and ethereal.

He stealthily approached a campsite where a bonfire flickered in the deep night, and shadowy figures moved in the dim light. Songmao slowly wagged his tail, murmuring to himself, "Kauko, are you hiding in this light and shadow?" Just as he prepared to dash toward the camp, a strange phenomenon appeared in the sky—several stars streaked across the heavens with breathtaking beauty, slowly falling and adding an incredible grandeur to the quiet night.

The stars grew brighter and larger, trailing long tails of fire as they hurtled toward the depths of the forest, where they exploded. The night sky was instantly torn apart by orange-red light, and flames and thick smoke danced like frenzied ghosts in the wind.

Songmao felt the treetops swaying wildly beneath his feet, as if panicked by the sudden fire. Waves of heat slapped his face, and the world turned red. He took off running, skirting the edge of the fire, leaping over sparks, and weaving through the smoke, silently chanting, "Don't let me die here. I don't want to become a wandering ghost."

Just then, a heart-wrenching scream pierced his ears, making him stop in his tracks. He looked around, seeing only twisted tree shadows dancing in the fire, unable to locate the source of the sound. He touched his chest, his heart pounding like thunder, as if the scream was his own fear crying out. He kept running, but an indescribable chill crept into his heart.

The sound came again! Desperate and panicked, it sounded just like Kauko's mournful cry when he was lost in the swamp and his scream when he fell off the cliff. Songmao's body instinctively turned toward the direction of the sound—it had to be Kauko!

However, the flames mercilessly licked at his feet, and the fire blocked his path. His vision was torn apart by the sea of fire, and despair flooded his heart.

What should he do? Songmao stood alone, the fire hissing around him, his heart tearing, struggling, and weeping.

***

The advisor sat cross-legged, intending to calmly review the battle plan once more, but his mind was gripped by an invisible hand, unable to find peace. This unease felt like a distant memory, harkening back to the gloom before the Sherkon army approached Sien City.

Unable to shake the ominous premonition, he quickly stood up, rolled up his sleeves, and wrote a note. He walked to the tent entrance and handed the note to a waiting guard, instructing, "Quick, deliver this to General Langkun!" As the guard disappeared into the night, the sky suddenly lit up with a strange phenomenon—a celestial fire, as if falling from the stars, streaked across the quiet night, heading toward the deep forest.

The advisor stood by the window, his gaze fixed on the sight, his shock unconcealed. The worry in his heart solidified into a heavy certainty: this was Fire Maiden's doing, a meticulously planned disaster. The man who once believed he could control the winds and clouds now felt an unprecedented sense of insignificance and defeat. He weakly leaned against the tent, his eyes filled with despair.

He knew he was powerless to save the princess and Prince Qin, who were far away, or to protect General Langkun and his hundred thousand troops. He immediately summoned his guards and led them toward a nearby stream, hoping to find a sliver of survival in the raging fire.

However, Kauko's figure was nowhere to be seen. Faint cries for help seemed to emerge from the fire, only to be swallowed by the roaring flames, leaving no trace. The fire grew fiercer, and no one dared to act recklessly. All they could do was shout in unison, "Kauko, come out!"

The once-cool stream was gradually overwhelmed by the heat, its flow weakening. The advisor, unable to bear the scorching heat and despair, collapsed into Tichu's arms, still murmuring Kauko's name.

Just as everyone was losing hope, a fiery figure burst through the wall of flames—it was Kauko! His body was engulfed in fire, as if he had just escaped from hell. Yet, when he emerged from the flames, the fire mysteriously extinguished itself. Without pause, he charged toward the flames on the other side of the stream, as if he had lost his mind. The advisor, seeing this, quickly ordered the soldiers to stop him and prevent him from re-entering the fire.

Kauko was tackled to the ground, his head submerged in the water. He suddenly lifted his head, howling in terror. At that moment, Songmao, who had followed the stream, arrived and saw Kauko struggling in the water. He shouted, "Stop! Don't hurt him!"

The soldiers, startled by the sudden command, released Kauko. Kauko scrambled to his feet, his eyes still closed, and asked urgently, "Songmao, is that you?"

"It's me. Don't be afraid of the fire!" Songmao leaped onto Kauko's shoulder and quickly tore off a piece of cloth, deftly covering Kauko's eyes.

Kauko calmed down slightly and asked, "Did Master send you?"

"Master? Isn't he with you?" Songmao was puzzled, but now was not the time for questions. He pulled out a copper flute from his pocket and handed it to Kauko. "This is your divine flute. Play it quickly. It can extinguish this demonic fire."

Kauko held the long-lost flute and sighed, "How can I play music in this state?"

The advisor, having caught his breath, noticed that Kauko showed no signs of burns, his clothes untouched. He said, "Kauko, don't you realize the fire hasn't harmed you at all?"

Kauko pulled off the cloth covering his eyes and patted his body. Then, with a look of surprise, he said, "Master, you're right! The fire didn't hurt me! Let me test it!" He ran to the edge of the roaring fire and extended a hand into the flames. There was no burning sensation, only a cool breeze. He stepped into the fire, his body engulfed in flames once more. "Haha, the fire I've feared all my life is just a mental demon!"

Kauko began to play "Cangshan Sister" on his flute. Wherever the beautiful melody reached, the fire silently vanished. A cool wind swept away the black smoke and scorching heat, and the bright moonlight returned to the ravaged forest. In the distance, the neighing of horses and the calls of soldiers could be heard.

***

Under the bright moonlight, Fire Rose and Prince Qin sat side by side on the soft grass in the forest, sharing stories from their hearts. Her stories, of course, were all about Bamei's legends.

Fire Rose had received Fire Maiden's final warning: she must retreat to the other side of the Red River, as "celestial fire" was about to descend, turning the vast forest into ashes. She should have left an hour ago, but she couldn't bear to part with the prince, enchanted by his dreamlike, heartwarming words.

She secretly planned to take the prince across the Red River with her, not just for herself, but to leave a kind-hearted prince for the world.

She suddenly suggested softly, "The moonlight is so peaceful. Why don't we take a walk to the Red River?"

Prince Qin hesitated. "The Red River is treacherous, with swift currents. It's not safe at night. Why don't we wait until tomorrow, and I'll accompany you then?"

Fire Rose insisted, "If we don't go tonight, there may be no tomorrow. Prince, if you're afraid, I'll go alone."

Prince Qin immediately stood up and called for guards to bring two horses. With a smile, he said, "How could I let the princess venture alone?"

They mounted their horses and, without any attendants, galloped toward the Red River under the night sky. Fire Rose quickly found the solitary iron-chain bridge—the escape route Fire Maiden had prepared for her. She turned to the prince and said, "Prince, let's dismount and listen to the river's roar on the bridge!"

Fire Rose got off her horse, and the prince followed. She grabbed his hand and urged, "Let's cross the bridge quickly, to the other side!"

Prince Qin was puzzled. "Why are we doing this?"

Fire Rose, knowing time was short, couldn't explain in detail. "Please trust me. Just follow me."

The prince still hesitated. "What about my men?"

Fire Rose, with no other choice, used her intoxicating fragrance to cloud the prince's judgment. He followed her onto the iron-chain bridge.

Just as they stepped onto the bridge, a fireball streaked across the sky and struck the bridge with a deafening crash. The bridge instantly shattered. Fire Rose and the prince were thrown into the air, and in a blinding flash of light, they plunged into the raging waves of the Red River.

Chapter 13

Nicknamed Chef

After releasing the fireball, Fire Maiden felt exhaustion wash over her like a tidal wave. She staggered back to Chinmi Garden, her sweat-soaked hair clinging to her cheeks, her steps heavy as if filled with lead. She chose a shaded spot beneath a stone wall and slowly sat down, the cold rock pressing against her back, sending a shiver through her body. She closed her eyes and let out a long breath. After a moment, a cold smile crept onto her lips, a mix of weariness and satisfaction.

"This fire attack drained me, but I hope it will solve things once and for all," she murmured to herself, her low whisper like a spell hanging in the air. She thought that as long as Kauko and those foolish remnants of the former dynasty were reduced to ashes, her world would return to peace, undisturbed by anyone.

Fire Maiden raised her hand, and her wand floated silently into her grasp. Her fingers slowly traced the length of the wand, and a faint light began to glow at its tip, gradually weaving a web of fine, hair-like threads that spread silently into the air. Moments later, the souls struggling and wailing in the flames were caught by the threads, drawn toward her with resentment and unwillingness.

As the dark, cold energy poured into her body, Fire Maiden's skin turned pale and translucent, her veins and bones faintly visible under the moonlight. Her eyes deepened like bottomless cold pools, as if every bit of the chilling force gathered into a cold light within them.

Suddenly, Kauko's flute music pierced the night sky, the sound waves striking Fire Maiden's chest like a thunderbolt. At that moment, she felt as if her insides were being torn apart, the searing pain instantly drenching her in cold sweat. The power within her seemed to be ripped away by an invisible hand. Gritting her teeth against the agony, she quickly retreated into a dark cavern, curling up against the cold stone wall, barely clinging to life.

Days passed, and she finally managed to pull herself out of the intense pain. Dragging her heavy body, she stumbled to the hall of Golden Mother. In a hoarse voice, she asked, "Mother, Kauko's flute music cuts through my heart and tears my soul. If he does this every day, how can I endure it?"

Golden Mother spoke calmly, "I warned you before not to provoke him."

Fire Maiden's eyes flashed with resentment and anger. "I'm already at odds with him. What's the use of saying that now? I've always offered you sacrifices. Please, give me a solution."

Golden Mother sighed softly. "Fire Rose might have been your cure, but you abandoned her."

"It's not my fault. She disobeyed me and brought this on herself," Fire Maiden said, her face pale, defending herself with a hint of grievance.

Golden Mother whispered, "She has been your accomplice. Only because she wanted to spare the prince she loved, you couldn't tolerate that. You were young once too."

Fire Maiden fell silent for a moment, then finally nodded. "If she were still here, I would try to make amends."

Golden Mother replied, "She is still alive, and she still owes you a debt, just as I owe you."

Fire Maiden returned to her bedroom in the palace, leaning alone on the large mandarin duck bed, softly calling Fire Rose's name, hoping for a response.

***

Fire Rose's body drifted with the Red River, like a leaf. Her skirt clung tightly to her legs, pulled by the current like a sad flag. Her long hair danced underwater, like a flock of crows circling aimlessly. The icy water seemed to drain all the warmth from her body. Yet, even in her weakened state, her life refused to succumb to the dark river. A small flame still burned in her heart, faint but unextinguished: in this life, she wanted to be a true princess and love a man who loved her. At some point, a small bubble escaped her lips.

In this moment of near despair, her hand touched a protruding rock. She hooked onto it and began to slowly pull herself toward the shore.

Her upper body finally lay on the slippery sand, a gentle breeze brushing over her, the tide kissing her lower body. The sound of the waves beside her was like a soothing lullaby, a tender sigh.

Too weak to stand, she crawled into a pile of rocks on the shore, leaning against a warm stone. She vaguely remembered the prince, face down, sinking into the depths of the river, carried away by the dark currents to a world without light.

She slowly fell into a deep sleep, her body feeling weightless, as if lifted by an invisible hand, swaying in the void. Surrounded by darkness, the only sound was her heartbeat, like distant drumbeats, echoing through the endless night.

In this empty, silent world, a faint figure gradually approached from the distance, as if crossing over from another time and space. It was Kauko, riding a white steed, like the moon in the night, quietly illuminating everything around her. His eyes shone with deep concern, a gaze that seemed to pierce through the darkness, reaching straight into her heart.

She struggled to open her eyes, wanting to see the figure clearly, to feel the warmth in his gaze. She reached out, trying to touch that warm face, but she could never reach it. Every attempt was met with emptiness, every hope turned to disappointment. The figure always dissipated into smoke just as she was about to touch it, vanishing into the darkness.

Finally, Fire Rose broke free from her deep sleep. The sky was so blue, as deep as Kauko's eyes. She remembered Kauko's gentleness, his doting on her, those moments from the past so clear yet so distant.

At that moment, Fire Maiden's voice echoed in her ears. It was as if Fire Maiden had read her thoughts, saying, "If you truly love Kauko, I won't stop you. You can return to him, but you must complete one more task."

A glimmer of hope rose in Fire Rose's heart. "You haven't harmed him?"

Fire Maiden's voice carried a hint of amusement. "I wanted to ask you! How is it that he's like a phoenix that can't be burned?"

***

Prince Qin's forces had suffered heavy losses, and the remaining soldiers, seeing no sign of the prince's return, fled to Annan to report the tragedy. General Langkun's troops, though also severely damaged, regained their confidence upon hearing of the mysterious force that had appeared, and they began to regroup.

The advisor stood by the window, gazing at the distant Red River bank, holding onto a sliver of hope that the princess and Prince Qin might have miraculously survived.

Hearing that they had last been seen near the riverbank, he immediately ordered a search team to scour the area. Kauko, anxious and desperate to join the search, was gently stopped by the advisor, who shook his head. "Kauko, at this critical moment, I need you by my side. Leave the search for the princess to me. I'll give you half a day to meet with Songmao and your friends from afar, then return quickly."

The advisor turned to Songmao. "Little spirit, you've performed a great feat. What reward would you like? Speak, and it shall be yours."

Songmao blinked his large eyes. "The credit belongs to Kauko! As for a reward, I'd like a bag of peanuts. You can leave it with Kauko."

The advisor squinted. "Why not keep it yourself?"

Songmao scratched his head. "I... uh... can't control myself. Once I start eating, I can't stop, and eating too much affects my spiritual energy."

The advisor smiled and nodded. "Very well, I'll give you an extra bag. Gather your friends and join the search for the princess."

Songmao flashed a bright smile. "As you command, Advisor!" He glanced at Kauko and said with a grin, "See how generous the advisor is?"

Kauko pretended to be displeased. "Songmao, are you saying I'm usually stingy?"

"Not at all, not at all," Songmao quickly waved his hands. "Just suggesting you be a bit more generous in the future."

Kauko laughed and patted Songmao's head. "So you want me to carry peanuts around for you all day?"

The advisor left the two playful companions, smiling as he walked away, letting them continue their banter.

In a hidden corner of the cave, the three monkey siblings had narrowly escaped disaster. Monkey Three, still shaken, couldn't hide his reproach. "Fourth Brother, this was all your idea. We didn't find Kauko, and we almost lost our lives."

Monkey Four's temper flared, and he turned sharply. "Third Brother, shouting a hundred times won't help! Don't forget, this trip wasn't just for Kauko. It was also to avenge our brother! If you're scared, why not go back to Annan and live your carefree life?"

The air grew tense, and even the usually cheerful Monkey Shang fell silent, her smile disappearing, her eyes slightly red, tears glistening at the corners.

Just as the tension peaked, a familiar figure appeared at the cave entrance like a ray of spring sunlight. Monkey Shang's eyes lit up, and she instantly shed her heavy emotions, rushing forward with a cheer. "Big Brother Kauko! Finally, we see you!"

Kauko opened his arms and gently hugged her, then pulled Monkey Three and Monkey Four into the embrace. The cave was finally filled with long-missed laughter and warmth.

After a moment of calm, Kauko's expression turned serious. "Who bullied our little Shang? Tell me, and I'll throw them into the Red River to feed the fish!"

Monkey Three and Monkey Four quickly waved their hands, hurriedly explaining, each claiming their innocence. Monkey Shang couldn't help but chuckle, tugging at Kauko's arm. "Big Brother Kauko, you misunderstood. It was just a small argument, nothing serious."

At that moment, Songmao leaped onto Kauko's shoulder and winked at Monkey Shang. "Kauko is just teasing you to cheer you up." Everyone laughed, and the atmosphere lightened.

Kauko's smile faded, and his expression turned grave. "You've all come at the perfect time. The princess is missing, and I can't join the search myself. I beg you to help me find her."

The three monkey siblings immediately straightened up, answering in unison, "Don't worry, we'll set out right away!" Songmao patted Kauko's shoulder. "I'll go with them. You wait here for good news."

Kauko clasped his hands in gratitude, his eyes filled with anticipation. "Then I'll await."

As he walked out of the cave, Songmao quickly caught up, leaping onto his shoulder and whispering mysteriously in his ear, "Open your mouth. I have a treasure for you to taste."

Kauko couldn't help but be curious. "What is it?"

Songmao smiled mysteriously. "Trust me, just open your mouth."

Kauko hesitantly opened his mouth, and Songmao dropped a golden pill left by their master into it. The pill had a faint sweetness and a cool sensation. Kauko swallowed it without hesitation, then joked, "I guess it's just a piece of rock sugar?"

Songmao covered his mouth and laughed. "Wrong, wrong. It's a peanut."

Kauko shook his head. "Since when are you willing to give away peanuts?"

Songmao smiled and explained, "Of course, it's not a peanut. This is a divine pill Master Dapeng left especially for you. He said it would help you resist demonic influences and enhance your power. To refine this pill, Master even offended the celestial realm, which is why he left in such a hurry."

After hearing Songmao's words, Kauko fell silent for a long time, his heart filled with gratitude and longing for Master Dapeng.

***

Deep in the camp, the advisor and General Langkun solemnly paid their respects to the fallen soldiers. Each took a jar of strong liquor and drank it in one gulp, then supported each other, sharing the weight in their hearts. The advisor's eyes glistened with tears, his voice low and self-reproachful. "General, my negligence failed to protect the princess. I am deeply ashamed."

The general's face was equally grave, filled with endless sorrow. "This is not your fault alone. I too am to blame for losing so many brothers-in-arms." He seemed to momentarily return to the hellish forest fire. After a pause, he worriedly added, "What's more urgent is that our army's provisions are exhausted. How will we deal with this crisis?"

The advisor adjusted his emotions, his eyes regaining their firmness. "General, we cannot drown in grief. Even if the princess is lost, our mission remains. I have a plan in mind."

"Please share your wisdom, Advisor," the general said eagerly.

The advisor spoke calmly, "The most urgent matter is to solve the food and supplies issue. The Sanba region in eastern Daze is the lifeline of our kingdom's grain supply. It's harvest season now, making it the perfect time for us to act."

The general frowned. "But that area is guarded by the Wolf Fang brothers of Sherkon, with fifty thousand elite troops. Although we have similar numbers in that region, most of our soldiers are new recruits. How can we win? Moreover, what if Fire Maiden herself takes the field?"

The advisor analyzed coolly, "She might be wary of the divine flute's power and hesitate to act rashly for now."

The general dismissed the surrounding attendants and continued to ask the advisor, "Should I lead reinforcements to General Dao Shan?"

The advisor shook his head. "You need to stay here and create a diversion to confuse the enemy, such as preparing boats to feign a river crossing. I plan to take Kauko with me to General Dao."

The general suddenly understood. "You intend to bring Kauko along?"

The advisor nodded. "Exactly. Kauko's abilities are extraordinary."

"Advisor, your insight is remarkable. You recognized Kauko's potential early on," the general praised.

The advisor smiled wryly. "It's not foresight, just a small talent for recognizing people."

As night fell, the advisor raised his arm, and a carrier pigeon cut through the dark sky, carrying his carefully crafted strategy to General Dao Shan's camp. The message, light as a feather, bore the weight of destiny.

At the break of dawn, before the sun fully rose, Kauko and the advisor set off on their journey. After three days and nights of relentless travel, they arrived at General Dao's camp just as the first light of dawn touched the horizon. Without resting, the advisor immediately wrote a challenge and handed it to General Dao, instructing him to send it to the Wolf Fang brothers of Sherkon.

The eldest Wolf Fang brother took the taunting challenge and read it aloud: "To the Wolf Fang Generals: You have occupied our land, oppressed our people, and wreaked havoc for years. Now, heaven has blessed Daze with a great chef, whose culinary skills are unparalleled. He specializes in cooking the heads of Sherkon's most heinous criminals, feeding them to the hungry eagles of Cangshan and the dragons of Erhai. If you believe this, leave Sanba immediately. If not, meet us on the battlefield at Paoma Mountain tomorrow. Signed, General Dao Shan."

The three brothers exchanged glances, their expressions a mix of disbelief and amusement. It was absurd—using a chef as a threat in a war challenge? The burly second brother grabbed the messenger like a chicken, his short sword gleaming. "Has your general lost his mind?" he sneered.

The third brother quickly intervened, turning to the messenger. "Countryman, does your general truly have such a remarkable chef in his ranks?"

The messenger replied firmly, "Absolutely. This chef is not only a master of cuisine but also wields a fire poker like a weapon."

The third brother waved the messenger away and carefully examined the challenge, beads of sweat forming on his forehead. After a moment of contemplation, he suggested cautiously, "We should be careful. After all, Fire Maiden recently fell to a young man who used a flute as a weapon. Could this chef be him?"

The second brother scoffed. "The three of us have conquered the snowy plateaus and subdued demons in Daze. Why should we fear a mere chef?"

The eldest brother slammed the table, laughing heartily. "Chef or flutist, it doesn't matter. Such tricks only scare women!"

***

Paoma Mountain wasn't actually a mountain but a vast, endless plain. On this expansive field, fifty thousand troops from each side formed battle formations stretching to the horizon. The thunder of war drums echoed through the skies, accompanied by waves of battle cries, enveloping the battlefield in unprecedented tension and fervor.

Once the formations were set, the Wolf Fang brothers rode to the front lines on their warhorses, heads held high. The eldest brother's voice boomed like a war drum: "General Dao, where is your great chef? Send him out!"

General Dao brandished his sword and replied, "No rush. It's been a while. How about I play with you first?" With that, he prepared to charge forward.

The advisor quickly stopped him. "General, wait! Today is Chef's stage. You and I are merely supporting roles." As soon as he finished speaking, the advisor waved his arm, and the sound of horns suddenly erupted, shaking the heavens. A steel-armored chariot was pushed out by soldiers, on which a mysterious figure in black sat, holding a copper flute, his face hidden under a hood, exuding an air of mystery. The Daze army seized the moment to chant, "Leave! Leave! Leave!"

The Sherkon army's ranks were thrown into chaos. The eldest Wolf Fang brother quickly roared to restore order and sent the second brother to face the challenge.

The second brother spurred his fierce warhorse, which shot forward like an arrow. Clad in heavy armor and gripping a long spear, his veins bulged with impatience and determination.

Kauko leaped down from the chariot with the agility of a leopard, landing precisely on the back of a snow-white warhorse. The horse's ears pricked up, its nostrils flaring as it seemed to smell blood and iron. It reared up, neighing to the sky, its mane flying in the wind as if ignited with battle spirit.

Kauko slowly removed his black hood, the setting sun casting a glow on his face, highlighting his furrowed brows and cold, gleaming eyes. At that moment, the world seemed to stand still, even the wind ceasing. The surrounding soldiers held their breath, stunned by the intense killing aura.

He leaned down and patted the horse, whispering a few inaudible commands. The horse began to trot briskly, its eyes fixed ahead, carrying its master step by step toward the second brother. When they were about twenty feet away, the horse suddenly stopped, its hooves firmly planted, muscles tensing slightly.

The second brother's lips curled into a sneer. He glanced coldly at the young man before him. "Just a brat," he muttered. Suddenly, he roared, "Don't blame me for being ruthless!" Without warning, he spurred his horse forward, his spear thrusting with a sharp whistle.

Kauko didn't meet the attack head-on. Instead, he leaned slightly to the side, letting the spear graze past him, bringing a chill wind. He gently guided his horse in a circle, his hands still empty, the flute securely tied at his waist.

The second brother chased him for several rounds but couldn't even touch a hair on Kauko's head. Humiliated, he spurred his horse recklessly, shouting incoherently, determined to end Kauko in one desperate charge.

The advisor's brow furrowed, sensing unease. Just then, Kauko suddenly executed a "Golden Cicada Sheds Its Shell" maneuver, instantly appearing behind the second brother and locking him in a tight grip. The two figures tumbled in the dust, their collision sending sand and stones flying, leaving a long scar on the ground.

A brilliant flame erupted, engulfing Kauko in blazing fire. The flames, like a fierce dragon, instantly consumed both men, shaking the entire battlefield.

The second brother, burning in agony, forgot who he was and screamed, "Chef, spare me!"

Kauko asked, "How should I spare you?"

"I'll leave, leave Sanba..."

"Your stench is unbearable when roasted. I'll spare you today, but not necessarily tomorrow. Now, leave!" Kauko released him and extinguished the flames.

The second brother scrambled back, helped by his men. Meanwhile, the eldest Wolf Fang brother ordered a volley of arrows at Kauko, who deflected them with his flute, transformed into a pig-faced demon, and stomped the ground, causing an earthquake.

At the advisor's command, war drums thundered, and General Dao led thousands of troops in a charge.

The second brother shouted to his brothers, "Run! He's a monster!"

Their forces were driven back a hundred miles, suffering heavy casualties.

The Daze army seized several large granaries left by the Sherkon forces and

170

quickly organized transport teams to move the grain to the mountains.

General Dao asked the advisor, "Since our army is so formidable, why not pursue the victory and push another hundred miles?"

The advisor replied, "General, in this battle, Fire Maiden did not appear, but we cannot predict when or how she will strike. Let's secure this granary first and wait for the right moment."

General Dao asked again, "Advisor, who is this Chef of yours?"

"Speaking of which, he's from your hometown. He's from Kau Village; his real name is Kauko. 'Chef' is just a nickname I gave him. His father is the famous Zhu Bajie."

"Ah, so he has an extraordinary background. My home is only thirty miles from Kau Village, but I never heard that Marshal Zhu had a son. Could I request to keep Chef here?"

"I can't decide that. He's the princess's man. You'd better let go of that thought," the advisor said, noticing Kauko nearby and beckoning him over. "Kauko, in today's battle, I only meant for you to sit on the armored chariot and intimidate the Wolf Fang brothers, but you put on quite a show. I was sweating bullets for you. How did you come up with that?"

Kauko smiled. "Master, I forgot to tell you, acting is my hobby. I learned it from the princess. I once played 'Zhu Bajie Carries His Wife' and did an even better job than today."

"Weren't you afraid of the volley of arrows? If something had gone wrong, how would I explain it to the princess?"

"Master, as long as I have the copper flute, nothing can touch me," Kauko said proudly.

The advisor, seeing Kauko's growing confidence, felt genuine joy.

***

After fetching water, Kau Lame brought a pot of strong wine to Wulong, enough to keep him drunk until dawn. Once Wulong was sound asleep, Kau Lame cooked a bowl of noodles, left the door slightly ajar, lit a lantern, and waved it a few times by the window before quietly sitting in a corner, waiting.

At midnight, he heard the faint sound of chains outside, as if someone was lingering. Kau Lame whispered, "Guest, come in quickly. It's not safe outside."

A dark figure stumbled in and collapsed on the floor. Kau Lame quickly turned the person over and recognized the pig-faced woman he had seen by the water earlier. She was soaked, cold, and weak, her hair disheveled.

Kau Lame hurriedly found the keys, unlocked her chains, and helped her into the bedroom, where she changed into dry clothes. He brought her a bowl of noodles and watched her eat slowly. When she had recovered somewhat, he asked gently, "Child, are you feeling better?"

She nodded timidly.

"Let me take you to rest." He supported her and led her to the wine cellar, entering the wine god's offering room. He pushed open a hidden door in the back wall, revealing a small bedroom. "Here, lie down," he said, helping her into bed and tucking her in.

Tears glistened in the princess's eyes as she asked softly, "Why did you save me?"

Kau Lame sighed. "Child, my heart aches for you." He continued, "I have a nephew who was just like you, with a pig's face, cute and lively. Sadly, he was killed when he was just a year old. Otherwise, he would be about your age now."

The princess thought of Kauko and asked, "Where are you from?"

"Kau Village. I was captured by the Sherkon to build this altar."

"The child you mentioned—was he Marshal Tianpeng's son?"

"Yes, how did you know?"

"He and I were childhood friends..." The princess wanted to say more but found her memories too hazy to continue.

"You mean my nephew is still alive? Where is he now?" Kau Lame pressed.

"I can't remember... Ever since I became a pig-head, I've lost most of my memories."

"Don't worry, child. Take your time. You've brought incredible news to our Kau family! What's your name?"

"People call me Bamei."

"Ah, you can call me Kau Lame."

"Then I'll call you Uncle Kau."

"Rest well and regain your strength. Tomorrow, I'll get you out of this devil's place."

As he stood to leave, he remembered the situation upstairs and turned back to warn her, "Bamei, there's a demon living upstairs—the prison warden. He's drunk and asleep now. Don't come out, and listen to me. The dangerous part is, he's invisible. We can't see him."

"Thank you, Uncle Kau, for the warning. I can already sense it—he must be some kind of demon," the princess replied.

Early the next morning, Kau Lame waited outside Wulong's door, holding a wine jug that emitted a rich, fragrant aroma. Soon, he heard Wulong's voice, "Lame, is that wine for me?"

"Yes, Warden," Kau Lame answered immediately, his voice tinged with respect.

Wulong chuckled. "You used to be so stingy, always using Fire Maiden to scare me. Why are you so generous today?"

"Warden, have you forgotten? You're the warden now. I wouldn't dare neglect you," Kau Lame said cautiously, handing over the wine jug. "From now on, whenever you want it, it's yours."

"What if I drink it all? Will Fire Maiden punish me?"

"As long as you're happy, I'll find a way."

"How?"

"I have a special pass that allows me to leave the camp once a month to gather materials for brewing. Warden, if you could change that 'month' to 'day,' I could come and go as needed, stock up on materials, and brew more wine. Then you could drink to your heart's content."

"Is that all? Then let me change one word for you."

Kau Lame took out the pass from his pocket and was about to hand it to Wulong when he noticed the character for "month" had already changed to "day." He couldn't help but praise, "Warden, you truly have divine powers! You changed the character without even lifting a brush!" He put the pass away and prepared to leave.

Suddenly, Wulong called out, "Wait, why do you need to bring a pig-faced person with you?"

Kau Lame smiled and explained, "Warden, that's approved by Fire Maiden. It's to make moving things easier."

Only then did Wulong feel reassured. "I'm off to my duties now, searching for the missing Daze princess. Don't forget to have wine ready for me tonight."

"What wine would you like tonight?"

"Qinghe Old Wine," Wulong's voice echoed from outside.

Hearing that he was truly gone, Kau Lame hurried down to the wine cellar and approached the princess, whispering, "Bamei, did you sleep well last night?"

The princess nodded, but Kau Lame noticed her red eyes and guessed she might not have slept at all. "Stand up and walk a few steps for me," he said, wanting to assess her physical condition.

Though puzzled, the princess stood up and turned in a circle, saying gratefully, "Uncle Kau, I do feel much better."

Kau Lame smiled slightly. "You seem fine. I'll get you out of here today to avoid any complications."

"That would be wonderful," the princess said, tears welling up in her eyes.

He picked up the iron chains from the corner and handed them to the princess. She hesitated for a moment but understood Kau Lame's silent gesture and quietly put the chains on herself.

Kau Lame prepared a horse shopping cart as usual. The princess sat at the back, her head lowered, her face smudged with soot, making her inconspicuous. As they passed the gate, the guard glanced at the princess and asked, "Lame, why are you bringing a small one today?"

Kau Lame quickly replied, "The warden sent him. All the strong laborers are at the construction site."

The guard didn't press further but announced unexpected news: "Lame, the warden has ordered that from now on, whenever you go out shopping, a prison guard must accompany you."

Kau Lame's heart skipped a beat, but he remained calm. "Why is that? Afraid I'll run away? Even if I run, the temple won't run with me..."

The guard impatiently cut him off and called over a grim-faced prison guard. "You've been wanting to get out for some fresh air, right? Go with them and keep an eye on them." The guard said nothing, only giving the princess a cold glance before getting into the cart and sitting opposite her.

The gate opened, and the guard instructed, "Go on, but don't forget to bring me some dried meat."

The princess lowered her head further, hiding her bright eyes. This sudden turn of events filled Kau Lame with panic. Escaping with the princess had just become much harder.

The cart jolted along the rugged mountain path, and the princess fell into deep thought. Her eyes flicked to the guard's gleaming waist knife, and for a moment, she considered snatching it. However, after careful consideration, she dismissed the idea, unwilling to put Kau Lame in danger for her own escape.

Halfway through the journey, they reached a cliff shrouded in mist, the path uneven from rainwater erosion. At this point, Kau Lame hatched a plan. He decided to let the princess off the cart and drive the cart, along with the guard, off the cliff, giving the princess a chance to escape. He felt he had lived long enough, and continuing to live as a humiliated prisoner was no life at all. Perhaps heaven would pity him and let him be reborn as a free eagle, soaring through the skies like the one above!

He turned to the guard and shouted, "Guard, hold on tight. This mountain path is treacherous." Then he said to the princess, "Kid, you're here to work, not to enjoy the ride. See how the cart is struggling uphill? Get down and help push!"

The princess, confused, raised her hands and asked, "How can I push with these chains on?"

"I'll unlock them for you," Kau Lame replied.

But the guard firmly refused, "No, push as you are!"

The princess got off the cart, and to her surprise, the guard also jumped down and followed her. "Push properly, no tricks," he warned. This reminded the princess of Kau Lame's plan—he was creating an opportunity for her to escape. However, things didn't go as Kau Lame had hoped. The guard was too cunning. Even if he hadn't been, the princess wouldn't have wanted Kau Lame to sacrifice himself for her. In the end, the cart made it over the hill, and the princess and the guard got back on.

Soon, a porter carrying a heavy load appeared on the mountain path. He walked steadily, humming a melodious mountain song: "The aroma of osmanthus wine wafts for miles, one bowl turns a ghost into an immortal..."

Kau Lame seized the opportunity and called out to the porter, "Excuse me, brother, is that wine you're carrying?"

The porter turned, his face lit with a simple smile. "Yes, it's homemade osmanthus wine. Would you like to try some?"

Kau Lame waved his hand. "With the official's here, I wouldn't dare. But I'd like to buy some for this gentleman to quench his thirst. How much?"

The porter said cheerfully, "Let me hitch a ride, and the gentleman can drink as much as he wants. Consider it my fare."

Kau Lame turned to the guard. "Sir, this wine is famous in ten villages. What do you think?"

The guard, who hadn't had a drink in days, was itching for one but hesitated. "What if the warden finds out?"

Kau Lame reassured him softly, "As long as I keep my mouth shut, how would he know?"

The guard nodded.

The porter placed the wine barrel on the cart and poured a jug for the guard. The aroma was intoxicating. The guard drank until he was thoroughly drunk and fell into a deep sleep. The cart continued on its way, soon arriving at the Phoenix Village market, while the guard remained lost in his dreams.

The porter left. Seizing the opportunity, Kau Lame unlocked the princess's chains, gave her some money, and bought her a sleek black horse and a sharp dagger from a farmer. He regretfully said to the princess, "Bamei, this is as far as I can take you. The rest of the journey is up to you."

The princess asked worriedly, "Uncle Kau, what will you do when you return?"

Kau Lame took a deep breath. "I've already thought of a way. It'll be fine. But you..." He hesitated, then spoke honestly, "There's one more thing. I heard from that Wulong that as long as he lives, his sorcery can't be broken. And he plans to ascend to the heavens with Fire Maiden, meaning his days are endless. Child, you must stay strong! Also, if you ever see my nephew again, tell him to come home and visit."

The princess nodded solemnly, her eyes filled with gratitude. She took one last look at him, mounted the horse, and galloped away.

Kau Lame picked up a brick from the ground and struck his own head with it.

***

By the Red River, General Langkun's troops had scoured the riverbanks multiple times, searching for any trace of the missing princess and Prince Qin. Despite their efforts, they found nothing.

Songmao and the three monkey siblings, like shrewd detectives, ventured into cliffs and hidden caves that the soldiers couldn't reach, exploring every possible clue.

As night deepened, Songmao stood on a towering rock, gazing at the dense forest on the opposite bank. A bold idea struck him, and he said to Monkey Four beside him, "Do you think they might have been swept to the other side by the river?"

Monkey Four looked up. "You might be right. But what can we do? That's Sherkon territory."

Songmao excitedly suggested, "Let's find a calm section of the river and cross quietly under the cover of night. What do you think?"

Monkey Four, recalling their previous bamboo raft adventure, was immediately interested. "Alright, let's have another legendary journey! I remember a good spot to cross."

The two adventurers didn't hesitate for a moment and set off toward the upper reaches of the Red River. After a full day of arduous trekking, they finally found a relatively calm section of the river. Here, tall bamboo grew densely, perfect for building a raft. They quickly and skillfully wove together a simple yet sturdy raft.

Under the moonlight, the river shimmered like silver. They carefully pushed the raft into the sparkling water, where it swayed gently, as if awaiting orders.

Songmao whispered, his voice tinged with excitement and anticipation, "Let's go!" He sat steadily at the front of the raft to navigate, while Monkey Four vigorously paddled.

The raft moved slowly across the rushing river. Late into the night, they finally reached the other side. Songmao nimbly jumped off the raft and tied the rope to a tree stump.

"Tie another knot, Songmao," Monkey Four reminded him. "If we lose the raft, we'll have to make another one."

Once the raft was secured, Songmao climbed a tall kapok tree nearby and surveyed the surroundings from above. The Red River, bathed in moonlight, resembled a silver dragon winding its way forward. Scattered along the banks were faint lights, perhaps from fishermen or Sherkon soldiers. "This search won't be easy," he muttered to himself.

Just as Songmao was about to look away, he suddenly noticed someone by their raft, frantically untying the rope. He asked in surprise, "Brother Monkey, are you untying the raft?"

But Monkey Four's voice came from below the tree. "I'm down here!"

Songmao instantly became alert and shouted, "Quick, someone's stealing the raft!"

Hearing this, Monkey Four rushed to the riverbank and saw a nimble figure already pushing the raft away from the shore. Without hesitation, he dove into the river to chase after it, but the woman struck him several times with the paddle, causing him to choke on water. He watched helplessly as the raft drifted further away under the moonlight. He climbed back onto the shore, dissatisfied with his performance, and said dejectedly to Songmao, "A female thief, but her skills are impressive."

However, Songmao's mind raced, and he laughed. "Brother Monkey, I think we came at the right time. Don't you think it's strange for a mysterious woman to cross the river in the middle of the night?"

"Yes, it is strange."

Songmao declared, "I bet that woman is the one we're looking for."

"Ah, could she be the missing Princess Wenxi?" Monkey Four exclaimed.

Chapter 14

The Butterfly Valley

On the sandy banks of the Red River, General Langkun's troops unexpectedly discovered Fire Rose. She lay quietly on the fine sand, like a withered leaf in the wind. Her black hair was disheveled, covering her pale face, and she looked exhausted and haggard. The soldiers carefully lifted her onto a horse and quickly brought her back to the camp, placing her on her bed.

The general rushed over, bringing a military doctor. However, Fire Rose refused to see the doctor. "General, I just need some rest. There's no need to disturb everyone," she said.

She waved her hand, signaling Tichu to close the door. "Guard the door. Don't let anyone in," she whispered. The door gently shut, cutting off all outside noise.

Inside, the candlelight flickered in the breeze, casting shifting shadows. She slowly sat in front of the mirror, her fingertips touching her face. The reflection showed her cracked lips, slightly red eyes, and an unmistakable weariness. She stared at the mirror, a wave of self-mockery rising in her heart: If Kauko saw me like this, would he feel a moment of pity? Or would he just find it laughable?

After two days of rest, her strength had somewhat recovered, but a sense of urgency lingered in her heart. Fire Maiden's mission was like a burning brand, reminding her that time was running out. She had to see Kauko as soon as possible.

The next day, she straightened her clothes and, with a calm expression, told the general her intention: "I need to visit the advisor. Let's set off quickly." Though hesitant, the general nodded and ordered Tichu to prepare the horses and arrange an escort.

On the way, Fire Rose curiously asked Tichu, "Is it true about Kauko using a flute to extinguish the fire?"

Tichu nodded indifferently. "It's true. That coward used a single copper flute to put out the flames of the entire forest."

Fire Rose pressed further, "What does the flute look like?"

Tichu thought for a moment. "It looks like an ordinary copper flute."

Fire Rose gazed into the distance and murmured, "That's a demonic flute."

She now understood Fire Maiden's obsession with it more deeply.

"I wish I had a flute like that," Tichu said.

Fire Rose shook her head gently. "You should be glad you don't. Stay away from anything demonic."

***

Kauko and General Dao had successfully defeated the enemy together. The victory that day became a heroic epic, celebrated among the soldiers. The nickname "Chef" also became a symbol of admiration.

As night fell, bonfires danced merrily in the twilight, casting a warm glow. Soldiers gathered around the fires, playing instruments and singing songs of victory, but Kauko sat apart, looking particularly lonely. He gazed at the stars and whispered to the gentle moonlight, "Princess, where are you? Are you looking at the same moon?"

At dawn, Kauko went alone to a nearby canyon, leaning against an ancient tree that had witnessed countless years. He gently patted the copper flute in his hand, his thoughts drifting back to carefree days with Bamei. He softly played the flute, its melody drifting through the morning mist, carrying a touch of sorrow and tenderness. Lost in the music, he forgot the flute's peculiarity—each time he played it, its life diminished.

In the distance, Fire Rose heard the unique flute melody and instinctively stopped her horse. "That tune is enchanting. Who's playing it?" she asked curiously.

Tichu replied with slight displeasure, "Who else? I don't even want to mention his name." He sighed inwardly, feeling that whenever Kauko appeared, his own importance in the princess's heart seemed to diminish.

"Yes, it's him," she murmured, then instructed Tichu to report to the advisor first while she followed the captivating flute melody, galloping away.

Before the melody ended, Fire Rose, dressed in a red gown, rode up to Kauko. Her eyes sparkled with joy and mischief. "Your flute sounds like it's scolding me."

Kauko's melancholy instantly turned into a smile. "Scolding you? Can't you tell it's longing? I was worried you'd be too frightened and age prematurely. But it seems you're still as radiant as ever."

Fire Rose's lips curved into a slight smile. "You've become quite the sweet talker. You didn't see how awkward I looked when I returned. You're lucky."

Kauko blamed himself. "It's my fault for not putting out the fire earlier, putting you through that."

Fire Rose's gaze fell on the flute in Kauko's hand. "I heard you used this flute to perform magic. Is it really that miraculous?"

Kauko simply smiled and handed the flute to her. Fire Rose hesitated for a moment, her fingertips touching the cool surface of the flute, as if sensing a hidden power within. She took the flute and examined it carefully but found nothing unusual.

She blew gently, but no sound came out. Fire Rose frowned slightly and looked at Kauko, waiting for an explanation.

Kauko saw her confusion and smiled faintly. "It only listens to me," he said calmly, with a hint of pride. "Master Dapeng and Songmao both tried. No one else can make it sound."

Fire Rose lowered her eyes, her fingers lightly tracing the flute's surface, as if sensing some deep secret within. A wave of unease washed over her, and her breathing became slightly hurried. She knew the flute's significance to Kauko and wanted to return it to him, but she hesitated. Fire Maiden's orders echoed in her mind—to make the flute disappear from Kauko's possession. It was an order she couldn't defy. But could she destroy Kauko's friendship? She remained silent, her heart torn between pain and fear, as if being ripped apart.

At that moment, a sudden gust of wind seemed to sense her inner turmoil and rushed toward her skirt, almost pulling her into the abyss of the cliff. Kauko reacted quickly, grabbing her wrist and steadying her. But her other hand lost control, and the flute, as if it had grown wings, flew out of her grasp and disappeared into the distant mist.

When Kauko turned his gaze back to Fire Rose, he was shocked to find that the hand he held was trembling, her arm flickering with a mysterious blue electric light. Her figure wavered between reality and illusion, her face sometimes clear as day, sometimes blurred like a dream, as if a rose and a ghost were intertwined in her. Fire Rose let out a piercing wail that echoed through the valley: "Kauko, let go!"

Songmao rushed over like a gust of wind. "Don't let go! She's not the princess!"

Kauko's eyes filled with confusion, and he tightened his grip. "Who are you? Why are you deceiving me?"

Fire Rose's struggles weakened in Kauko's grasp; her face twisted in pain. She finally managed to utter a few words: "I admit... I'm not the princess..."

These words struck Kauko like a thunderbolt, and his hand involuntarily loosened. Fire Rose fell to the ground, clutching her wrist and gasping for breath. Kauko looked down at her, his face a mix of disbelief and anger. "Then where is the real princess? Where is Princess Wenxi?"

Fire Rose looked up, her eyes unfocused, as if all her strength had been drained. "I don't know... She might be imprisoned in some concentration camp."

Kauko's expression darkened, his voice cutting into Fire Rose's heart like an icy blade. "I treated you so well. How could you help the enemy?"

Fire Rose knelt there motionless, her fingers clutching her sleeves helplessly, tears slowly streaming down her cheeks. "I never wanted to hurt you... My feelings for you were real, truly..."

Kauko closed his eyes, breathing heavily, as if suppressing the emotions surging within him. When he opened them again, his tone was chilling. "No matter what, you betrayed me and hurt the princess. Leave. I don't want to see you again."

Songmao jumped in frustration. "Kauko, you can't just let her go! She deliberately threw your flute away!"

Fire Rose's shoulders trembled slightly, and she lowered her head, choking back sobs. "Yes... I threw it on purpose... I don't deserve to explain..."

She slowly stood up and walked heavily toward the edge of the cliff. Each step was filled with suffocating despair. "Since you hate me so much," she said softly, like a wisp of wind, "maybe I... really should die..."

Just as she was about to step off the cliff, Kauko grabbed her. "Fire Rose, if you truly regret it, why take this path? Help me find the princess and redeem yourself!"

Hearing Kauko's hint of forgiveness, Fire Rose was moved. She wanted to throw herself into his arms and pour out her endless grievances, but she feared the merciless electric shock. She gently wiped the tears from her face, walked to her horse, and mounted it without looking back. The sound of hooves gradually faded, disappearing into the depths of the forest.

***

The news of Sanba's fall reached Sien City, shocking many generals. Prince Duan and a dozen veteran generals, who had spent their lives on the battlefield, jointly wrote a lengthy letter pleading with Fire Maiden to take action and suppress "Chef's" momentum.

After days of silence, Fire Maiden finally learned that Fire Rose had succeeded in removing the deadly flute. She gladly summoned them to the palace for a strategic discussion.

However, when the generals entered the grand hall, they found no sign of Fire Maiden. Instead, a long banquet table was set, laden with delicacies and fine wine, the hall illuminated as brightly as day.

Attendants respectfully seated the generals, and courtesans emerged, their gauzy dresses fluttering like celestial maidens. Their dance was graceful, their songs melodious.

Prince Duan scanned the opulence but saw no trace of Fire Maiden. He whispered to his deputy, "What is Fire Maiden playing at?"

The deputy smiled slightly and whispered back, "Sir, with fine wine and beautiful women, why worry about Fire Maiden's plans? Just enjoy the festivities." The other generals were already immersed in the revelry.

Unbeknownst to them, Fire Maiden's plan had already been set in motion.

A few days earlier, General Tian Gou stood before Fire Maiden's desk, his anxiety evident. His brows were furrowed, and beads of sweat clung to his temples. "Governor, are you really not leading the army yourself? With only twenty thousand men, how can I deal with the legendary Chef?"

Fire Maiden didn't answer immediately. She slowly looked up, her eyes behind the mask as deep as a dark lake, impossible to read. "Wipe your sweat," she said calmly, her tone carrying undeniable authority. "Don't overestimate him. That Chef is just a clown playing with fire."

General Tian Gou wiped his sweat with his sleeve, barely suppressing his unease. "But it's said that he..."

Fire Maiden raised a hand, cutting him off. "He'll try to scare you with fire. Just have your men pretend to be frightened and retreat quickly to Butterfly Valley."

"Retreat to Butterfly Valley... and then?"

Fire Maiden stood and walked to the map, her finger tracing a curve along a valley. Her voice was low but chillingly calm. "Once you reach the top of the valley, just do as I say. Make these movements. And then... it won't be your concern anymore."

General Tian Gou stared at her gestures, his doubts lingering, but Fire Maiden's composure left him no room to question. He nodded reluctantly. "Understood, Governor."

As he turned to leave, a slight shiver ran down his spine, as if he were walking into an unpredictable storm. He wasn't sure if he would make it out unscathed.

***

In the tent, the advisor was carefully studying the battlefield map, his fingers lightly tapping the location of Sanba. "General Dao, the Sherkon army's movements are too hasty, almost reckless," the advisor said calmly. "It reminds me of their tactics during the battle by the Red River."

General Dao stood nearby, his hand resting on the hilt of his sword, brimming with confidence. "Advisor, even if they caught us off guard, they only have twenty thousand men. They're no match for us..."

The advisor raised a hand, stopping him. "General, just hold your position. Don't attack rashly. We need to fully understand the enemy's intentions before making any decisions."

General Dao nodded. "Understood. I'll go to Butterfly Valley to set up defenses." He quickly left the tent.

The advisor remained alone, his gaze returning to the map. He sighed softly.

"This land is our defensive zone, but given the current situation, retreat might be the wiser choice." He had already made up his mind to discuss the matter with the princess before deciding.

"Tichu!" the advisor called.

Tichu hurried in and asked respectfully, "Advisor, what are your orders?"

The advisor asked urgently, "It's been a while. Why hasn't the princess returned?"

Tichu replied with a hint of displeasure, "I'm afraid the princess and Kauko are still on that cliff."

Hearing this, the advisor's expression turned grave. He immediately ordered, "Tichu, take a fast horse and go to the mountain. Make sure they return quickly." Tichu nodded and left the tent, mounting a horse and galloping away.

***

Kauko watched Fire Rose leave, his heart turbulent and unsettled. He turned to Songmao, confused. "In the past, whether I carried her or held her hand, nothing unusual ever happened. Why was today so different?"

Songmao scratched his head, a hint of mystery in his eyes. "Perhaps it's the effect of Master Dapeng's pill."

"That pill is so miraculous?" Kauko couldn't help but ask.

Songmao nodded firmly. "Its wonders are far greater than you think."

Kauko sighed deeply. "Master, you've done so much for me!"

Songmao leaped onto Kauko's shoulder and whispered, "Then do what you must! For now, you need to return to camp and report Fire Rose's actions to the advisor."

Kauko blamed himself. "How can I face the advisor? I was supposed to protect the princess, but I failed..."

Songmao interrupted his self-reproach. "Running away won't solve anything. We have to face it. No matter what, go back first."

Kauko shook his head. "No, I must find the real princess."

Songmao looked at Kauko with confusion. "Do you know where she is?"

Kauko shook his head helplessly. At that moment, Tichu came galloping on a black horse, panting heavily and shouting, "The advisor's urgent order! You must bring the princess to the camp immediately!"

Kauko stammered, his tongue tied, "The princess... she..."

Songmao quickly interjected, "The princess has already gone back ahead of us."

Kauko awkwardly grinned, then leaped onto his horse and caught up with Tichu, asking, "What's the emergency?"

Tichu's expression was grave as he scolded, "General Dao has personally gone to face the enemy! You've been gone for so long. Don't you understand the stakes?"

Kauko's face showed shock, and he defended himself, "How is that possible? Chef is clearly still here. Why would General Dao go alone?"

Tichu had no patience for his excuses and barked, "Stop dawdling! The advisor is summoning you urgently."

However, Kauko said, "I'll go straight to the front lines!" He turned his horse and galloped toward Butterfly Valley.

When Kauko arrived at the battlefield, he saw General Dao gripping his sword, ready to face the Sherkon general. Kauko quickly rode over and blocked General Dao, saying resolutely, "General, since Chef is here, why do you need to go yourself?"

General Dao looked into Kauko's determined eyes and shook the sword in his hand, about to hand it to him. But Kauko smiled faintly, "Chef isn't skilled with swords." With that, he rode straight toward the Sherkon vanguard general.

The Sherkon general sat firmly on his horse, wrapped tightly in a thick, wet blanket, revealing only a pair of sharp eyes that scanned the surroundings warily through the gaps in the blanket.

Kauko stood not far away, his gaze lingering on the general's cumbersome attire, a hint of a smirk playing on his lips. He bent down, picked up a dry branch from the ground, and twirled it casually between his fingers, his movements nonchalant yet provocative. He called out, "General, that wet blanket seems tight. Are you afraid of my fire? How about a taste of this stick?"

The Sherkon general's eyes flashed with anger, his lips twitching slightly before he let out a low roar. He spurred his horse, and the steed reared up, charging at Kauko like an arrow released from a bow. His massive hammer swung in a wide arc, aiming to split Kauko in two.

But Kauko remained calm, guiding his horse to the side with ease, slipping past the general like a gust of wind. The hammer struck empty air.

The dry branch continued to twirl in Kauko's fingers, as if it were nothing more than a toy.

The Sherkon general quickly turned his horse and charged again. Kauko's eyes narrowed, and with a flick of his wrist, the branch sent a pinecone flying like an arrow. With a dull thud, the pinecone struck the general squarely between the eyes. He grunted, the hammer slipping from his grasp as he lost his balance and fell heavily from his horse.

Kauko didn't stop. The branch in his hand danced nimbly, sending pinecone after pinecone flying like a relentless rain, striking the general's prone form. The general struggled on the ground, the wet blanket restricting his movements, but it couldn't shield him from the barrage of pinecones. The dull thuds of impact mixed with the general's cries of pain and his frantic attempts to roll away. Gradually, the thick blanket was torn apart by the pinecones, leaving the general fully exposed. His expression shifted from anger to panic, and finally to utter helplessness.

General Dao, seeing this, grew excited and forgot the advisor's warning. He signaled for an attack. The Sherkon army, caught off guard by the sudden turn of events, quickly retreated in disarray. The Daze army surged forward, launching a full-scale pursuit.

General Tian Gou, standing atop a high mountain, looked down at the dense ranks of Daze soldiers in Butterfly Valley. His eyes gleamed with cunning as he followed Fire Maiden's plan. He faced the valley and, in a grand gesture, urinated toward the Daze army below!

The Daze soldiers felt deeply humiliated. They roared in anger, charging up the mountain like a pack of wolves. However, their shouts were soon drowned out by a louder, more earth-shaking rumble. A massive flood surged down from the upper reaches of the valley, unstoppable.

General Dao, sensing the enemy's sinister magic, urgently called out to Kauko, "Kauko, where's your divine flute? Use it to break this spell!"

Kauko frantically felt around his waist, only to remember that the flute was lost. His face turned pale, and he stammered, "The flute... it's gone."

General Dao's gaze turned icy, piercing Kauko like a blade. "Tell me, what else can we do?"

Kauko shook his head weakly. "There's nothing."

General Dao took a deep breath and decisively ordered, "All troops, retreat! Retreat!"

In the valley, the massive flood crashed against the mountain walls, the roar echoing in all directions. The Daze soldiers' tight formation was instantly shattered by the floodwaters. Some desperately waved their arms, trying to grab their comrades, only to be swept away by the relentless current. Others bent down to pick up dropped weapons, only to be knocked over by the surging water and disappear into the churning waves.

The cold from the flood seeped into their bones. The soldiers' terrified screams were drowned out by the deafening roar of the water. They ran up the slope like headless flies, the slippery mud causing many to fall, get up, and fall again. Above them, arrows rained down from the Sherkon army, piercing armor and skin. One by one, the Daze soldiers fell, their blood mixing with the muddy water, staining the flood a deep red.

Kauko's gaze pierced through the rain of arrows and the churning waves, suddenly catching sight of a figure on a large rock—General Dao. He stood alone on the rock, surrounded by the rushing floodwaters. His armor was covered in mud, his face streaked with blood and water, his eyes hollow and dazed. He was clearly exhausted, swaying unsteadily.

Without a second thought, Kauko plunged into the flood. The icy water instantly submerged his lower body, the powerful current nearly knocking him over. He pushed against the water with his legs, his arms paddling, resisting each oncoming wave. Finally, he grabbed General Dao's arm and pulled him onto his back. The general's body was stiff, his arms hanging limply. Kauko gritted his teeth, struggling against the current. The waves crashed into him, making it hard to stand, and the weight on his shoulders slowed him down even more. The cold wind whipped water droplets into his face, stinging his eyes.

He managed to climb to slightly higher ground and set General Dao down. His whole body was trembling, but he only wiped the water from his face and looked back at the chaos in the valley—there were still more people to save. He took a deep breath and stepped back into the raging flood.

The mud beneath his feet loosened in the water. Countless people struggled in the flood, some trying to climb rocks, others clinging to floating tree trunks. His vision blurred as rain and tears mixed, making the whole world seem to tremble. He wanted to reach out and help, but he didn't know who to save first. The cold and exhaustion gradually overwhelmed him, his legs aching and his arms refusing to obey.

A deep, unnatural rumble filled the air. He turned to see a towering wave rushing toward him, dark and alive with malevolence. Before he could act, it crashed over him, dragging him into its cursed depths. The water coiled around him, heavy and relentless, sapping his strength and clouding his senses.

***

General Dao led the exhausted remnants of his troops through the treacherous mountain paths, finally finding a hidden valley where they hastily set up tents in the pouring rain. The advisor arrived safely with a group of knights. As soon as General Dao saw the advisor, he knelt, his forehead nearly touching the ground, his voice filled with despair. "Advisor, I have failed! I didn't follow your instructions, and... I lost Kauko." His voice choked with tears.

The advisor gently walked over and helped General Dao to his feet, his voice soft but heavy. "General, you did your best. My disciple failed, didn't he?"

General Dao's eyes filled with tears as he sobbed, "He said he lost the divine flute."

The advisor took a deep breath, his expression grave. "Is that so? I'll get to the bottom of this."

General Dao's eyes flickered with hope. "Then... do you think Kauko might still be alive?"

The advisor nodded firmly. "I believe he may just be confused and unwilling to face us for now."

***

The princess, now free, felt lost and helpless. She rode alone through the deep mountains, avoiding populated areas. The sound of her horse's hooves clicking against loose stones echoed in the quiet. She tightly wrapped her scarf around her face, trying to hide her appearance and the pain in her heart.

Occasionally, the mountain wind would lift a corner of her scarf, revealing part of her pig-like face. She would nervously tighten the reins, afraid of being discovered. In the distance, she heard the laughter of villagers and instinctively hid in the bushes, peering through the leaves with her bright but sorrowful eyes as the happy villagers passed by.

After days of wandering, her food supply was nearly gone, and hunger made her feel increasingly weak. When she reached a small village and saw children playing with iron hoops and women chatting at their doorsteps, a glimmer of hope rose in her heart. But as she dismounted and approached, a child accidentally rolled an iron hoop to her feet. The child looked up at her heavily wrapped head and screamed in fright.

The women noticed the unusual visitor and hurriedly gathered their children, closing their doors with a creak. The princess felt a pang of sadness. She bent down, picked up the iron hoop, and gently placed it at the doorstep of one house. She raised her hand to knock but silently gave up.

She knew her appearance had caused panic and couldn't blame the villagers. Silently wiping the tears from the corners of her eyes, she tightened the reins and continued her lonely journey.

As night fell, the bright moonlight illuminated her solitary path with a silvery glow. She removed her scarf, revealing her cursed, deformed face and unusually large ears. The cold night wind brushed her face as she and her loyal black horse, like two lonely travelers, moved like dark shadows along the desolate mountain road.

The road twisted and turned, the surrounding hills and vegetation blurred and indistinct in the darkness. Her face was wet from the wind and tears, and though her body was exhausted, her eyes still shone with determination. Her fate had been cruelly rewritten, and she had endured discrimination and violence that words could not describe.

She vowed to find Kauko, her companion who had also been toyed with by fate. She vaguely remembered the last time she was with Kauko, in a lush forest near an abandoned ancient temple, located in the direction where the sun and moon rose. So she followed a little-traveled path in that direction, letting the silver moonlight light her way.

Late at night, the princess followed the lakeshore and arrived at a quiet little village. A few thatched cottages stood peacefully, exuding a sense of tranquility. After dismounting, she chose to sit quietly on a nearby ridge, pondering whether to "borrow" some food from the villagers to stave off her hunger. She had no intention of stealing, only wanting to fill her stomach and leave some copper coins as compensation.

As she hesitated, a small dog happily ran toward her, barking incessantly. The princess gently waved her hand, and the dog quieted down, sitting in front of her with curious eyes. She reached out and patted its head, whispering, "You're a smart little one, aren't you? You can sense my sincerity." The dog seemed to understand, licking her hand before leading her to a thatched cottage, cleverly pushing the door open with its nose.

The aroma of food wafted from inside, and the princess's stomach growled. She tiptoed in, lifted the pot lid, and took out a bowl of leftover rice. Sitting at the table, she ate it all in one go, tasting taro, wild vegetables, and rabbit.

After eating, she placed a few copper coins on the table and was about to leave the comforting little cottage when suddenly lights appeared outside, and the sound of people broke the night's silence. She hurried to the door, only to find it locked.

She peeked out the window and saw several adults and children staring back at her. They held no weapons. An old woman walked to the window and cried, "My child, you've come back! Don't run away anymore. No matter how you look, I don't care. You've suffered so much all these years outside." The old woman reached out to touch the princess's face, but the princess shrank back in fear.

The princess heard the young woman's sobs: "Husband, don't run away. The children miss you." She peeked out again and saw the woman forcing three children to kneel on the ground, their wails rising and falling.

The princess understood that they meant no harm; they had simply mistaken her for someone else. Perhaps there was another pig-faced person in their family who had suffered the same fate as her? At this thought, tears streamed down her face—for herself and for others. The old woman's hand touched the princess's face, her palm damp. She took out a handkerchief and wiped the princess's tears, murmuring, "I've missed you." The cries around them grew even more mournful. The princess held the old woman's hand, pressing it to her cheek, unable to speak for a long time.

The old man called out to the family, "Stop crying! What if the soldiers hear us?" The outside quickly quieted down.

The princess turned to the kind old woman, her voice tinged with helplessness. "Grandma, you've mistaken me for someone else. I'm just a traveler passing through."

The old woman's eyes were filled with stubbornness as she shook her head. "Don't lie to your mother. Whether you're a pig's head or a dog's head, it doesn't matter. Just stay home."

The princess sighed softly, trying to explain. "Grandma, your son might have suffered the same misfortune as me, turned into this by some evil force. But I'm really not him. You've mistaken me."

The old woman remained unmoved. "I don't believe it. You are my son. Even if you turned to ash, I'd recognize you."

The princess, seeing no other option, confessed, "Grandma, I'm actually a girl, seventeen years old."

Her words brought a moment of silence. The old woman took the lantern from the old man and examined the princess closely, her voice filled with tenderness. "Son, has your mind gone bad? You need to stay home, don't go anywhere."

The princess felt a wave of helplessness and said softly, "Grandma, I'll have to take it off." The old woman quickly replied, "Don't, you'll catch a cold. Even if you take it off, I won't believe you."

So the princess hid behind the wall, took off a red undergarment from her waist, and carefully waved it in front of the window. The old woman took the garment and examined it closely. It was indeed something a girl would wear. She immediately realized her mistake and apologized, "Young lady, I'm so sorry!" She then called for the children to get up and told her daughter-in-law to open the door. The family filed into the room, and the princess instinctively retreated to the corner by the stove, trembling slightly. The old woman slowly sat at the table, her eyes filled with concern. She gestured for the princess to sit beside her and gently stroked the back of the princess's hand. "Child, what's your name?"

The princess replied softly, "I don't have a name. Everyone calls me Bamei."

"Bamei?" The old woman's eyebrows raised, as if recalling something. "There was a beloved child in the opera troupe with that name. Is that you?"

The princess nodded and smiled. "Yes, it's me."

The old woman's eyes welled up with tears. She tenderly touched the princess's face, her voice trembling. "Child, who did this to you?"

"I don't know," the princess replied, her voice filled with resignation.

The old woman sighed, her eyes clouded with sorrow. "My poor son, I don't know where he is or what he's suffering." She noticed the copper coins on the table and quickly handed them to the princess. "You'll need money out there. Keep it. Child, where are you planning to go?"

"I'm looking for another pig-faced person. He's alone and helpless. I want to help him," the princess said.

The old woman nodded, her eyes filled with approval. "Good child, still thinking of others."

That night, the family insisted that the princess stay. They brightened the oil lamp and gathered around her, sharing many warm words. The straw scarecrow on the wall seemed to smile at her, and the aroma of fried cakes filled the room.

Late into the night, the princess lay on a soft straw bed, wrapped in a warm quilt. The chirping of crickets and the occasional sound of cowbells outside created a peaceful rural night melody.

The next morning, sunlight streamed into the room, its warmth gently waking the princess. She slowly sat up from the straw bed.

Beside the bed was a vibrant floral dress, its hem embroidered with blooming chrysanthemums. A bamboo basket nearby was filled with freshly baked corn cakes and a few pieces of brown sugar.

The child's mother pushed the door open and looked at her with gentle eyes. "I wore this dress once at the market but thought it was too flashy, so I put it away. It's been stored for too long. I think it'll suit you well, so I'm giving it to you."

The princess was deeply moved by this selfless kindness. She gently picked up the dress, her eyes sparkling with joy. She stood up and bowed deeply to the woman, her heart filled with gratitude.

As the princess set out on her journey again, wearing the bright floral dress, her sorrow seemed to lessen.

Chapter 15

The Princess's Fangs

The sun gradually rose higher, its scorching rays bathing the undulating sand dunes in a golden glow, as if cloaking the earth in a shimmering garment. The princess wiped the sweat from her brow and pressed on with determination. Amid the golden dust, a small, dark shadow began to emerge, flickering in and out of sight like a ghost.

The princess glanced back inadvertently, and the tiny shadow immediately hid behind a dune. Her brow furrowed slightly. The horse, sensing her unease, quickened its pace without prompting.

A gray wolf peeked out from behind the dune, its eyes bright and cunning, locked onto her. In the sunlight, its fur swayed in the wind, glinting like sharp needles.

As night fell, the moonlight spilled over the dunes, creating a patchwork of light and shadow. Every time the princess turned around, those eyes, cold as stars, seemed to leap in the darkness, always watching her silently, sending chills down her spine.

The princess didn't know whether, in its eyes, she was a lonely traveler or a much-anticipated meal. She clung tightly to the saddle and whispered to her horse, "Faster, I don't like those eyes." The horse, as if sensing her fear, suddenly surged forward, its hooves kicking up sand that scattered like rain.

The wind howled in her ears as she kept looking back. The gray wolf had gradually disappeared behind the dunes. She breathed a sigh of relief, slowed her horse, and began searching for a suitable place to rest.

However, just as she was about to dismount, the horse suddenly stomped the ground nervously and let out a tense whinny. Following its gaze, the princess saw the gray wolf sitting calmly on a small mound nearby. The desert's silence and the wolf's gaze seemed to mock her helplessness. Its shadow, like her unfortunate past, clung to her relentlessly. Every time she tried to shake it off, it felt as though an invisible chain pulled her back.

The princess gripped her whip, a glint of determination in her eyes. Since she couldn't escape, she might as well face it head-on. She resolved not to be haunted by it anymore, accepting the wolf's presence and continuing her journey, curious to see how much worse fate could get.

The wolf, however, began to feel a sense of loss and unease. It found it difficult to face the solitary, proud traveler alone. One day, as the sun set in a haze, it lifted its head and let out a long, mournful howl. The sound echoed through the silent valley, causing the distant trees and grass to tremble. The princess and her horse were resting in a cave, and the wild, lonely cry stirred a sense of melancholy in her heart.

The next morning, as the princess stepped out of the cave at dawn, she was shocked to see a dozen wolves waiting not far from the entrance. As she emerged, they began to circle her, their steps predatory, their growls filled with hunger. Seeing these vile creatures, the princess felt an unexpected surge of courage. She tore off her headscarf, threw it to the ground, and drew a short knife from her back. She slashed it through the air in a crescent moon shape, bared her teeth, and shouted, "Come on!" Her roar shook the valley, startling birds and beasts into fleeing. The wolves, seeing this, tucked their tails, cowered, and retreated before finally scattering.

After traveling another hundred miles, the princess began to recognize familiar places, where she had performed, lived, laughed, and cried in Auntie Wei's arms.

One night, she stopped to rest at a god temple. Everything felt so familiar—the temple's eaves, the guardian deity's portrait, and the stage in the front courtyard. She took a candlestick and moved from room to room, reminiscing about a beautiful memory. It was here that she had met little Pighead Brother. She regretted carelessly calling him a monster, hurting his feelings, and even more, leaving him alone in the kitchen, subjecting him to immense fear and humiliation.

The princess thought of the small loft in the kitchen, where her friendship with Kauko had blossomed. She stepped into the kitchen, where everything remained as it had been, clearly still in use. The stairs to the loft were covered in years of dust. Had no one set foot there since they left? She carefully climbed the creaking stairs and stopped at the top step. The loft seemed much smaller than she remembered; as an adult, she couldn't stand up straight. Yet, in her childhood eyes, it had been vast enough to hold their entire world.

Her gaze fell on a dusty wooden box, which she remembered as being brown. She bent down to examine it, wanting to confirm that it was indeed brown, that everything from the past was real. She gently wiped away a corner of the dust, revealing the brown wood, and a long-lost smile spread across her face. She remembered—this was her secret. She had stored something inside. She hoped that when she opened it, she would find those treasures.

Yes, they were there, lying quietly for ten years, like a miracle! What treasures could make the princess's heart race and bring tears to her eyes? They were two masks—one of Zhu Bajie and one of Zhu Bajie's wife. The princess placed the candlestick on the floor and picked up the two exquisitely crafted, lifelike masks, feeling as though she were holding two warm faces.

Little Bamei had begged Auntie Wei to make these masks and stored them in this box, always hoping that Kauko would return to her side. She would ask Auntie Wei to let him stay, and they would perform together, singing "Cangshan Sister".

The princess placed the masks back in the box. They were too small, belonging only to two clever little kids with tender faces. She descended from the loft, unable to shake the melancholy in her heart. By the light of the moon, she walked to the stage in the front courtyard, unconsciously moving her feet and swaying her hips, recalling the lively days with the theater troupe. Yes, a silent little boy had once sat on the stone lion to the left of the stage. Who could have guessed, at first glance, that he could change faces?

The poplar tree by the courtyard wall rustled in the breeze, as if echoing the stories of the past, vying for the princess's attention. But the princess didn't want to see it. Painful memories should be forgotten, especially those of childhood. Yet the tree seemed to have recorded everything, and seeing it brought the past vividly to life.

***

After more than half a month of travel, the princess finally arrived at Jingxin Temple, where she and Kauko had once stayed. She was greeted by a flock of crows nesting in the dilapidated temple. They flapped their wings and flew into the woods, disturbing the serene world.

The weeds and vines were more overgrown than before, clinging to the walls and even climbing onto the roof. The princess's heart grew heavier at the sight of this desolation, and the sky seemed to mirror her mood, covered in thick, dark clouds.

She didn't dismount immediately but stood for a long time in front of the abandoned temple, looking around. Finally, she couldn't help but shout, "Kauko! Kauko!" She knew it was a futile call, but her voice echoed through the empty temple and the surrounding mountains, carrying an endless sorrow. As her cries faded, tears wet her cheeks, but her heart felt somewhat calmer.

The princess dismounted and tied her horse to the old stable. Just then, a fierce wind blew, and rain poured down, turning the day as dark as night. She took shelter in a cellar, curling up on a bed in the corner, clutching a blanket.

All night, she listened to the sound of the wind and rain, but she couldn't recall where she had gone after parting with Kauko, nor when she had turned into a pig-faced person. Rainwater seeped through cracks in the rock walls, disappearing silently into hidden channels.

When sunlight finally streamed into the cellar, the princess gradually fell asleep. A gentle breeze carried a warm, peaceful aura, softly caressing her face and lulling her into a tranquil sleep. In the corner where wild roses had once grown, unknown little plants now sprouted, trying to climb the broken wooden barrel on the rock wall, as if they too wanted to have a story.

***

The frontline battle report was swiftly delivered to Fire Maiden. She closed her eyes, sniffed the envelope, took a deep breath, and said to the messenger, "Too much bloodshed! Take it directly to the complaining generals."

Prince Duan took the report tied with a red silk thread and asked the messenger, "This is addressed to Governor Fire. Why didn't she open it? Did she not read it?"

The messenger replied, "I don't know. I only followed Governor Fire's orders."

The generals whispered among themselves, wondering if Governor Fire didn't want to see how General Tian had been mocked by Chef.

Old General Qiang Heng, standing beside Prince Duan, took the letter from the prince's hands. "Let me read it to everyone," he said. He tore it open and read aloud, "Governor, great news! In this battle, I fought Chef for ten rounds, making him cry for his parents. Then, in front of everyone, I urinated on his head. My urine miraculously turned into a flood, sweeping away the enemy's army of a hundred thousand. At this moment, the remnants of the Sanba rebels are fleeing..."

The generals didn't believe it and burst into laughter.

"Did he borrow the Dragon King's water cannon?"

"Let's have him come tomorrow and urinate for us to see!"

"Annihilating that many enemies? We can retire now!"

"My beloved generals!" Governor Fire suddenly appeared behind a translucent curtain. "No need to nitpick. The rebels are truly defeated, and Sanba is in our hands. Old General, what else does the letter say?"

"...All credit goes to the governor's brilliant strategy."

Hearing this, the generals realized that Governor Fire had already taken action and cheered, "Governor, you are mighty!"

She waved them off. "Alright, go back and lead your troops. Don't bother me with such trivial matters."

***

After Fire Rose discarded Kauko's divine flute, a weight was lifted from Fire Maiden's heart. She felt much more at ease and thought that the little demon's experience and loyalty could be put to greater use. She summoned Fire Rose,

"Return to your master's side, Fire Rose."

However, Fire Rose didn't respond, having hidden herself away.

Fire Maiden continued, "Come back, and I'll reward you. I'll make you the Princess of Daze."

Still, there was no reply.

Fire Maiden's tone turned warning. "If you don't answer, I'll have to punish you! Whether it's a reward or punishment is up to you."

Hearing this, Fire Rose grew anxious. She knew what Fire Maiden's punishments entailed, and the thought sent a shiver down her spine. She spoke, "Master, I just want to be myself, a little flower fairy. Please, let me be."

Fire Maiden sighed softly. "I don't blame you for feeling this way. You think you've hurt the one you love and severed a lifetime of affection, don't you?"

Fire Rose sobbed, "Isn't that true, Master?"

Fire Maiden spoke slowly, "Listen, Fire Rose, you're too young. I've been through this. Kauko and I are alike—we love only one person. Who does he love? You know."

Fire Rose wept silently.

Fire Maiden continued, "Kauko loves a princess Bamei. No matter how you treat him, even if you favor him, you won't win his heart. Because you're not Bamei."

Fire Rose trembled and asked, "Then why did I come to the mortal world?"

Fire Maiden replied gently, "There are more men in the world than just Kauko. I originally had Prince Qin in mind for you, but he opposed me and lost his life. I think there's another man who's quite good—the one named Tichu. Hasn't he been loyal to you? His care for you, in every little way, isn't it more than Kauko's? Though he's unknown, he's always been steadfast, whether you noticed or not."

Fire Rose responded softly, "I have feelings for them, but not as deeply as I do for Kauko."

Fire Maiden smiled and explained, "Master isn't asking you to choose between them. These are just examples. I want to help you move past Kauko's shadow and see that there are warm, caring people beyond it. As for who it might be, that's up to fate. Men are fascinating creatures. When you meet the right one, you might forget all about Kauko."

"Really? Can love come again?" Fire Rose raised her confused eyes, her voice tinged with hope.

Fire Maiden shared her own secret: "It's my own experience! Back in the heavens, I fell in love with Marshal Tianpeng, but he didn't love me at all. Because I loved him too much and couldn't let go, it led to a great disaster for both of us, and we were banished to the mortal world. I thought I'd never love again! But when love returned, it struck like a bolt from the blue, just as intense as before."

After hearing Fire Maiden's words, Fire Rose, though still feeling a bit lost, returned to her side.

Fire Maiden announced to the world that "Princess Wenxi" had pledged allegiance to the Sherkon regime. To foster a sense of unity between the royal family and the people, Fire Maiden ordered a month-long festival in Sien City, with the celebrations to be arranged by the princess. During the festival, citizens were allowed to drink, gather in the streets, and celebrate, while soldiers were forbidden from killing or harassing the people.

Fire Rose appeared before the public in lavish princess attire.

Wherever she went, she was the dazzling center of attention. She wore a long red silk dress embroidered with delicate gold and silver threads, sparkling like starlight. The dress was adorned with various gemstones, emitting a subtle glow, like a dancing rainbow. Her hair was intricately styled, decorated with gold and silver hairpins and jeweled ornaments. Silk ribbons hung from her hair, embedded with gemstones, making her hairline particularly striking. Her earrings swayed gently with her steps, like a melody in music. The bracelets on her wrists jingled softly, like silver bells.

Her joyful demeanor seemed to embody the spirit of the festival. Every laugh she shared ignited joy in those around her. She appeared like a fairy from a fairy tale, spreading the magic and happiness of the festival to everyone she encountered.

At first, the citizens were shocked to hear that the princess had pledged allegiance to Sherkon. Many came to see her with disappointment and anger, some even carrying hidden weapons. But when they saw a beautiful, charming princess who loved to dance and laugh with them, they quickly accepted her as their own.

***

Songmao and Monkey Four, tasked with a critical mission, quietly infiltrated Sien City, determined to uncover the mystery of Princess Wenxi's whereabouts. Under the cover of night, Sien City was ablaze with lights and bustling with activity, yet beneath the surface of this prosperity, there seemed to linger a sorrow of a fallen nation. Monkey Four cleverly concealed his monkey face, while Songmao obediently perched on Monkey Four's shoulder like a small pet. The two moved through the crowd, their eyes searching.

Soon, in the square before the palace, Songmao's gaze locked onto a woman dancing gracefully. Her movements were elegant and passionate, and she danced with the people, earning cheers and applause. Songmao immediately recognized her as Fire Rose.

Monkey Four, however, was skeptical. He whispered, "Didn't you say before that it's hard to tell the real princess from the fake one? Why are you so sure she's not Princess Wenxi?"

Songmao firmly retorted, "Would Princess Wenxi ever side with the Sherkon people?"

Monkey Four pondered for a moment and proposed another possibility: "Perhaps the princess has her reasons, using this as a way to infiltrate the enemy camp as a spy."

As the two debated, the woman, surrounded by attendants, hurried into the palace. Songmao urgently said, "Follow her!" Immediately, they leaped onto the rooftops, moving swiftly between buildings, closely tailing the woman.

The woman passed through courtyards and arrived at a secluded place. She respectfully bowed to a woman in a red robe and a black mask: "Master, what are your orders?"

The red-robed woman slowly turned, her voice low and cold, "Princess, are you enjoying yourself?" Songmao's heart tightened as he recognized her—Fire Maiden, the former lover of Dapeng.

Fire Rose respectfully replied, "Thank you, Master. I'm very happy. But I often wonder, am I truly the princess?"

Fire Maiden sneered, "I don't like hearing that. Of course, you're the princess. Princess Wenxi died long ago in the pig demon camp."

Songmao felt as if struck by lightning. He finally confirmed that the woman before him was not Princess Wenxi but Fire Rose.

Fire Rose was also shocked. Her eyes widened, and her voice trembled as she asked, "Ah, did you kill her?"

Fire Maiden's tone carried a hint of regret: "I only meant to imprison her to prevent her from causing trouble. But an accident occurred, and I deeply regret it. I had planned to take her as my disciple."

Hearing this, Fire Rose choked back tears: "Poor princess! Her death is partly my fault. Master, I really don't want to impersonate the princess anymore."

"Fire Rose! Princess! You mustn't act like a child. Do you know how important it is for you to be the princess? You've eased the hatred many Daze people feel toward Sherkon, and you've convinced many to leave the rebel army and return home. You've saved so many lives!"

Initially, Fire Rose wanted to become the princess for love. But recently, she had gained widespread affection from the people, hearing countless tragic stories and heartfelt confessions. These stories awakened her innate kindness and compassion. Her thoughts shifted—if she continued to be the princess, she decided it wouldn't be for herself but for the people who adored her.

She followed Fire Maiden's words: "Master, if I continue to be the princess, I need a token."

"What token do you want?" Fire Maiden asked.

"A token that allows me to punish Sherkon people who harass the citizens," Fire Rose replied.

Fire Maiden pondered for a moment and said, "I agree, but not now. I still need the Sherkon people to help me deal with the rebels. Give me some time. Once I master the Great Demon Art, I won't need them anymore."

Fire Rose thought she had no choice but to wait patiently and asked, "Master, what did you need me for?"

"The Sherkon king will visit Sien City in a few days. I remember there's a very festive play in Daze. Find someone to rehearse it, and we'll have the Sherkon king watch it."

"Are you talking about 'Zhu Bajie Carries His Wife'?" Fire Rose asked.

"Exactly that one," Fire Maiden confirmed.

"I'll do my best," Fire Rose replied.

At that moment, a guard rushed in to report: "Governor Fire, Prince Duan reports that several of our granaries have been burned down recently, allegedly by Chef."

Monkey Four winked at Songmao, and the two silently acknowledged that this was the work of the Monkey Army, unrelated to Chef.

"Chef? He was already drowned in a flood of urine!" Fire Maiden said disdainfully.

Fire Rose asked in confusion, "Who is the chef?"

To prevent Fire Rose from falling into an emotional whirlpool, Fire Maiden casually made up an excuse: "Just a thief skilled at scaling walls."

***

In a quiet corner of the jungle, Monkey Three and Monkey Shang silently watched Monkey Four and Songmao busy themselves. The clamor of war seemed like a distant drama to them, and they felt helpless to participate. Monkey Three felt a surge of desire to contribute to the efforts of these brave warriors, even if in a small way. But fighting and killing weren't his strengths, and the thought of scaling walls filled him with fear.

One leisurely afternoon, Monkey Three took Monkey Shang for a walk in the woods and stumbled upon a group of monkeys who made their living mining and forging. As they chatted, an idea suddenly struck Monkey Three: he had once been a skilled craftsman. Why not pick up the trade again?

"I can make bronze mirrors," Monkey Three excitedly told Monkey Shang.

Monkey Shang beamed: "Then the money we earn can support Kauko and the rebel army. We can be part of the fight too."

Filled with enthusiasm, Monkey Three used his savings to buy an abandoned bronze workshop and hired some monkey craftsmen. They began making bronze mirrors, with Monkey Three personally wielding the hammer, feeling a deep sense of accomplishment.

Meanwhile, Monkey Shang took on the responsibility of sales. She cleverly established connections with middlemen, pushing these exquisite bronze mirrors to distant markets. Every time she saw the mirrors being sent far away, she felt a surge of pride.

***

Monkey Four and Songmao hurried back to their hideout from Sien City.

Before catching his breath, Monkey Four urgently called out to Monkey Three: "Third Brother, Kauko and the princess, they..."

Monkey Three sat up straight, his gaze sharp as an eagle's, locking onto Monkey Four. "What about them?"

Monkey Four's eyes flickered for a moment, as if weighing his words. "They... might have already..." He trailed off, lowering his head, his Adam's apple bobbing as if swallowing something bitter.

Monkey Three pressed, "Don't beat around the bush! Did they follow their predecessors?"

Monkey Four quickly waved his hands. "No, no. I mean, they might... no longer be in this world."

Monkey Three handed him a ladle of water, comforting him: "Drink some water first, then tell me what happened."

Monkey Four took the ladle, tilted his head back, and drank it all in one go. He put the ladle down, wiped his mouth, and then recounted everything he and Songmao had seen and heard in the capital, along with their speculations. The room fell into a dead silence, broken only by the sound of wind whistling through the cracks in the window.

"Ridiculous!" Monkey Three slammed the table, the sound echoing in the small room. "That guy Kauko, even fire couldn't harm him. How could mere floodwaters take him down?"

"Right, Big Brother Kau seems like he has nine lives!" Monkey Shang, who had been quietly weaving a bamboo basket, chimed in softly, her voice tinged with reluctant hope.

Songmao crouched in the corner, fiddling with a stick in his hand, his expression growing serious. He slowly spoke: "Perhaps... Kauko, unable to save the princess and failing to fulfill General Kau's trust, felt so guilty that he gave up on living."

"Gave up on living?" Monkey Three's eyes flashed with complexity. "That's just your speculation. We can't jump to conclusions based on guesses. Instead of sitting here making wild assumptions, we should go to Butterfly Valley and see for ourselves."

"Right, we need to see it with our own eyes!" Everyone nodded in agreement.

Songmao looked up at Monkey Three: "You mentioned Kauko, but what about the princess? Do you think she... might still be alive?"

Monkey Three's face darkened, his gaze dropping as if avoiding the question. He sighed deeply, "The princess's situation... is hard to predict. We might need to prepare for the worst."

Songmao's brow furrowed, his lips trembling slightly. "So, you agree with our investigation? If that's the case, the advisor needs to know immediately."

Monkey Four nodded heavily and stood up. "Songmao, you're fast. This task is yours. We'll meet at the river valley as planned."

Without another word, Songmao darted into the night like an arrow, heading into the mountains to find the advisor and General Dao's hiding place.

After the princess's mysterious disappearance, Tichu stayed by the advisor's side, temporarily serving as his personal guard. His heart was filled with worry for the princess, and whenever he thought of Kauko, a nameless anger surged within him. In Tichu's eyes, Kauko seemed like the embodiment of misfortune. He clearly remembered that every time the princess and Kauko were together, disaster followed. He was convinced that the princess's disappearance was intricately linked to Kauko.

As Tichu sank deep into thought, a nimble figure leaped down from a tree in front of the advisor's tent. It was Songmao, his face filled with anxiety.

Seeing Tichu lost in thought, Songmao tried to slip past this gatekeeper into the tent. But to his surprise, Tichu's large foot suddenly blocked his path.

Tichu looked down, his cold gaze piercing Songmao as he demanded, "Don't you know that to see the advisor, you must first get past me?"

Songmao was startled, taking a sharp breath. He quickly forced a smile and said playfully, "Brother Tichu, I saw you were lost in thought and didn't want to disturb you. But I really have urgent news to report to the advisor."

Tichu's eyes were as sharp as an eagle's, his voice tinged with barely concealed resentment. "Then tell me first, what exactly did Kauko do to the princess?"

Hearing this, Songmao finally understood that Tichu's emotions stemmed from his deep affection for the princess and his misunderstanding of Kauko. He took a deep breath and replied honestly, "Brother Tichu, I was just about to report the princess's current situation to the advisor. Would you like to come in with me and hear it for yourself?"

Tichu's curiosity was instantly piqued, and he nodded. They entered the tent together, where the advisor sat behind a simple wooden table, clutching a jade hairpin left by the princess. Seeing Songmao enter, a glimmer of hope flashed in the advisor's eyes. He lightly tapped the table, signaling Songmao to approach, and then asked urgently, "Songmao, tell me quickly, what have you discovered?"

Songmao cleared his dry throat, his tone heavy with unspoken weight. "Master, Kauko sent me to the capital to investigate Princess Wenxi."

"Have you found any clues?"

"Master, the princess met with misfortune on her way back from Annan. The one who spent so many days with us was not the real princess but Fire Rose, a spy sent by Governor Fire."

The advisor's expression instantly turned grave, his stern features as if covered in frost. "This... is this true?"

Songmao nodded, as if bearing a thousand-pound burden. "Just a few days ago, Fire Rose tricked Kauko into giving up his flute and threw it into an abyss. Kauko caught her in time, and on the edge of the cliff, she confessed her identity and crimes."

The advisor slammed his hand on the table in anger, the loud sound venting his inner fury and grief. "This... this explains so many of the previous doubts." He paused briefly and asked, "What about our Princess Wenxi?"

Songmao choked back tears. "Master, Governor Fire herself said that the princess had been turned into a pig-faced person and sent to a dark, sunless concentration camp. There... she has left us."

This news struck the advisor like a bolt from the blue. His arms stiffened as he leaned on the table, as if trying to steady his trembling body. The princess—the jewel and hope of Daze—had met such a tragic end, dying in humiliation. His eyes became vacant and lost, the path ahead seemingly shrouded in endless darkness. After a moment of silence, he spoke slowly, "This matter... must not be leaked to outsiders."

He handed Songmao a small bag of peanuts as a gesture of comfort, saying, "Songmao, don't cry." Then, the advisor slowly retreated into the depths of the tent, allowing sorrow to envelop him.

Tichu said nothing. He left the tent, mounted his warhorse, and galloped toward Sien City.

Songmao could feel that everyone had fallen into a deep pit, each struggling within it. He pocketed the peanuts, dusted himself off, and decided to reunite with the Monkey siblings to search for Kauko. Perhaps only by finding Kauko could they bring a new hope to everyone.

***

In the desolate Butterfly Valley, Songmao and the three Monkey siblings rode tirelessly under the scorching sun, covering over a thousand miles. Among the numerous bodies on the riverbed, they found no trace of Kauko. This seemed like a small comfort, as it meant Kauko might not be among the casualties. But where had he gone? Faced with the dry riverbed and the relentless heat, even the horses were exhausted, losing the will to go on.

Monkey Three dismounted, crouched down, and touched the cracked, drought-stricken earth. He looked up at the cloudless sky, where only the blinding sun and scorching heat remained. He announced helplessly, "We've done all we can by coming this far." Though the others were reluctant to admit it, they knew that persisting further wouldn't change the outcome.

Ahead, there was a large mound of earth, standing out starkly, as if someone had moved a family grave there. Songmao couldn't help but call out, "Let's go there to take shelter from the sun, rest for a bit, and think."

They stumbled forward and knelt in the shade of the mound, as if bowing to it. A gentle breeze brushed past, bringing a hint of coolness.

Songmao's furrowed brow relaxed slightly. He asked, "Have you thought about how we'll tell Kauko about the princess if we really find him?"

Monkey Four fanned himself with his clothes and said, "We'll have to tell him the truth. How can we conjure up a princess out of thin air?"

But Monkey Shang shook her head. "Don't mention that the princess is gone. Let Big Brother Kau keep a sliver of hope in his heart."

As they were sighing, the mound behind them began to shake, clumps of earth falling off. Startled, they jumped back and moved away, only to hear Kauko's voice emerging from the earth, "Quick, help me out. This blanket is so heavy..."

They rushed back in surprise, dug out a hole, grabbed two legs, and pulled out a person covered in dirt. It was indeed the lively Kauko!

Kauko wiped the dirt off his face and kicked the mound, saying, "I was sleeping inside, thinking it was the Dragon King's bed. If you hadn't woken me up, this might have been my grave."

Songmao climbed onto Kauko's shoulder, brushing the sand off his head, and asked, "A huge flood swept away tens of thousands of people. How did you survive?"

Kauko waved his hand. "I almost didn't! When I was first submerged, I somehow turned into a turtle, feeling like I'd become the Dragon King's son-in-law. I was about to follow the water to the sea, but then I heard a shout and snapped out of it."

Everyone asked, "Who shouted at you?"

"The princess! I heard her yell, 'Kauko, take off Fire Maiden's turtle shell! The old demon is sending you to the South Sea to feed the sharks!'"

Whether the princess had truly shouted or Kauko's longing for her had conjured the voice, Kauko believed it, and he had escaped Fire Maiden's sorcery once again.

"The princess..." Songmao was about to mention the heartbreaking news—that the princess had passed away—but at the last moment, he closed his mouth.

Kauko, anxious and relentless, pressed on, "Do you have any trace of the princess?" His sharp eyes scanned everyone present, desperate for any clue. The group exchanged glances, remaining silent, afraid to touch on the sensitive topic.

Finally, Songmao took a deep breath, gently wiped the sweat from his nose, and said, "The last place the princess was seen was near the pig demon concentration camp outside Sien City."

Kauko immediately took off his shirt, shook off the sand, and draped it over his head without pulling it down. Songmao gently comforted him, "Kauko, we're like family. If you're in pain, let it out."

"Why should I cry?" Kauko's tone was firm. He quickly put his clothes back on. "I'm thinking. The news you've brought is crucial to me. Leave the next steps to me." He had made up his mind to face Fire Maiden himself and rescue the princess from the jaws of death. He turned to Songmao and decisively instructed, "Go back and inform the advisor."

Everyone looked at Kauko's resolute expression, knowing it was futile to try to dissuade him. They could only watch as he leaped onto Monkey Four's horse, whipped the reins, and galloped away, disappearing into the dust in the distance.

Chapter 16

The Thirty-First

After days of relentless travel, Tichu finally caught sight of the towering, majestic walls of Sien City, the capital. To avoid drawing attention, he gifted his horse to a farmer in exchange for a carrying basket, disguising himself as a vegetable vendor. He blended into the bustling crowd at the city gate.

Near the gate, a large group of people crowded around a notice posted on the wall, craning their necks to read it. Tichu wanted to push through to see what it was about, but the heavy basket on his back made it difficult. He had to stand on the outskirts, relying on the chatter around him to piece together the situation. People were saying that Princess Wenxi was forming a theater troupe and recruiting male leads. Hearing the princess's name, Tichu's heart stirred, and he couldn't help but shout, "Make way, let me see!" Seeing his urgency, the crowd parted for him. He squeezed through to the notice board and, sure enough, saw Princess Wenxi's name. His heart leapt with joy—this was the perfect opportunity to get close to the princess. He reached out to tear the notice down and take it with him.

"Don't touch the notice!" a Sherkon soldier barked.

"I want to sign up," Tichu declared loudly.

"If you want to sign up, follow me. But I'll warn you, if you're not up to it, leave now before I beat you with a plank," the soldier sneered.

Tichu confidently replied, "I'm willing to try."

He was taken to the theater troupe and handed over to the female manager. She asked him to demonstrate a few theatrical moves and was quite pleased with his performance. She then handed him a spear and asked him to show some basic techniques.

Tichu's skilled display drew a crowd, and everyone praised him. The manager then asked, "Have you ever performed in 'Zhu Bajie Carries His Wife'?"

Hearing this, Tichu laughed so hard his shoulders shook. "Give me a chance to meet the princess, and you'll see if I've done it or not."

The manager retorted, "Don't get ahead of yourself. I haven't decided to use you yet."

Tichu fell silent. He tightened the belt around his waist and muttered, "Scaling walls and leaping rooftops." With a nimble jump, he vaulted onto a pillar as tall as a man. Then, chanting "Dragon soars, tiger leaps," he flipped three times in the air, landing as lightly as a swallow. As he landed, he swept the manager off her feet and lifted her onto his shoulders.

She was so impressed by his dazzling moves that she giggled, tugging at his sleeve. "Put me down, or you'll break my old back!"

Tichu gently set her down and clasped his hands in apology. "I meant no offense. I just wanted to prove my skills."

The manager's tone softened. "You seem quite capable, but can you sing 'Cangshan Sister'?"

Tichu frowned. "Ma'am, are you testing me? That's a song for female roles."

"How is that a test?" she explained. "If the female lead can't sing it, the male lead has to teach her."

Tichu took a deep breath and nodded. "Then I'll try." He closed his eyes, summoning the memory of Bamei singing on his back in the past. Her clear, melodious voice still echoed in his ears. He couldn't help but sing the long-forgotten tune: "On the peak of Cangshan lies my home, my brother carries me back to my mother's house..."

Not far away, Fire Rose was strolling through the garden with Fire Maiden. Suddenly, she heard the familiar, comforting melody and was struck with confusion: Could that be Kauko's voice? Her heart raced, and she hurriedly excused herself from Fire Maiden.

Seeing this, Fire Maiden smiled. "It seems you've finally found your male lead for the troupe."

Fire Rose rushed back to her palace and ordered her servants to find the singer. While waiting, she quickly touched up her makeup and stood behind an ornate screen. If it was Kauko, she wouldn't let him touch her hand; if it was someone else, she wouldn't even bother seeing him.

A maid entered and reported, "Princess, the man has been brought."

"Have him wait inside," Fire Rose said, her heart fluttering with both anxiety and anticipation.

The door opened, and in walked Tichu. As soon as he entered, he eagerly called out, "Princess! Princess!" At that moment, Fire Rose's heart sank.

She was disappointed but then remembered Fire Maiden's advice about emotions and men. Perhaps she should give Tichu a chance.

She slowly stepped out from behind the screen, wearing an inquiring smile. "What brings you to this place of trouble?"

Tichu's eyes were firm as he countered, "Are you Fire Rose or Princess Wenxi?"

Fire Rose realized then that Tichu hadn't come out of admiration for her but to find the missing true princess. A bitter feeling rose in her heart as she understood that she still hadn't made people forget the real princess. Reluctantly, she resorted to her old trick, releasing a faint mist of perfume as she walked past Tichu, replying, "There is no Fire Rose. Only Princess Wenxi stands before you."

"My apologies, Princess. I was wrong to believe the rumors," Tichu said, his eyes filled with remorse as he gazed deeply at the "princess."

A small, mischievous secret was turning in his mind, bringing a playful smile to his lips.

Fire Rose seemed to want to decipher something from his smile. "Why are you so happy?"

"Tell me, if I play Zhu Bajie, will you play his wife?"

"Really? If you're willing to teach me, I'd like to try."

Tichu seemed surprised. "Princess, have you forgotten everything?"

Fire Rose said mysteriously, "Does it matter if I remember? Just tell me, will you teach me or not?"

Tichu nodded enthusiastically, smiling. "Of course! Whatever role you want to play, I'll be by your side!"

A glint of excitement flashed in Fire Rose's eyes. "Then it's settled!" She pointed to a chair nearby, signaling Tichu to sit. She leaned in, staring into his eyes as if trying to find an answer. "Tichu, tell me, did you come here just for me? Or are you a spy for someone else?"

Tichu answered firmly, "No, I came for the princess."

She pressed further, "Do you know I'm currently serving Governor Fire?"

Without hesitation, Tichu replied, "You must have your reasons. I'll always stand by you."

She smiled faintly. "Alright, you can stay as my personal guard. But I need Governor Fire's permission. She knows about your involvement with the resistance."

After settling Tichu, Fire Rose went to see Fire Maiden to report that Tichu had come to join her and asked if he could stay. Fire Maiden said, "This is good news. You've gained a loyal companion, and the rebels have lost a warrior. Two birds with one stone. But he'll have to do something for me first."

"Master, please instruct me."

"Write a letter of amnesty in the princess's name and have Tichu deliver it to General Dao."

Fire Rose, worried about Tichu's safety, made an excuse. "He's rehearsing with me. How can he leave? I'll arrange for someone else to handle this."

"Fine," Fire Maiden said. "I just wanted to test his loyalty. Rehearsals are more important. The Sherkon king arrives soon."

***

During the Golden Valley Festival celebrations, the "princess" joined the people in merrymaking—drumming, dancing, and watching bullfights. On the surface, she seemed full of joy. However, whenever citizens eagerly asked her about driving out the Sherkon, she fell silent, her inner anxiety and turmoil shadowing her every move.

As the festival activities ended, she rode back to the palace with Prince Duan along a tree-lined avenue, Tichu and his guards following closely behind. Even the ragged, frowning citizens smiled and waved when they saw her. These simple interactions warmed her heart but also deepened her guilt, as she knew she was merely a manipulated stand-in.

Ever since Kauko had grabbed her arm, the surge of positive energy had dispelled the dark energy Fire Maiden had planted in her. She felt she had grown a lot, no longer muddle-headed or unable to distinguish right from wrong. She now felt more compassion and care for others.

Suddenly, several women rushed to the center of the avenue, kneeling before her horse and crying, "Princess, save us! Save our daughters!"

Tichu instinctively moved to disperse them, but Fire Rose signaled him to step back. She dismounted and kindly helped the women up, asking them to explain. They tearfully said their daughters had been forcibly taken by the authorities.

Fire Rose turned to Prince Duan, who was still on his horse, and asked, "Prince, do you know about this?"

Prince Duan looked uneasy and repeatedly denied it. "No, I don't."

Fire Rose promised the women she would investigate and told them to go home and wait for news. As she watched them leave in tears, she remounted her horse. Just then, Prince Duan whispered in her ear, "Princess, don't get involved. This was approved by Governor Fire, and I'm in charge of carrying it out. Those thirty women are gifts for the Sherkon king."

Fire Rose asked in confusion, "Why use force?"

Prince Duan replied with a hint of disdain, "Princess, you don't understand. This is how it's always been done. It's easy, and no one can stop it."

"What's the difference between this and banditry? How can I help you build goodwill with the people of Daze?" Fire Rose couldn't contain her indignation and whipped her horse forward. Tichu and the guards chased after the "princess," leaving Prince Duan alone. Prince Duan noticed the hostile glares from passersby and grew anxious, regretting not bringing his own guards. He hurried to catch up with the "princess."

After returning to the palace, Fire Rose sought an audience with Fire

Maiden and immediately asked, "Master, do you know about Prince Duan forcibly taking those women?"

"Fire Rose, women are like property. The strong take them. Besides, these women are lucky. From now on, they'll be the king's women," Fire Maiden explained.

"Master, you and I are also women. How can we not feel compassion for them?" Fire Rose found Fire Maiden's words jarring. The image of her revered master lost its majesty in her heart, leaving only fear.

"This compassion will be your downfall! I've always taught you that as a princess, you should indulge in pleasures, not pity. How could you forget?" Fire Maiden's expression darkened.

Afraid of angering her master, Fire Rose quickly said, "I'll put away my compassion. Master, can I at least go see those women and offer them some comfort?"

"They're locked up in the southern palace. Go and console them, but you can't save them. The Sherkon king loves beautiful women."

***

Fire Rose took Fire Maiden's written order, changed into plain clothes, and looked like an ordinary maid. She hurried to the southern palace and presented the order to the guards.

The guard eyed her suspiciously, finding her somewhat attractive, and asked with ill intent, "Did you steal this order?"

Fire Rose glared sharply. "How dare you! Watch your tongue, or you'll lose your head."

The guard, intimidated by her presence, didn't dare say more and immediately opened the gate, leading her to a gloomy area in the backyard—the palace prison. High stone walls were embedded with sharp iron hooks that glinted coldly in the sunlight.

Pushing open the heavy wooden door, they entered a dim, damp corridor lined with flickering torches that occasionally crackled. On either side were rows of small, cramped cells.

Fire Rose clutched her skirt tightly, taking a deep breath to calm herself.

From the depths of the prison, low sobs pierced the cold walls, carrying helplessness and despair, echoing in Fire Rose's ears. She tiptoed closer, and pairs of eyes behind the iron bars glimmered faintly, filled with unspoken fear and loss.

A trembling voice broke the silence: "Who... is there?"

Fire Rose replied softly, "It's me. I've come to see you." Her voice carried warmth like sunlight.

A young voice pleaded urgently, "I have a child... she's still very young. I don't know how she is. If possible, please tell my family not to worry about me."

Another prisoner added, "My fiancé and I were supposed to marry in two months. Please tell him to wait for me."

Fire Rose listened to their pleas; her heart deeply moved each time. Her throat tightened, and her voice choked with emotion. "I'll do my best."

She visited each small cell, and every woman, unaware of why they had been captured, begged this sudden visitor to send a message of peace to their families.

As Fire Rose turned to leave, one prisoner suddenly asked, "Why are you helping us?"

Fire Rose stopped and whispered, "Because I, too, am a woman."

At the end of the corridor, in a cold dining hall, stood a large wooden barrel filled with murky water. On a nearby wooden table were scattered bowls, chopsticks, food scraps, and moldy buns.

Fire Rose angrily questioned a guard, "Is this what they're eating? Moldy food?"

"Yes, it's to break their spirits," the guard replied coldly.

"Break their spirits?"

"Crush their will to resist until they submit."

Tears welled up in Fire Rose's eyes. The cries from the cells continued to strike her heart, each one like a blade cutting into her soul. Trembling, she left the prison and returned to her palace. Once inside, she collapsed in a corner.

Tichu, seeing that the "princess" hadn't emerged from her room for a long time, knew she was still troubled by the fate of the thirty women. He gently knocked on her door and comforted her from outside, "Princess, you don't need to grieve too much for those women. As lowly commoners, they should have known their fate."

"Tichu!" Fire Rose suddenly opened the door and shouted in his face, "Are you also so cold-hearted, spouting the same words as Governor Fire?"

Tichu lowered his head and replied, "Princess, I'm not cold-hearted. I, too, come from generations of poverty, just like them. The poor can only endure."

Hearing his pitiful explanation, Fire Rose softened her tone. "I'm thinking of how to save them. Give me some ideas."

"Princess, I'm not clever, but I have one idea. It might scare you, though."

"Tell me."

"I thought, if I kill Sherkon King, those women would naturally be set free."

Fire Rose shook her head. "You have such a foolish mind, always coming up with rotten ideas. If Sherkon King dies, Governor Fire will have those women buried with him."

"Princess, it's better if you come up with a plan, and I'll carry it out," Tichu said, his voice tinged with shame.

"There's only one way," Fire Rose said, a cold smile curling at the corners of her lips. "Let's go rehearse the play."

Tichu followed behind Fire Rose as they made their way to the rehearsal hall. He couldn't understand why the "princess" had suddenly lightened up, and it made him uneasy. After a couple of hours of practice, Fire Rose went to see Fire Maiden. When Fire Maiden saw Fire Rose's hurried demeanor, she asked, "Princess, are you still here for those women?"

"Master, this will be the last time I trouble you," Fire Rose said, bowing respectfully as she spoke.

Fire Maiden warned her, "This is truly the last time, or I will be deeply disappointed in you."

"If Sherkon King agrees to let go of those thirty women, can I set them free?" Fire Rose asked.

Fire Maiden looked at Fire Rose, thinking her naive and poorly taught. Old men might risk their lives, but they would never give up beautiful women. She decided to let Fire Rose learn her lesson the hard way. "I agree. If he truly pities them and lets them go, he must tell me himself."

Fire Rose nodded. "Master, give me a moment. I'll be right back." With that, she hurried off.

She went alone to Sherkon King's residence and knocked on the door, requesting an audience.

Sherkon King was frolicking with his dancers when he heard that Princess Wenxi had come to see him. He quickly rose to greet her at the door. Seeing the rare beauty standing before him, he couldn't help but take her delicate hand and lead her to the sitting room. Though he was over seventy, his tall and robust frame still bore traces of his former grandeur, though a slight hunch, sagging shoulders, and a drooping neck had diminished his charm. His face, weathered by years on the high plateau, resembled that of an eagle, with dark, rough skin and long hair that fell to his shoulders, covering half his face. His deep-set eyes gleamed as they fixed on his prey.

He smiled warmly at Fire Rose. "Princess, has Governor Fire sent you to check on me?"

Fire Rose pursed her lips. "I came of my own accord. Is there something wrong with that?"

Sherkon King laughed even more boldly, a hint of mockery in his words. "Princess, do you know that Governor Fire once warned me that of all the women in Daze Kingdom, you are the one I must not touch. It seems she favors you the most."

Fire Rose blinked. "Your Majesty, how many women have you had in your life?"

Sherkon King chuckled. "That's a difficult question to answer."

Fire Rose pressed on. "Then how many more women will it take for you to be satisfied?"

A flicker of contemplation passed through Sherkon King's wandering eyes. "Satisfied? That word doesn't suit me."

Fire Rose smiled faintly. "It sounds like Your Majesty is a natural romantic. How interesting."

The light in his eyes grew more intense as he leaned closer to her ear. "If you're willing, you can return to Sherkon Kingdom with me. I promise to make you the most honored woman there."

Fire Rose gently pushed him away, pretending indifference. "I heard Your Majesty has prepared thirty beauties. I suppose I would be the thirty-first. What fun would that be?"

"No, no, with you alone, I would be content. I need no one else," he said, reaching out to touch her waist.

She pushed his hand away. "If you want me to go with you, you must agree to two conditions. First, have Governor Fire release those thirty women so I can be at ease. Second, give Governor Fire a gift. Only when she is pleased will she let me go."

"That's easy enough. Wait for me, Princess," he said, disappearing into the inner room. Moments later, he returned and said, "Princess, help me up. Let's go see Governor Fire. We can talk intimately on the way."

Fire Maiden was reviewing the progress report on the Heavenly Altar construction when a guard announced that Sherkon King and the princess were at the door. She put away the blueprints and welcomed them in.

Before Sherkon King could speak, Fire Maiden signaled him to remain silent. She slowly walked around him, her nose twitching slightly as if sniffing something.

"Governor Fire, your nose is quite sharp. Have you caught the scent of the treasure on me?" Sherkon King said with a laugh, sitting down on a chair. He pulled out a silk-wrapped object the size of an egg from his chest and handed it to Fire Maiden. "This is for you. Open it and see."

Fire Maiden didn't take it directly but gestured for Fire Rose to receive it. Fire Rose carefully unwrapped the silk, revealing an oval-shaped, translucent purple cat's eye stone. Fire Maiden finally took it and held it up to the light, examining it closely. The mysterious cat's eye within the stone seemed to gaze back at her, as if trying to draw her soul into it. She turned to Sherkon King. "This doesn't seem ordinary. What is its purpose?"

"It is the Tear of the Moon God, connected to mysterious yin energy. I've kept it with me for years. Many women have tried to harm me, but none have succeeded. I think it will be of greater use to you. When you practice your yin arts, keep it close, and it will double your effectiveness."

"Your Majesty has given this to me. What will you do if another woman tries to harm you?" Fire Maiden asked with a smile.

"From now on, I will only have one woman. How could anyone harm me?" Sherkon King said with a grin.

"What do you mean?" Fire Maiden asked curiously.

"Governor, I've given you this treasure as a dowry. Now, I ask you to give me your treasure in return," he said, pulling Fire Rose between them.

"Your Majesty, you wish to marry the princess?" Fire Maiden asked in surprise. But when she saw the calm look in Fire Rose's eyes, it seemed they had already discussed this. She scolded him with a laugh, "Your Majesty, I was just worried that my little princess might play a trick on you, perhaps using some bewitching incense. But it seems your old lecherous nature hasn't changed. You've managed to get your hands on the flower I so carefully cultivated. If it weren't for the cat's eye stone, I would have parted ways with you."

"So, you agree?" he asked, his eyes narrowing with delight.

"Your Majesty, you may leave first. Let me speak with the princess alone before giving you a definite answer."

Fire Rose stopped Sherkon King as he was about to leave. "Your Majesty, what about the other thing you promised me?"

"Ah, yes. Governor, I only want the princess. Quickly send those women you prepared for me back to their homes," he said, then happily left.

Fire Maiden turned her gaze back to Fire Rose and motioned for her to lift her head. "My beautiful princess, you've played a dangerous game. Do you not understand the consequences?"

"I'm not joking. At worst, I'll become a queen for a while," Fire Rose replied calmly.

"He's already halfway in the grave! Can't you learn a bit of your master's pride and choose a worthy man to love properly?" Fire Maiden said, shaking her head in disappointment.

Hearing this, Fire Rose began to sob. "How can I be proud? You're always punishing me. The Sherkon people don't treat me like a princess. To free those captured women, I have to sell myself. What am I?"

"Then let fate decide!" Fire Maiden waved her sleeve and left Fire Rose behind, returning to her Chinmi Garden.

***

Under Fire Rose's urging, Fire Maiden released the women, allowing them to step out of the cold, dark prison and reunite with their families. Soon after, shocking news spread through the palace: the princess would marry Sherkon

King, and the two would embark on a long journey to the snowy highlands.

The news spread like wildfire through the streets of Sien City. People stopped what they were doing to discuss it. How could their princess, a woman as beautiful as a flower, both inside and out, marry the notoriously cold and ruthless Sherkon King?

Tichu came before the "princess," his eyes filled with confusion, seeking confirmation of whether the rumors were true. Fire Rose nodded, confirming the news. Tichu said nothing, his expression heavy as he left. But within a day, he returned, clad in his guard's armor, standing watch by the princess's side. During rehearsals, he and Fire Rose would take to the stage, passionately performing their gripping play.

After one such rehearsal, as the others dispersed and the stage fell silent, Fire Rose picked up a floral mask and put it on, signaling for Tichu to follow. They sat on the cool stone steps at the side of the stage.

Seeing Tichu's furrowed brow, as if he had a thousand words to say but couldn't bring himself to speak, Fire Rose broke the silence. "If I really leave, what will you do?"

Tichu pondered for a moment. "I... haven't thought about it."

Fire Rose said calmly, "I think you can't return to the advisor. It's all my fault. You should leave this place, find a good woman, and settle down."

"There's already someone in my heart, but I don't necessarily need to settle down," he said, not daring to look at the "princess".

A hint of sadness flashed in Fire Rose's eyes. "I envy her!"

"Princess..." Tichu tried to explain, but Fire Rose cut him off.

In a low voice, she said, "I understand what you mean, but you don't understand me." She took a deep breath and decided to reveal her secret. "Tichu, I am someone who lives behind a mask. I am not the princess you know."

Tichu's eyes filled with confusion, thinking she was speaking in riddles. "Why?"

Fire Rose slowly removed her mask, revealing her delicate face. She gently brushed aside the hair on her forehead, showing her smooth skin. "Look, do you see any scars here?"

Tichu examined it closely and shook his head. "No."

"Does Bamei have any?"

"Yes," Tichu replied firmly.

"Bamei's acting skills are impeccable. Could she forget this grand play in such a short time?"

Tichu sighed. "No."

Fire Rose pressed closer. "The princess's parents died because of Fire Maiden. Could she forget her hatred for her enemy and bow to her as a master?"

"She wouldn't," Tichu's voice grew heavier.

Fire Rose lowered her head slightly, then raised it again, her eyes filled with resolve. "Then you should know. I am not the princess in your heart. I am the legendary Fire Rose, Fire Maiden's puppet, controlled and used by her."

Tichu's gaze sharpened like a blade, fixed on Fire Rose. His voice was low and filled with accusation. "Are you the one who harmed the princess?"

Fire Rose's voice trembled with guilt. "Fire Maiden ordered me to find the princess. That day, on the caravan road, I found you. While the princess was briefly alone, I secretly sprinkled rose perfume on her. Fire Maiden used her dark arts to turn her into a pig-faced person."

"What happened after?"

Fire Rose lifted her tear-filled eyes to Tichu. "I never saw the princess again. But rumors say she was imprisoned in that pig demon camp. I also heard she disappeared there, possibly... no longer alive."

Tears welled up in Tichu's eyes, streaming down his rugged cheeks. His voice broke as he said, "Fire Rose, why are you telling me this? You're stabbing me in the heart!"

Fire Rose's eyes were full of remorse, her voice trembling. "I never wanted to hurt anyone, especially the princess. Fire Maiden made me live in a daze. It's only recently that I've begun to understand. I also hope to find a way to atone..."

Tichu interrupted her angrily. "How can you possibly make up for this? The princess and I grew up like siblings. I swore to go through fire and water for her, but I failed to protect her. I couldn't stop her from suffering such a fate!"

Fire Rose hung her head, tears falling. "You and Kauko hate me. I might as well die."

Tichu took a deep breath and shook his head. "No, I won't harm you. Seeing you willing to sacrifice for those women, I know there's still light in your heart. For that, I still see you as the princess."

Under the pale moonlight, Fire Rose's eyes held a trace of sorrow as she whispered, "I can't play the princess much longer. These last few days, let's perform the play well. It will be our final bond."

The night deepened, and Tichu, as usual, escorted Fire Rose back to the palace.

As they walked home, the lights flickered in the windows along the road. His subordinates, seeing him, winked and teased, "Boss, did you and the princess have a little scene tonight?"

"I heard the princess is getting married soon. Does she still have time to play around with you?"

"Once the princess leaves, what will you do?"

These jokes usually made them all laugh, and Tichu would join in. But tonight, each jest felt like a needle piercing his heart. He swallowed his sobs.

When he returned to his room, he didn't turn on the light. He collapsed onto the bed, his heart filled with longing and pain for the princess. He bit down on the corner of the blanket, tears streaming uncontrollably.

Suddenly, the room lit up, but Tichu didn't notice until a familiar voice whispered in his ear, "I never thought a tough guy like you could cry."

He sat up abruptly. Standing before him was Kauko, his familiar mischievous grin making Tichu freeze. "You... are you a ghost?"

Kauko chuckled. "A few days apart, and I've turned into a ghost?"

"Didn't they say you'd become a turtle?"

"Being a turtle isn't fun. I came back."

Tichu frowned. "Then why are you here?"

Kauko's smile faded, and he said seriously, "Like you, I'm here for the princess."

Tichu's voice was heavy with grief. "I just heard the princess is gone."

Kauko gripped his shoulders firmly. "Don't listen to that fake princess. The princess is still alive."

"Then find her and show her to me."

The room fell silent, only the distant chirping of insects and the rustling of wind accompanying their conversation. Kauko broke the silence, repeating, "Believe me, she's still alive."

Tichu looked up, his eyes filled with confusion and pleading. "I want to believe you. I'll help you. But I have one request: don't harm Fire Rose."

Kauko smiled faintly. "Don't worry. My business with her is already settled."

"Then what do you need me to do?" Tichu asked.

"I need to meet Fire Maiden," Kauko said, a glint of cunning in his eyes. He slowly extended his hand and added in a low voice, "As long as I can hold her hand."

Tichu studied Kauko, puzzled by his confidence. "That's it?"

Kauko clenched his fist, his gaze resolute. "Once I hold her hand, she'll have no escape. She'll have to hand over the princess."

Tichu was silent for a moment, his eyes somber. He warned, "You can't defeat Fire Maiden."

Kauko smirked. "I can now summon lightning and fire. One of them will be enough to subdue her."

Tichu shook his head. "Fire Maiden's Heavenly Demon Arts are no joke. We may bicker often, but I don't want to see you walk to your doom. You should practice your father's skills more before facing her."

Kauko pressed on. "Do you think the princess can wait? She's suffering. How can I wait? You might not care, content to fool around with the fake princess."

Tichu knew he couldn't argue with Kauko, so he reluctantly nodded, agreeing to create an opportunity for him.

The plan was this: at the farewell banquet for Sherkon King the following night, after the play ended, the lead actors would present an exquisite floral mask to Fire Maiden and Sherkon King. Tichu's idea was to switch places with Kauko backstage. Once the mask was on, Kauko could approach Fire Maiden unnoticed.

Chapter 17

The Wounded Beast

In the backstage dressing room, the troupe members changed into their costumes one by one, donned their masks, and eagerly awaited the start of the performance. Tichu suddenly remembered Kauko, who was hiding in a corner. He quietly grabbed a set of the male lead's costume and slipped over to Kauko's hiding spot. "Put this on quickly and be ready for my signal," Tichu whispered, handing over the elaborate costume.

Kauko, still his mischievous self, smirked and swiftly tapped Tichu's pressure points. Before Tichu could react, he fell into a deep sleep. Kauko changed into the costume and confidently walked into the dressing room, squeezing in next to the female lead.

He had once asked Tichu who would play the role of the wife, but Tichu had only smiled mysteriously and refused to answer. Kauko stared into the female lead's eyes, trying to discern something. Ah, a woman's eyes could be so beautiful when only they were visible, as beautiful as a princess. But this couldn't be the princess—the princess would never stoop to such a role. Nor was it the fake princess, for the fake princess couldn't perform this play. He tentatively asked her, "Are you nervous?" The female lead seemed lost in her own world, paying him no mind. She was clearly a cold and aloof character.

The play began, and Kauko still had no answers. No matter, there would be chances to carry her, lift her, hold her, and embrace her. He would surely figure it out then. He was eager to find out, fearing he couldn't wait to uncover the true identity of the female lead. What a shame it would be if he didn't.

Once the play started, the female lead's every move, every song, and every dance reminded him so much of Bamei. The way they looked at each other during their embrace was both familiar and strange. The long melody of "Cang Sister" lacked the joy of Bamei's version but carried an extra layer of sorrow.

Gradually, Kauko became immersed in the emotions of the play, temporarily forgetting his quest to uncover the female lead's identity. Their performance won rounds of applause from the audience.

Sitting in the front row, Fire Maiden watched the male lead's performance, her brow furrowed. His acting, his demeanor—it all felt familiar, unsettling her.

She unconsciously reached into her pocket, pulled out the cat's eye stone, and clutched it, trying to calm herself. Suddenly, in the reflection of the stone, she saw a familiar figure—Kauko, the troublemaker who had always been a thorn in her side. Her heart skipped a beat as she realized this little imp was right before her eyes.

She began to scheme, thinking of how to deal with him. According to Golden Mother, she couldn't destroy Kauko, this little sprite, until she mastered the Heavenly Demon Arts. She had no choice but to believe Golden Mother's words—fire hadn't killed him; water hadn't drowned him. So, she decided to toy with him, to leave a scar on his heart.

She called over a guard and gave him a task, then continued to watch the play with Sherkon King by her side.

Tichu, leaning against the corner, had a good nap and was awakened by a burst of applause. He realized Kauko had stolen his role again. But this time, he wasn't angry; instead, he felt a bit grateful, as it had allowed him to sneak away.

After the play ended, the male and female leads returned to the stage. They gently held the glowing opera masks, waiting to present them to Fire Maiden and Sherkon King.

Just as they were about to leave the stage and enter the audience area, one of Fire Maiden's armored guards stormed onto the stage. His eyes were cold as he barked at the leads, "By Governor Fire's order, remove your masks!"

Fire Rose immediately took off her mask, while Kauko hesitated. The guard swiftly reached out and roughly yanked off his mask. In that instant, Fire Rose's eyes widened, as if she wanted to call out Kauko's name, but she quickly realized that doing so would only endanger him. So, she feigned composure, acting as if there was no connection between them.

Kauko, upon seeing that the female lead was Fire Rose, looked surprised. He didn't understand why she was no longer afraid of physical contact with him or how her acting had improved so much. No wonder he kept having illusions of Bamei.

Aside from Fire Maiden, no one in the audience recognized Kauko. They thought the princess had invited some prince to perform with her, so they cheered enthusiastically.

Kauko was thrown off by the sudden turn of events. After a moment of hesitation, he tried to rush toward Fire Maiden. But she stood up calmly, raised her hand, and gave a slight wave.

Dozens of red lanterns, hoisted on bamboo poles, were lifted high by guards, illuminating the stage so brightly that it dazzled Kauko's eyes.

"Everyone," Fire Maiden's voice emerged from beneath her dark hood, "the man next to the princess may look human, but he's actually a monster! How ugly is he? Do you want to see?"

"Yes, yes!" the crowd shouted excitedly.

Fire Rose was dragged away, leaving Kauko alone on the stark white stage.

Fire Maiden's hoarse voice rang out again, "If you want to see, shout 'monster' together, and he'll reveal his true form!"

"Monster! Monster!"

The thunderous humiliation felt like stripping him naked, tearing his flesh apart, and throwing his fragile soul before a pack of wolves. He lost control and revealed his pig-faced form, like a beast from Cang Mountain.

The crowd began throwing shoes and food at him, their jeers like thunderbolts striking him until he was battered and bruised. He covered his head, curled into a ball, trying to hide his face and escape the barrage of light and shadow. He let out a childlike cry for help, "Master! Bamei! Songmao!"

"Get out!" Fire Maiden's shrill voice was especially piercing, startling him into leaping up. He stepped on people's heads to escape the crowd, stole a horse, and fled into the dark night.

Fire Maiden laughed heartily. She hadn't expected that the little secret Fire Rose had inadvertently revealed about Kauko would become his fatal wound.

The audience, thrilled by the spectacle, suddenly heard a scream from the crowd. They turned their attention away from Kauko's escape, wondering what another drama was unfolding.

Sherkon King collapsed onto Fire Maiden, his body sliding down to the ground as something warm splashed onto her skirt. She was about to help him up when she saw a shadowy figure fleeing through the crowd. She wanted to use her weapon but feared harming her esteemed guests. She immediately ordered her guards to give chase.

***

Sunlight filtered through the cracks in the rocks, casting dappled shadows inside the cave. The princess slowly opened her bleary eyes and sat up. On the stone shelf against the wall, earthen jars were neatly arranged. She remembered clearly what each jar contained: rice, flour, and dried vegetables. Her gaze lingered on the stove in the corner, and in her mind, she saw Kauko bustling about there.

A whinny broke her reverie. The horse above seemed to know she was awake, its urgent calls betraying hunger and thirst. The princess took down a bow and quiver from the wall, slung them over her back, grabbed a handful of dried rations from a jar, stuffed them into her pocket, and began eating as she walked lightly up to the temple hall. She saw fragments of Buddha statues scattered on the ground and felt a pang of pity. She picked up the larger pieces and placed them on the altar, whispering, "When my pig-headed brother comes, he'll surely restore you to your former glory."

She led the black horse to the familiar slope by the edge of the woods. The horse happily lowered its head to graze, while the princess sat on the grassy slope, her eyes distant. Her gaze seemed to pierce through time, seeing her past self chasing and playing with Kauko here, their laughter still echoing in her ears. She frowned, a wave of confusion washing over her. Why had they been separated?

The horse's nostrils flared with contentment as it slowly moved toward the stream. Water droplets splashed onto its lips, exciting it. The princess, infected by its joy, happily got up and followed, stepping into the stream. The cool sensation under her feet felt so familiar.

She tossed a bunch of flowers into the water, watching their graceful forms dance along the stream until they disappeared into a forest. The princess grew curious. Why had she never ventured into that forest? She decided to follow the stream and see what she could discover. When she met Kauko again, she could tell him the story of that place. She nimbly mounted the horse, not bothering to hide her pig face, and followed the stream slowly, her mind filled with fragmented memories, drifting like debris in the water.

Before she knew it, she had traveled dozens of miles. A ridge loomed ahead, and the stream had carved a gap through it, forming a waterfall that cascaded into a ravine. The princess let the horse rest by the water while she climbed the slope to see where the waterfall led.

Just then, she heard voices. A small monkey-faced man, carrying a white squirrel on his shoulder, hurried out of the woods and onto a path running parallel to the stream. The monkey-faced man set up a tripwire on the path, while the squirrel climbed a tree ahead. The princess hid behind a tree, waiting to see what they were up to.

Soon, the sound of hoofbeats approached from a distance. As the rider neared the tripwire, the squirrel used a mirror to reflect light into the rider's eyes. The horse tripped, and the rider was thrown several feet. The monkey-faced man pounced on the fallen rider, trying to tie him up, but the rider suddenly reacted, flipping over and pinning the monkey-faced man down. He pulled a dagger from his waist and was about to strike.

At that moment, an arrow shot through the air, accurately hitting the rider's neck. His movements froze, and his body went limp. The monkey-faced man pushed the corpse aside, knelt on the ground, and called out to the woods, "Thank you, hero! May I ask your name so I can repay you in the future?"

The squirrel had already jumped onto the tree where the princess was hiding, curiously examining her. "Hero, you look a lot like a friend of mine," he said.

The princess, intrigued, put away her bow and smiled. "What's your friend's name?"

"Kauko," the squirrel said proudly.

The princess was startled and blurted out, "Then you must be Songmao!"

The squirrel's eyes widened in surprise. "How do you know my name?"

"Because I'm Bamei!" the princess exclaimed excitedly.

Songmao cheered, "Monkey Four, the princess is here! Come quickly!"

Monkey Four rushed over, took the princess's hand, and said excitedly, "Princess, everyone said you were gone, but Kauko always believed you were alive."

The princess looked puzzled. "Why do you call me princess?"

Songmao explained, "Don't you remember? Bamei is the princess. It was Fire Maiden who turned you into this. No matter what, you're still our princess."

The princess touched her face, deep in thought. "Since I got this face, I've forgotten many things. Tell me everything slowly. Where's Kauko? Where is he?"

Monkey Four replied, "Kauko went alone to Sien City to confront Fire Maiden and demand your return."

The princess grew worried. "Even if it's for me, he shouldn't take such risks."

"Don't worry, Princess," Songmao explained. "Kauko is improving every day, and his courage is growing. Fire Maiden can't handle him."

The princess hugged Monkey Four and had Songmao sit on her shoulder. She said happily, "Without you two clever devils, I wouldn't know who I am or when I'd find Kauko. You two were in danger today. Why did you ambush that soldier?"

Songmao answered, "He was Fire Maiden's messenger. He went to the Daze army's camp and surely didn't do anything good. We wanted to capture him and interrogate him, but he died."

The princess said, "Search his body."

They found a letter and handed it to the princess.

The princess opened it and read, "To Governor Fire and Princess Wenxi."

Songmao interjected, "The princess mentioned here can't be you. It must be the fake princess."

The princess continued reading, "My troops, numbering over thirty thousand, have unanimously agreed to submit to the imperial court and immediately cease hostilities with the Sherkon Army. We hope the court can send troops within ten days to join us and collaborate on the grand plan of reviving the nation. General Dao Shan respectfully submits."

Songmao and Monkey Four asked in unison, "General Dao is surrendering? Is he becoming a puppet?"

"That's what it means," the princess replied.

Songmao and Monkey Four anxiously asked her, "Princess, what should we do?"

"Let's go. Follow me, and we'll discuss it on the way back," the princess suggested.

Monkey Four pushed the soldier's body into a deep pit, then mounted the soldier's horse.

Songmao climbed onto the princess's horse and sat in her arms. The elegant black horse led them back to Jingxin Temple.

They sat on the princess's bed and began discussing their next steps. However, faced with a long list of names—"Advisor," "General Lang Kun," "General Dao Shan"—the princess seemed at a loss. These names felt familiar, yet she couldn't connect them to herself. She said dejectedly, "I'm so confused. Just tell me directly how I can help you."

Songmao reminded her, "Princess, you're not just helping. The entire Daze army is yours to command."

The princess's gaze swept over their faces, catching the deep disappointment in their eyes. She smiled faintly, with a hint of self-mockery. "Alright, if I am the princess, what should I do?"

Monkey Four scratched his head. "We should arrest General Dao Shan and quell this rebellion."

The princess asked, "Then, which warrior has the ability to do this?"

Songmao's eyes showed a flicker of uncertainty. "In theory, the entire army would obey your command without hesitation. But now..." His gaze drifted over the princess's face.

The princess nodded slightly. "You mean, as I am now, they wouldn't recognize me, let alone trust me."

Songmao pondered, "There are still a few important figures. Advisor Midd, but he's with General Dao, so he must be under control. Then there's Kauko, but who knows when he'll return. However, there's also General Lang Kun, who is utterly loyal to the princess."

The princess asked eagerly, "Where is General Lang Kun now? If I write him a letter, can it reach him?"

"He's stationed thousands of miles away," Monkey Four said. "But I can send a carrier pigeon."

"Then I'll issue an order in the princess's name!" The princess still didn't believe she was the princess, feeling like an imposter.

Monkey Four and Songmao rummaged through the room, found paper and ink, and prepared everything. The princess wrote, "Urgent! To General Lang Kun: General Dao Shan intends to lead all troops in surrendering to the puppet court. Please use any means necessary to eliminate Dao Shan and his accomplices, rescue our Advisor, and save our tens of thousands of soldiers. Additionally, I have escaped danger and will return to lead the army soon. Sincerely, Princess Wenxi."

After finishing, the princess asked, "How is it? Does it look like something the princess would write?"

They happily said it was exactly what the princess would write! Songmao reminded the princess to add a thumbprint with her right thumb to prove it wasn't a forgery.

***

The shadowy figure who attempted to assassinate Sherkon King was none other than Tichu. He didn't get far before being cornered by over a hundred Sherkon soldiers in a narrow dead-end alley.

With high, unscalable walls on three sides and the only exit blocked by advancing soldiers armed with spears and swords, Tichu found himself trapped. Pressed against the cold, unyielding stone wall, he knew there was no retreat. In a desperate move, he took a deep breath, let out a fierce roar, and charged at the soldiers. Miraculously, he dodged the first fatal strike, wrestled a sword from one of the soldiers, and the first Sherkon soldier fell at his feet. The others, intimidated by his ferocity, hesitated and stepped back, only to be pushed forward again by their governor. Once blood was drawn, Tichu forgot his fear and fought with everything he had. He grabbed another sword, wielding both blades with deadly precision, turning the narrow alley into a brutal battlefield.

After fighting for what felt like hours, Tichu was covered in wounds, his body a bloody mess, and his strength nearly spent. Just as he was about to collapse, an order came from Prince Duan: capture him alive. Soldiers climbed onto the rooftops and cast a net over him, finally subduing him.

He was thrown into a dungeon, his hands and feet shackled in chains. A physician tended to his wounds just enough to ensure he wouldn't die in captivity.

Fire Maiden summoned Fire Rose for questioning. "Were you involved in this? How is it that Tichu and Kauko both appeared by your side and caused trouble at the same time?"

Fire Rose immediately knelt before her. "Master, I had no idea! If I had known, I would have stopped them."

Fire Maiden's expression remained cold and unreadable. "It's best if you weren't involved. Otherwise, I won't go easy on you."

Fire Rose cautiously asked, "What will happen to Tichu?"

"The Sherkon people plan to use him as a sacrifice to their banner," Fire Maiden replied indifferently.

***

General Lang Kun opened the secret letter from the princess and was shocked by its contents. He thought, *How could General Dao Shan be so foolish as to ally with foreign invaders? I also received a letter urging me to surrender, but I never wavered. The princess orders me to eliminate Dao Shan and his faction, but wouldn't that mean our armies would destroy each other? And what would be left to fight the Sherkon Army?* He called his deputy, Bai Cai, to discuss the matter.

Bai Cai read the letter and voiced his suspicions. "Could this letter be a fake? Perhaps it's a trick by the Sherkon people. Besides, if the princess has escaped danger, why hasn't she returned?"

"I share your doubts," General Lang Kun said, deep in thought. He retrieved a letter from the puppet court supposedly written by the "princess" and compared it to a genuine letter from the princess before her disappearance. After examining the three documents side by side, he said, "The handwriting looks the same, but if you look closely at the thumbprint, I can tell which is real!"

The deputy asked, "How? They look the same to me."

"There's a story behind this. When I escorted the princess back, she was riding a horse and cut her thumb on a bamboo leaf. Although it healed, her thumbprint always had a slight unevenness, a mark from the scar." General Lang Kun pointed out that the thumbprint on the recent letter matched the princess's previous one, while the one from the puppet court did not.

After much deliberation, they decided against a direct confrontation between their armies. Instead, General Lang Kun would take twenty guards and go to General Dao Shan's camp.

They set off immediately, riding hard for three days until they reached General Dao Shan's camp. Half a mile away, General Lang Kun took out a double-eagle flag from his waist and ordered his soldiers to raise it high on a pole. This flag, bestowed by the puppet court, signaled their surrender to the regime. From a distance, they could see the same flag flying over General Dao Shan's camp.

When they arrived at the camp's entrance, General Lang Kun coldly addressed the guards. "Tell General Dao Shan to come out and greet me! He's got quite the nerve, making me wait at his gate."

The guards hurried through the camp to General Dao Shan's tent and reported, "General, General Lang Kun has arrived unexpectedly. He's at the gate, waiting for you to welcome him."

General Dao Shan was visibly surprised by the sudden visit. "How many men did he bring?" he asked warily.

"About twenty," the guard replied.

"What was his demeanor like?" General Dao Shan pressed.

The guard recalled the scene. "He seemed displeased that you weren't there to greet him."

General Dao Shan frowned. "Did he seem hostile?"

"No hostility, but I noticed they were flying the same new flag as us."

Hearing this, General Dao Shan relaxed slightly and smiled. "So, the old fox has switched sides too," he muttered to himself. He quickly ordered the guards, "Assemble the honor guards and go welcome General Lang Kun at the gate."

The guards sprang into action, and soon the honor guards were assembled. General Dao Shan stood at the front, his chest puffed out, his expression solemn.

"General, my apologies for not welcoming you sooner!" General Dao Shan clasped General Lang Kun's hand, feigning warmth. "What brings you here unannounced?"

"Forgive the intrusion, but the matter is urgent. Let me in to quench my thirst and fill my stomach first," General Lang Kun replied.

General Dao Shan waved his hand, and drums and music sounded as they entered the camp. Once inside, he pulled General Lang Kun aside and whispered, "Tell me, why are you really here? I can't rest until I know."

General Lang Kun lowered his voice. "I've received intelligence that the princess at court is an imposter. The real princess has escaped and is rallying forces to deal with traitors like us. You know I once had an army of a hundred thousand, but after recent defeats, I'm down to sixty thousand. If the princess attacks us one by one, we're in grave danger. But if we join forces, she might not be able to defeat us."

General Dao Shan's eyes lit up with relief. "I've been worried too. The court's reinforcements are taking too long. Before you arrived, I was afraid you might come to attack me. But seeing you flying the new flag, I feel much better."

General Lang Kun smiled faintly. "The advisor was always watching me, so I had to act loyal. Did you really think I believed we could drive out the Sherkon people? By the way, what have you done with the advisor?"

General Dao Shan tilted his head slightly and whispered, "I've placed him under house arrest, planning to hand him over to the court later."

General Lang Kun said calmly, "I think it's best to convince him to join us."

General Dao Shan shook his head, looking somewhat helpless. "I doubt I can persuade him. Perhaps you can. But before that, let's eat and drink, and then we can discuss the details."

General Lang Kun seized the opportunity. "I think it's better to invite your closest allies to join us. We can talk while we eat."

General Dao Shan's eyes showed a hint of approval. "Good idea!"

Soon, he gathered a dozen of his most trusted men, and a feast was set up in a small courtyard. General Lang Kun was surprised to see Dao Yin, General Dao Shan's deputy, among the group. Dao Yin had always been close to the advisor and was deeply trusted by him. Years ago, the advisor had sent Dao Yin to General Dao Shan's side under the pretext that they were distant relatives.

General Lang Kun spoke passionately, encouraging everyone to drink and dream of promotions and marrying into noble families. At an opportune moment, he stood up, walked over to Dao Yin, patted his shoulder, and whispered, "Where's the restroom? Can you show me the way?"

Dao Yin stood up and led General Lang Kun to the restroom. After making sure no one was around, he whispered urgently, "Old General, why are you taking this path?"

General Lang Kun pretended to be drunk, slurring his words. "Why... why shouldn't I?"

Dao Yin's eyes flashed with disappointment. "Anyone can, but not you. You're the pillar of the advisor and the princess!"

The general raised an eyebrow. "And you? Can you?"

"No," Dao Yin replied without hesitation. "I will never join your ranks! I'm waiting for my chance."

General Lang Kun's lips curled into a sly smile. "Don't you think I'm giving you that chance now?"

Dao Yin stared at the general, his gaze sharp, and suddenly understood. He said gratefully, "Thank you for the guidance, General! I'll go now."

General Lang Kun returned to the table and continued to encourage drinking. He raised his cup and asked, "What will you all do after surrendering? No more battles to fight."

"Take more wives."

"Have more children."

General Lang Kun turned to General Dao Shan and asked casually, "What about you, General Dao?"

General Dao Shan smiled mysteriously. "I haven't decided yet."

General Lang Kun probed further, "Do you want to be king?"

Everyone laughed, as if anything were possible. Just then, a guard announced, "General Lang Kun, a stunning woman has arrived at the camp gate, asking to see you."

General Lang Kun feigned excitement, standing up unsteadily and pointing outside. "Such good fortune! I'll take a look and be right back."

General Dao Shan, believing the act, laughed. "Don't take too long. We'll be waiting."

As soon as General Lang Kun stepped out of the courtyard, Dao Yin quickly pulled him aside and signaled his men to pour oil around the house and set it ablaze. In moments, the courtyard was engulfed in flames. Those who tried to escape were shot down by archers.

Dao Yin successfully took control of the troops. When the soldiers learned the truth, they cheered with joy. Most of them harbored deep hatred for the Sherkon occupiers and their collaborators but had been too afraid to speak out. Now, they finally had a leader to follow.

Chapter 18

The Bewitched Woman

After a brief afternoon nap, the advisor woke up feeling still disheartened. Before even opening his eyes, he called out, "Go, summon General Dao at once! If he still doesn't come to his senses, I'll..." Before he could finish, a familiar, resonant voice sounded by his bedside.

"Advisor!"

Startled, the advisor sat up abruptly and saw Generals Dao Yin and Lang Kun standing side by side at his bedside, their expressions tense, as if they had been waiting for some time.

"Is it really you?" the advisor's voice trembled, his gaze lingering between the two men as if he couldn't believe his eyes.

The two generals had never seen the advisor in such a disheveled and vulnerable state. They immediately knelt down; their voices respectful yet tinged with guilt. "Advisor, we've let you suffer!"

The advisor composed himself and waved for them to rise, a hint of relief finally entering his tone. "This isn't a dream, is it?"

Dao Yin quickly replied, "Absolutely not! Dao Shan and his accomplices have all been dealt with."

The advisor let out a long sigh, his gaze complex as he looked at the two men. His voice carried a mix of emotions. "These past few days, I've wondered countless times if I had misjudged you. Would you betray my trust like Dao Shan did? All my efforts would have been in vain."

Hearing this, Lang Kun responded with a touch of playfulness, "Advisor, has someone been speaking ill of me in your presence? Have you lost faith in me too?"

The advisor chuckled and waved his hand. "No, no, it was just a fleeting thought. Dao Shan truly caught me off guard and nearly destabilized the entire situation. I'm not ashamed to admit it—this time, I truly felt moments of despair. If it weren't for your timely intervention, the consequences would have been unimaginable! I must reward you for your merits..."

However, Lang Kun's smile suddenly faded, and he spoke meaningfully, "Advisor, if we're talking about rewards, the greatest credit doesn't belong to

General Dao or me."

The advisor was slightly taken aback. "Oh? Who do you mean?"

Lang Kun's eyes flashed with respect as he said, "The princess."

"The princess?" The advisor leaned forward, his tone becoming urgent. "Tell me more!"

General Lang Kun took out a letter from his robe and handed it to the advisor. "It was the princess who ordered me to rescue you and quell the rebellion."

After reading the letter, the advisor was filled with emotion. He had always worried that the princess was too fragile to withstand such trials and feared he might never see her again. Now, his confidence was restored, and he couldn't help but say, "The princess has crossed the first major hurdle of her life."

General Lang Kun asked with concern, "Advisor, why do you think the princess hasn't returned to the camp?"

The advisor, of course, had an idea but simply said, "The princess has just escaped. She must be unwell and not fit for a long journey."

Lang Kun then asked, "What about Kauko? Ever since you gave him the nickname 'Chef,' he's disappeared without a trace."

"His path is a longer one. That boy can't sit still; he won't achieve much staying at home," the advisor explained. "Fortunately, he's thick-skinned. I gave him that nickname to stir him up, to let him go out and experience the world, face some hardships, and quickly learn about himself and his enemies. He has many hurdles to overcome, and it won't be easy for him. It all depends on how much time Fire Maiden leaves him."

"I see. I thought he had run away like Tichu," General Lang Kun said, finally understanding.

The advisor spoke firmly, "He was born for this chaotic era. He cannot escape his fate." His sharp gaze fell on the two generals. "The celestial signs have been chaotic these days. You two must stay vigilant."

They nodded repeatedly. Afterward, General Lang Kun left to return to his base, while General Dao Yin was promoted to the Commander of the eastern front.

***

Monkey Four brought news of the princess's whereabouts, and Monkey Three and Monkey Shang were overjoyed, eager to visit her. However, Monkey Four waved his hand and frowned. "Don't go just yet. The princess only remembers being 'Bamei' now. She has no recollection of her past, and her emotions are still unsettled. If you rush to see her, it might only confuse her more."

Monkey Three stroked his chin thoughtfully. "Brother Four, it seems the princess has a psychological issue. I happen to know a powerful sage who might be able to help."

The sage was the accountant at the workshop, usually sitting in a corner flipping through ledgers. His grayish-white hair almost covered his face, making his age hard to discern. But his deep, abyss-like eyes, paired with his flowing white beard, gave the impression that he understood everything about the world.

Monkey Three and Monkey Four sat down beside him. Monkey Three took out a copper coin from his pouch and pushed it toward the sage, whispering, "Brother Four has an important matter to consult you about."

Monkey Four described the princess's condition. "She's neither old nor injured, yet she's forgotten everything recent. What's the reason for this? And is there any hope for her to recover?"

The sage closed his eyes and silently calculated for a moment before speaking slowly. "This woman has suffered a tremendous blow. Her liver and lung souls have been injured and have left her body. Listen, this is a self-preservation mechanism. The trauma was too great, and her emotions became uncontrollable. If she remembered everything too clearly, the pain would crush her. The anger and sorrow would become too much to bear. Thus, her liver and lung souls temporarily left to protect her. What she has forgotten is precisely what she couldn't endure."

Monkey Four asked urgently, "Is there any hope for her to regain her memories?"

The sage slowly opened his eyes and spoke calmly. "There is, but it depends on the environment. If she remains trapped in suffering, forgetting might be a blessing. If the situation improves, we can help her souls return, open her heart, and reconnect her emotions. Then, she may recover. The method is simple: find someone or something she loves, let her come into contact with it naturally, and her heart will open."

After listening, Monkey Four nodded thoughtfully and handed over another copper coin. In his mind, he already pictured Monkey Shang—her past demeanor as a hostess might help trigger the princess's memories. He decided to have Monkey Shang dress up and prepare to take her to see the princess.

Monkey Shang tilted her head, puzzled. "You just said not to disturb the princess. Why are you dragging me to see her now?"

Monkey Four smiled and waved his hand. "You've met the princess before. She'll be happy to see you; it won't cause any trouble."

The two of them rode horses along a mountain path, the pine forests and valleys rushing past on either side, the wind whistling in their ears. After half a day's journey, they arrived at Jingxin Temple.

At that moment, the princess and Songmao were sitting on the grass, basking in the soft sunlight, while a black horse grazed nearby. Suddenly, Songmao jumped up and waved, shouting, "Monkey Four, Monkey Shang!"

The princess turned her gaze and saw the girl beside Monkey Four. Her eyes softened as the familiar face gradually became clearer in her mind. She remembered the girl who had once served guests at Kauko's small shop.

The princess stood up and walked forward, helping Monkey Shang dismount from her horse. She smiled warmly and said, "I remember you, Monkey Shang! I didn't expect you to come all the way to Daze."

Monkey Shang took her hand and replied excitedly, "Princess, ever since you left with Kauko, we closed the shop and followed you here."

The princess's gaze was gentle and affectionate as she examined Monkey Shang. She sighed softly, "Monkey Shang, you've become even more beautiful. As for me... do I still look like a princess?"

"You will always be our princess, no matter how you look!" Monkey Shang exclaimed, wrapping her arms around the princess's waist.

The three of them sat down on the soft grass, bathed in the glow of the setting sun. Laughter and conversation flowed in the breeze, as if even the surrounding grass blades were moved to dance.

The princess smiled as she reminisced, saying softly, "Do you remember when I ordered that bowl of Three Delicacies Noodles at the shop? You were running around, searching for ingredients, and by the time you finished, I had already left. Did it make you and Kauko angry?"

Monkey Shang recalled the scene and couldn't help but laugh. "We weren't angry, just a bit puzzled. Kauko even brought the noodles out himself, wanting to see who had ordered them. When he couldn't find anyone, he looked so disappointed. He asked me what the customer looked like. I said, 'A great beauty.' But he just shook his head and said, 'If she's not eating, then you have it.'"

The princess burst into laughter, her eyes glistening with nostalgic tears. "I didn't want to see him back then, afraid he'd get dragged into this mess. But I couldn't help wanting him to know I'd been there. I thought ordering the Three Delicacies Noodles might give him a hint."

Monkey Shang shook her head with a smile. "He didn't figure it out. But maybe he knew deep down and just didn't mention it to me."

As soon as Monkey Shang finished speaking, the princess raised an eyebrow and declared, "That fool definitely didn't guess."

Songmao, who had been listening, chimed in, "Princess, when was the last time you saw Kauko?"

The princess's expression darkened slightly. "It was in the caravan. That morning, I spoke a few words with him. Little did I know that from that day on, my life would completely change, and I'd never see him again."

Seeing the princess's memories gradually returning, Monkey Four clapped his hands excitedly. "Princess, you're remembering! Look, you've recalled almost everything!"

The princess was momentarily stunned, as if something was slowly surfacing in her mind. She spoke slowly, "It's true... so many images are coming back: the advisor, General Lang Kun, Tichu, Fire Maiden... and the battles on the eastern and western fronts..." She suddenly looked up and asked, "How is the situation on the eastern front?"

Monkey Four took out a letter from his robe and handed it to her with a smile. "Good news! General Lang Kun just sent this."

The princess read the letter and clenched it tightly, her eyes shining. "Everyone has done so well! I can't stay idle any longer. I must see the advisor as soon as possible. But in my current state, how can I return to him?"

The group exchanged smiles, each knowing in their hearts—their princess had truly returned. Songmao comforted her softly, "The advisor already knows about your condition, Princess. He's kept it secret for you. He won't be surprised when he sees you."

Hearing that the princess was preparing to depart, Monkey Four quickly said, "Princess, there's one more urgent matter. The Sherkon people have rebuilt a massive granary at Three Dams, storing all the grain they've plundered. If we can destroy the granary, the Sherkon army will run out of supplies, and our Daze resistance forces will have a chance to retake Three Dams."

The princess's eyes sparkled with excitement. "Oh? Tell me more."

Monkey Four immediately reported, "My monkey troops have burned down many granaries across Daze, but this one is untouchable. I've sent several groups of brothers, but they've all been blocked. They've set up sentry posts a mile away, and the paths leading to the granary are coated with oil—black, sticky, and slippery."

The princess narrowed her eyes, deep in thought. "That's tar. It ignites upon contact with fire. They're clearly targeting your monkey troops, trying to seal off all entrances."

Monkey Four nodded with a bitter smile. "When we encounter tar, we monkeys have no choice but to retreat."

Suddenly, the princess had an idea. Remembering that the Monkey family made mirrors, she asked Monkey Four, "Have you ever used mirrors to reflect sunlight and start a fire?"

Monkey Four nodded. "Yes, it's faster than using flint. Are you thinking of using a mirror to ignite the granary?"

The princess's eyes gleamed as she explained, "In ancient times, there were methods of using large mirrors to focus sunlight and ignite enemy camps from a distance. We don't need one that big—just enough to focus light from two miles away."

"Will one large mirror be enough?" Monkey Four asked, slightly doubtful.

"One will suffice," the princess nodded.

Monkey Four smiled. "Don't worry, Princess. This isn't difficult. Monkey Three is an expert. I'll discuss it with him. But the mirror will be quite large, and it'll take a few days to make the mold and polish it."

The princess nodded in satisfaction. "Good. The operation to burn the granary is in your hands. I'll set off for the eastern front tomorrow to meet the advisor."

Monkey Four and Monkey Shang exchanged glances, then took their leave and headed into the mountains while there was still daylight. That evening, the princess asked Songmao about Kauko's recent activities, listening with great interest. When Songmao mentioned that Kauko had become a renowned "Chef", she couldn't help but laugh, her eyes curving with amusement. Just as they were engrossed in conversation, a clear horse neigh broke the silence.

Songmao agilely climbed up a crevice in the rocks and, under the moonlight, saw a shadowy figure dismount and sneak toward the princess's stable. He glanced back and whispered to the princess, "A horse thief has come. I'll deal with him."

Songmao climbed up the crevice and quietly circled behind the figure. Spotting some pine cones on the ground, he suddenly shouted, "Horse thief, take this!" Before the words had fully left his mouth, he kicked the pine cones like a rapid-fire volley toward the shadow. The pine cones thudded against the figure, but the shadow remained motionless, allowing the cones to hit him. Then, the figure looked up and choked out, "Songmao..." The voice, filled with familiar pain, instantly froze Songmao in place.

Songmao paused, recognizing Kauko. His heart tightened, and he quickly jumped up before him. Kauko slowly sat down, leaning against a wooden post, his shoulders trembling slightly. Seeing the tear stains and swollen eyes on his face, Songmao immediately understood and asked softly, "Did that old witch bully you again?"

Kauko looked up, his voice hoarse with resentment and pain. "Songmao, I called for you, I looked for you... but where were you..."

Songmao's expression darkened, and he couldn't help but apologize. "I'm sorry, Kauko. I was careless."

Just as he bowed his head in guilt, a gentle figure emerged from the moonlight. It was the princess. She looked at Kauko, weathered and worn, her eyes filled with tenderness. She sat down quietly beside him and called softly, "Kauko."

Kauko froze, then slowly turned his head. His eyes met the princess's in the night, and he stared at her as if unable to believe it was real. He reached out a trembling hand and gently touched her piglike face, whispering, "You... are you really the princess?"

The princess nodded slightly; her eyes soft as water.

Tear stains still fresh on his face, Kauko broke into a relieved smile and said joyfully, "Could it be... that my dream has come true?"

The princess gently patted his hand. "You're so happy."

Songmao felt his presence was no longer needed and said, "You two talk. I'll spend the night in the forest." With that, he lightly patted Kauko's shoulder and disappeared into the woods.

The princess held Kauko's hand as the two of them walked slowly toward the cavern. Under the dim glow of an oil lamp, Kauko could no longer dwell on his grievances; he simply gazed at the princess, entranced. The princess did not shy away, allowing him to examine her face, which had been cursed into a "pig's snout," with calm acceptance.

"Princess, your appearance is quite similar to what I imagined," Kauko couldn't help but laugh, his voice tinged with playful delight.

The princess raised an eyebrow, feigning reproach. "There are rumors that it was Fire Maiden who transformed me like this. Now I wonder if it was you who played a trick on me?"

Kauko leaned his head gently toward her and blinked. "Though I didn't cast the curse, seeing you look like me... I can't help but feel a bit proud. Who says we don't look good together?" With that, he pulled out a small mirror from his waist, a gift from Monkey Three, and handed it to the princess. "If you don't believe me, take a look. I mean it."

The princess glanced at the mirror, pursed her lips, and pushed it away. Seeing her reluctance, Kauko quickly explained that it was a gift he had prepared for her long ago but never had the chance to give. Hearing this, she finally accepted it, though she didn't examine it closely, simply tucking it into her pocket.

"If you really like this appearance, you might have to look at it for the rest of your life," the princess said with a hint of self-mockery, sighing.

"What kind of sorcery could transform someone like this?" Kauko frowned as he asked.

The princess replied softly, "Fire Maiden has taken in a monster called Wulong. He never shows himself, only manipulating curses through eerie voices. At her command, thousands have been transformed to look like you. I don't know why she favors your face so much... Your Uncle Kau told me that this curse cannot be broken unless Wulong is killed."

Hearing this, Kauko's expression darkened, his hands tightening slightly. He spoke with determination, "Princess, don't worry. I will find that Wulong and make sure he disappears forever!" Then, curiosity sparked in his eyes. "By the way, you mentioned you've met my uncle? How did that happen?"

The princess's eyes flickered in the lamplight, carrying a trace of lingering sorrow. Her voice was soft but trembled with emotion. "In the pig demon's concentration camp..." She began to recount the painful memories in fragments. Kauko held her hand tightly, as if his grip could erase all her nightmares. The princess took a deep breath, steadying herself, and asked gently, "What did Fire Maiden do to you?"

Kauko lowered his head, his expression revealing a hidden pain. His voice was hoarse, each word seeming to carry a wound. "She mocked me in front of everyone, calling me 'ugly.' At that moment, it felt like my heart had been pierced by a blade..."

The princess reached out gently, caressing his face. "Kauko, do you remember? I told you that you are the one and only immortal in this world."

He closed his eyes, as if committing her words to memory, and whispered, "But back then, you weren't there. I... I was truly lost."

The princess smiled softly, her gaze warm yet resolute, and squeezed his hand. "Even when I'm not by your side, my heart is always with you."

Kauko took a deep breath, a look of determination crossing his face. "Next time she comes, I'll tell her, 'Old witch, I have the princess in my heart. I'm not afraid of you!'"

The princess laughed, her eyes filled with both relief and a trace of worry. "But what if the fake princess comes to disturb you again, leading you astray? Would you still be at a loss?"

Kauko grinned, pretending to be helpless. "Then what should I do?"

The princess blinked, her eyes sparkling with mischief. "I'll teach you a trick. Remember it well! If Fire Maiden attacks your weakness, you can counterattack hers."

Kauko's eyes lit up with a sly smile. "Good idea. If she dares to mock me again, I'll threaten her, 'Say one more word, and I'll rip off your mask!'"

The princess couldn't help but laugh, her voice ringing like a bell in the night. "That would surely scare her out of her wits!"

The two shared a smile, their eyes reflecting each other's joy. In that moment, their laughter held not only rare happiness but also shared courage, as if they no longer feared any storm.

The princess stopped laughing and asked, "I heard your martial arts have improved greatly, and you've earned a formidable reputation?"

Kauko's eyes brightened with pride, his eyebrows lifting slightly. "That's right. Now I can control natural elements like water, fire, wind, and lightning. I've also mastered techniques like the Golden Cicada Shedding its Shell and using an opponent's strength against them, turning the tangible into the intangible. When I was young, Master Dapeng taught me these, but I was too impatient to grasp them. Thanks to the advisor's guidance, I've finally understood. It's just a pity my headaches haven't gone away, or else—" He paused, then smiled. "I might have caught up to my father."

The princess listened with admiration, her eyes filled with wonder. "You've learned so much! Tell me, how does 'turning the tangible into the intangible' work?"

Kauko narrowed his eyes, a hint of pride in his voice. "For example, if you punch me, taking the hit directly would hurt like hell. But if I subtly redirect your force, making it land nowhere, then the punch won't have any effect."

The princess nodded in understanding, smiling. "No wonder you dare to provoke Fire Maiden now." She reached out and took his pulse, feeling it carefully. "Your pulse is much calmer than before. So... can you fly now?"

Kauko chuckled wryly and shook his head. "Fly? Just thinking about it makes my headaches worse."

Their conversation flowed naturally, occasionally touching on painful memories, and a few tears were shed. Kauko, exhausted from days of travel, gradually leaned against the princess and began to doze off. The princess watched his half-closed eyes and quietly helped him to the bed, carefully tucking him in. She tidied up the room, then bent down to gaze at his peaceful sleeping face. Her face drew close, as if she wanted to kiss him gently, but in the end, she only tenderly brushed his hair.

She walked softly to the oil lamp and sat down. Her fingers unconsciously touched her own face, and she couldn't help but take out the small mirror Kauko had given her. Staring at the "pig's snout" in the reflection, she sighed, her eyes dimming. This unfamiliar face had brought her countless humiliations and helplessness. A faint pain stirred in her heart, wondering when and who could break this merciless curse for her.

In truth, Kauko had woken up when the princess moved him, but he kept his eyes closed, pretending to sleep, savoring her tenderness. He quietly opened his eyes and saw the princess repeatedly touching her face, silently shedding tears as she looked into the mirror. Kauko's heart ached. The princess, who always wore a smile, seemed to hide so much sorrow and loneliness beneath it. Her vulnerability, masked by her strength, pierced his heart.

He waited until the princess had fallen asleep before getting up and heading to the temple. Noticing the fragments of the Buddha statue neatly arranged on the altar, he guessed it was the princess's doing. Seeing the moon sinking in the west and realizing dawn was still two hours away, he found a clay pot, fetched half a pot of mud from the stream, and repaired the Buddha statue. He then knelt and kowtowed, asking for the Buddha's protection over the princess.

As he stood to leave, he heard the Buddha's voice in his ear: "Patron, wait. Beneath the lotus seat behind me, there is something you will love."

Kauko walked around to the back and reached out, finding a copper flute. He asked the Buddha, "I gave this to you. Why are you returning it to me?"

"This flute is not the same as the one you gave."

"Could it be..." Kauko pressed the flute to his face, feeling its warmth against his lips. "My own flute! How did it end up here?" he asked joyfully.

"It was left by a nameless wild magpie."

"Where is the bird?"

"The Heavenly Mountain has crumbled, and fate has run its course. He has returned to the west," the Buddha intoned.

It turned out that Master Dapeng, unable to let go of Kauko, had used the last breath of his life to transform into a wild magpie, watching over Kauko until the Heavenly Mountain's energy was exhausted and turned into a vast sea.

***

The Sherkon soldiers carried out a indiscriminate massacre across Daze. The land was stained with blood, and new graves were scattered across the fields. The wind carried a pungent stench, attracting wild dogs that roamed hungrily, sniffing the scent of blood as they prowled through abandoned villages and alleys. Prince Duan had inherited the throne of Sherkon King and was preparing to escort the coffin back to their homeland. But the flag covering the coffin required the blood of Tichu.

Fire Rose's heart was torn with grief, but she was powerless to change Tichu's fate. Summoning her courage, she went to the prison to bid him farewell. However, the Sherkon soldiers coldly blocked her. "Prince Duan has ordered that no one is allowed to visit the condemned," they said.

Fire Rose's eyes turned cold, and she secretly used a sedative to slip past the grim prison gates. The cold, damp stone walls of the narrow corridor felt like an endless abyss, the flickering torchlight casting eerie shadows that seemed like silent curses. She walked step by step, her heart pounding like a drum, until she finally saw the familiar yet desolate figure—Tichu. Once tall and strong as a mountain, he was now hunched in a corner, shackled and exhausted. The sight broke her heart. Yet, when he saw her approach, he struggled to his feet, dragging the chains on his feet, and moved to the iron bars. His eyes, filled with tenderness, gazed at her.

Fire Rose stepped forward, her fingers gently touching his scarred face. Tears rolled down her cheeks, dripping from her fingertips. She knew every wound on his body was for her sake—and she was nothing but a fake princess. Her eyes stung as she whispered, "Why were you so reckless? I agreed to marry him as a ruse. I had my own plans. But you threw your life away."

Tichu smiled weakly, but his eyes shone with unwavering determination. "I don't regret it, Princess. I would give everything to protect you." He paused, his gaze drifting to the distant past, a soft smile on his lips. "Do you remember when Bamei was seven, and the troupe leader wanted to sell her? I was just a child, but I caught a venomous snake and put it in his shoe, hoping it would do the job for me."

Fire Rose's tears flowed even more fiercely. She gripped his hand tightly, her other hand gently touching the cold chains. Her eyes were filled with pain and guilt. "You've always protected me, but... I can't save you." Her voice was low, carrying an endless despair, like a wisp of a ghost trembling in the air.

She kissed his hand lightly, her eyes deeply imprinting his face. Biting back her tears, she stepped away, each step feeling like her heart was being torn apart. The last image in her eyes was of him standing silently in the darkness, lonely yet smiling.

***

Kauko quietly left the princess, a flame of determination burning in his heart. He was heading to the capital, his target clear: Wulong. He couldn't bear to see the princess suffer another day of humiliation. He arrived at Phoenix Village, where the princess had mentioned, hoping to find his Uncle Kau at the village market. But strangely, the villagers were all heading out of the village, their expressions grave. He stopped an old man and asked what was happening.

The old man sighed. "Today, in Sien City, the Sherkon people are going to execute a hero from Daze. We're going to see him off."

"What kind of hero?" Kauko asked urgently.

The old man's eyes shone with reverence. "He killed Sherkon King for us! Now, the Sherkon people are using him as a sacrifice."

Kauko's heart stirred with respect. "Does this hero have a name?" The old man shook his head.

Kauko made up his mind. Such a hero couldn't be left to die. He was sure the princess wouldn't mind waiting one more day. He mounted his horse and galloped toward Sien City.

Outside Sien City, a grim execution platform had been erected. On the high platform, black, yellow, and white cloth strips fluttered in the wind, surrounded by Sherkon soldiers armed with axes. A corner was tightly sealed with black cloth, likely the cage holding the hero. Below the platform, Sherkon soldiers formed a tight perimeter, and black eagle flags fluttered on the city walls, their flapping sounding like the laughter of death. People from all around had gathered, pushing to the front to catch a glimpse of the hero's face, to remember him and tell his story to future generations. Many brought paper money, ready to send him off in his final moments, hoping he would walk the path to the afterlife with peace and without the harassment of evil spirits.

On his way, Kauko encountered an old monk in yellow robes. Seizing the opportunity, he borrowed the monk's attire, wrapping prayer beads around his wrist and holding a staff. He tied his horse to a distant poplar tree and entered the execution ground in the guise of a monk, his head bowed and hands clasped, softly chanting, "May the Buddha have mercy." The crowd, seeing a monk approach, respectfully made way for him, allowing him to slowly approach the platform.

Just as Kauko was about to step onto the platform, the Sherkon soldiers coldly blocked him, the glint of their spears flashing with a deadly chill.

"Go and report to your superior," Kauko said calmly to the soldier in charge. "This monk is here by order of Governor Fire to perform rites for the deceased."

The soldier frowned slightly, his eyes showing a hint of disbelief. "Governor Fire did not issue such an order. Step aside now. We Sherkon people do not believe in such superstitions."

Kauko raised his hand, seemingly accidentally brushing the soldier's arm. In that instant, a cold, eerie chill seeped through the soldier's skin into his bones, making him shiver uncontrollably. A cold wind seemed to pierce his heart. Kauko spoke in a low, deliberate tone, "Today, the celestial signs are ominous. The sun is obscured, and a cold wind blows. This man is no ordinary person," he pointed to the black-shrouded iron cage on the platform, his voice dropping even lower. "He is a reincarnated demon, a harbinger of doom. The spirits are already tugging at your arm... Look, beneath the king's flag on the city wall, dark flames flicker..."

The soldier's face turned pale, his mind in turmoil. He quickly waved his hand. "Enough, enough! Go up and perform the rites quickly, lest his vengeful spirit causes trouble. You have the time it takes to smoke a pipe!"

Kauko nodded and stepped past the soldiers onto the platform. He slipped under the black cloth and saw Tichu trapped in the iron cage, his clothes torn, his face haggard, but his jaw clenched tightly, his eyes filled with unyielding determination. Kauko whispered to him, "I'm here to get you out."

Tichu's eyes widened in surprise, but then he smiled faintly. "It's really you! But I'm badly injured. I can't go far."

Kauko placed a hand on Tichu's back, channeling a surge of energy into his meridians. He whispered, "Stay calm. I'll take your place. When they take me to be executed, you slip away in the chaos. There's a horse tied to a poplar tree not far from here. Ride southeast to find the princess. She's returned to the camp. As for me... after today, the princess won't have to worry about this calamity anymore."

Tichu was stunned, his eyes filled with complex emotions as he looked at Kauko. He rasped, "You... you should go! I'd rather die here than have you die in my place. If you're gone, the princess will hate me forever."

Kauko smiled and patted his shoulder reassuringly. "The princess sent me to save you. She said she'd only feel at ease if you returned."

A glimmer of hope appeared in Tichu's eyes, and he finally nodded. "Since the princess ordered it, I can't give up lightly."

Kauko smiled faintly. "I won't let myself die in vain either." With that, he used a secret technique to quickly switch places with Tichu. He then took a handful of yellow soil from his sleeve and smeared it on his face, disguising his handsome features with a dull, earthy appearance. He locked the cage door firmly and sat in the corner, assuming Tichu's posture, waiting for the soldiers to arrive.

The deep, resonant sound of drums seemed to rise from the ground, shaking the air and tightening the hearts of the crowd below. As the horns blared, several burly men quickly ascended the platform, tearing down the black cloth and shoving the "monk" aside. They opened the iron cage and dragged out the prisoner, forcing him to the front of the platform. Tichu took advantage of the chaos to slip down from the side, silently weaving through the crowd. He found Kauko's horse, mounted it, and swiftly disappeared into the distance.

Kauko was held by the burly men, facing the execution tools, but he stubbornly refused to kneel. The men grew angry and struck his knees with a rod, but Kauko shouted, "It tickles!" and jumped up, still refusing to kneel. The soldier in charge, furious, signaled to the city wall and soon received a response: "Cut off his legs!"

The executioners no longer held back. The axeman swung his blade at Kauko's legs, but the blade clanged as if striking iron, reverberating loudly. Kauko scratched his legs exaggeratedly and shouted, "It tickles! It really tickles!" The executioners' faces changed, and they surrounded him, hacking at him with their blades, but not a single wound appeared on his body.

Kauko calculated that Tichu must have gotten far enough by now. Unable to contain his anger any longer, he shouted, "You're breaking the rules! A prisoner can only be executed once. You've hacked at me a hundred times, and you still won't stop?" The crowd, initially shocked, began to cheer and grow angry, chanting, "Let him go! Let him go!"

At that moment, a flag waved from the city wall, and a thousand arrows whistled toward the crowd. Kauko suddenly broke free of his chains, leaped off the platform, and waved his hand. A fierce gale swept up, hurling arrows, the execution platform, and soldiers into the sky. This move, taught by Master Dapeng, was one he had recently mastered. Now, testing it for the first time, its power was undeniable.

Just as he was about to turn and chase after Tichu, a sharp female voice rang out from the city wall. "Ugly freak, you think you can escape so easily?" He turned and saw Fire Maiden standing on the city wall, dressed in black, her face filled with mockery as she looked down at him.

"Who are you calling ugly?" Kauko shouted back, not backing down.

"You, ugly freak!" Fire Maiden sneered, expecting the crowd to join in her ridicule. However, the surroundings fell silent, and no one echoed her words.

Kauko laughed heartily and boldly exposed his pig-like face to the crowd. "I am the son of the Rake King, born this way. Whether I'm ugly or not, I know it myself. It's not for you to judge! But you, Fire Witch, dare you remove your mask and let the people of Daze see your true face?"

The crowd joined in, chanting, "Dare you? Dare you?"

Fire Maiden covered her mask with her hand, turned away, her eyes flickering with fear.

Kauko laughed even more heartily, deliberately spinning around on the platform, flipping several somersaults, and enjoying the crowd's cheers.

Fire Maiden, thoroughly enraged, snorted disdainfully and hurled a massive fireball at Kauko's head. Unprepared, Kauko was engulfed by the fireball and sent tumbling into the sky, disappearing into the clouds.

The courage that had just ignited in the crowd was instantly extinguished, like eggplants frostbitten. Everyone fell silent, not daring to make another move.

Chapter 19

Smell as Water

Songmao had spent the night resting on a thousand-year-old tree, comfortably lying on a bed woven from branches, his heart filled with joy at the reunion of the princess and Kauko. He took out a precious pill he had been saving, holding it between his fingers. It emitted a faint, colorful glow, like a star fallen from the sky into his hand, releasing a delicate fragrance that wafted through the leaves. Master Dapeng had gifted this masterpiece of his life's work to Songmao, but Songmao had never met his destined love. Perhaps this was fate's arrangement. Songmao knew that now, someone needed this pill more than he did.

"This treasure is truly magical!" Songmao heard a delicate voice and looked around, but saw no one. He only caught a whiff of a captivating, feminine fragrance.

"Look up, I'm here!" Songmao raised his head and saw a beautiful little squirrel girl hanging upside down from a branch, smiling at him.

"Why are you hanging there?" Songmao asked, gazing at the friendly little girl.

"I couldn't find a nest tonight. Can I squeeze in with you?" she asked.

"Then come down," Songmao said, putting away the pill and making room for her.

The little girl sat down beside him, leaning close. "Can I see your treasure again?"

Songmao hesitated. Her beautiful eyes seemed only interested in the treasure, but he found it hard to refuse her request. He said mysteriously, "That's the Lover's Pill. It's only for the eyes of a destined lover."

"Why not let me see it? Maybe I'm the one you've been waiting for," she said, her bright eyes shining in the darkness, filled with anticipation.

Songmao obediently took the pill from his ear and handed it to her. She held it in her palm, examining it closely, then complained, "Why doesn't it look as beautiful as before?"

Songmao said, "The closer your heart is to mine, the brighter it will glow. It seems your heart is still far from me."

"Then let me hold it while I sleep. Maybe our hearts will come together. Is that okay?"

"Alright, I'll let you try," Songmao said, turning over to sleep, testing the beautiful little girl.

The next morning, Songmao woke up to find the little girl gone. He thought it was a dream, but when he reached into his ear, he realized one of the pills was missing—though it was a fake one. He always kept a fake pill for emergencies.

What a pity. Such a charming little girl, a rare beauty, but her heart was as cold as ice, only interested in material things. He touched the spot where she had slept—it was already cold. A small tuft of her orange tail fur hung from the branch, with dewdrops clinging to it, glistening like tiny pearls in the morning light.

Songmao nimbly jumped down from the tree and scanned the stables. He immediately noticed that Kauko's horse was missing. His heart tightened, and he quickly crouched down, slipping into the crevice and descending into the cavern. The cavern was silent, with only the princess curled up on the bed, sleeping soundly. Songmao gently touched Kauko's bed—it was cold, clearly long abandoned. He shook the princess's shoulder. The princess rubbed her sleepy eyes and looked at him with a hint of confusion.

"Where's Kauko? Where did he go?" Songmao asked in a low voice, his eyes filled with concern.

"I don't know," the princess said after a moment's thought. "He probably went to Sien City again!"

Songmao's face was full of unease. "What about me? What if he calls for me?"

The princess smiled and gently patted his shoulder. "Songmao, let him go on his own. Don't you think he's grown up? He's learning to take responsibility for himself and others. Come, let's go to the advisor—he's waiting for us."

Before setting off, the princess straightened her grass-flower skirt and carefully wrapped her long, gray-brown scarf around her head, trying to cover her large ears, upturned nose, and mouth. But her ears were stubborn, still poking out from the cloth. Songmao, feeling sorry for her, jumped onto her shoulder and said, "Princess, let your mouth show. I'll give you a peanut for good luck."

The princess smiled. "Alright, Songmao, you always take such good care of me." She pulled the cloth aside and opened her mouth, waiting. A sweet little thing fell into her mouth and slid straight down her throat. "Thank you, Songmao," the princess said, continuing to wrap her head until only her eyes were visible. She then draped a black veil over her head.

The princess mounted her horse, and Songmao jumped into her arms, sitting in front. After riding for a while, Songmao reminded her, "We should rest for a bit."

The princess patted his head. "We just set out."

"I need to go into the woods for a moment," Songmao said, blinking.

The princess had to stop the horse. He jumped down but didn't hurry into the woods. Instead, he said to the princess, "Princess, you're sweating on your face. Why not loosen the scarf and get some air?"

The princess replied, "It's not easy to wrap it up. I'll wait a bit." Songmao had no choice but to jump back onto the horse without going into the woods. The princess was curious. "You forgot to go into the woods!"

"I'm not in a hurry anymore," he said, brushing her off.

After traveling a hundred miles, Songmao pointed to a small stream by the roadside and said he was thirsty, very thirsty. Why not stop and drink some cool stream water and rest for a while? The princess also felt her mouth dry and agreed.

They crouched by the stream, and the princess untied the scarf, unwrapping it layer by layer. Songmao held his breath, quietly waiting for a miracle.

The princess stared at her reflection in the water, which wavered like her current mood. She wanted to look but couldn't bear to. If only she could see her original self, how sweet that would be. Suddenly, she felt that the wavering outline in the water looked familiar. One hand holding the scarf loosened, and she slowly reached out to touch her cheek, then her ears, nose, and mouth. She cried out, "Songmao, do you see it? Is it real?"

Songmao replied triumphantly, "Princess, it's real!" He regretted not giving it to her sooner, all for Kauko, wanting him to see the princess looking just like him.

The princess pulled off the scarf and threw it into the water, where it seemed reluctant to leave, clinging to the water plants. She sat on a nearby rock, took out the small mirror Kauko had given her, and looked at herself over and over, left and right, examining every part. She pursed her lips and smiled, then called out, "Songmao, come here. I need to make sure this is real."

Songmao's little head pressed against the princess's beautiful face, and both inside and outside the mirror, everything was real. Seeing his sly smile, the princess asked, "Little clever one, was this your doing?"

Songmao said proudly, "Yes and no. The peanut you ate was actually a pill, crafted by Master Dapeng. He meant to give it to his beloved but never did, so he gave it to me. What would I do with it? It's magical—not only did it make you beautiful, but it also keeps you forever young."

"Ha, whoever marries me will have a hard time," the princess laughed. "He'll grow old, and I'll still look like I'm seventeen or eighteen. People will point at him and say, 'Are you her grandfather?'"

Songmao wagged his tail and laughed. "That's not necessarily true. It depends on who you marry!"

"How so?" the princess asked, her eyes wide.

"Kauko also got one. Not only is he strong in martial arts, but he'll also stay forever young. You can ask him if you don't believe me."

***

Fire Maiden had temporarily driven Kauko out of sight, but she knew deep down that he would return soon, more brazen than ever. His humiliation stung like needles, unbearable like the heat of a volcano. Fire Maiden clenched her fists, a flash of ruthlessness in her eyes—she had to intensify her cultivation of the Heavenly Demon Technique, forcing all gods and demons to bow before her, or else she would reduce them to ashes.

She arrived at the pig demon camp, originally intending to question Wulong about the progress of the celestial altar's construction. But when she arrived, she found the camp eerily silent and empty. She looked around, suppressing her anger, and coldly ordered her subordinates to find Wulong.

Her subordinates looked uneasy and whispered, "Governor, we can't see any trace of him."

"Ugh, I have to do everything myself!" Fire Maiden said coldly, taking out her cat's eye stone from her robe. Through it, she saw Wulong leisurely drinking in the cellar beneath the celestial altar. Furious, she led a group of guards straight to the altar.

The celestial altar towered into the clouds, connecting heaven and earth, emitting a cold light under the sun. Standing before the altar, Fire Maiden felt a surge of excitement, momentarily forgetting her plan to punish Wulong. At that moment, Wulong hurried over, his rough voice calling out, "Governor! Congratulations!"

She raised an eyebrow and asked indifferently, "Congratulations for what?"

Wulong smiled obsequiously. "I was just about to report the good news. The celestial altar is complete, waiting only for you to activate it."

Fire Maiden's anger dissipated, and she laughed heartily. "Good! I'll forgive your crime of drinking during the day. Let's go inside and take a look!"

Wulong led her into the altar, pointing to a stone staircase with a tone of reverence. "This staircase leads directly to the top, with 9,999 steps. Normally, it's sealed and only opens when transporting sacrificial items."

Fire Maiden frowned slightly and asked mockingly, "Are you telling me I have to climb all the way to the top every time?"

Wulong smiled obsequiously and explained, "Governor, for your convenience, we specially designed a celestial ladder." With that, he led Fire Maiden to a hidden door. When opened, a beautifully carved seat embedded in the center of the staircase came into view, shimmering with silver light. Wulong said respectfully, "You only need to sit in, pull the handle, and in the blink of an eye, you'll reach the top. Once there, light the torch. When you see the sun, moon, and stars revolving around the torch, you can begin your cultivation."

Fire Maiden raised an eyebrow, slightly skeptical. "Is it really that magical? Why don't you come up with me and try it?"

Wulong quickly shook his head, as if Fire Maiden could see him, his voice tinged with awe and fear. "Governor, forgive me. The energy there is too intense. With my level of cultivation, I'm afraid I couldn't withstand it."

Fire Maiden said no more, smiling slightly, her eyes gleaming with excitement. "Then I'll try it! If it works well, I might cultivate there for a few days. During that time, no one is to disturb me."

Wulong cautiously added, "Governor, there's one more thing. We have many pig demons in the camp, but we don't need so many now. Why not set up an arena, select a dozen pig demons to fight each day, and sell tickets to earn silver? We can use the proceeds to serve you. What do you think?"

Fire Maiden nodded appreciatively. "Not a bad idea, but keep a hundred or so pig demons to maintain the altar."

Wulong felt so excited, watching as Fire Maiden gracefully sat on the celestial ladder seat and disappeared into the ascending track.

***

After crossing a small hill, the clamor of Daze military camp could be faintly heard. The clashing of weapons and the shouts of soldiers reverberated through the air. Songmao instinctively slowed his pace, glancing at the princess beside him, a hidden worry rising in his heart. The soldiers all believed that Princess Wenxi had defected to the Sherkon. If the real princess appeared suddenly, it might lead to misunderstandings or even danger. He turned his head and whispered, "Will they recognize you?"

The princess's gaze darkened, her voice calm but tinged with anxiety. "Does the fake princess really look that much like me?"

"Exactly the same," Songmao replied in a low voice. "Even Kauko and the advisor were fooled."

Hearing this, the princess frowned, stopped her horse, dismounted, and led the reins as she slowly walked up the hill, her eyes fixed on the camp under the shade of the trees. She quickly calculated her next move. After a long while, she looked up, her tone firm. "Songmao, go and bring the advisor here. He has the wisdom to distinguish the real from the fake."

Songmao nodded, nimbly leaping onto the treetops and disappearing into the forest. Moments later, he landed in front of the advisor, panting as he called out, "Advisor, I've found Kauko and the princess!"

The advisor, who had been dozing, was startled. He looked up, his eyes lighting up. "Where are they?"

"Kauko ran off again, probably to Sien City."

"Let him run around," the advisor said, gesturing with his hands to indicate a large head. He asked, "What about that... that..."

Songmao understood. "You mean the pig-faced princess? She's outside the camp, waiting for you to fetch her."

Hearing this, the advisor stood up abruptly, grabbed his cloak, and hurried out. After a few steps, he suddenly remembered his cane and turned back to get it, waving off the guards who were about to follow. "No need, I'm just going out for some fresh air with Songmao."

When they reached the hill, the bamboo grove was quiet, with only a black horse tied to a tree, gently swishing its tail. The advisor looked around in confusion, about to call out, when he heard a familiar voice behind him. "Advisor, I'm here."

He turned sharply, but instead of the pig-faced princess, he saw a human-faced princess. His cane clattered to the ground, and he stared at her, demanding, "You... how did you come back?"

The princess bent down to pick up the cane and handed it to the advisor. He hesitated for a moment before taking it. The princess smiled gently and explained, "Advisor, it seems Fire Rose has done you great harm. I am actually the pig-headed princess."

The advisor's confusion deepened. "Where is the pig head?"

Songmao interjected, "I've already broken the pig-head curse."

The princess nodded, confirming Songmao's words.

"Since when could you break curses, Songmao?" the advisor asked, still half-doubting. He probed further, "If you're really the princess, you shouldn't mind me asking about two distinctive features on your body, right?"

The princess smiled. "Advisor, please ask."

The advisor cautiously asked, "The princess has a scar on her hairline, right?"

The princess gently lifted her hair, revealing her forehead. "See for yourself." Her expression was calm and confident.

The advisor stared at her forehead but found no scar. He said in confusion, "Why is there no scar? Am I seeing things?"

The princess was puzzled. She knew there had been a prominent scar on the left side of her forehead. She reached up and gently felt her forehead but couldn't find the familiar mark. She turned to Songmao, a hint of anxiety in her voice. "Can you check for me? Is it there?"

Songmao examined her carefully and shook his head. The advisor spoke again, his tone serious. "I remember you had a scar on your thumb. Can I see it?"

The princess nodded. "Yes, on my right thumb." She extended her hand to show the advisor.

The advisor took her hand and examined it closely under the bright sunlight, but his face gradually showed disappointment. He motioned for Songmao to come closer and asked, "Do you see a scar?"

Songmao regretfully replied, "I don't see one."

The advisor sighed deeply. "I don't see it either. I thought I was seeing things." He looked at the princess and sighed again. "If you're Fire Rose, you'd better leave now. You might fool Songmao, but you can't fool me. Don't wait for Kauko to return. If he sees you and scratches you, it might cost you half your life."

Songmao quickly defended her. "Last night, Kauko was with the princess. I swear on my life that this is the real princess." The princess remained calm and suggested softly, "Advisor, why not ask me something Fire Rose couldn't possibly know?"

The advisor listened, gripping his cane tightly, his chin resting on his hand as he pondered. "Alright. What did you call me when we first met?" the advisor asked.

The princess answered without hesitation. "Uncle."

"Who was the first general you appointed?" the advisor continued.

The princess answered just as quickly. "General Dao Shan."

"What is the princess most afraid of eating?" the advisor asked, a hint of anticipation in his voice.

"Grasshoppers," the princess replied smoothly and naturally.

Hearing these answers, the advisor's doubts were mostly dispelled, but there was still one final question. "Princess, you don't have magic now, do you?"

"Of course not. I know you've always been concerned about those two scars, but I really can't explain it," the princess said helplessly.

Songmao jumped onto the princess's shoulder and exclaimed excitedly, "I can explain! It's because the princess ate a divine pill today!"

The advisor asked curiously, "What kind of divine pill?"

"A pill crafted by Master Dapeng over his lifetime. After the princess swallowed it, the curse was lifted, the scars disappeared, and she became even more beautiful and youthful," Songmao explained with great enthusiasm.

"That makes sense!" the advisor exclaimed, gripping the princess's hand tightly, his eyes filled with emotion and relief. Tears streamed down his face. "Princess, I shouldn't have sent you to Annan Kingdom, making you suffer so much."

The princess's face softened into a gentle smile as she patted the advisor's hand reassuringly. "I see this as a trial fate has given me. You didn't see how happy Kauko was when he saw my pig-headed appearance. He kept his pig face close to mine, refusing to pull away." She pointed to her cheek, her eyes sparkling with mischief.

From the princess's calm tone, the advisor sensed her unyielding spirit and felt immensely relieved.

Songmao nimbly leaped onto a bamboo branch, overjoyed that the advisor had recognized the princess. However, a lingering doubt tugged at him, and he couldn't help but ask the advisor, "Fire Rose and the princess look exactly alike. Will you have to ask so many secret questions every time you see the princess to prevent imposters?"

"That is indeed a problem," the advisor mused, studying the princess. "Fire Rose spent many days with me, and I had no idea she was a fake. Songmao, let me ask you first—how do you think we should guard against this?"

"In my opinion, I'll just stay by the princess's side every day. The princess I'm with will always be the real one!" Songmao declared confidently.

"That won't work. You might fall asleep, and then another fake could come and cheat me," the advisor retorted.

The princess interrupted them, saying, "Actually, it's quite simple. Fire Rose was transformed from a rose spirit, so she carries the scent of roses, which she can't get rid of. As for me, I never use perfume. I'm as light as water." She extended her arm for the advisor and Songmao to smell, and they were immediately convinced. "Since I'm the real one, Advisor, take me to the camp."

***

When Prince Qin fell into the raging currents of the Red River, he was fortuitously saved by a river dolphin that had gained sentience.

As the iron chain bridge snapped, Prince Qin tried to grab the "princess", but she had already fallen into the torrent ahead of him. Though he desperately wanted to save her, the rushing waters repeatedly pulled him under, making it impossible to keep his eyes open. Gradually, exhaustion and cold overtook him, and his struggles grew feeble, his limbs heavy as lead.

Finally, he succumbed to the relentless river, tumbling like a leaf in the waves for over a hundred miles before being washed into a small inlet.

This inlet was home to a young river dolphin, who had once worked as a servant for the Dragon King of the South Sea. Not long ago, it had followed the Dragon King on an inspection of the Red River. While the Dragon King dozed, it slipped into this inlet and saw a young, beautiful woman sitting by the shore, her feet playing in the water. Enchanted by her, it couldn't resist kissing her toes when she wasn't looking. After returning to the South Sea, it couldn't forget the encounter and sneaked back to claim the inlet as its own, hoping to see the woman again.

The woman's name was Ayee, just seventeen years old, the only daughter of a wealthy family in a riverside village. She disliked needlework and books, preferring to hunt in the forest and fish in the river. After the river dolphin touched her toes, she fell seriously ill. Her father forbade her from playing by the water, as villagers often saw a strange creature swimming in the depths of the inlet. Occasionally, it would surface, revealing its translucent body, colorful scales, and obsidian-like eyes. The ethereal, shimmering creature seemed to watch the passersby on the shore.

The river dolphin spent its days in loneliness. The lifeless arrival of Prince Qin sparked its imagination. It circled his body, observing him with fascination, and couldn't resist a daring plan. If it could merge its soul with this human body, it might have a chance to go ashore and find the woman it adored. Gathering all its energy, it charged into Prince Qin's floating body, reviving him.

Prince Qin instinctively floated to the surface and slowly swam toward the shore.

***

Ayee hadn't been to the small inlet in a long time, but she still yearned for the feeling of playing in the water. The cool river flowing through her fingers had once brought her endless joy. She loved to let her long, chestnut hair fan out on the water's surface, gazing at the lazy clouds drifting across the sky, the sunlight casting red highlights on her strands. But she hadn't experienced that joy in a long time.

She thought that even if she couldn't play in the water, just walking by the river would be nice—feeling the breeze from the river, watching the golden ripples, the mist on the opposite bank, and smelling the damp scent of earth and wildflowers. However, her father, Jeddi, had assigned a maid to watch her constantly, making her feel suffocated. One day, she lied to her father, "Dad, I've lost my sapphire necklace!"

Jeddi was shocked. "How did you lose it? That was your mother's, may she rest in peace."

"I think I lost it at the small inlet, the last time I played in the water."

"I'll send Bei Xi to look for it."

"I should go too. I know where I've been," Ayee pleaded.

"Don't go near the water," Jeddi said sternly. "I don't want you encountering any water spirits again."

"Yes, Dad."

Ayee and Bei Xi each mounted a horse and rode to the inlet, leaving the horses to graze on the riverbank as they walked into the rocky shore.

Bei Xi warned Ayee, "Ayee, don't go any further, or your father will have my head!"

Ayee looked at the poor maid and stopped, choosing a flat rock to sit on, facing the tranquil inlet. She closed her eyes, savoring the slightly damp, warm breeze of the late autumn afternoon brushing her cheeks.

"Aren't we here to look for the necklace?" Bei Xi asked.

"No need. It must have been stolen by the water spirit," Ayee said mysteriously.

Bei Xi sat close to Ayee, afraid the water spirit might reach out with long arms to grab them. But her wandering eyes kept glancing at the water, hoping to catch a glimpse of the strange creature people talked about. She saw a dozen seagulls circling and squawking in the distance, and something strange crawling toward the shore. She nudged Ayee, "Look, is that the water spirit?"

Ayee stood up and looked in the direction Bei Xi pointed. "That's a person crawling. Maybe something happened. Let's go see." Before Bei Xi could stop her, Ayee was already running over.

It was Prince Qin. He reached out a hand to Ayee as she approached, then passed out. Ayee realized the stranger needed help and knelt beside him. His face was pale, but his features were handsome. His chest rose and fell with each breath, but he lay motionless, the water lapping at his legs. She shook him vigorously, trying to wake him, but to no avail. She grabbed his arm and, with all her strength, dragged him to the riverbank.

Bei Xi, standing nearby, urged nervously, "Alright, let's leave quickly. What if he's the water spirit?"

"Have you ever seen a water spirit like this? He's drowning. Quick, let's take him back to the village," Ayee said.

Ayee secretly brought Prince Qin home, and Bei Xi and the other servants hid him in the woodshed, tending to him for several days. When he could get up, he started working with the servants.

Seeing his diligence, Ayee was inspired and brought her father to watch him chop wood. She said he was a wanderer looking for a meal and begged her father to let him stay.

Her father observed that he was honest and clean-cut, so he agreed.

Ayee asked him where he came from and what his name was, but he remembered nothing. His soul was entangled with the river dolphin's, leaving his memories in chaos. She named him Azar, meaning "stranger." Azar quickly adapted to his new role as a servant. Though he sometimes felt confused by his lack of memories, he was happy to chop wood, fetch water, and tend to the horses, especially since Ayee often came to see him and praised him, which made him happiest.

One day, Ayee's father, Jeddi, was teaching her archery in the backyard, with Azar serving them. Ayee noticed Azar seemed interested in archery and let him try. He shot three arrows in a row, all hitting the bullseye. Jeddi asked him, "Were you a hunter in the past?"

Azar shook his head. "I don't remember."

Ayee had been pestering her father to go hunting in the forest, and Jeddi was considering who would be suitable to accompany her. He said to Azar, "Tomorrow, Ayee will go on a hunting trip into the mountains. You will accompany her."

Ayee's eyes sparkled with excitement. "Great! Azar, you can teach me archery."

Jeddi cleared his throat loudly. "Young man, you must protect my daughter in the forest. She tends to be reckless, so you must take good care of her."

"Yes, Master," Azar replied politely.

Ayee took Azar into the forest, where she immediately revealed her true nature, flitting about like a happy bird.

She led him to a small waterfall she had discovered as a child. She loved the shaded valley by the babbling stream, where purple lilacs bloomed year-round.

"It's so peaceful here," Ayee sighed contentedly, sitting among the lilacs. She motioned for Azar to sit beside her, noticing his gentle demeanor, his deep, tender eyes, his black hair casually falling over his forehead, and the mysterious story hinted behind his firm lips.

Azar noticed her gaze. "Ayee, why are you looking at me like that? Did I do something wrong?" he asked cautiously.

Ayee blushed. "I don't know. I feel... different when I'm with you."

Azar was silent for a moment, then said, "I'm just a servant, Miss." But as he spoke, another voice in his mind said, "Fool, pick a flower for her!" Without thinking, he plucked a lilac and tucked it behind Ayee's ear, saying, "Compared to your beauty, this flower pales."

Ayee's eyes widened, and a shy smile appeared on her lips. Before he could react, she kissed his cheek and ran into the woods. Over the next few days, they continued their hunting trip. Ayee's kiss stirred Azar's mind, and though he tried to focus on his duties, he found his gaze constantly drawn to her. She moved through the forest with confidence, light and graceful. When she turned her radiant smile toward him, he had to look away to keep from getting lost in her bright eyes.

One morning, as they chased a wild rabbit, Ayee slipped on some moss and tumbled down a slope, eventually falling into a lake. It happened so quickly that by the time Azar reached the lake, Ayee was gone. Without hesitation, he dove into the water, risking entanglement in the weeds, and searched the depths until he found the unconscious Ayee. He urgently pressed her philtrum until she finally coughed up water and slowly woke up.

Azar carried her to a sunny spot on the grass and sat down. Ayee leaned weakly against him, whispering, "Azar, where are you from?" Her eyes were filled with dependence.

"I don't remember. Maybe somewhere far away," he replied softly, a hint of confusion in his eyes.

"Maybe you came here just for me," she said, cupping his face, her gaze firm and tender. "You've already stolen my heart."

Azar's heart raced. "Ayee, I... I don't know what to say," he stammered, his emotions surging like a tide, but his reason told him he was just a servant and shouldn't entertain such hopes.

"I want to hear what's in your heart," she said earnestly, her eyes burning with intensity.

A voice in Azar's mind said, "If you can't speak, then don't say anything. You know what to do!" Suddenly, he was filled with passion, his eyes shining, his face radiant with joy. He held Ayee tighter, feeling her heartbeat.

When they returned home, Ayee bravely announced their relationship to her father, hoping for his approval. Her father was furious, demanding, "Sneaking around with a servant... aren't you ashamed?" He glared at Azar. "I gave you a job, and this is how you repay me?"

Azar lowered his head but spoke firmly. "It's not her fault! I was the one who confessed. If you must blame anyone, blame me."

Jeddi angrily told Azar, "You are not to approach my daughter again, or I'll send you to the authorities!"

Ayee was heartbroken and locked herself in her room, refusing to eat or drink. One day passed, then two... Jeddi pretended not to care, but seeing his daughter grow increasingly haggard, he finally relented on the seventh day. Though he was deeply reluctant, he agreed to their marriage and prepared several sets of fine clothes for Azar, choosing an auspicious date for the wedding.

The night before the wedding, Azar changed into his new clothes and looked at himself in the mirror. The reflection felt eerily familiar, and suddenly, he remembered who he was—he was Prince Qin of Annan!

He recalled his childhood betrothal to Princess Wenxi. How could he marry Ayee? "I have to tell Ayee!" Prince Qin thought frantically.

"You can't do that. She saved you. How can you betray her?" the river dolphin's voice reminded him.

Prince Qin and the river dolphin's soul wrestled with each other, unsure of what to do.

The next morning, everyone discovered that the groom was gone, and a horse was missing.

Ayee thought her father had driven Azar away and angrily confronted Jeddi.

Jeddi, feeling sorry for Ayee, comforted her, "My dear daughter, how could I break my promise to you? Let's go find him together!"

"The world is so vast. Where should we look?" Ayee asked, tears in her eyes.

"Where is he most familiar with?" her father asked.

"That would be the forest!" Ayee replied with certainty.

Chapter 20

The Shaking Bridge

Prince Qin hid in the forest, his horse carrying him slowly along the hunting path. Memories of his time with Ayee flashed through his mind, reminding him that she was waiting for him. Yet, deep in his heart, the shadow of the princess lingered, driving him forward, further and further away from Ayee.

The sound of hooves crunching on fallen leaves echoed softly, while the distant sound of flowing water seemed to guide him. Towering trees surrounded him, their dense foliage blocking the sunlight and casting dappled shadows on the ground. The path ahead was draped with low-hanging vines that occasionally reached out as if trying to pull him from his horse. Strange bird calls echoed through the forest, both alluring and chilling.

As night fell, the last traces of sunset disappeared, and a thick fog slowly rose, shrouding the forest in mystery. At that moment, a strange, flickering light appeared before Prince Qin, piercing through the mist with an inexplicable magnetism, as if beckoning him.

Drawn by the enchanting light, Prince Qin urged his horse forward, gradually approaching the mysterious source. Before him was a massive ring of light, as large as a barn. The rings shimmered with different hues, slowly rotating and emitting a low hum, like a lullaby. The surrounding trees leaned in the same direction, as if struck by a powerful force.

At the center of the rings, a figure gradually appeared, lying on its back, facing the sky, as if immersed in a sweet dream. As the rings rotated, the figure slowly rose and then vanished into the light. When the figure reappeared, Prince Qin was shocked to recognize it as the familiar pig-faced Kauko.

Prince Qin immediately realized that something terrible must have happened to Kauko. "Kauko!" he called out anxiously, a surge of courage driving him to charge toward the mysterious rings. But the power of the rings seemed insurmountable, repelling him again and again, as if an invisible barrier stood in his way. Just as he prepared to try once more, Ayee appeared like a shadow, gripping his hand tightly. Together, they charged forward, finally breaking through the rings, which exploded into a kaleidoscope of colors before dissipating into the air.

At that moment, Jeddi arrived with a torch, illuminating the surrounding darkness. Kauko fell heavily to the ground, waking from his dream. Prince Qin bent down to help him up, but Kauko jumped to his feet, exclaiming in surprise, "Prince Qin, it's been a long time!"

Prince Qin sighed in relief. "Kauko, how did you end up here, asleep?"

Kauko noticed the others present and shook his ears, transforming his face. He turned to Ayee and said, "Don't be scared. I'm not a monster."

Ayee replied, "Are you the famous Chef? Everyone in Daze praises you!"

Kauko chuckled. "I guess I am a bit famous! But to be honest, I've been trapped here for days, unconscious, all thanks to that old witch, Fire Maiden. Those strange rings are actually yin-yang Lock. If it weren't for you and Prince Qin breaking through, I'd still be stuck. Thank you, dear girl! What's your name?"

"My name is Ayee," she said excitedly. Saving the "Chef" was an honor!

Kauko turned to Prince Qin. "I won't thank you. Do you know why?"

Prince Qin asked, "Why not? I risked my life to save you, and you can't even spare a word of thanks?"

"Prince Qin, listen. Even though I was unconscious, I sensed that your body had been invaded by a little demon. Don't you feel like you've been controlled?"

"It's true. I couldn't remember anything and couldn't control myself," Prince Qin admitted. "But now I'm fully awake!"

"That's because the power of the rings drove it out of your body. You see, if you hadn't run into me, you'd be in trouble!"

"Brother Kau, what kind of demon was it?" Ayee asked curiously.

"It was a river dolphin from the South Sea Dragon King's court. It escaped and became a demon, trying to marry you through Prince Qin," Kauko explained. "Ayee, you almost married a river dolphin. Prince Qin, you have a betrothal to the princess. You almost became a traitor."

Hearing this, Ayee grabbed Prince Qin's hand and began to cry. "Even if you're a prince, you can't just leave me like this. You owe me an explanation. Otherwise, my father won't let it go!"

Prince Qin walked up to Jeddi and said sincerely, "My actions earlier were out of necessity, but I truly care for Ayee. I want to take her as my sister and bring her back to Annan to meet my parents. What do you think?"

Jeddi smiled slightly and patted Prince Qin's shoulder. "Thank you for your kindness, Prince. My daughter is mischievous, so you must take good care of her. But for tonight, why don't you all return to the village? Let me play the host and treat you properly."

Kauko, however, shook his head. "You three go ahead. I have urgent matters to attend to."

Seeing Kauko's urgency, Jeddi offered him a horse, suggesting that Ayee ride with him. But Ayee had already happily run to Prince Qin's side, grabbing his sleeve and insisting on riding with him. Jeddi watched this scene with a faint smile, a hint of helplessness in his eyes.

Kauko turned to Jeddi and asked, "How many days does it take to reach the capital by horse from here?"

Jeddi calculated for a moment. "At least ten days."

Kauko frowned and sighed. "Ten days? Even three days would be too late. If only I could fly." As soon as he said this, he suddenly felt a lightness in his body, and his feet lifted off the ground. Startled at first, he touched his forehead, feeling normal. Recalling recent events, he realized—Fire Maiden's powerful strike must have unblocked the stagnation in his body!

He silently recited his master's mantra and a gust of wind lifted him into the air. He spun a few times, flipping joyfully, testing this newfound freedom. After a moment, he calmed himself and landed back by the forest. He cupped his hands in farewell and said loudly, "Until we meet again!" Before the words faded, he had transformed into a gust of wind, swiftly disappearing into the clouds.

In just a few moments, Kauko arrived in Sien City.

Hovering high above, he looked toward the north of the city and saw a vast expanse of darkness, with no stars above and no lights below. He suspected that this was the location of the celestial altar. He flew closer and saw a dark wind rising from the ground and black clouds descending from the sky, converging into a swirling vortex that flowed into a black hole. Kauko tried to follow the wind and clouds to find the entrance but was blocked by an invisible wall, unable to pass no matter which direction he tried. Puzzled, he decided to find someone who could explain.

He went to the "princess'" palace, where guards were stationed everywhere. He landed lightly on the roof, skillfully moved a few tiles, and silently slipped into Fire Rose's chamber.

Moonlight streamed through the window, casting a serene glow on Fire Rose's peaceful face as she slept. Kauko lit a candle, and the soft light gradually filled the room, creating a gentle ambiance. He walked quietly to the bedside, bent down, and gently shook Fire Rose's shoulder.

Her eyelashes fluttered, and she slowly opened her eyes. In her drowsy state, she saw Kauko's familiar pig face swaying in the candlelight, as if she were still dreaming. She rubbed her eyes and reached out to touch his cool nose, realizing it wasn't an illusion. She sat up abruptly and said urgently, "I thought... I'd never see you again..." Before she could finish, tears streamed down her cheeks.

Kauko sat on the edge of the bed, watching her cry. His heart ached, and he couldn't help but pull out a silk handkerchief, handing it to her. He scratched his big ears and said teasingly, "Don't cry, don't cry. I'm terrified of women's tears."

Fire Rose covered her face and sobbed, as if all the pent-up grievances were pouring out. Kauko scratched his head, flustered, and tried to comfort her. "Ah, Fire Rose... dear Fire Sister!" As he said "sister," he conjured a vibrant red rose and handed it to her. "Don't cry. This is for you."

Fire Rose was captivated by the rose, a faint smile appearing on her face. She gently took it, but the rose instantly turned into petals, warm with the candlelight, scattering in her hair.

"Ha, you've learned my tricks?" Fire Rose chided, though her eyes sparkled with joy.

"Not at all, not at all! Yours is real skill. I'm just using illusions to make you laugh."

"Kauko... thank you," Fire Rose finally smiled sincerely, her eyes glistening. "I never thought I'd see you again. Tell me, how did you survive this time?"

"It was close, but Prince Qin saved me."

Fire Rose looked incredulous. "Prince Qin is alive?"

"Not only alive, but he's doing well, with a beauty by his side."

"He's married?" she asked, surprised.

"Not exactly. She's a lovely adopted sister," Kauko said playfully. "I see your eyes lighting up. Do you have feelings for Prince Qin?"

Fire Rose sighed. "I'm just a flower demon pretending to be a princess. How could I dare to hope?"

"Don't belittle yourself," Kauko encouraged her. "I've heard the people say you've done many good deeds, showing the grace of a princess."

"Enough about me," Fire Rose said. "You must have a reason for coming. What is it?"

"I have a question for you. Answer if you will; if not, I won't blame you. I want to enter the celestial altar. Do you know how?"

Fire Rose frowned slightly and whispered, "Since Fire Maiden activated the altar, a magical barrier has appeared around the camp and its surroundings. It's like an invisible wall. No one can get in."

Kauko nodded. "Yes, I just experienced it. I ran into a wall."

Fire Rose suddenly smiled slyly. "I have an idea. Every night, the Sherkon soldiers take ten pig-faced men from the camp to the arena in the south of the city, forcing them to fight to the death. The winner is sent back to the camp. Maybe this is your chance."

Kauko grinned. "This plan... could work." He looked at Fire Rose seriously. "Why don't you come with me and escape this misery?"

Fire Rose was stunned, her eyes darkening. She whispered, "I can't. My life is in Fire Maiden's hands. I have no choice... but I won't harm you."

Kauko nodded, bid farewell to Fire Rose, and was going to head to the arena.

"Remember to fix the hole in my roof before you leave!" she called after him, a playful smile in her eyes.

Kauko entered the arena in the south of the city. The high stone walls were illuminated by the flickering light of torches, casting shadows on the dark crowd. The midnight air was thick with the smell of alcohol, sweat, and blood. The audience cheered excitedly, as if this deadly spectacle were the night's main event.

On the stage, two pig-faced gladiators fought, one in red and the other in black, wielding heavy swords with wild but clumsy movements. The red gladiator, covered in blood, staggered but still fought back. The black gladiator hesitated, seemingly reluctant to continue, but under the crowd's urging, he finally swung his sword. The red gladiator fell to the ground, his dimming eyes fixed on his opponent, as if with a glimmer of relief. The black gladiator panted, raised his sword, and let out a hoarse roar to the crowd, as if celebrating his survival.

Suddenly, there was a clanging sound from the iron cage at the side of the arena. The guard peeked inside and was stunned. "Huh? Is there another one in here?"

Kauko reached out a hand from the cage and tossed out a string of copper coins. "See? This money is real, right? Let me out. I'm itching for a fight!"

The guard grinned and pulled Kauko out of the cage, removing his shackles and throwing a red coat over his shoulders. He handed Kauko a sword. The drums beat loudly, drowning out the crowd's murmurs. The black gladiator charged at Kauko, sword in hand.

Kauko dodged easily and whispered in his ear, "Be careful. Don't run into my blade."

The black gladiator took this as a challenge and swung his sword even more wildly. Kauko sidestepped and eventually disarmed him, tossing his own sword aside and fighting bare-handed. When the time was right, Kauko grabbed the black gladiator, tapped his pressure points, and then lifted him, pretending to break his spine.

The crowd erupted in wild cheers. Kauko became the night's champion, and the guard proudly ordered his subordinates, "Make sure this guy fights tomorrow night! He's quite the entertainer."

Kauko was locked in a prison cart and jolted back to the camp, where he was thrown into a small cell. Once everything was quiet, he carefully removed the heavy shackles and slipped out of the cell, locking the guard inside. With a small spell, he gave the guard a pig's head. He changed into the guard's uniform, pushed open the prison door, and saw the towering silhouette of the celestial altar in the distance.

Kauko crept along the wall, reaching the altar's entrance, where four guards stood watch. He calmly approached and lightly tapped them, secretly placing "sleeping bugs" on them. The guards blinked, their eyelids growing heavy, and they slumped against the wall, falling into a deep sleep.

Kauko entered the altar, groping through the dim corridor until he reached his uncle's room. He quietly pushed the door open, and smoke wafted out. The faint light of an oil lamp illuminated the room's vague outlines. An elderly figure crouched by the bed, smoking, the air thick with the scent of tobacco. The old man slowly looked up, his eyes calm but piercing through the haze, silently observing the intruder.

"Uncle, it's me, Little Pig Head!" Kauko said softly, his voice filled with warmth. But the old man just stared at him blankly, his eyes empty. Kauko smiled slightly, flicked his ears, and transformed back into his familiar pig-faced appearance.

Uncle Kau's eyes instantly lit up, and he struggled to stand. Kauko helped him up, and they sat side by side on the bed. Uncle Kau's trembling hand gently touched Kauko's face, as if tracing a long-lost memory. "You look like your father... and your mother," he murmured, his eyes filled with emotion. "You've finally returned! Did Bamei send you?"

Kauko nodded. "Yes, Uncle. Thank you for saving her."

Uncle Kau's face softened with a loving smile. "We're family. No need for thanks. That girl cares deeply for you."

Kauko smiled, his eyes gentle. "She truly is a remarkable girl."

"Then your uncle has done a good deed," Uncle Kau said, his eyes brimming with pride.

Kauko smiled along with his uncle, "Yes, that was quite a feat. Uncle, how long have you been here?"

Uncle Kau's expression darkened, and he sighed softly. "Over a decade. Every day I hope, but I don't know when it will end."

"It won't be long now, Uncle," Kauko said, his eyes burning with determination, his back straight. "In just a few days, I'm going to turn this place upside down!"

Uncle Kau was stunned, his face paling. He grabbed Kauko's hand, his voice filled with urgency. "Nephew, Governor Fire is incredibly powerful. I'm afraid you might..."

"Uncle, I've seen the world. My powers have grown recently—I can summon wind and rain, control sand and stones, and command lightning.

There's nothing I can't do!" Kauko grinned confidently, his face full of pride.

Uncle Kau's heart finally settled, and he looked at Kauko with gratitude. "Thank the heavens! Nephew, if you have such abilities, what can I do to help you?"

Kauko thought for a moment, then lowered his voice. "I have two tasks to accomplish. But first, I need to deal with that little demon, Wulong."

Uncle Kau frowned and nodded. "That Wulong is elusive. How can we deal with him if we can't even see him?"

Kauko's lips curled into a sly smile. "The princess said he's a heavy drinker, right?"

Uncle Kau nodded. "That demon is always pestering me for alcohol, from morning till night."

Kauko leaned closer to Uncle Kau's ear and whispered a few instructions. Uncle Kau's eyes lit up with amusement, and he led Kauko to the underground wine cellar. Before parting, he patted Kauko's shoulder. "Rest well. Tomorrow, Wulong will have a 'treat.'"

Early the next morning, Kauko faintly heard a hoarse voice outside the door, impatiently urging, "Hey, Cripple! Where's the wine?!"

"Just a moment, sir! I'll fetch it!" Uncle Kau responded, grabbing a jar and heading into the cellar.

Kauko leaned in and poured more than half a jar of wine into the pot, then secretly added a splash of urine. He shook the jar a few times, opened the lid, and sniffed it. Worried the urine smell wasn't strong enough, he dipped his finger in and tasted a drop, then nodded in satisfaction.

Uncle Kau carried the jar out carefully. Wulong eagerly grabbed it, brought it to his lips, and took a big gulp. His eyes widened in shock, and he let out a cry, "Cripple, what kind of wine is this?"

Uncle Kau's face turned pale, thinking their plan had been exposed. He didn't dare speak, only reaching out as if to take the jar back.

However, Wulong's face soon broke into a drunken smile. He smacked his lips in delight. "Ah, today's wine is different! It's even stronger than usual—what a fine drink!" With that, he greedily clutched the jar and gulped it down. As the wine entered his system, strange ripples formed around Wulong's body, and his vague outline gradually solidified into a monstrous, glowing mantis-like creature! The "mantis" was taller than a man, its antennae twitching slightly, its chin dripping with wine, and its eyes gleaming with malice. Uncle Kau, witnessing this, widened his eyes in terror, his legs giving way as he collapsed to the ground, trembling uncontrollably before finally fainting.

Just as Wulong raised the jar, still unaware of the full extent of the change, Kauko emerged from the shadows, coldly watching him. "The wine tastes good, doesn't it? Too bad you won't get to drink it tomorrow."

Wulong was startled and reflexively threw the jar at Kauko, then turned to flee. But no matter which direction he ran, Kauko always appeared in front of him, like an invisible wall. Wulong, sweating profusely, finally collapsed to the ground, begging for mercy. "Spare me, good sir! I don't know you. Why are you tormenting me?"

Kauko sneered. "You've harmed countless people, even the princess. How many more will cry out for justice because of you?"

Wulong slumped to the ground. Kauko took out his copper flute, pointed it at Wulong, and gave it a light flick. Wulong's body shuddered violently, then turned into a wisp of green smoke. It swirled in the air for a moment, let out a few shrill screams, and finally dissipated into nothingness.

Kauko carried his unconscious uncle to the bed and settled him down. He then set out to explore how to reach the top of the celestial altar and bring Fire Maiden down from her divine throne. He discovered the celestial ladder but found it impossible to enter, blocked by an invisible barrier. He tried the stone staircase but was similarly thwarted by an unseen force. Frustrated, he returned to his uncle's side and shook him awake.

As soon as Uncle Kau woke up, he asked, "Did you catch him?"

Kauko smiled faintly. "Don't worry, Uncle. He's been reincarnated."

The worry in Uncle Kau's eyes faded slightly, and he chuckled. "That urine trick of yours is deadly. Whoever touches it is doomed. Even Fire Maiden wanted to make him reveal his true form but couldn't. I suspect it was because you peed on me when you were little that I ended up here."

Kauko laughed. "Uncle, you're amazing too! The celestial altar you designed is full of traps. I wanted to go to the top, but there's no way!"

Uncle Kau shook his head slightly. "It's not me. The altar has its own spiritual energy. Since Fire Maiden activated it, it's been protected by divine power. It's nearly impossible for anyone to enter at will."

Kauko frowned, his eyes filled with urgency. "Then how do I get up there? If she stays up there cultivating, won't she become the 'Heavenly Demon Star'?"

Uncle Kau pondered for a moment, his eyes flickering. "Nephew, I've prepared for this. If we destroy the altar, she'll have to come down." He pulled out a roll of blueprints from under the bed, carefully spread them out, and pointed to a spot. "The celestial ladder is powered by underground water from a subterranean river. If we dig a hole in the cellar and divert the water, the altar will collapse."

Kauko looked down at the blueprint, frowning in thought. "It's a good plan, but if Sien City gets flooded, it'll be a disaster."

Uncle Kau explained calmly, "There's an ancient riverbed outside Sien City.

The water will flow out there. The only thing to be careful about is that the people imprisoned here don't get swept away by the flood."

Kauko nodded, a glint of determination in his eyes. "I'll make sure they're safe, but it's best to evacuate them beforehand. When I'm fighting Fire Maiden, I won't be able to look after them."

Uncle Kau clapped his hands, relieved. "Good! Nephew, I'll go to the prison and arrange their escape. You focus on dealing with Fire Maiden." With that, he calmly extended his wrists to Kauko. "Here, make it look convincing. Put the shackles on me."

Kauko smiled slightly, put on the ill-fitting prison guard uniform, and cuffed his uncle. He led him out and approached the still-sleeping guards, shouting, "Wake up! The warden has ordered this man to be locked up and closely guarded!"

The startled guards didn't dare ask questions and quickly escorted Uncle Kau to the prison area.

Inside the prison, the atmosphere was already tense. Behind the iron bars, the prisoners gathered, their faces filled with anger as they banged on the bars, shouting, "Let us out! Let us out!" The guards were at a loss, staring in shock— the "pig-headed demons" had transformed back into humans overnight. The cells were filled with figures, and the noise was deafening.

As soon as Uncle Kau was thrown into the cell, he seemed prepared. He pulled out a few small keys from his sleeve and quickly handed them to the people around him, whispering, "When the altar collapses later, take the chance to break out of the cells, break through the back wall, and escape home!"

The prisoners' eyes sparkled with hope, their hearts filled with long-lost anticipation as they held their breath, waiting for the moment of upheaval.

In the damp underground cavern, Kauko carefully followed the red line on the blueprint and finally stopped in front of a stone wall. According to the blueprint, this was the weakest section of the underground river.

He listened intently. The underground river roared like a thousand wild beasts crashing through the rocks. He held his breath, focused his mind, and a beam of light shot from his fingertips. The light pierced through the darkness, penetrating the stone wall. Water droplets flowed out like diamonds, but Kauko knew this wasn't enough. He gently scratched the rock with his flute, creating a small crack. Then, with a deafening explosion, the rock shattered, and Kauko was thrown into the air by the powerful blast. The wild water surged out like a released beast, rushing fiercely.

Kauko floated in the air, swiftly waving his flute. A stone wall rose from the ground, separating the guards from the prisoners. Then, he drew a few symbols with his flute, and the powerful water flow seemed to follow his command, concentrating its force on the altar's foundation. As the foundation loosened and shook, the altar began to sway. The sky suddenly turned dark with thick clouds, as if sensing the earth's upheaval, and let out a low roar.

Fire Maiden was deep in her magical cultivation, her body frozen like an ice sculpture. Her skull mask glowed faintly with a purple light. Her red dress fluttered gently in the wind, like dancing flames, hot and enchanting. She seemed to merge with the cold aura around her, establishing a mysterious connection with the vast universe.

Suddenly, Fire Maiden felt as if the celestial altar had grown wings, carrying her through the clouds. The sensation made her heart race and her blood boil. She was overjoyed, thinking she had reached the pinnacle of the Heavenly Demon Technique, as if victory was within her grasp.

However, the cold reality shattered her beautiful illusion like frost. The altar began to shake violently, like a small boat in a storm, jolting her out of her deep meditation. She opened her eyes abruptly and saw the altar's stone pillars collapsing, boulders falling like rain. The runes on the altar, which had been glowing, flickered a few times before extinguishing completely, falling into silence.

Fire Maiden's eyes filled with terror and helplessness. She struggled to stand, but her body was still numb from the cultivation. She stumbled and fell several times, like a drunkard. Despair and rage intertwined in her heart, turning into a shrill, desperate scream. Then, she and the altar plunged into the surging flood, swallowed instantly, leaving only silence and desolation.

Kauko had originally planned to engage Fire Maiden in a life-and-death battle, but to his surprise, she never appeared. The victory came too quickly, leaving him disoriented and lost, like a lone goose wandering in a flooded area. Only when he saw no trace of Fire Maiden did his restless heart finally calm down.

Concerned for the safety of the princess, the advisor, and Songmao, Kauko decided to return quickly. However, he didn't forget Fire Rose. Before leaving, he went to the "princess' palace". The courtyard was eerily quiet, the gates wide open, with not a single guard in sight. He slipped into the palace silently, searching everywhere, but found no one.

Fire Rose's makeup box was still open on the table, a brow pencil lying on the floor. Kauko picked it up and carefully placed it back in the box. He guessed she had left in a hurry, perhaps fleeing with the other palace staff. "Fire Rose, did you grow wings? You ran so fast!" he muttered to himself. He had planned to take her with him this time, to make her the princess's sister.

Kauko flew back to Sanba on a cloud. Looking down from above, he saw General Dao Yin's troops chasing the fleeing Sherkon soldiers like tigers. The

Sherkon soldiers ahead were panicking, scrambling into a canyon, but General Dao Yin quickly ordered his troops to halt. He approached the advisor and the princess, who were on horseback, "Advisor, we must not repeat our mistakes in this canyon. What do you think?"

"General, you're wise. Let's stop here," the advisor replied, watching his tens of thousands of soldiers standing quietly at the edge of the canyon, knowing they were overcome with fear of the place.

As soon as he finished speaking, a wild neigh echoed through the valley. A fiery red horse burst out from the ranks, charging straight into the canyon without hesitation! The rider was none other than Tichu, his imposing figure towering, a golden leopard flag fluttering on his back, his spear gleaming as it stirred up a whirlwind of sand and stones.

"It's the Butcher!" shouts of joy erupted from General Dao Yin's troops. The soldiers, seeing Tichu's familiar figure, felt their morale soar! Without needing orders, tens of thousands of Daze soldiers surged forward like a flood, following Tichu's lead, rushing deep into the canyon.

General Dao Yin, seeing this, smiled with a mix of helplessness and admiration. He bowed to the advisor and said, "Advisor, Princess, please wait here! I'm going with them!" He plunged into the surging crowd, leading the charge with his sword drawn, heading straight for the enemy lines.

Meanwhile, the Sherkon army had climbed to the other side of the canyon. The archers stood ready, forming a dense defensive wall, their cold, gleaming arrows waiting for Tichu to enter their range.

However, from high above the clouds, Kauko watched it all. He chanted softly, ancient incantations stirring up wind and thunder. In an instant, a sandstorm swept toward the Sherkon position, throwing the enemy into chaos. The sudden display of heavenly power pushed the Sherkon soldiers' fear to its limit. The Butcher's fearsome reputation weighed on them like a mountain. They dropped their weapons and fled in disarray.

The Daze army's morale soared even higher, their battle cries shaking the heavens as they pursued the fleeing enemy relentlessly, like a storm. The advisor, watching the distant troops, turned to the princess and said, "Let's follow them."

The princess smiled faintly and nodded. "Alright. They charged ahead so quickly, leaving us far behind." She looked ahead and added playfully, "If only there were a bridge, we could save half a day's journey." The advisor squinted, pretending to ponder. "Maybe there is a bridge." He had already sensed a familiar magnetic fluctuation and knew Kauko was nearby. Sure enough, a long iron chain bridge suddenly appeared on the riverbank not far away, ancient and sturdy, spanning the canyon as if whispering to them, "Come and try me."

"Princess, look. As you wished, there's a bridge waiting for us," the advisor said with a smile, leading the princess and their horses onto the bridge. The bridge swayed slightly underfoot, giving a strange sense of floating. The princess, feeling curious, couldn't help but ask, "This bridge is unusual. It spans such a long distance. Advisor, do you know who built it?"

The advisor looked at her and smiled. "The builder is likely a master who wouldn't easily reveal himself."

The princess, deep in thought, gazed at the opposite bank. "After driving out the Sherkon, we should invite him to build a stone bridge, one wide enough for two carriages, to transport supplies."

"Noted. If he can't build it, I'll throw him in prison," the advisor said with mock seriousness. The bridge trembled slightly at his words.

The advisor wasn't in a hurry. He and the princess walked leisurely, chatting and occasionally tapping the chain railing. The princess gradually felt the bridge becoming less stable. Though there was no wind, it swayed as if in a breeze. She said to the advisor, "Let's cross quickly. This bridge doesn't feel safe."

The advisor deliberately raised his voice. "I agree. In the future, we should build a sturdy one."

They quickened their pace and crossed the bridge. The advisor couldn't hold back his laughter any longer and shouted, "Kauko, stop playing tricks. Come out now."

Before the words faded, the iron chain bridge dissipated like mist. Kauko flipped through the air and landed in front of them, rubbing his sore back. "Master, I wanted to surprise you and the princess. How did you figure it out?"

Chapter 21

The Dancing Shadow

The night sky over Daze was suddenly torn apart by a once-in-a-millennium meteor shower. Streaks of silver brilliance trailed across the heavens, like ancient and mysterious prophecies slowly unfurling across the celestial canvas. Children rushed out of their homes, eager to chase the falling stars, as if racing against them. Meanwhile, the elders, clutching their weathered wooden staffs, stood in solemn silence, their eyes filled with deep concern. They knew that such a spectacular celestial event was no mere coincidence—it might well be an omen of an impending storm.

Just as magnificent as the meteor shower, the flames of rebellion spread like wildfire across the vast lands of Daze. For over a decade, the iron hooves of Sherkon had trampled this land, leaving it in darkness. But now, that once-unshakable rule was like a crumbling ship in a storm, riddled with cracks and on the verge of collapse.

The assassination of the King of Sherkon was like a blazing torch, instantly igniting the fire of resistance in the hearts of every inhabitant of Daze. Soon after, the once-mighty Governor Fire, who had struck fear into the hearts of many, was driven into hiding by a novice "Chef," leaving his generals scattered and leaderless, like frightened birds.

Over four thousand warriors who had broken free from the pig-demon concentration camps chose not to return to their homes. Instead, they gathered under the banner of Kau Lame, forming an unstoppable force that surged toward Sien City like a raging flood. Their assault was relentless, and they even managed to breach the city's fortified northern gate, shaking the seemingly impregnable city to its core. On the city walls, the portrait of Sherkon King, once hung high, was torn down and trampled underfoot. In the streets, the towering statue of Sherkon King, which had once looked down upon the people, was toppled, its massive head rolling to the ground, stripped of all dignity. Though this lone army was eventually forced to retreat under the pressure of Sherkon's forces, their bravery and fearlessness became a spark that ignited the fighting spirit and hope in the hearts of the city's inhabitants.

***

On the eastern front of Daze, the princess stood in gleaming armor, the sunlight reflecting off her resolute face. The advisor's brown robe fluttered in the wind, his staff adding an air of authority. Warhorses neighed, their iron hooves crushing dried branches and leaves, kicking up clouds of dust. The golden leopard banner flapped in the wind, intertwining with the smoke of battle, creating a magnificent scene.

On the southern front, General Langkun's troops had successfully crossed the treacherous Red River and passed through the dense Naxi Forest. He stood at the edge of the forest, watching his soldiers march across the abandoned Sherkon camps and onto the open plains.

On the western front, Prince Qin led fifty thousand Annan cavalry, racing day and night toward Sien City. They were a formidable force, striking fear into the hearts of their enemies wherever they went. Prince Qin, clad in silver armor and a golden helmet, rode a tall white horse, looking like a god of war descended to earth. Villagers lined the roads, waving and cheering, while children ran after his troops, hoping to catch a glimpse of the heroic prince.

After several fierce battles, the forces of Daze grew stronger, like bamboo shoots after the rain, full of vitality. The princess stood atop a mountain, gazing into the distance, a hint of worry in her eyes. She turned to the advisor beside her and said, "Advisor, though our army is growing in strength, we lack capable commanders. This concerns me."

The advisor smiled faintly, as if he had already considered this. "Princess, have you thought about Tichu? He is brave and experienced in battle."

The princess nodded. "Tichu is a good choice. But do you have anyone else in mind?"

The advisor's tone carried a hint of amusement. "Are you thinking of Kauko? In my opinion, he is better suited to remain in the kitchen."

The princess frowned slightly. "What do you mean, Advisor?"

The advisor mysteriously turned his gaze toward the direction of the cooking fires and said softly, "Why don't you ask him yourself?"

The princess quietly made her way to the camp's kitchen. The stove fire burned brightly, and steam filled the air. Kauko stood by the stove, skillfully stirring a pot of soup, the aroma wafting through the tent. Sunlight filtered through the cracks in the tent, casting a warm glow on his focused and composed expression. The princess leaned against the doorframe, quietly observing the scene, as if beginning to understand the advisor's cryptic words. Just as she turned to leave, Kauko's voice broke the silence. "Princess? I was just thinking of you, and here you are."

The princess smiled softly and replied, "Thinking of me for what?"

Kauko smiled and ladled a spoonful of soup, offering it to her. "Taste this new soup I've made. See if it suits your taste."

The princess took a sip, the warm broth spreading across her tongue. She sighed in genuine admiration. "Kauko, your cooking skills have truly improved."

Kauko's smile faded slightly, as if he sensed something amiss in her expression. He asked quietly, "Princess, did you come here just for a bowl of soup?"

"Just for a taste," the princess replied with a smile, turning to leave, a hint of disappointment in her heart.

Kauko stepped forward and said in a low voice, "Princess, you seem distracted. I doubt you even truly tasted the soup."

The princess stopped and looked directly at him. "Kauko, I am in need of a commander. Would you be willing to take on the role?"

Kauko answered honestly, "The work of a general is too bloody."

The princess pressed further, "Then are you content to spend your life by the stove, cooking and stewing, without finding it dull?"

Kauko smiled without hesitation. "As long as I can stay by your side, even as a cook, what does it matter?"

The princess challenged him, "If Tichu is made a general, and you remain a cook, won't you feel even the slightest bit of resentment?"

Kauko smiled calmly and replied with serene confidence, "I don't care."

The princess relayed this conversation to the advisor. As soon as she finished, the advisor chuckled, as if everything had gone exactly as he had anticipated. He knew that the strange celestial phenomena foretold turbulent times ahead, and he needed Kauko to remain by the princess's side as her steadfast protector.

Soon after, Tichu was appointed as a general and sent to the front lines to fight alongside General Daoyin. At first, he was filled with reluctance, believing that he was the best protector for the princess. When the princess told him that she had found a new personal guard, Tichu couldn't help but ask, "Who could possibly be more suited for this role than me?"

The princess smiled gently. "Kauko."

Tichu sighed, as if he had already guessed. "I thought as much." Though his words carried a hint of resignation, he also knew deep down that he could never compare to Kauko.

***

The underground tunnel beneath Chinmi Garden led to a dry riverbed, where a labyrinth of caves of various sizes interconnected. Fire Maiden had named this complex underground world the "Dragon Palace," for it was here that she had hidden the unconscious king in a secret cave. To enter the Dragon

Palace, one had to pass through the underground tunnel, and those who knew of its existence had long been eliminated by Fire Maiden. Even Fire Rose was unaware of the tunnel and the maze.

That dramatic day, while Fire Maiden was deep in meditation, she suddenly felt the ground shake beneath her. Before she could react, she was thrown into icy water. As she struggled, countless boulders came crashing down from above, pinning her to the bottom. Though her mind quickly awakened from her meditative state, her body remained stiff and unresponsive. She closed her eyes in the murky water, using the tortoise-breathing technique to conserve energy, lying still as if she had turned to stone.

Days and nights passed, and Fire Maiden felt a long-lost vitality surge from the depths of her dantian (lower belly). Her joints slowly loosened, and her stiff body gradually regained its flexibility. Strength gathered within her like molten magma. With a sudden burst of energy, she struck out with her palm, and with a low rumble, the boulders shattered, sending sand and water swirling around her. Fire Maiden's figure flashed, and she silently slipped through the water, disappearing into the depths of the underground current. Moments later, she emerged in the dark Dragon Palace, her form blending into the shadows like a ghost.

Exhausted, she dragged herself to the sleeping king and cradled his face in her hands, tears streaming down her cheeks. "For loving you, I've become like this. How I wish you could protect me, just once!" The king continued to sleep peacefully, a faint, tireless smile on his face, making Fire Maiden reluctant to complain further. She gently stroked his hair, her fingers tracing his forehead, whispering, "Sleep, sleep."

She wandered between the caves, standing by the rocks and gazing at the ancient murals that had faded with time. She pried a black stone from the wall and began carving strange symbols into the rock, each one resembling a curse.

The cracks in the cave seemed to grin at her, telling stories she did not wish to hear. At times, she clung to the cave walls like a bat; at others, she leaned against the skeleton of a sunken ship. Her eyes flickered with emotions—sometimes volcanic rage, sometimes the sorrow of a lone swan. Her lips moved softly, as if reciting ancient incantations.

She picked up a long bone from the ground and gently tapped it against the cave wall, each strike following a rhythm. As she tapped, she hummed a self-composed tune, "The Little Red Fox":

Under the moonlight, the little red fox dances,
Lost in the lonely forest mist.
She heard an ancient tale,
And sought the light that belonged to her.

His bright eyes,
Shining with the light that was hers.
The deep lakes, flowing with enchanting stories,
The stars of the bright night, hiding mysterious adventures.
The little red fox defies the heavens, chasing the fiery light,
Whether it be a lantern or the fires of hell.
But with each step filled with hope,
Two shadows follow, hearts intertwined.

After singing, she suddenly burst into laughter, the sound echoing through the maze, filled with madness and despair, causing even Chinmi Garden to tremble.

The Sherkon soldiers stationed at Chinmi Garden huddled in their guard posts, too afraid to look toward the garden. Shadows flitted across the night sky, and eventually, the soldiers could bear the terror no longer. They fled with a passing Sherkon patrol.

Fire Rose was summoned to Chinmi Garden by Fire Maiden, but she could not find her. Instead, she heard Fire Maiden's eerie voice echoing all around. Left with no choice, she spent her days by Golden Mother's side. During the day, she burned incense for Golden Mother, and at night, she lit lamps, trying to calm her own fears. She asked Golden Mother, "Why don't you help the Governor? She's suffering."

Golden Mother replied, "My child, I have given her good advice and have been fair to her and to you. If I were to offer bad advice now, I would be no better than her."

"Why would you give bad advice? Why not show her the right path?"

"I eat the offerings you provide, so naturally, I must cater to your wishes," Golden Mother answered helplessly.

Suddenly, Fire Maiden appeared before Golden Mother. "I heard everything! I want to hear your bad advice." She then turned to Fire Rose and said, "Don't be afraid of me. Though I may have lost my way, I am still your master. You look exhausted. Why don't you rest in your rose-scented place and wait for my orders?"

After Fire Rose left, Fire Maiden urged Golden Mother, "Speak quickly!"

Golden Mother sighed. "If I tell you, all the incense I've received over the years will have been for nothing."

Fire Maiden retorted, "If you don't help me, Chinmi Garden will surely fall with me. Where will you go then?" Seeing Golden Mother remain silent, Fire Maiden took out a cat's eye gem from her robe and placed it on the altar. "I offer you my third eye. What do you say?"

"Your sincerity is rare. I will break my rule." Golden Mother then whispered something to Fire Maiden. "Even without the heavenly altar, you can still reach the highest level of the Heavenly Demon Art."

After hearing this, Fire Maiden felt her energy flow more smoothly, and her madness subsided somewhat. She woke Fire Rose, who was sleeping under a rose tree, and brought her to the king's bedside. "Fire Rose, remove your eyepatch," Fire Maiden said gently.

Fire Rose saw a dignified and handsome man lying peacefully in bed and guessed that he was the king, as he matched Fire Maiden's descriptions perfectly. For the first time, she truly understood Fire Maiden's deep love and meticulous care for the king, and she was deeply moved. She looked up at Fire Maiden and saw love and tenderness in her eyes.

Fire Maiden led Fire Rose out of the king's room and said, "I am exhausted and fear I cannot care for the king properly. I want to entrust him to his daughter, but I cannot let go until he wakes. What do you think, my disciple?"

"I think if you can forgive Princess Wenxi for joining the rebel army, she will surely come to care for her father," Fire Rose said.

"Of course I will forgive her. She is just a child. You know I never intended to harm her."

"Master, what are your plans now? The rebel army is closing in on Sien City."

"I will no longer involve myself in these conflicts. Let the Sherkon people deal with their own fate. As for me, when the king awakens, I will take you with me to find a pure land where we can cultivate in peace, hoping for a better fate in the next life. Will you still follow me?"

Listening to her master's calm words, Fire Rose felt as if she were seeing a new side of her, much like the moment she herself had once experienced a sudden enlightenment. She had prayed countless times before Golden Mother, hoping that her master would discern good from evil and turn toward the light. Seeing her master's change of heart today, Fire Rose felt a surge of excitement. She said eagerly, "Master, I will follow you to the ends of the earth."

***

After Prince Duan returned to Sherkon to ascend the throne, the old Sherkon general, Qiang Heng, became the military counsellor for the occupying forces. Knowing that defeat was inevitable and unsure of the Governor Fire's fate, he decided to retreat as soon as possible. He left thirty thousand soldiers under the command of General Tian Gou to defend Sien City, planting the king's banners on the city walls to create the illusion of a hundred thousand troops. Meanwhile, he led eighty thousand soldiers back to Sherkon. General Tian Gou once asked Qiang Heng in confusion, "You've already lost half of your two hundred thousand troops, and now you're taking so many with you. What's the point of leaving me with only thirty thousand?"

Qiang Heng's eyes gleamed with cunning. "You were trusted by the Governor Fire. She will help you."

General Tian Gou frowned deeply. "Do you really believe she's still alive? Even if she is, getting her to help me is no easy task! Why not let me leave with you?"

Qiang Heng whispered in Tian Gou's ear, "Leaving with me is a death sentence. I'll leave someone with you who knows how to summon Fire Maiden."

Meanwhile, the advisor and the princess arrived at Phoenix Village, only half a day's journey from Sien City. Standing on a small hill behind the village, the princess gazed into the distance, where the outline of Sien City could faintly be seen. She couldn't help but recall how Uncle Kau had helped her escape in this very place.

The mountain breeze brushed against her face, but the advisor's brow was furrowed as he stared at the setting sun, a sense of foreboding brewing in his heart. He suggested to the princess that they halt their march. "The signs today are unusual. Let us rest and wait for clearer omens."

In the village, the advisor stayed at a local household, burning incense and casting divination. The result was a single ominous character: "忌" (taboo). His expression darkened, and he quickly called for Kauko, instructing him in a low voice, "Go to Sien City and scout. I have a bad feeling."

A short while later, Kauko returned from Sien City, his face grave. "Though it is broad daylight, the skies above Sien City are shrouded in dark clouds, and the air is icy. It feels just like when we were trapped by Fire Maiden's demonic flute."

Hearing this, the princess sighed. "The advisor's foresight is indeed profound. Let us delay our advance."

Kauko nodded and left to relay the orders.

The villagers, hearing of the princess's arrival, rushed to beat drums and gongs, gathering around the small house where she was staying. The princess, hearing the commotion, stepped out with a smile and waved to them.

An elderly woman with a wrinkled face grasped the princess's hand and said excitedly, "The king and queen once visited our village. You look just like your mother! Are they truly gone? You must avenge them, and all the people of Daze!"

The princess's eyes welled with tears as she replied softly, "I will."

In the crowd, she noticed an old man with a weathered face and approached him. "Grandpa, are you still raising horses?"

The old man was astonished. "How does the princess know I raise horses?"

"Of course I know," the princess said with a smile, pointing to the sturdy black horse in the courtyard. "This is one of yours. It has carried me through many trials."

The old man quickly walked over to the black horse and lovingly stroked its mane. "I remember now! You were the one wrapped up tightly next to Kau Lame back then, weren't you?"

"That's right," the princess replied with a mysterious smile. "Thanks to your fine horse, it protected me all the way."

The old man patted the horse's back and sighed with emotion. "This horse won't let you down, Princess."

The princess spent a warm hour surrounded by the villagers, their laughter drifting through the cool evening air. When it was time to leave, she turned back repeatedly, seemingly reluctant to part with these simple, smiling faces.

As she turned to head back to her room, Songmao leapt down lightly from a peach tree. His gaze was suddenly drawn to a bright red glow in the corner of the courtyard—a cluster of roses blooming abruptly in the shadows, their vibrant colors out of place. Suspicious, Songmao approached and gently parted the petals, revealing a letter pouch with the words "For the Princess's Eyes Only" written on it.

He took the letter and quickly delivered it to the princess. When she unfolded the letter, her expression immediately turned grave. "Where did this come from?"

Songmao led her to the spot where the rose bush had been, only to find, to his astonishment, that the tree had vanished. The princess whispered, "Don't mention this to anyone."

She hurried back to her room, swiftly changed into men's clothing, tied her long hair up high, and covered her face with a scarf. She turned to Songmao and instructed, "I need to meet someone. I'll be back soon. Stand guard outside and pretend I'm still resting inside. Don't let anyone in, understand?"

Songmao's face was solemn as he answered without hesitation, "Don't worry, Princess. I'll cover for you!"

Kauko had gone to deliver orders, a task that should have taken only the time of a meal. But as he walked, he chatted along the way, and it ended up taking him a long time. When General Langkun saw Kauko, he asked him to demonstrate some of his skills. After watching, the general didn't praise Kauko but instead boasted about himself, "Heh, back in Annan, I already saw your potential." Prince Qin, upon meeting Kauko, insisted on matchmaking his sworn sister, Ayee, with him. To escape Ayee, Kauko had no choice but to take her to Tichu's tent and leave her in his care.

When Kauko returned to the camp, he wanted to report to the princess and hurried toward her room, only to be stopped by Songmao. Songmao stood at the door, his expression serious, his arms crossed. "The princess has given orders. No one is to disturb her now."

Kauko asked in surprise, "When did you replace me?"

"This afternoon!" Songmao seemed like a completely different person, unyielding and unemotional.

Seeing Songmao's unrelenting stance, Kauko sighed helplessly and had no choice but to return to his own room. But not seeing the princess left him unable to relax.

At dinner time, he cooked a bowl of the princess's favorite three-delicacy noodles and brought it to her door, trying once more to enter. Songmao glanced at him coldly, his tone tinged with displeasure. "Kauko, don't you understand what 'do not disturb' means? With your attitude, no wonder Tichu always finds you annoying."

Kauko had no choice but to force a smile, set the bowl down, and walk away. However, as the night deepened, the princess's room remained eerily quiet. His anxiety and confusion grew stronger, and he couldn't help but approach the door again.

Songmao was curled up by the door, seemingly dozing. Kauko tiptoed closer, about to push the door open to investigate, when Songmao's eyes snapped open, like an impenetrable barrier blocking his way.

Kauko looked at Songmao's tired face and said softly, "Songmao, you should rest. Let me take over for a while."

Songmao shook his head, his tone still calm. "Kauko, thank you, but the princess ordered me not to leave my post without her command."

Seeing Songmao's stubborn expression, Kauko knew he couldn't persuade him. He went straight to the advisor and asked in a low voice, "Master, did the princess have dinner tonight?"

The advisor stroked his chin and replied slowly, "It seems I haven't seen her come out tonight."

Kauko's frown deepened. "Don't you think it's strange? The princess didn't even have dinner, and she specifically replaced me with Songmao as her guard?"

The advisor's brow also furrowed with suspicion. "It is indeed unusual."

Kauko hesitated, then asked, "Master, Songmao won't let me in. Can I... take a look?" He pointed to the roof.

The advisor coughed twice, tacitly giving his approval. With this hint, Kauko quickly climbed onto the roof, carefully lifted a tile, and peered inside. The room was empty. He hurried down to report to the advisor. The two of them cornered Songmao and interrogated him, forcing him to reveal the truth.

***

Deep within the underground palace, a hidden passage loomed faintly, like a gateway to another world. Beyond the stone door lay a natural hot spring, nestled quietly in the embrace of the rocks, with a gentle mist permeating the air.

The spring water emitted a soft green glow, reflecting off the rock walls as if merging the stone with the water. The pebbles at the bottom, smoothed by time, were as round as jade, complementing the moss on the shore and adding a touch of vitality. Drops of water fell from the ceiling into the spring, creating ripples and a soothing, melodic sound, like a tranquil symphony of nature. In this hidden realm, time seemed to flow slowly, allowing one to forget the noise of the world and simply immerse themselves in the peace.

Every night, Fire Maiden would enter this secret place alone. She would gently remove her robe and mask, revealing her true self. As she slid into the water, the green spring enveloped her like a soft lotus leaf, tenderly surrounding her. Fire Maiden closed her eyes, letting the magic of the spring wash away her fatigue, as if every bubble whispered to her, lulling her into a deep trance.

Normally, the underground palace was shrouded in darkness, but tonight was different. Fire Maiden had lit torches throughout the chambers. The flames were particularly glaring in the dark, and whenever a cold breeze passed, the torches swayed, casting twisted and eerie shadows.

Fire Rose, having delivered the letter, returned to the underground palace. Fire Maiden gave her an approving look and said, "You've done well. I can sense that the princess is on her way."

A flicker of joy crossed Fire Rose's face. "Master, should I go up to meet her?"

But Fire Maiden shook her head. "No, go to the hot spring. Cut some branches from your rose bush and place them one by one in the water. Then scatter the rose petals on the surface."

Fire Rose went to the hot spring and, while carrying out the task, couldn't help but wonder what the hot spring and the roses had to do with the princess. Nevertheless, she carefully followed Fire Maiden's instructions. When Fire Maiden came to inspect, Fire Rose couldn't resist asking, "Master, what's the purpose of putting so many thorny rose branches in the water?"

Fire Maiden leaned over the pool, her fingers gently playing with one of the rose branches, a strange smile on her lips. "You'll know when the princess arrives."

From Fire Maiden's expression, Fire Rose already understood most of it. "Master, you're not going to harm the princess, are you? If you do, the king will be heartbroken!"

Fire Maiden sighed. "I didn't want to hurt her, but I have no choice."

Hearing this, the dam in Fire Rose's heart seemed to burst, and tears immediately blurred her vision. Her trust in her master had completely vanished. She couldn't believe she had once again become an accomplice in harming the princess!

She wanted to vent all her pain and anger, then die a quick death at Fire Maiden's hands.

***

Under the moonlight, the princess rode swiftly to the silent Chinmi Garden. The high walls blocked her view, and a few old trees swayed in the moonlight. She dismounted and pushed against the rusted iron gate, but it didn't budge.

Through the crack in the gate, she could vaguely make out the outlines of several ancient buildings, and a shadowy figure flashed briefly in front of one of them. The horse, sensing something, neighed uneasily. Summoning her courage, the princess knocked on the gate, breaking the eerie silence.

The heavy iron gate creaked open as if moved by invisible hands, and a spectral flame with no visible source guided the princess into the courtyard. The light suddenly became blinding, forcing her to close her eyes. When her vision returned, she found herself in the underground palace, face to face with Fire Rose.

The princess had heard that Fire Rose resembled her, but seeing her in person was still a shock. If not for Fire Rose's different attire, she might have thought she was looking at her own reflection.

Fire Rose, feeling guilty, introduced herself, "Princess, I am Fire Rose." Standing before the princess, she felt immense shame—shame for stealing the princess's appearance, impersonating her identity, and repeatedly harming her.

The princess gently took Fire Rose's hand and said softly, "Fire Rose, let me take a good look at you." Both of them felt a warm energy flowing from each other's hands, an indescribable sense of closeness instantly binding their hearts together. Fire Rose also took the princess's other hand, holding it tightly as if unwilling to let go. The princess sighed, "I've always felt so lonely. I never thought I'd have such a beautiful sister!"

Fire Rose was deeply moved by the princess's warmth. She had expected to be scolded, but instead, she was met with such kind words. "Princess, having you as my sister, I have no regrets in this life."

Fire Maiden, hiding in the darkness, watched the tender interaction between the two girls. Something in her heart was stirred, and she quietly wiped away a tear from the corner of her eye. In a hoarse voice, she said, "You two chat. I'll be back in a moment." She went to see the king, as she too had many emotions to express.

The princess asked about the king's condition, and Fire Rose replied that he was still alive and that Fire Maiden had been taking good care of him. But she whispered to the princess, revealing Fire Maiden's plot. "Princess, you must leave, or you'll die here tonight." Fire Rose already had a plan in mind, and she shared it with the princess.

"I came for my father. How can I leave without saving him?"

"The king will be fine. She won't harm him. You can save him later."

"What about you?"

"I'll manage. She's my master, after all. She won't do anything to me." Though Fire Rose said this, she had already prepared for the worst. She continued, "Do you feel that gentle breeze heading toward that cave? That should lead to an exit." She flicked her sleeve, and a stream of rose petals floated out, drifting like smoke toward the cave. "Follow the petals and run. I'll hold off Fire Maiden."

Soon, Fire Maiden returned, hidden in the shadows. "You two have been talking for a while. Were you speaking ill of me? Fire Rose, take the princess to the hot spring for a bath. Afterward, I'll take her to see the king."

Fire Rose agreed and led the princess into the hot spring cave, helping her remove her clothes. Fire Maiden watched as the princess donned a snow-white bathrobe, her skin like jade, her hair cascading like a waterfall, her eyes shimmering with a mysterious light that matched the spring's glow.

"Alright, Fire Rose, you may leave now," Fire Maiden's voice echoed from a corner of the hot spring cave.

Fire Rose obeyed and left. The princess walked slowly toward the spring, her pale toes dipping into the water. The green glow of the spring seemed to brighten, and a look of contentment crossed her face. She continued deeper into the water, the rose petals gathering around her. She gently parted them with her hands and began to hum Fire Maiden's tune:

Under the moonlight, the little red fox dances,
Lost in the lonely forest mist.
She heard an ancient tale,
And sought the light that belonged to her.

"Stop!" Fire Maiden's masked face appeared among the rocks. "You're not the princess!"

"Master, I'm not the princess. I'm your obedient disciple. I can sing your song." Fire Rose continued singing:

His bright eyes,
Shining with the light that was hers...

Fire Maiden stared coldly at Fire Rose, her voice filled with cruelty. "My obedient disciple, you've truly angered your master!" She then began to chant an eerie spell. Fire Rose's legs suddenly lost their strength, and her body uncontrollably sank into the water. But she refused to fall without a fight. Summoning her last ounce of strength, she stood up and shouted, "Master, if you're going to punish me, make it harsher!"

Fire Maiden's eyes flashed with madness. "You asked for it. Don't blame me for being merciless!" She intensified the spell.

Fire Rose struggled in the water, but Fire Maiden had already turned and was hurrying away to find the princess.

Chapter 22

The Flames of Hell

After hearing Songmao's description, Kauko learned that the letter had come from a rose bush, which had then vanished without a trace. His mind quickly pieced together the fragments of this mysterious event, and a sense of foreboding rose within him: Fire Rose must be behind this—or more likely, the scheming Fire Maiden was pulling the strings.

He leapt into the night, his figure gliding like an owl through the silent skies above Sien City. Moonlight bathed the city walls, casting a cold, metallic sheen over the tightly shut gates and the motionless guards, making everything seem icy and lifeless. He paused for a moment, deducing that the princess would not be able to enter the city.

He then turned his attention to the outskirts, searching the fields and forests for any possible clues. When he reached the back mountain of Chinmi Garden, he suddenly stopped. Under the moonlight, a swarm of colorful butterflies fluttered in the air, forming a floating ribbon of flowers. The scene was eerily beautiful, piquing his curiosity. With a swift movement, he flew into the swarm, only to discover that what he thought were butterflies were actually rose petals, carrying the distinct fragrance of Fire Rose.

"Fire Rose..." he murmured. "She must be trying to tell me something!"

Kauko followed the trail of petals, landing on a thorn-covered rocky outcrop where he found a narrow crevice shaped like the gaping mouth of a hungry fox, continuously spewing petals. He stomped hard on the crevice, and the ground cracked open, revealing a large hole.

He agilely jumped into the hole, following the rugged path marked by the petals. Suddenly, faint glimmers of light appeared in the darkness ahead. Kauko hid behind a rock and saw a figure holding a torch, looking panicked, rushing toward him. As the figure drew closer, he recognized the princess and stepped out from behind the rock, blocking her path. Startled by the sudden appearance of a large shadow, the princess instinctively threw the torch at him. The torch traced a bright arc through the air, heading straight for Kauko.

Kauko deftly caught the torch and called out in a low, urgent voice, "Princess!"

The princess froze, then her face lit up with surprise and relief when she saw it was Kauko. "How did you get here?"

Kauko waved the petals in his hand. "Fire Rose led me here."

The princess spoke hurriedly, "You came just in time. Fire Rose helped me escape, but I don't know what's happened to her. We need to save her!"

The two of them quietly made their way back to the hot spring cave. Inside, the cave was eerily silent. Fire Rose's body floated in the center of the hot spring, face down, motionless except for the gentle ripples caused by the rose petals drifting around her.

Kauko pulled Fire Rose out of the water and laid her on the ground. The princess carefully cradled Fire Rose's upper body, letting her rest in her arms. She brushed Fire Rose's hair aside and felt for her breath with her fingers.

Seeing the princess shake her head in disappointment, Kauko said, "Princess, hold her steady. Let me try something." He placed his hands lightly on Fire Rose's back and slowly channeled a surge of yang energy into her. This force temporarily summoned Fire Rose's dissipating spirit, bringing her a moment of peace.

Fire Rose gradually opened her eyes and, seeing the princess and Kauko beside her, managed a pale but contented smile. Summoning the last of her strength, she whispered something into the princess's ear, then tried to reach out to Kauko. He quickly took her hand, noticing a single tear glistening in her eye.

Kauko thought of all the complicated history between him and Fire Rose, and at this moment, he felt an overwhelming sense of regret. He reached out to wipe the tear from her face, but the tear transformed into a rose petal before his eyes, floating into the air with a faint glow. Then, Fire Rose's entire body dissolved into thousands of petals, swaying gently in the breeze as if bidding a final farewell before disappearing entirely.

As they prepared to leave with heavy hearts, Fire Maiden, clad in a red robe, blocked the exit of the hot spring cave. Her face was hidden behind a black-and-white mask, and she pointed a bone at Kauko, saying, "You and I are truly fated to meet everywhere!"

Kauko pushed the princess behind him and drew a copper flute from his sleeve. "Fire Maiden, today I only wish to take the princess away. I have no desire to fight you. Step aside, or else..."

Fire Maiden laughed maniacally, her mask tilting askew. "And if I don't, what then?"

"Then I'll give you a small warning," Kauko said, raising the flute to his lips and watching her reaction.

"Still playing childish games! Go on, blow it," she sneered.

Kauko, not believing she could be unaffected, began to play. But Fire Maiden showed no sign of discomfort, seemingly enjoying the music. Kauko stopped and asked, "What have you been practicing?"

"That's my secret. Now, taste this!" Fire Maiden's eyes shot out a stream of fire, like a dragon's breath, heading straight for Kauko and the princess.

Kauko immediately extended his right hand, absorbing the flames into his palm. Seizing the moment, he released the accumulated thunderous energy, sending Fire Maiden flying dozens of feet. She crashed into a stone pillar, and the ceiling above her began to tremble, threatening to collapse.

Fire Maiden struggled to her feet but did not retaliate. Instead, she shouted at Kauko, "Stop!"

"Do you finally understand my power?" Kauko asked.

"Ridiculous! I just didn't expect you to have mastered the art of energy absorption. Didn't I seal your heavenly gate?"

"Indeed, but the firestone you threw at my head a few days ago reopened it."

"Oh no no... I'll let you go today. Take the princess and leave," Fire Maiden said reluctantly.

Kauko took the princess's hand and warily walked past Fire Maiden. After putting some distance between them, he called back, "You're being reasonable today! But don't follow us, or I'll return and destroy your lair!"

"Just get out of here. I can't be bothered to chase you," she replied, extinguishing all the lights in the underground palace and making no move to pursue them.

Back at the front gate of Chinmi Garden, the princess's horse was still waiting obediently. Kauko scolded her gently, "Why didn't you bring me along for such a dangerous mission?"

"The letter said that if I told anyone, I wouldn't be able to see my father."

"How could you trust Fire Maiden?"

"I shouldn't have, but for my father, I had no choice."

"I understand," Kauko said, thinking of his own poor mother. If someone had told him, "Come, your mother is here," he would have done the same.

Kauko was relieved that the princess was safe and that he had been given a chance to play the hero, at least making up for some of his past guilt. The last time, the princess had been turned into a pig's head and had suffered greatly. He asked her, "For the journey back, would you like me to carry you, or shall we ride the horse?" Of course, Kauko wanted to show off his flying skills.

But the princess replied, "I'm just a mortal. Let's ride the horse."

"Princess, there's only one horse. Can I squeeze in with you?"

The princess mounted the horse without a word, her smile hidden in the darkness. She didn't realize that Kauko, with his night vision, could already see

282

her expression. He leapt onto the horse behind her. The princess cracked the whip, and the black horse galloped like a whirlwind into the mountain path. Kauko tentatively reached for her waist, then grew bolder, finding the same confidence and closeness he had once shared with Bamei. He held her tightly.

A long-lost sweetness rose in the princess's heart, a kind of intimacy only Bamei had ever known. She closed her eyes, and the memories she had buried deep within came flooding back. She saw herself again as the carefree Bamei, with Kauko, in the fields, the forests, the theater. After becoming the princess, that unbridled joy and closeness had felt like a distant world, separated by a veil. But now, every touch, every breath from Kauko felt so real. The princess felt a sense of fulfillment and sweetness she had never known before. She took a deep breath, savoring the happiness, and unconsciously loosened the reins, letting the horse wander freely under the moonlight, carrying her and Kauko into those beautiful memories.

The moonlight spilled over the open ground at the village entrance. In the deep silence of the night, Kauko nimbly dismounted and took the reins from the princess. He had to be careful not to be seen by the advisor, who might disapprove. Their eyes met in the moonlight, each wearing a knowing smile.

Seeing his innocent expression, the princess couldn't help but want to pinch his ears. She deliberately brought up a topic, "Do you know why Fire Maiden didn't fight you head-on today?"

Kauko looked smug and replied with a laugh, "Maybe she's afraid of losing to a rising star like me?"

The princess shook her head gently. "You don't understand. Fire Maiden was actually worried, just like me, that you might act impulsively and bring down the underground palace, endangering my father."

Kauko was struck by this realization. "So that's it. I was indeed a bit reckless. Princess, punish me!"

The princess's eyes sparkled. "How should I punish you?"

"Anything, slap me?" Kauko said like a child seeking attention.

The princess laughed and shook her head. "That would hurt my hand. I'd rather pinch your big ears." With that, she reached out and gently tugged at his ear.

Their light laughter echoed in the night, as if even the air was tinged with sweetness.

***

Hidden in the back mountains of Phoenix Village was a thousand-year-old mysterious cave. Deep within, candle flames danced like spirits in the thick darkness. The three monkey siblings sat around a stone table carved with the marks of time. They had discovered the Sherkon's hidden grain storage in Sien

City and were discussing how to destroy it.

"Let's stick to the old method—set it on fire!" Monkey Four's voice echoed in the cave.

Monkey Three crossed his arms, his brow furrowed. "But the grain is stored underground. Fire might not reach it."

Monkey Shang also voiced her concern. "Right, how can we make the flames dig into the ground?"

As the three siblings reached an impasse, Songmao rushed in, panting. After hearing their plan, he quickly said, "I understand your urgency to help the princess, but fire isn't the best solution."

"Why not?" Monkey Three asked, puzzled.

Songmao's expression grew serious. "Remember when Fire Maiden set that fire? She wanted to burn down Kauko's family estate, but in the end..."

"Oh, I heard about the fire at Kau Village," Monkey Three said, understanding Songmao's concern.

The monkeys exchanged glances and fell silent. They were all thinking the same thing: Who could guarantee that the fire wouldn't spiral out of control and engulf all of Sien City?

"Then what should we do?" Monkey Four looked to Songmao for a new plan.

Songmao stood before the three monkey siblings with a relaxed demeanor, a bag of peanuts in his hand and a playful smile on his lips. "Don't worry. I just got back from prison, not only with clues but also some snacks. Leave this big operation to me. You go find the princess and Kauko. There's plenty else to do."

Monkey Four laughed and patted his shoulder. "What, you want to hog all the glory? No more brotherhood?"

Songmao scratched his head. "Listen, the war is almost over. Give me a chance. I want a heroic story to tell my descendants."

Amid the laughter of the monkey brothers, Songmao disappeared into the forest. As he ran, he gathered every squirrel he encountered, excitedly sharing, "I found a huge grain storage, enough to feed us for ten years! Follow me, let's take it all home."

The news spread like wildfire, and soon, hundreds of squirrels, each carrying a small bag, formed a long line behind him. They scurried through ditches, climbed rooftops, and dug tunnels, emptying the entire grain storage in one night.

When General Tian Gou of Sherkon woke up, he found the grain gone. His face turned pale, and despair washed over him, nearly driving him to collapse. He wanted to flee Sien City, but the thought of his family being held hostage by Qiang Heng, the military counsellor, filled him with dread. In desperation, he urgently ordered his soldiers to requisition grain from the surrounding areas and pressed the mysterious man who knew the king's whereabouts to find the entrance to the underground palace. He planned to steal the king and pin the blame on the rebel army, forcing Governor Fire to step in, as only she could turn the tide.

***

Fire Maiden wandered like a lonely ghost through the shadows of the night. She sealed the exposed exit of the underground palace and dug a new tunnel leading to the volcanic crater north of the city. In the cold, dark passage, her mind churned with new schemes.

Her goal had never changed—to capture the princess and bathe in her blood. According to Golden Mother, the princess's blood contained powerful spiritual energy. When combined with Fire Maiden's dark energy, it would become the key to unlocking the secrets of heaven and earth, allowing her to reach the pinnacle of the Heavenly Demon Art.

Fire Maiden sat on the edge of the volcanic crater, her eyes filled with determination as she tried to awaken the lazy guardian god sleeping deep within the volcano. As the night deepened, she tried again and again, but the god remained unresponsive, leaving her feeling disheartened. She had once considered a mad plan—to jump into the crater and wake the god directly. But the terrifying abyss of the volcano made her hesitate.

In desperation, she took out a long bone from her robe and gently tapped the edge of the crater, humming her favorite tune, "The Little Red Fox". The notes drifted into the depths of the volcano, as if carrying some kind of magic.

When she sang the line, "The little red fox defies the heavens, chasing the fiery light," sparks began to rise from the crater, as if awakened by her song.

The sparks grew in number, swirling around her. The ground trembled faintly, like the breath of a giant beast beneath the earth, signaling an awakening. The tremors grew stronger, and Fire Maiden's heartbeat quickened, a mix of anticipation and excitement.

She leapt into the air, elongating the tune, singing with even more fervor. The melody seemed to open the gates of the volcano, and magma surged out like wild horses, massive fireballs and ash clouds rolling into the sky.

The thousand-year dormant volcano, like a giant beast lurking beneath the earth, had once been a distant legend in the villagers' tales. They had worked and sung at its foot, welcoming the seasons, never imagining that the silent giant would awaken, turning legend into nightmare.

The streets of Sien City had already become a vortex of panic. Cries and hurried footsteps filled the air as men carried luggage and women held their children, all rushing toward the city gates like panicked ants fleeing a flood.

Outside the city, the villages near the volcano were eerily silent, their doors wide open, the wind banging the shutters with a mournful sound. Only a few elderly men, their faces lined with deep wrinkles, stubbornly sat on broken wooden chairs in front of their homes, staring at the distant red glow with determined eyes, vowing to perish with their land.

Though the volcano was dozens of miles from Phoenix Village, the sky was already filled with volcanic ash, fine as dust, drifting in the night breeze. Under the faint moonlight, the ash shimmered with a dark golden glow, mysterious and unsettling.

On a high slope, the advisor held a short staff, his gaze fixed on the crimson fire clouds in the sky. He asked calmly, "Kauko, this commotion is extraordinary! Can you tell if it's the wrath of heaven or the work of demons?"

Kauko stood still, letting the wind whip his robes. He listened intently, and amidst the rumbling of the mountain, he faintly heard intermittent human voices, indistinct and surreal. He opened his eyes and asked the advisor, "Master, may I fly into the clouds to investigate?"

The advisor nodded slightly, waving his sleeve. "Go."

Kauko leapt into the night sky, his figure disappearing into the clouds like a wild goose.

However, after waiting for a long time on the high ground, the advisor still saw no sign of Kauko. He shook his head, sighed, and turned to walk back to the village. Just as he was about to close the door to his house, he heard the princess's urgent voice, "Advisor, wait!"

The princess hurried in, dragging a tall, dark figure behind her. Her face bore a mysterious expression. "Advisor, take a look. Who is this blackened figure? I can't recognize him."

The advisor was startled. He raised his lantern and brought it closer to the figure. The person was completely charred, with only a pair of white eyeballs gleaming in the candlelight, a terrifying sight. When he heard the figure's soft chuckle, he gasped and exclaimed, "Kauko? Did you fall into the volcano and get roasted?"

Kauko coughed dryly, his expression tinged with embarrassment. "Master, you really have a knack for guessing! As soon as I reached the clouds, I saw Fire Maiden at the volcano's mouth, humming some demonic tune and stirring the flames. I tried to stop her, but the magma seemed alive, lunging at me, almost swallowing me whole! Luckily, I escaped in time using the Five Elements Escape Technique, or I wouldn't even be ashes now." He pointed to the scorch marks on his body, his tone a mix of frustration and urgency. "Didn't you say fire couldn't harm me? Why did it almost kill me this time?"

The advisor's gaze was grave as he slowly examined Kauko's charred body, the burns in several places horrifying to behold. His brow furrowed, and after a long pause, he said, "This is the Hellfire, the most intense demonic flame in legend. If Fire Maiden can control such a fire, it means her power is nearing its peak."

Kauko's expression turned serious, and he asked urgently, "What should we do then?"

The advisor set down the oil lamp, his tone thoughtful. "Hellfire cannot be blocked by anything; it turns all it touches to ash. Yet you escaped with only minor burns, which means that while it is fierce, it may not be untamable. The next time you encounter it, don't flee or resist it head-on. Instead, try to use your inner energy to divert it."

Hearing this, Kauko's eyes lit up, and he blurted out, "Then I'll go try it now!"

The advisor raised his hand, his expression stern. "No. Your vitality is damaged. If you fight now, you'll only harm yourself further."

Kauko wanted to argue, but under the advisor's unwavering gaze, he could only mutter, "A few minor burns, and you're treating me like an invalid." He flicked his sleeve, a hint of defiance in his gesture, and headed back to his room.

The advisor watched Kauko leave, the authority in his eyes gradually replaced by worry. He turned to the princess and said in a low voice, "Fire Maiden and Kauko have been fighting back and forth. I'm worried about the king's safety. I want to find a way to rescue him first."

The princess replied anxiously, "Father has been unconscious all this time. Even if we rescue him, how can we keep him alive?"

The advisor pondered for a moment, his fingers lightly tapping the table. "Fire Maiden may have her tricks, but I have my methods." His tone was confident, carrying a hint of self-assurance. He pointed to an old leather bag hanging on the wall and continued, "Do you know what's inside this?"

The princess shook her head.

"This is a silver needle case, something I've carried for most of my life." The advisor's gaze softened, as if recalling something. "Before you were born, the queen once fell into a coma due to poisoning. The king personally summoned me to the palace. At the time, her breath was extremely weak, and it was this silver needle technique that helped her wake up. Since then, I've been serving by the king's side."

The princess's eyes lit up, and she asked eagerly, "In that case, what should we do next?"

The advisor took a deep breath, his gaze resolute. "Princess, let me think about it a bit more."

***

As dawn slowly rose, Fire Maiden's frenzy gradually subsided, and her hoarse voice grew quieter. She finally returned to her underground palace, exhausted, searching for a place to rest. Meanwhile, the volcano also calmed, with only the scorching magma quietly reminding people of what had just happened. As people began to calm down, they noticed yellow spirit papers scattered on the ground, each bearing the same message:

Truth is false, false is true,
Truth and falsehood confuse the world.
Where is Princess Wenxi now?
A painted skin laughs at your foolishness.
If you want peace, catch the ghost first,
On New Year's Eve, offer it to the fire dragon.

In Sien City and the surrounding villages, whispers spread like wildfire, and mysterious speculations filled every household. Villagers gossiped and debated: Were these events some kind of divine warning? Was it the Bodhisattva reminding them, or the volcano god issuing a warning? The princess had disappeared from the palace, and the princess riding the black horse in Daze army—was she real or fake?

Curiosity and unease drove the villagers to investigate, and they actually found some clues. The most puzzling was the black horse, which was said to be possessed by magic at night, moving like lightning, and its rider was always just a silhouette, their face blurred, like a black ghost. Some witnesses claimed they had seen this figure dancing with wolves among the graves. This rumor spread quickly, and many people gathered in Phoenix Village, surrounding the princess's residence, demanding that the rebel army hand over the so-called "fake princess" to be sacrificed to the volcano god.

To protect the princess, Kauko drew an invisible boundary around the outer wall of her house. Anyone who tried to cross it would be violently repelled by an unseen force.

This miraculous scene deepened the villagers' suspicions, convincing them that the fake princess was indeed possessed by evil.

Inside the house, the princess anxiously confided in the advisor, "Fire Maiden undoubtedly wants me dead, and now even the common people are hostile toward me. None of this makes sense!" Her voice was filled with frustration.

The advisor replied calmly, "Princess, there's no need to worry. This is just Fire Maiden's trickery." He then instructed Kauko, "Go outside and invite someone in—an old man wearing a horned hat, named Wang Xing. He's a well-known local gentry man. I want to talk to him."

The gentry man, aware of the advisor's reputation and having met him years ago, gladly followed Kauko into the house. He recognized the advisor and was about to bow when he noticed the young woman beside him, whose beauty was otherworldly. He froze, fear creeping into his heart. The advisor smiled at him, helped him sit down, and said, "Sir, please cast aside your doubts and take a closer look at the princess before you. Isn't she the spitting image of the queen, a celestial being? Don't you trust me?"

Wang Xing still had doubts. "I've heard that the real and fake princesses are indistinguishable. How can you be so certain?"

"The story is long," the advisor said. "I see you're holding one of those bewitching papers. Come over to this dark corner and hold the paper up to the candlelight. Look closely at the back."

Wang Xing did as instructed and was shocked to see a masked figure appearing and disappearing on the back of the paper, someone he felt he had seen before but couldn't quite place.

"Let me give you a hint," the advisor said. "Isn't it the demon Governor Fire?"

"Yes, yes! I saw her once during a play not long ago," Wang Xing nodded.

"Now, set the paper on fire," the advisor instructed.

Wang Xing held a corner of the paper and lit it. As it burned, a sound like the squeaking of mice came from the paper, and a series of child-sized shadows flickered before his eyes.

Terrified, he dropped the remaining piece of paper and exclaimed, "Advisor, what is this?"

"This is what I wanted to tell you, Sir," the advisor explained. "Governor Fire isn't dead. She's trying to make a comeback. This paper is one of her wicked tricks. Every word on it is a little demon, so anyone who reads it falls under her spell. She's tried to frame the princess repeatedly but failed. Now she's trying to use the people of Daze, because the princess is our guardian, and she's irreconcilable with Fire Maiden."

Wang Xing suddenly understood. He bowed deeply to the princess and said shamefully, "I've been blind. I'll go explain this to the villagers at once."

The advisor stopped him. "Sir, there's no need to clarify things just yet. Why not add fuel to the fire?"

Wang Xing's eyes swept over the princess's face, and a look of confusion crossed his features. His tone carried a hint of reproach. "Advisor, wouldn't that make me complicit in injustice?"

The princess smiled gently; her eyes filled with understanding. "Sir, listen to the advisor."

The advisor spoke earnestly, "I have a favor to ask of you, and I hope you'll lend your full support."

Wang Xing replied, "Advisor, as long as it's within my power, I'll do my best."

The advisor then detailed a plan to turn Fire Maiden's scheme against her. Wang Xing listened and agreed without hesitation.

After Wang Xing left, he spread a story that led the bewitched villagers away.

The advisor, the princess, and Kauko sat around a wooden table. Moonlight streamed through the window, casting a silver glow over the room.

The advisor, both excited and anxious, said, "Tomorrow, we'll steal the king. Fire Maiden will surely go mad, and that will be the moment of our final battle with her. Tell me, how should we handle this?"

Kauko gently tapped the table and said firmly, "Master, since you've already laid out this plan, trust in my strength. I can handle Fire Maiden's madness."

The princess's gaze met Kauko's, then turned to the advisor. With confidence, she said, "Advisor, we've been preparing for this moment. You don't need to worry too much."

The advisor's furrowed brow relaxed. "With the princess and my disciple by my side, I'll play the spectator once more."

That night, the volcano erupted again, and the world seemed to be scorched by flames. People were in a panic. Kauko wanted to join the fight, but the advisor stopped him, advising him to conserve his energy and wait for the right moment.

The next day, Wang Xing gathered several strong men from the village and quietly ambushed the path the princess often took. Sunlight filtered through the sparse leaves, casting dappled shadows on the ground, as if foreshadowing an impending storm.

When the princess and Kauko returned on horseback, an arrow shot through the air, striking Kauko in the chest. He fell heavily from his horse, but a glint of cunning flashed in his eyes before he closed them, pretending to be unconscious.

The princess cried out in alarm, dismounted, and rushed to check on Kauko, but the strong men quickly surrounded her and tied her up. Wang Xing then sent someone to Chinmi Garden, where they posted a notice on the rusted front gate. The notice fluttered gently in the breeze; its words clear:

To the Great Fire Dragon: For the peace of the people, I have captured the demonic princess. At the late hour today, I will bring her here and offer her to you for judgment. —Wang Xing, local gentry.

As soon as the notice went up, villagers from near and far gathered around Chinmi Garden, waiting for the spectacle to unfold. They wanted to see the fake princess with their own eyes, hoping the fire dragon would take her away and spare them further volcanic eruptions.

Fire Maiden arrived early, disguised as a village woman with a bulging belly, walking clumsily. No one paid her any attention; her face was hidden under a scarf, revealing only a pair of cunning eyes. She hated the glaring sunlight and summoned a dark cloud to roll over Chinmi Garden. She loved the eerie atmosphere, feeling a thrill as she saw the fear on people's faces.

Meanwhile, the princess and Kauko, along with a few capable subordinates, quietly made their way to the back mountain of Chinmi Garden. Kauko chanted an incantation, summoning the local land god. "Where is the king hidden?" he asked.

The land god hesitated, stammering, "It's just... just..."

Kauko barked, "The princess is here. What are you hesitating for? Aren't you afraid the heavens will punish you for siding with demons and abandoning righteousness?"

The land god, already short in stature, shrank further in shame. His tongue tied; he could only glance toward an old tree nearby. Kauko understood and ordered, "Go, stay away from Fire Maiden. Her days are numbered."

Kauko approached the old tree and, with a wave of his flute, uprooted it. Beneath it was a dark hole. "I'll be back soon. Prepare the carriage," he said before disappearing into the hole.

He landed gently at the bottom, facing an open door. Inside, a dignified man lay on a bed. Kauko assumed this was the king. Just as he reached out to carry the king, two black-clad figures appeared behind him, each holding a sword and thrusting toward him. Startled, Kauko spun around and delivered a backhand punch, sending the two men sprawling. One of their swords accidentally pierced the other's stomach, and blood splattered onto the bed and floor.

Kauko bared his fangs and roared, "I don't want to kill anyone. Get out!"

Kauko carefully picked up the unconscious king, moving slowly and cautiously, as if afraid to disturb the sleeping monarch. Once back above ground, he and the princess gently placed the king in the waiting carriage. Suddenly, the princess noticed bloodstains on the king's clothes. Her face turned pale, and her legs seemed to give way.

"Princess!" Kauko quickly reached out to steady her, his voice urgent but soothing. "This blood isn't the king's. Don't worry."

The princess widened her eyes in confusion. "Then where did the blood come from?"

Kauko explained, "I just fought two Sherkon infiltrators in the dark. The blood is theirs."

The princess's heart finally settled, and she took a deep breath, trying to calm herself.

Kauko then walked over to the uprooted tree, chanted a spell, and the tree slowly re-rooted itself in its original spot, as if nothing had ever happened.

Chapter 23

The foolish Child

As the final hour approached, the clouds above Chinmi Garden pressed lower. The sound of hurried hoofbeats echoed from a distance, drawing the attention of the crowd. Among them, Fire Maiden snorted coldly, her body transforming into a shadow in an instant, flying into the churning dark clouds.

A drenched and panting horse galloped to the gates of Chinmi Garden, kicking up a cloud of dust. The rider looked up and shouted to the sky, "Great Dragon King! Master Wang sent me to report that the princess is on her way. She will arrive within the hour!"

Fire Maiden felt a surge of displeasure. Lightning flashed and thunder roared within the dark clouds, startling the horse, which reared and threw the rider to the ground. The rider quickly knelt and said, "Great King, please calm your anger. Master Wang only wishes to please you. He saw the princess's extraordinary beauty and thought you might want to marry her rather than skin her. He prepared a grand sedan chair, had her bathed and dressed, and adorned her with makeup, all to present you with a radiant bride."

Fire Maiden thought to herself, *the old man is being presumptuous. What do I need a bride for?* But considering his intentions, she patiently said, "Go and hurry him up. The princess doesn't need to be dressed up; natural is better."

After another hour, the sound of wedding suona horns drifted from afar, alternating between joy and sorrow, stopping and starting intermittently. Fire Maiden initially wanted to grab the princess and leave, but she thought it would be more entertaining to let the play unfold. So, she called out from the clouds, "Why the delay? Why the hesitation?"

Hearing her voice, Wang Xing bowed to the sky and said, "Great King, the princess is in hysterics. She's wet herself and is crying uncontrollably. The bridesmaids are changing her clothes and fixing her makeup."

"Hurry up, or I'll take her by force!" Fire Maiden grew impatient, and the dark clouds churned violently, terrifying the onlookers.

Wang Xing replied, "We're almost there." He ordered the princess to be tied up and placed on a horse.

In a flash, the princess was brought to the gates of Chinmi Garden.

Fire Maiden saw that it was indeed the princess and said, "Master Wang, what did you say to make the princess cry so much?"

Wang Xing replied, "I only spoke well of you. If you don't believe me, ask the bride."

Fire Maiden turned to the bride and asked, "What did he say to make you so distraught?"

The bride opened her mouth but remained silent, holding back her words. She couldn't speak. In reality, she was Songmao, transformed into the princess by Kauko. The advisor had instructed him and Wang Xing to deceive Fire Maiden, luring her away from the underground palace so that Kauko and the real princess could rescue the king. As long as Songmao didn't speak, he could maintain the princess's appearance. This was difficult for Songmao, who was naturally talkative and found it unbearable to stay silent.

When Fire Maiden saw the bride's peculiar front teeth—sharp and shiny— she grew suspicious and shouted, "What kind of little demon are you? Show your true form!"

Songmao, intimidated by Fire Maiden's authority, let out a startled "Ah!" and reverted to his squirrel form, shocking everyone. He quickly let out a fart, causing chaos among the onlookers, and took the opportunity to escape.

Fire Maiden, seeing Wang Xing still sitting on the carriage, questioned him, "Were you conspiring with them to deceive me?"

"Yes, so what?" Wang Xing replied calmly.

"Then you've lived long enough, unless you have nimble feet like that squirrel." Her eyes shot out a ball of fire, heading straight for Wang Xing.

At that moment, Kauko descended from the sky, standing in front of Wang Xing. He extended a hand and absorbed the fireball into his palm.

Seeing this, Fire Maiden realized why Kauko hadn't impersonated the princess himself and why he had arrived late. A cold sweat broke out on her back.

She immediately disengaged from Kauko and fled underground to check on the king. But she found the king's chamber door wide open, his bed empty, and both the bed and floor stained with blood. A bunch of violets that had been beside the bed now lay in a pool of blood on the ground.

Fire Maiden's heart felt as if it had been sliced by a sharp blade. Overwhelming pain and despair surged through her. As her trembling hand touched the cold bloodstains on the bed, she felt the courage and confidence that had sustained her for years slipping away, as if her soul had been ripped out. Her world plunged into deep darkness, everything becoming meaningless, leaving only seething hatred.

Staggering, she followed the blood trail, which led her to the palace exit.

There, she saw a dark figure on the ground—a dead man who resembled a Sherkon tribesman.

She tore open the man's sleeve and saw an eagle tattoo on his arm, a mark of the Sherkon loyalists.

On a dusty path, Kauko escorted Wang Xing home, keeping an eye on the desolate surroundings. Suddenly, a frail little girl emerged from the ruins of a burned village and stopped in front of his horse.

"Big brother, the villagers say you're a hero!" the girl's voice trembled, her small, dusty hands clutching Kauko's sleeve. "Please help me defeat the fire dragon!"

Kauko reined in his horse and dismounted, crouching down to face the girl. Her dirty face bore a striking resemblance to the younger Bamei's when she was a child. His heart trembled, and he said kindly, "Little one, I have tasks to complete today, but I promise to defeat the fire dragon tomorrow, okay?"

"No!" the girl shook her head vigorously. "The fire dragon will come again tonight. We can't wait!"

Wang Xing sighed and whispered, "Her mother died the night before yesterday, and last night her home was burned by the fire dragon. This child..."

Hearing this, the girl wiped her tears and tugged at Kauko's sleeve. "Please!"

Kauko looked into the girl's tearful eyes and, after a moment of silence, stood up and said to Wang Xing, "The child is right. I'll go now. Please inform the royal advisor and the princess that I might be late."

Wang Xing, worried, said, "Are you sure? Whether you succeed or not, don't take too long!"

Kauko patted Wang Xing's shoulder, then turned to the girl with a smile. "Wait here. I'll go and seek justice for you."

As he prepared to leave, his expression suddenly froze, as if he were listening to something. Then, in a flash, he transformed into a gust of wind and disappeared.

In the blink of an eye, he returned, carrying a sack on his shoulder. He called out to the crowd, "Quick, catch this! It's full of treasures. Don't drop it!"

The crowd carefully took the sack, treating it as if it were a precious baby. When they opened it, they found it filled with glittering gold, silver, and jade.

Wang Xing asked in confusion, "Where did these treasures come from?"

Kauko pointed to the hill behind the village and said with a smile, "These must be treasures left by your ancestors. The ancient tomb was cracked open by volcanic rocks, and some thieves were looting it."

"Ah! That's the burial ground of our ancestors from eight generations ago!" the crowd exclaimed.

Kauko continued, "I've driven away the thieves and sealed the tomb. These treasures might have been left by your ancestors to help you."

Seeing the girl still standing there, gazing at him expectantly, he said, "I must go now. I'll see if there are any treasures near the fire dragon." With that, he soared into the sky and disappeared into the twilight clouds.

Kauko hovered in the scorching air, staring down at the volcanic crater. The heat waves rising from below forced him to conjure an icy cloak around himself. He folded his arms and dove headfirst into the depths of the volcano like a swooping falcon.

When he was a hundred feet from the boiling lava, his icy cloak had almost completely melted. The heat scorched his skin, and every bone in his body felt as if it were about to melt. He tried to summon another icy cloak, but the extreme cold dissipated into white mist upon contact with the intense heat.

Enduring the searing pain, he looked around. The scene before him was like a hellish landscape. The lava churned and roared like thousands of ferocious beasts breaking free from their chains. The alternating dark red and golden light was almost blinding. Bubbles occasionally rose from the lava, bursting into sparks that exploded at his feet. He held his breath, afraid that the slightest touch of the heat would turn him into a wisp of smoke.

He couldn't find the dragon palace the royal advisor had mentioned and wondered if he needed to go deeper. Just as he was about to take the risk, the lava suddenly churned violently. With a low rumble, a massive figure emerged from the depths.

It was a giant dragon, its body glowing with golden-red flames. It had turned over in its sleep, its massive form faintly visible in the lava. The molten flow around it danced wildly. The dragon seemed to calm down quickly and began to sink back into the lava.

Kauko swiftly drew his copper flute, focused his energy, and locked his eyes on the dragon's neck. With a sudden burst of strength, the flute emitted a blinding golden light. In an instant, an ear-splitting roar echoed through the depths of the volcano. The golden light pierced the dragon's neck, severing its massive head from its body.

The headless dragon thrashed wildly in the lava, its blood-like flames pouring out like a waterfall. Its enormous tail slammed against the volcanic walls, shaking the entire mountain. The severed head, however, did not remain still. Its crimson eyes blazed with fury as it opened its flaming maw and lunged at Kauko from the lava, moving as fast as a bolt of lightning.

Kauko initially thought of fleeing but found his body irresistibly drawn toward the dragon's head. Resigned, he gripped his copper flute and charged forward, thinking to himself, *Princess, I'm afraid we'll meet in the next life.*

The dragon's head collided with the flute, exploding into countless sparks that showered Kauko, stinging like thousands of needles. He momentarily lost consciousness, but it was only for a second.

The volcano began to shake violently, the lava boiling like an angry sea. The walls of the volcano cracked with terrifying sounds. Kauko looked up and saw that the passage above was mostly blocked by collapsing rocks. Clenching his teeth, he gathered his remaining strength and shot upward.

Rocks rained down from above, and scorching smoke filled his lungs, making it hard to breathe. Several large boulders nearly hit him as he dodged one danger after another.

Finally, he burst out of the volcano's crater. The fierce wind, carrying volcanic ash, hit him in the face. He stumbled in mid-air, then turned to look back. The crater had collapsed into ruins, and thick smoke billowed into the sky.

Kauko's chest heaved violently, his face covered in sweat and dust. He wiped the grime from his forehead, closed his eyes, and felt the cool evening breeze and the pounding of his heart after surviving the ordeal. He murmured, "Haha, Princess, it seems I really do have nine lives."

***

Fire Maiden, draped in a red robe, stood with the hem of her garment fluttering in the wind like flickering flames. Behind her mask, her eyes, glowing like molten lava, locked onto General Tian Gou, pinning him in place. His breathing grew rapid, and beads of sweat formed on his forehead. The silver ingots in his hand slipped to the ground, clinking as they fell. He hastily bent down to pick them up, stammering, "Th-These ingots... are for you..."

Fire Maiden glanced at the ingots; her gaze icy. "Silver? Can silver buy your life? Tell me, where is the King of Daze?"

Tian Gou trembled, his lips quivering as he struggled to speak. "I... I don't know... I really don't know what you're talking about..."

Before he could finish, Fire Maiden pulled out a severed arm from her robe and tossed it onto the pile of ingots. The arm bore a vivid eagle tattoo, seemingly mocking Tian Gou's feeble attempts to hide the truth.

Seeing the familiar tattoo, Tian Gou's face turned pale. His knees gave way, and he collapsed to the ground, kowtowing repeatedly, his voice choked with sobs. "Governor, spare me! I... I sent them to protect the king..."

Fire Maiden stepped forward, grabbed Tian Gou by the collar, and lifted him to his knees. Her eyes burned with fury as she hissed, "Why did you know the king was in the underground chamber?"

"It... It was Military counsellor Qiang Heng who told me," Tian Gou stammered incoherently.

Fire Maiden's gaze pierced through him like a blade. "What else did he say?"

"He said..." Tian Gou's words were fragmented, tears and snot streaming down his face. "He said... without the King of Daze, you would focus on dealing with the rebels..."

Fire Maiden let out a cold laugh, a cruel smile curling her lips. "You dared to plot against my king?"

Tian Gou waved his hands frantically, crawling backward. "No, no! It was... it was that pig-faced man... he took the king! It wasn't me!"

Fire Maiden released him, and Tian Gou crumpled to the ground, gasping for breath. Her eyes grew colder, and a murderous intent simmered behind her mask. "Where is Military counsellor Qiang Heng now?"

Tian Gou swallowed hard, his voice tense. "He... he sent a message by carrier pigeon. He's camping at Shawan Town near the border tonight and plans to return to Sherkon tomorrow."

Fire Maiden chuckled; her voice laced with cruel mockery. "You think he'll return to Sherkon safely? How laughable!"

Before the words had fully left her mouth, she tore off her cloak and raised her arms. Flames ignited in her palms, quickly coalescing into two blazing fireballs. With a flick of her wrists, the fireballs shot into the sky, trailing fiery tails as they streaked toward Shawan Town in the north.

Tian Gou stood frozen, watching the fireballs grow smaller and smaller in the distance, their fiery trails seemingly splitting the night sky. His legs began to shake uncontrollably, and his mind was consumed by the thought of escape. As Fire Maiden turned her back, he crept toward the door, sweat dripping from his temples and blurring his vision.

Outside, his horse pawed at the ground restlessly. He gritted his teeth and made a final dash, his hand reaching for the saddle. But just as he touched it, he felt a heavy weight on his shoulder. A searing hand clamped down like a vice, the heat of the flames spreading instantly. His knees buckled, and he fell to the ground, his strength draining away like water.

He looked up weakly to see Fire Maiden's cold eyes staring down at him as she leaned in and asked, "Running? Where do you think you're going?"

***

At the village entrance under the moonlight, the princess's jade crown reflected a cold glow. She sat atop a tall, sleek black horse, her snow-white dress swaying gently in the night breeze. Her eyes were filled with worry and anticipation. Kauko returned to Phoenix Village like a gust of wind, his figure almost like a beam of light in the darkness. He appeared before the princess and asked hurriedly, "Am I too late?"

The princess took a deep breath and said softly, "Not too late. But you, who used to be so cautious that it worried me, now act so boldly that it worries me even more."

Kauko chuckled. "Thank you for your concern, Princess! But I have something to tell you, though I'm afraid it might scare you..." Before he could finish, the sky suddenly lit up with a crimson glow, like a meteor shooting from Sien City toward the north. Kauko's expression turned grave, and he clenched his fists. "That must be Fire Maiden's doing! Princess, I must go!"

***

The evening glow vanished instantly, and the stars and moon dared not show themselves. A sinister aura spread a thick black curtain, merging heaven and earth into a chaotic, nightmarish abyss. Fire Maiden, like a ghost, hid within, quietly waiting for someone. When Kauko arrived above Sien City, everything was pitch black. Even his owl-like eyes were useless, as if blinded by Songmao's cloth strips. However, Kauko grinned, realizing it was Fire Maiden's dark barrier.

He activated his keen vision and scanned Sien City. The streets and alleys were eerily quiet, not even the wind dared to blow loudly. Every window was tightly shut, but faint shadows moved behind the curtains. People's eyes glowed faintly, as if searching for answers or waiting for something.

The nightingales in the trees stopped singing, their eyes wide open as they scrutinized the dark night. Stray cats climbed onto rooftops, sniffing the air.

Where was Fire Maiden hiding? Was she the nightingale, the stray cat, or the eyes behind the curtains, waiting to strike?

Kauko decided to stop searching for her. He waved his hand lightly, and an orange auspicious cloud appeared in the sky. He gracefully sat on the cloud, placed his copper flute to his lips, and began to play. The clear, playful melody of "Cangshan Sister" floated through Sien City's night sky.

People peeked out from their homes, looking up at the sky. In the night mist, a faint moon seemed to rise slowly from the horizon, stopping above the treetops. Who was in the moon, and who was playing this enchanting melody in the sky? No one knew.

Of course, only Fire Maiden understood that this was Kauko's challenge to her.

Fire Maiden smiled coldly, choosing a purple cloud for herself. Her red robe, bathed in purple light, exuded an eerie and mysterious aura, giving her an advantage in presence. She floated leisurely to a spot a few feet away from Kauko before stopping.

Kauko stopped playing the flute and stood up, waiting for her.

Fire Maiden immediately confronted him, "Did you steal the king?"

Kauko retorted, "The father and daughter reunited—it's only natural. How is that stealing?"

"What a motherless child! You dare to justify your thievery? I should teach you a lesson on behalf of your father..."

Before she could finish, Kauko interrupted, "You've played so many tricks on me—snake demons, bewitching incense, fire attacks, water attacks, the yin-yang lock. What else do you have? Show me your best move."

Fire Maiden smirked, "Then let me show you something new." Her red lips parted slightly as she blew a cold breath toward Kauko.

Kauko stood his ground, feeling the cold breath like an evening breeze, so he paid it no mind. He thought Fire Maiden was gathering energy for a major attack. But she stopped there, tilting her head back and laughing loudly, her voice echoing over the empty city like the grinding of a millstone in the quiet night. "Foolish child, you still don't realize you're about to die?"

As soon as she spoke, Kauko felt a chilling cold spread through his heart. In the blink of an eye, he turned into an ice statue from head to toe, his body as stiff as stone, unable to move. No matter what spells he tried to summon to escape, none worked.

Fire Maiden circled around him, gloating, "I could take your life, but that wouldn't be fun. I have a better way to punish your disrespect." She pulled a silver needle from her sleeve and held it up to Kauko's eyes. "Poor child, you suffered from this magic needle since you were young, and now you'll have to endure it again. This time, I won't be merciful. I'll give you a few more." She pulled out another needle, and then another...

She continued to ramble, "I guarantee you'll never fly again, never use your skills, never laugh, never have children. You'll only cry and obey my commands."

Kauko stared at the cold, glinting needles in Fire Maiden's hand. A trace of regret flashed in his eyes as he recalled their many confrontations. He realized he had been too arrogant, underestimating Fire Maiden's power.

He took a deep breath, his pupils reflecting the cold light of the needles. Just as he was about to close his eyes, the familiar face of the princess appeared in his mind. He thought, *Who will protect her in the future? Who will guard her pure, jade-like world?*

Then, the princess's gentle voice echoed in his heart, like sunlight breaking through dark clouds, dispelling all the gloom in his mind: "I'm with you. What are you afraid of?" Her voice, like a spring breeze, restored Kauko's determination and courage.

He suddenly realized, *Why should I fear her? Those needles made me lose my composure! Now that I'm invincible, why fear a few small needles? Let her try!* As his mind relaxed, he felt a strange sensation in his legs, as if insects were biting him, or perhaps needles pricking him. But Fire Maiden's needles were still in her hand, and she was still pulling more from her sleeve. What could it be?

Kauko suddenly understood—it was the sparks of underground fire! A few must have slipped into his pants earlier and hadn't escaped. He immediately focused his energy, drawing those sparks into his body and catalyzing them, instantly breaking Fire Maiden's ice spell.

Taking advantage of Fire Maiden's distraction, Kauko grabbed her hand holding the needles and shook them loose. He then activated his energy-absorbing technique, intending to drain her essence. Fire Maiden panicked briefly but quickly regained her composure. She grabbed his other hand and sneered, "Pig boy, energy absorption is my specialty! I was a bit slow earlier, but let's see if you can escape this time."

Under the dark night sky, their figures intertwined like a sudden crack in the heavens, a dazzling lightning bolt tearing through the night. They plummeted to the ground, creating a massive crater as flames erupted and spread rapidly. They leaped over the flames, darting through the lightning and thunder, like two dragons engaged in a thrilling battle across the heavens and earth.

After a fierce struggle, silence fell, the echoes of the battle still ringing in their ears. As the smoke cleared, the two figures crashed to the ground, raising a cloud of dust. Kauko's clothes were torn, flames still flickering on them, emitting a faint red glow. He struggled to breathe, each breath accompanied by sharp pain. A long wound on his arm dripped blood. Fire Maiden's skirt was shredded, her disheveled hair clinging to her sweaty forehead. Her mask was gone, and her scarred face bore a new, deep gash, twisting her features further. She tore a piece of her skirt and tied it around her cheek.

Neither could stand anymore, using their last bit of strength to prop themselves up against the scarred city wall. Kauko raised his head with difficulty, his eyes meeting Fire Maiden's. Both pairs of eyes were filled with exhaustion but also defiance. They seemed to be searching for answers in each other's gaze, or perhaps just a sliver of comfort.

Kauko gritted his teeth and pointed at Fire Maiden, "Old demon, I could have beaten you if you hadn't used that dirty trick, freezing my limbs."

Fire Maiden's eyes flickered with residual flames as she replied, "Pig boy, even your father respected me. How dare you call me an old demon? If it weren't for your father's sake, I would have destroyed you long ago! I didn't finish you off earlier because I had already expended much of my energy launching those fireballs. Let me catch my breath, and then I'll deal with you!"

Kauko struggled to stand, shaking his arms defiantly, "Next time, you won't be so lucky. Now that my limbs are free, I'll beat you back to your true form."

Fire Maiden laughed, "Haha, you're not as skilled as your father, but your mouth is just as foul. If I were your mother, I'd slap that mouth of yours every day."

Kauko glared at her, his voice filled with deep anger, "Don't mention my mother! She was the one who loved me most in this world."

When Kauko mentioned his mother, Fire Maiden saw a glimpse of vulnerability in him, like a young boy. Her eyes gleamed with cunning, and she hatched a plan.

"You poor child," Fire Maiden said, pretending to understand, "Why would I speak ill of your mother? I know her better than you do. I've seen her! She was a beautiful woman, a loving mother. When you were young, she was always by your side. Even now, if you calm your heart, you can see that she hasn't gone far. She's still nearby. Can you see your mother? Look ahead, in that halo of light. Isn't that your mother?" She cast a hypnotic spell, transforming herself into the image of Kauko's mother, beckoning to him from within a soft, beautiful glow.

Kauko stood up and walked toward his mother, reaching out to take her hand. But his mother took a step back, withdrawing her hand, and said, "My child, we are separated by the boundary of life and death. We cannot touch. The reason I haven't moved on is because I have one unresolved matter."

Kauko asked, "Mother, I'm doing well. What is it that troubles you so much?"

His mother pointed at him with her sleeve, "I want to see you married."

"Mother, I haven't found the right person yet. I'm afraid you'll have to wait."

"You're not being honest with me!"

"Please forgive me, Mother. There is a woman in my heart, but I don't know if she feels the same. If you insist, I'll take you to see her."

"Is the woman you speak of the princess? Very well, my son, lead the way."

Kauko and his mother, each riding a colorful cloud, floated to the open-air arena south of the city in an instant. His mother asked, "It's pitch black down there, empty. Are you deceiving me?"

"Please be patient, Mother. The princess and her entourage must be hiding in fear, probably in some corner. Let me light the way." As he spoke, Kauko raised his right hand and transformed the divine energy he had gathered into a fist-sized orange fireball, shooting it into the sky.

His mother looked up at the fireball and laughed, "It seems this little light won't do. Let's go down and look."

Kauko stopped her, saying gently, "Wait a moment, Mother. It's too dark, and we might scare the princess."

At that moment, the small fireball in the night sky suddenly transformed into a massive, blazing white sun, hanging in the heaven. Its light was not the warm golden glow of the sun but a blinding white radiance, instantly illuminating the entire world. The grass, trees, streams, and distant mountains, all hidden in darkness, became vividly clear under the intense light.

Kauko's mother let out a terrified cry, revealing Fire Maiden's true form. The sudden brightness filled her with extreme fear. She instinctively covered her eyes and curled up, no longer able to maintain her disguise, and tried to flee. However, the fields, treetops, rooftops, and hillsides were all covered with mirrors, reflecting beams of scorching light toward her. It was the princess, who had commanded the monkey army to set up these mirrors in advance. They worked in groups of three, operating large copper mirrors.

Fire Maiden tried to escape underground, but Kauko blocked her every move. She thrashed wildly in the air like a mad cow, but no matter which direction she fled, she couldn't escape the beams of light. Finally, like a bundle of burning red grass, she slowly descended toward the arena, trailing smoke and fire.

Kauko hovered in the air, confirming that Fire Maiden's demonic powers had been broken, and finally relaxed. Only then did he realize that the wound on his arm was bleeding profusely. His vision blurred for a moment, and he saw Tichu approaching. He landed in front of Tichu, blocking his path.

Tichu reined in his horse and demanded, "Why are you blocking my way? Are you here to settle things with me?"

Though exhausted, Kauko forced himself to stand straight and smiled faintly, "Tichu, I'm here for the princess..."

"Of course I know you're here for the princess! But if you want to fight, I'm ready." Tichu knew he was no match for Kauko, but he was determined to defend his dignity.

Kauko laughed, his tone light, "Butcher, when did I say I wanted to fight? I just want to borrow your orange robe. I don't want the princess to see me covered in blood and get scared."

Tichu was momentarily stunned, then burst into laughter. He took off his robe and tossed it to Kauko, "Such a small matter!"

Kauko caught it and said cheekily, "I know you dislike me, but I'm like a sticky plaster—you can't shake me off."

Tichu extended a large hand, inviting Kauko onto his horse, "Get on, hero!"

Kauko leaped onto the horse, sitting behind Tichu. Tichu cracked the whip, and the horse galloped toward the arena.

The princess and Songmao had already arrived at the arena. They watched as the fiery mass slowly descended before them, turning to ash. Songmao couldn't help but shout, "Haha, Princess, Chef has roasted the demon today!"

The princess responded excitedly, "Who says otherwise!" But then she looked around, "Why don't I see Kauko coming down?"

At that moment, Kauko seemed to emerge from the ground, appearing like a shadow behind the princess. He smiled at Songmao, raising a finger to his lips, signaling him to stay quiet.

Songmao deliberately raised his voice and said to the princess, "Princess, Kauko once told me that once Fire Maiden was dealt with, he would return to his Tian Mountain. I think he might have left without saying goodbye."

The princess was stunned, her brow furrowed, "Is that true?"

Songmao feigned mystery, "Actually, it was just a dream. It might not be real."

"You rascal, Songmao! Are you teasing me? Kauko has accomplished a great feat. I must thank him!"

Songmao smiled slightly, "Princess, if you only have a 'thank you' for Kauko, I can pass it on for you."

The princess laughed, "Haha, go find him quickly. I still have a general's position waiting for him!"

Just then, Kauko leaped in front of the princess, laughing heartily, "I only want to be the general of the kitchen troops, not some bloody general!"

The princess was startled, then beamed with joy. She grabbed Kauko's hand and asked urgently, "Are you alright? I only saw you flying around, but I couldn't see clearly what happened!"

Kauko laughed, patting his chest, "Princess, Fire Maiden couldn't do anything to me. She was unlucky to run into the two of us working together." However, his face was pale, and his steps were unsteady.

The princess noticed Kauko wearing Tichu's robe and saw the blood seeping from his arm. She gasped, "Heavens, how can you still laugh!"

She quickly helped Kauko remove his upper garment and took off her own scarf to gently bandage his wound, her movements tender and careful.

Kauko winced slightly, pretending to be in pain, "Ouch, Princess, be gentle." He continued with a playful smile, "Blow some fairy breath on it, and the pain will go away."

"I'm not a fairy. Where would I get fairy breath?" the princess retorted, pretending to be annoyed.

"Just try it. Blow gently!" Kauko blinked.

The princess chuckled, took a deep breath, and gently blew on the wound. She asked with concern, "Does that feel better?"

Kauko's eyes sparkled with joy, "It doesn't hurt at all! With the princess's fairy breath, who needs a doctor?" His voice was filled with happiness.

As the two flirted, Songmao rummaged through the pile of ashes. Suddenly, a small red fox emerged from the ashes. Songmao shouted, "Fire Maiden isn't dead!"

The little fox lowered its head and tucked its tail, trying to sneak away, but the crowd quickly surrounded it. Tichu drew his sword, ready to strike it down, but the princess stopped him, signaling to wait for Kauko's decision. Kauko crouched down and looked into the fox's eyes. They were clear, like a mountain spring, with no trace of evil. He sniffed with his keen nose and detected no demonic aura. He stood up and made way for the fox.

The fox darted away, and no one knew if it was still the same fox, its reincarnation, or its current life.

The princess saw Kauko staring blankly in the direction the fox had gone, worried that he might be lost in the mindset of life-and-death battles on such a beautiful night. She patted his back and asked loudly, "Do you know what day it is today?"

Kauko turned back and saw the joyful faces around him. He replied, "The day of victory!"

The princess said, "Yes, but it's also New Year's Eve! Kauko, put away that sun in the sky and let the people of Daze have a happy New Year's Eve celebration." She called Songmao over and said, "Set off three fireworks and order the troops to enter the city."

Songmao and Monkey Four climbed a tree and launched the first firework into the clear night sky. The long arc streaked across the heavens, leaving a beautiful trail of colors from red to purple, like a rainbow descending to earth.

Next was the second firework, blooming like a hundred flowers in the sky. The beautiful blossoms slowly opened, their petals scattering in all directions with the sparks—vivid reds, dazzling yellows, and fresh blues, each petal like a fairy's gift from above.

The third firework revealed a smiling face, a long-lost smile that filled the night sky with joy and celebration.

The princess looked up at the beautiful sky and reached out to grab Kauko's hand, but found only empty air. She turned around and saw Kauko lying face down on the cold ground, unconscious.

Chapter 24

Farewell Gazes

The remnants of the Sherkon army in the city were completely routed. Soldiers panicked, dropping their swords and shields, shedding their heavy armor, and scattering like headless flies. They pushed and shoved each other, desperately surging toward the north gate. The howling north wind and the enveloping darkness seemed like a giant maw ready to devour every fleeing soul. Those who fell were trampled mercilessly by the crowd behind them, never to rise again. The fleeing soldiers resembled a panicked herd of sheep, running in all directions.

The moment the city gates opened, the long-suppressed citizens felt a signal of liberation. Under the cover of night, they climbed the towering city walls, tore down the Sherkon eagle banners, and angrily threw them into roaring flames. The leopard banner of the King of Daze was promptly raised, proudly fluttering in the light of torches and lanterns.

In the city streets, every household opened their doors, spilling warm light into the dark alleys. Children held hands, running joyfully through the streets, their laughter echoing through the night. On this night of great change, past wounds and memories were temporarily set aside. Every face was filled with anticipation for the future.

Meanwhile, the puppets who had once occupied the palace hurriedly changed into civilian clothes. Those who couldn't escape in time tried to hide. The surviving royal relatives, filled with joy, embarked on their journey to the capital.

***

Morning light spilled over the green-tiled roofs and upturned eaves. The princess, dressed in a white silk gown, stepped out of her fragrant chamber and walked gracefully to the palace entrance. Kauko was already waiting there, clad in deep blue armor. Golden threads embroidered with cloud patterns and flying dragons danced across his breastplate, and the crimson plume on his helmet fluttered like a burning flame. The sword at his waist swayed gently, as if narrating his honor and duty. The royal advisor had organized a special palace guard called the Forbidden Army, and Kauko was its commander.

Their eyes met, and they shared a knowing smile, saying more than words ever could. She lightly brushed the back of his hand with her silk handkerchief, a gesture so subtle it was almost imperceptible. He was momentarily startled but quickly composed himself, walking side by side with her into the palace.

The princess approached the king's bedside and sat down. Her slender fingers gently touched his pale, cold forehead, trying to sense the faint breath of life. The king's chest rose and fell slightly, but his snow-like complexion hinted at a grim prognosis. Nearby, the sandalwood incense burner emitted a faint fragrance, mingling with the scattered herbal scents to create a unique atmosphere.

The princess's eyes reflected her father's aged face. Tears quietly gathered at the corners of her eyes. She looked up and met the royal advisor's gaze, as if conveying endless hope, anxiety, and even helplessness. The advisor nodded slightly, understanding the princess's concerns.

One day, Kauko went to the herbal medicine room to visit the advisor but found him lying on the floor, foaming at the mouth and unconscious. Kauko smelled the herbal scent on the advisor and knew he had been experimenting with new medicines, likely poisoned.

He shook his head, quickly lifted the advisor, and placed his palm against his back. Channeling his inner energy, a warm current flowed from his palm into the advisor's organs, forcing the toxins out.

After a while, the advisor's breathing stabilized, and the bluish-purple hue on his face faded. He slowly opened his eyes and, seeing Kauko, gave an awkward smile.

Kauko picked up a broken herbal jar from the floor and sighed, "Master, what medicine are you trying to find?"

The advisor's eyes showed a trace of weariness as he coughed dryly, "I'm searching for a divine herb—one that can invigorate without burning the heart, detoxify without draining energy."

Kauko narrowed his eyes, "Master, are you referring to the immortal grass?"

The advisor's eyes flickered, and he stared at Kauko in surprise, "Kauko, you know of it?"

Kauko took a deep breath, as if reliving a painful memory, "Yes. I fell off a cliff searching for it, and Master Dapeng lost his life saving me."

The advisor pressed on, "Have you seen the immortal grass?"

Kauko shook his head, "No, but it might exist on Tian Mountain."

The advisor smiled, "If it does, the king can be saved. Otherwise, I'll have to keep searching."

"Master, give me a few moments, and I'll find it for you." Kauko flapped his large ears and soared into the sky, arriving at the Tian Mountain region.

Below the clouds, he saw a shimmering lake but no towering mountain that had haunted his dreams. Thinking he had come to the wrong place, he circled a few times, confirming this was indeed the spot.

Seeing an old man and a child herding cattle by the lake, he transformed his face and quietly landed, approaching them. He asked the elder, "Was there once a tall mountain here?"

The elder squinted, curiously examining the tall young man before him, "I don't know about a tall mountain, but there used to be thick clouds here, blocking the sun. Strangely, half a year ago, the clouds suddenly dispersed, revealing this vast lake."

The elder's words reminded Kauko of the Great Buddha at Jingxin Temple mentioning the "collapse of Tian Mountain." Now, Kauko was certain Tian Mountain was gone. Remembering his master and the beautiful memories of his childhood and youth, he couldn't help but kneel and weep, tears streaming down his face. The elder, seeing the young man's sorrow, helped him up and asked, "Did you have a connection with the immortals in the clouds?"

"No," Kauko wiped his tears, not wanting to mention Master Dapeng. "I came to find the immortal grass. Not seeing the mountain, I was overcome with grief."

"What do you need the immortal grass for?"

"To save a loved one who has been unconscious for many years."

The elder called to the child on the ox, "Shunzi, come here." When the child approached, he took a handful of green grass from the child's hand and handed it to Kauko. "This is the immortal grass. Take it."

Kauko joyfully accepted it and asked, "Such a rare item—why do you carry it with you?"

The elder laughed, "We grow an acre of immortal grass. It's not rare. We carry some to save the oxen if they eat the wrong grass and get sick."

Kauko thanked them and hurried back, delivering the immortal grass to the advisor.

The advisor prepared a new medicine and tested a small amount himself. Immediately feeling clearer in mind and sharper in hearing, he decided to administer it to the king. After several days of careful treatment, the king's complexion grew rosier, and his breathing became steady and strong.

On the fifth day, the advisor, filled with hope, suggested the princess stay by the king's bedside, hoping the king would see her first upon waking. However, the king remained unconscious, his eyes moving rapidly beneath closed lids, as if lost in a deep dream.

The princess waited patiently by the king's bedside for half a day. At lunchtime, Kauko personally prepared a bowl of three-delicacy noodles and brought it to the princess. The princess and the advisor politely declined the bowl, and Kauko, embarrassed, said, "How could I forget about the master!" At that moment, as if drawn by the aroma, the king's eyelids slowly lifted. His vision was blurry, but he mumbled, "My love, help me sit up."

Hearing the king's voice, the princess held back tears of joy and gently helped him sit up, leaning against the headboard.

The advisor knelt and kowtowed, his voice trembling slightly, "Your servant Midd pays homage to the king."

The king's gaze turned to the advisor, "Advisor, why are you so unkempt? You've aged."

The advisor replied with a mix of joy and sorrow, "Your Majesty, you have been asleep for over sixteen years. I have suffered greatly all these years. How could I not age?"

The king's eyes wandered to the princess, and he softly said, "Then why does my beloved look as young and beautiful as ever?"

The princess, her heart filled with mixed emotions, took his hand and pressed it to her cheek, sighing gently, "Father, I am Wenxi, your daughter."

The king gasped, his hand gently brushing her cheek, as if confirming his memory, "Wen'er (endeared calling), how have you grown so much? And... where is the queen?"

Tears welled up in the princess's eyes as she whispered, "Mother has left us."

"Why?" he asked, his voice fragile, almost inaudible. Perhaps he didn't need an answer; he already knew.

His eyes wandered around the room, as if searching for someone else—a betel nut girl.

He must have been deeply disappointed, for she was nowhere to be found. Everyone in the room knew who he was looking for, but no one dared to mention her name.

His gaze fell on Kauko's distinctive pig-like face, and his brow furrowed. He asked the advisor, "Who is this?"

The advisor replied, "His name is Kauko. He is a blessing to Daze."

The king's expression darkened, "Since when does the palace of Daze harbor monsters? Drive him out at once!"

The princess defended Kauko, "Father, Kauko saved all of Daze. He is not a monster!"

The king glared, his tone firm, "I said out, and out it is!"

The advisor nodded slightly, signaling Kauko to leave. When the door closed behind him, the princess and the advisor exchanged looks filled with regret.

The king, seeing their silence, sighed slowly, "Advisor, you must remember the last time a pig demon appeared, Daze fell into ruin. Now, another pig-headed creature appears. Is misfortune upon us again?"

Fearing the king's recovery would be affected, the advisor reassured him, "Your Majesty, rest assured. I will keep him far from the palace."

Kauko walked heavily out of the palace's golden gates. He handed his sword and token to a servant, instructing him to return them to the princess.

With a heavy heart, he left the familiar capital and headed straight for distant Phoenix Mountain, where his friends Songmao and the monkey siblings lived. Seeing Kauko's dejected state, Songmao jokingly asked, "Did the princess find another love?"

Kauko collapsed onto a straw bed, his voice tinged with bitterness, "It's not about the princess. The king woke up, took one look at my face, and banished me from the palace."

Monkey Three's anger was evident, "I always said the people of Daze and Sherkon are no different. That's why I prefer to stay in this cave rather than go to Sien City."

Monkey Shang asked with concern, "What about the princess... did she let you go?"

Monkey Four shook his head, "Royal rules dictate the king's word is law. The princess has no say. She can't do anything."

Kauko said softly, "Anyway, aren't we fine together?" He tried to sound lighthearted, but they all heard the resignation, loss, and longing in his voice.

Though the king had just awakened from his long slumber, he recovered quickly. Within days, he was seated in the palace's council hall, reading congratulatory letters from various nations. A letter with a red base and gold edges caught his attention. Opening it, he found it was a personal letter from the King of Annan. "To strengthen the deep friendship between our nations, shall we consider the previously agreed-upon marriage alliance, laying a cornerstone for future alliances?" it read. Looking at the advisor standing before him, the king inquired, "As for Prince Qin, I have only heard of his name. What is he truly like?"

The advisor reported truthfully, "Prince Qin is loyal, kind, and righteous. He has risked his life for Daze."

Hearing this, the king decided to meet the prince in person. He ordered, "Invite Prince Qin to the palace."

As night fell, the palace lanterns lit up one by one. The king and Prince Qin conversed warmly until late into the night.

The next morning, bathed in sunlight, the king's eyes were filled with contentment. He said to the advisor beside him, "Prince Qin and I have reached an agreement on the marriage alliance. He is willing to marry into Daze for the harmony of our nations. Advisor, draft a royal letter inviting the King of Annan to preside over the wedding."

The advisor bowed and withdrew. In the corridor, he encountered the princess, who had come to pay her respects to the king. Greeting her, his smile carried an unprecedented awkwardness and sorrow. The princess noticed the advisor's unusual expression but attributed it to exhaustion.

Morning light filled the palace as the princess and the king shared breakfast. The table was laden with delicacies prepared especially for her, giving her a sense of unease. The king's eyes sparkled with a mysterious light.

After the meal, the king said softly, "Wen'er, accompany me to the garden." The princess immediately stood and obediently supported him as they walked out of the dining hall.

Holding the king's warm but heavy hand, the princess could sense the unspoken sorrow in her weathered father's heart.

They arrived at a pavilion overlooking a pond shimmering with golden ripples. The king smiled faintly, pointing to a pair of mandarin ducks, his tone calm but laden with meaning, "Wen'er, do you know what those birds are?"

"Mandarin ducks," the princess replied, recalling a play she had once performed called *The Beating of the Mandarin Ducks*.

The king said softly, "Wen'er, watching them inseparable is enviable. I have also found a suitable match for you."

The princess looked up, startled, "Father, you've chosen someone for me?"

The king's smile remained as he nodded, "Wen'er, the person I've chosen for you is the most suitable. He will protect you and give you happiness. Trust me."

The princess's face froze, and she blurted out, "Father, I wish to decide my own marriage."

The king's brow furrowed, the warmth in his eyes gradually replaced by authority, "Wen'er, you are my daughter. The person I've chosen for you will not be wrong."

Tears streamed down the princess's face as she sobbed, "Father, though your intentions are good, only I know what brings me happiness."

"You!" The king, not expecting his daughter's defiance, felt a pang of disappointment, and anger flashed across his face.

The princess, not daring to look at the king any longer, fled the garden and sought out the advisor, pouring out her grievances.

The advisor knew whom she loved but understood it was a forbidden hope. He could only tell her the harsh truth, "Princess, the king has made his decision. There is no turning back. If you refuse, according to royal tradition, you will be bound and sent to the bridal chamber."

"Then I have no choice but to accept my fate?" the princess asked tearfully, her voice filled with despair.

"Yes, even I, your old servant, have no solution," the royal advisor handed the princess a handkerchief. "Perhaps the mistake lies with me. I shouldn't have brought you back from the opera troupe."

After Kauko disappeared from the princess's sight, the palace became eerily quiet. The princess grew restless day by day, unable to eat or sleep. Finally, with the help of the royal advisor, she disguised herself as a man, left the palace, and rode a horse out of the city toward Phoenix Mountain to find Kauko.

Monkey Shang was outside the cave drying clothes when she saw a horse approaching from a distance. At first, she didn't recognize the rider, but when the person removed their headscarf and let their long hair flow freely, she exclaimed joyfully, "Ah, it's the princess!"

She tossed the clothes aside and ran happily toward the princess. Hearing Monkey Shang's call, everyone gathered at the cave entrance to welcome her.

Surrounded by everyone, the princess entered the cave. She looked around but didn't see Kauko.

Songmao sensed her urgency and stepped forward, whispering, "Princess, he was just here sleeping. He must have gone to the woods to relieve himself. Let's wait for him."

The princess nodded gently and found a comfortable spot on the straw pile to sit. Her voice was soft, "What are your plans now?"

Monkey Shang immediately replied, "We've discussed it with Brother Kau. We're planning to return to Luding in Annan."

Hearing this, the princess's smile stiffened slightly, and a faint disappointment and reluctance flashed in her eyes. "That's so far away. Won't it be difficult for us to meet in the future?"

Monkey Four sighed, his eyes filled with melancholy. "It's indeed a tough decision. We don't want to leave either, but Daze has never truly been a place for us outsiders."

At that moment, the princess took out a piece of paper with a secret code from her sleeve and handed it to Monkey Four. "This is a new decree about to be issued by the palace. Read it aloud so everyone can hear."

Monkey Four took the paper and began to read, "By the order of the King of Daze: From the day this decree is issued, all people residing in Daze, whether outsiders or foreigners, shall enjoy equal rights as long as they abide by the law. This includes the freedom to choose residence, occupation, business, marriage, and faith, as well as protection under the law."

As Monkey Four read, the atmosphere in the cave shifted from heaviness to joy. Their faces lit up with happiness and relief, and laughter echoed through the cave. Everyone realized that this meant they no longer had to leave for

312

distant Annan.

Monkey Three asked in confusion, "Princess, why has the king changed his mind at this time?"

The princess smiled gently, "Because your contributions and courage cannot be ignored."

However, behind her smile, the princess's heart was filled with endless sorrow. Only she knew that these efforts alone could not truly shake her father's deep-rooted prejudices.

In truth, what truly changed the king's decision was the compromise she had made with him. Recalling that conversation felt like reliving a tear-filled night.

***

When the princess realized she couldn't escape the arranged marriage with Prince Qin, she decisively decided to use this opportunity to negotiate with her father, seeking equal rights for all outsiders.

With tears in her eyes, she said to the king, "Father, if you insist on marrying me to Prince Qin, I beg you to grant me one condition—I hope Kauko and other outsiders can be granted equal rights. They are the unsung heroes of our victory. It was their sacrifices that brought us peace. If we cannot honor them, I will have no face to face my comrades-in-arms. I would rather end my life."

The king's expression darkened, his tone cold and harsh, "Wen'er, you are too willful! It seems I have failed to teach you properly over the years. Advisor, lock her up and starve her for three days. Let's see if she remains so stubborn!"

The royal advisor, trembling with worry, stepped forward to plead for the princess, "Your Majesty, please reconsider! You and the princess have endured so much hardship. Do not let this harm your relationship. The princess is still young. If she has erred, please show mercy. Allow me to counsel her."

The king waved his hand impatiently, "Advisor, my family affairs are none of your concern! Take her away!"

The advisor knelt on the ground, pleading urgently, "Punish me instead, Your Majesty. This is all my fault. I should not have allowed the princess to associate with such people."

The princess crouched down and gently helped the advisor to his feet. "Advisor, you have been like a father to me. What fault is yours? Please rise."

She turned and bowed deeply to the king, her voice filled with despair and determination, "Your Majesty, it seems your heart holds only yourself. You do not need a daughter. I might as well grant your wish and let you live alone!"

With that, the princess removed her crown and threw it onto a chair. Her long hair cascaded down, covering her sorrowful face. She drew a short sword from her waist and resolutely moved to slash her own throat.

"Wen'er!" the king cried out in anguish.

At that critical moment, the advisor swiftly struck a pressure point on the princess's arm, and the sword clattered to the ground.

The king rushed forward and embraced the princess, "Wen'er, why would you do this? Your father only wanted to teach you some discipline... Ah, you are as fiery as your mother. Never do such a foolish thing again. You are the only one in your father's heart."

***

Songmao couldn't help but sigh, "When Kauko hears this unexpected good news, he'll be overjoyed."

Hearing Songmao mention Kauko, the princess instinctively looked around again, a hint of anxiety in her voice, "Why hasn't Kauko returned yet? How long does it take to relieve oneself?"

Seeing this, Songmao suggested, "Princess, should I go look for him in the woods?"

The princess nodded, and Songmao immediately transformed into a shadow, disappearing outside the cave.

The princess waited for a long time, but neither Kauko nor Songmao returned. Helpless, she opened the bag beside her and took out exquisitely packaged candies and pastries, arranging them on the small table in front of her.

She forced a smile, trying to sound cheerful, "Tomorrow, I will marry Prince Qin. I know it's inconvenient for you to attend my wedding, but I still want to share this news in advance and thank you for your companionship along the way." Though her voice carried joy, her eyes betrayed her disappointment. "I had hoped to tell Kauko this news in person, but since he's not here, please convey it to him." With that, the princess quickly stood up and walked out of the cave, leaving behind a trail of surprise and confusion.

The monkey siblings exchanged glances, unsure of what to do. They knew the bond between Kauko and the princess had weathered many storms, and they had thought it was unbreakable. Yet now, they had to face the fact that the story of the princess and Kauko seemed to have come to an abrupt end at this moment of victory.

***

The princess wore a red wedding dress, vibrant and deep. The dress was embroidered with golden and silver threads of longing, shimmering under the light as if telling a glorious tale. Her hair was meticulously styled, tied high on her head, adorned with a golden hairpin embedded with pearls and gemstones that sparkled dazzlingly.

Long golden earrings dangled from her ears, swaying gently with her light steps, as if whispering a secret of love. Around her neck was a string of crystal-clear pearls, complementing her jade-like skin. Her wrists were adorned with delicate golden bracelets, one after another, and she held a red embroidered fan studded with gemstones.

As she slowly walked out of the magnificent palace, the maids on either side bowed their heads in reverence, their delicate hands holding golden trays filled with rose petals, scattering them to create a floral path. A group of musicians played ancient wedding melodies, the solemn tunes as if ancient deities were blessing the ceremony. Her steps were calm and dignified, each step in harmony with the rhythm, blending seamlessly with the surrounding music.

In the shadows of the palace's glazed roof, Kauko and the monkey siblings hid silently.

The monkey siblings' eyes sparkled with curiosity and excitement as they pointed at the lively scene below, occasionally exclaiming in awe.

But Kauko stood quietly, his eyes filled with indescribable sadness and loss. He silently watched the woman he deeply loved; his heart filled with unspeakable bitterness. From now on, his beloved Bamei would no longer be the free-spirited girl who shared his heart. Those carefree, joyful days would forever remain in the past.

The princess walked through the palace garden path, where roses, and peonies bloomed on both sides, emitting a faint fragrance. The trees were adorned with colorful silk lanterns, shimmering in the sunlight, complementing the flowers in the garden.

On one side of the garden path stood another heartbroken man. Tichu had led his troops north to pursue the remnants of the Sherkon army, driving them out of Daze for good. But upon returning to Sien City, he arrived just in time to see the princess in her wedding dress. He had experienced too much and began to understand that many things could not be forced, especially matters of the heart. Watching the woman he loved deeply walk hand in hand with another man, the sense of defeat was like a bitter wine he had to swallow. Who could have guessed? He had thought the princess would marry Kauko, but instead, Prince Qin was the groom!

Ayee, as the bridesmaid, followed closely behind the princess in her exquisite attire. As she passed Tichu, a sudden breeze lifted the hem of her skirt, catching it on a nearby branch. Tichu reacted quickly, stepping forward to gently free the hem and carefully smooth it out. Though a small gesture, it conveyed warmth to Ayee. She paused and gave Tichu a deep, affectionate glance, her eyes filled with tenderness. The icy layers in Tichu's heart seemed to melt slightly, rippling with emotion.

After Ayee walked away, Tichu noticed a handkerchief on the ground. He picked it up and saw the delicate embroidery of "Ayee" on it. He clutched it tightly, Ayee's enchanting gaze lingering in his mind.

Kauko and the others moved like cats, leaping from one rooftop to another, hiding under eaves, their eyes fixed on the princess's every step. The sunlight cast golden rays, accidentally reflecting off the silver ornaments on Monkey Shang, sending a beam of light into the princess's eyes. She instinctively looked up at the roof. In that instant, Kauko's gaze met hers. This sudden farewell struck her heart like an electric shock. Her steps faltered, and she swayed unsteadily. The maids around her gasped and rushed to steady her.

Songmao jumped down from the roof, swiftly navigating through the dense trees and flower beds, silently following the princess. As the princess slowly approached the bridal sedan, about to step inside, the world seemed to stand still. Her picturesque figure became the most beautiful sight in everyone's eyes. With one more step, she would enter a different world. Yet, Kauko's passionate, melancholic gaze, though it traversed the crowd, time, and space, could not stop her steps.

She resolutely stepped into the bridal sedan. The red silk fluttered in the wind as the sedan gradually moved away, disappearing down the secluded path leading to Prince Qin's palace.

After losing sight of the princess, Kauko and his companions, disheartened, made their way to the outskirts of the city. They anxiously awaited Songmao's return, but he was nowhere to be seen. Eventually, they returned to Phoenix Mountain with heavy hearts.

On the hillside, Kauko stood alone in the wind, letting the cold breeze blow through his sorrow, the melancholy in his eyes undiminished. His heart felt as if it had been torn apart, the pain indescribable.

Monkey Three and Monkey Four busied themselves planning their mirror shop in Sien City, hoping that keeping busy would help Kauko move past his pain.

Monkey Shang, who seemed to understand Kauko's feelings best, quietly approached him and gently held his arm, wanting to comfort him. In the cool breeze, Monkey Shang's eyes sparkled with a hint of cleverness as she softly said, "Yesterday, I saw the princess sitting in the cave with us, restless, constantly glancing at the entrance. Even when the wind blew outside, she would turn her head, hoping to see something."

Kauko took a deep breath, the clouds in the sky seeming to stir with emotion. He said in a low voice, "I understand. That's why I hid, so her gaze wouldn't waver because of me, so her heart wouldn't suffer more."

Monkey Shang bit her lip, her face curious. "Then... Brother Kau, what will you do next?"

Kauko gazed into the distance, silent for a moment before whispering, "I... truly don't know."

Monkey Shang smiled gently and said, "I've heard that a girl often watches you from the shadows. Do you know who it is?"

Kauko smiled bitterly, "Shang, are you talking about Ayee? Thank you for your kindness, but..." He gently patted Monkey Shang's head. "Some feelings aren't so easily replaced."

Monkey Shang frowned slightly; her innocent eyes filled with confusion. "The princess clearly loves you so much. How could she marry someone else?"

At that moment, Songmao returned with light steps, holding a pale purple letter in his hand. He handed it to Kauko and said softly, "The princess asked me to give this to you. She wants you to go to Chinmi Garden. At dusk today, burn this letter in front of Golden Mother Goddess and make a wish for her."

Kauko took the letter with a heavy heart. Seeing no words or seal on the envelope, he asked Songmao, "Did the princess say if I could read what's inside?"

Songmao hesitated for a moment before replying, "The princess didn't mention it."

Kauko smiled faintly, "Alright, tell the princess I will fulfill her request." Though the princess was now married, at least she still remembered him, and that brought him a small comfort.

Chapter 25

The Immortal Maiden

Before nightfall, Kauko arrived at Chinmi Garden, holding the princess's letter in his hand. The letter fluttered gently in the breeze, as if whispering secrets yet unspoken. His fingers lightly touched the envelope, sensing the emotions pulsating within. Yet, he did not open it, for he understood that some wishes needed no words.

As dusk deepened, the candlelight in Chinmi Garden swayed in the night wind, casting a mysterious glow over the golden curtains. Golden Mother Goddess appeared even more solemn and warm in the night.

Kauko carefully arranged the offerings and lit the paper money. The flames danced in the night, like messengers bridging the human world and the divine. He brought the pale purple letter close to the candle, ready to burn it for Golden Mother. Suddenly, Golden Mother's voice, filled with concern, asked, "Have you opened the letter?"

Kauko was startled, looking at the motionless statue of Golden Mother, momentarily nervous. "No, I haven't."

Golden Mother's voice came again, tinged with reproach, "Then how will you make a wish for the princess?"

"Thank you for reminding me, Golden Mother. I'll take a look now." Kauko carefully opened the envelope and pulled out the letter. To his surprise, both sides of the paper were blank, devoid of any ink.

"What wish is written in the letter?" Golden Mother asked again.

"Golden Mother, it's a blank sheet of paper," Kauko said, puzzled.

Golden Mother, as if seeing into his heart, said gently, "Perhaps the princess believes you can understand her heart's desire?"

"Of course, I can guess," he replied with unwavering certainty.

Golden Mother seemed unconvinced. "Is that so? Then tell me."

Kauko said sorrowfully, "But I think it's too late now. There's no point in saying more."

Golden Mother reminded him, "Since the princess entrusted you, how can you break your promise?"

Kauko took a deep breath, as if summoning a lifetime of courage. "I think the princess hopes Golden Mother will bless our pitiful pair, even if it's in the next life..." His voice was filled with deep sorrow.

"And what is your wish?" Golden Mother pressed.

Tears welled up in Kauko's eyes as he choked out, "It goes without saying—it's the same as the princess's!"

Golden Mother's voice became even more melodious and caring. "Truly a pitiful pair of mandarin ducks! Since the princess has asked me, I might as well grant your wish." Her words carried rare compassion. "Now, close your eyes and sincerely call the princess's name until she hears you."

Kauko obeyed, closing his eyes and devoutly chanting "Princess" in his heart. At that moment, the princess gently stepped out from behind the curtains and stood before Kauko. She was dressed in a pure white gown, her hair flowing like a moon fairy descending to earth. Kauko opened his eyes and saw the beautiful princess, unable to believe what was before him. "Are you some immortal maiden? Please don't tease me anymore."

"Pig-head brother, open your eyes wide. I'm Bamei!" The princess smiled sweetly, taking Kauko's hand and reaching out to touch his upturned nose.

When Kauko felt the princess's gentle touch, a warm, familiar sensation spread through his body, dispelling the doubts and unease in his heart like mist under the sun. Without thinking, he pulled her into his arms, his voice low and filled with emotion. "Princess, this time, no matter who tries to take you away, I won't let go."

The princess gently patted his back, a loving smile on her face. "Pig-head, don't worry. No one will fight you for me."

Hearing this, Kauko narrowed his eyes and said seriously, "I'm just afraid Prince Qin won't let go so easily."

The princess lightly poked Kauko's chest. "He can't beat you." As soon as she finished speaking, she turned to the shadows and called out, "Songmao, come out now!"

Songmao leaped out of the shadows, landing lightly on the princess's shoulder. He asked with a hint of pride, "Princess, how was my performance?"

The princess smiled fondly, scratching his little head. "Perfect, little one."

Kauko, observing their tacit understanding, frowned slightly and asked curiously, "What's going on? Did you two plan this?"

The princess chuckled mischievously, revealing the secret. "Haha, Songmao played a little act, pretending to be Golden Mother."

Noticing the princess yawn, Songmao quickly turned to Kauko. "Kauko, the princess is very tired today. Where should we rest tonight?"

Kauko suggested, "How about returning to Kau Village?"

The princess shook her head, her voice soft as the wind. "I'd rather go to

Jingxin Temple. Let's find some peace there tonight and set off tomorrow."

Songmao immediately jumped into the air, declaring in an exaggerated tone, "Let's listen to the princess!"

They exchanged smiles, the joyful atmosphere resonating within the temple. Kauko, in high spirits, leaped lightly into the night sky, carrying the princess and Songmao with him. The stars seemed to flow beneath their feet, and the moon felt close enough to touch. Soon, the familiar and tranquil outline of Jingxin Temple came into view.

As usual, Songmao preferred to spend the night in the woods, enjoying the serenity of nature alone, leaving the temple's underground chamber to Kauko and the princess.

In the mystical little world of the underground chamber, the candlelight flickered softly, illuminating the ethereal space. Kauko gently took the princess's hand and guided her to sit on the bed, saying tenderly, "Princess, sit down first. I'll make some noodles."

But the princess held his hand and said softly, "Wait, I have something to tell you."

Kauko sat down beside her, quietly waiting for her to speak.

"Kauko, don't call me princess anymore," she said, her voice light but filled with determination. "From the moment I left the palace, I only wanted to be a free-spirited Bamei, following you, living a life of farming and weaving."

Her eyes sparkled, her smile growing brighter. "During the farming off-season, we can form a theater troupe in the village, and I can even sing a few lines." Her voice was full of anticipation and happiness, as if she could already see that joyful and peaceful future.

Kauko smiled playfully. "I've been thinking about that too. Imagine, when we meet the elders in the village, and I say, 'Princess, come and bow to the elders,' they'd be so scared their legs would shake. And when I'm working in the fields, and you bring me food, if I say, 'Thank you, Princess,' the villagers would laugh their heads off!"

The princess laughed, adding, "That's nothing. If my father finds out the princess is hiding in Kau Village, we'll be in big trouble!"

"Bamei, you are right. I'll remember that," Kauko said with a warm smile, then blinked playfully. "Bamei, any more pearls of wisdom? If not, I'll start making the noodles."

"Wait, of course there's more," the princess said with a light laugh, gracefully standing up from the bed, her skirt swaying with her movements. She walked to the old stone stove, her eyes curiously wandering over the iron pot and cooking utensils. Then she turned to Kauko with a radiant smile. "Kauko, I want to cook a meal for you. Although I've never been in a kitchen before, I want to learn."

Kauko was deeply moved by her words, a glimmer of surprise in his eyes. He smiled and replied in a gentle tone, "The princess cooking—this will be a legendary tale. Let me be your little assistant." Under Kauko's guidance, the princess began her culinary adventure. Though she accidentally burned her hand and added a bit too much salt, she eventually managed to make a fragrant bowl of three-delicacy noodles! Her technique might still be a bit clumsy, but the love she poured into it warmed Kauko's heart. As they sat side by side, savoring the noodles the princess had made, they were sharing more than just a meal—they were sharing their hearts.

In the quiet after the meal, the princess took out a small bronze mirror and gazed deeply at her reflection. The bright candlelight illuminated her face, making her features appear especially pure and natural.

She said slowly, "Back then, I used this mirror to see my pig-headed self. That moment truly broke my heart."

Hearing her words, Kauko walked over to her, gently caressing her cheek, his eyes filled with deep affection. "Do you know? When I saw you then, I even thought you had become like me, even cuter than me. But when I accidentally saw you crying in the middle of the night, I instantly understood how much pain and struggle you had endured."

Tears glistened in the princess's eyes, but a sweet smile appeared on her lips. "That pain was indeed indescribable, but it made me understand you better. Come here, lean your head closer. I want to see what we look like together."

***

Kau Village had risen from the ashes of a fire over a decade ago. The ruins were gone, replaced by bamboo and thatched cottages neatly lining a stone path that ran east to west.

In the early morning, as the sun peeked over the eastern mountains, the night mist quietly dissipated, revealing the towering mountains to the east, the emerald lake, and the trees in the valley. The lake's reflection turned the village into a harmonious dream. To the north, a vast expanse of green grass stretched out, where children and sheep ran freely. Beyond the grass, the hills and forests guarded the meandering river that flowed from the north, winding along the village's western side like a graceful maiden.

To the southwest lay endless fields of rapeseed. As far as the eye could see, golden rapeseed flowers swayed gently in the breeze, like golden waves, their fragrance carried by the wind.

As soon as Kau Lame got up, he heard magpies chirping in the tree at the village's western entrance. Leaning on his cane, he sat down in the stone pavilion at the village entrance, facing the wooden bridge and the endless rapeseed fields beyond the river. He thought to himself, "Now that the princess and the king have returned to the palace, the Sherkon people are gone, and Governor Fire has been dealt with, Pig-head should be coming home."

The sun warmed his back as he smoked a pipe, dozing off until he was awakened by a group of children playing in the water nearby.

The sound of hoofbeats grew closer.

A little boy with curious eyes tugged at Kau Lame's robe. "Uncle, someone's coming on horseback. Is it the great hero you mentioned?"

Kau Lame looked up, his eyes shining with excitement. "Shui Wa, you're fast. Go and see. If he has a pig's head, he's your big brother. Bring him to me."

Shui Wa nodded excitedly and scampered off.

Soon, Kauko rode up on horseback, accompanied by the princess and Songmao. Seeing Kauko, Kau Lame was so excited he could barely stand, tears glistening in his eyes. "Nephew, you've finally returned!"

Kauko quickly dismounted and steadied his uncle, smiling. "Uncle, why were you waiting at the village entrance so early in the morning?"

Kau Lame's eyes crinkled into a smile. "I heard the magpies calling, and I knew my nephew was coming back."

At that moment, the princess gracefully dismounted and stepped forward, greeting softly, "Hello, Uncle!" Her voice was as gentle as a spring breeze, tinged with shyness.

Kau Lame studied the beautiful girl before him, as if trying to recall something. "Young lady, I feel like I've seen you before, but I can't quite remember."

The princess smiled sweetly and replied softly, "It must be hard for you, Uncle. I'm Bamei."

Kau Lame was stunned for a moment, then suddenly understood. "Oh, so it's Bamei!" He drew out his words, both surprised and delighted. "Welcome back with us." He turned to Kauko and said, "Nephew, she must be your wife, right?"

The question caught Kauko off guard, but he quickly grinned. "Uncle, yes, but we're not married yet." His voice was full of pride.

Hearing this, the princess's cheeks flushed, but her eyes sparkled with happiness.

At that moment, Songmao chimed in, "And me, Uncle!" He jumped on the horse, drawing everyone's attention.

Kau Lame looked over and saw the adorable white squirrel, his face lighting up with joy. "Come here, let me take a look."

Songmao leaped onto Kauko's shoulder, wagging his tail.

Kau Lame said to Songmao, "Songmao, it's rare for you to have taken care

322

of my nephew for so many years. You're a hero of the Kau family." Then he turned to the children gathered around. "You see, I told you the Kau family has a squirrel immortal, and you didn't believe me. Now you see!"

The children cheered and crowded around, gently touching Songmao, eager to play with him. Kauko and the princess exchanged smiles and nodded. Songmao happily jumped down and scampered off with the children.

Kau Lame turned to Kauko and the princess. "Let's go home. First, we'll pay respects to your great-grandmother. She's the one we consult for all major and minor matters in the village."

Seeing his uncle's difficulty walking, Kauko picked him up and effortlessly placed him on the horse. Kau Lame chuckled, a bit embarrassed. "This old bone of mine, just a few steps, and you're already fussing over me."

As they passed a newly built house in the western part of the village, Kau Lame called for a stop and pointed to the house. "Kauko, this house was built brick by brick by the villagers for you. Everyone has been hoping for your return."

Soon, they arrived at the gate of a spacious mansion. Great-Grandmother was already sitting quietly in the main hall, waiting. The children had already spread the news, and villagers flocked to catch a glimpse of Kauko's grown-up heroism and the new maiden's charm.

Great-Grandmother's hair was neatly coiled, and she wore an exquisite blue robe embroidered with intricate patterns. Her face bore a serene and gentle smile as she sat in the grand chair, exuding both dignity and kindness.

Kauko and the princess walked up to Great-Grandmother, knelt down, and respectfully bowed. "Greetings, Great-Grandmother!" they said in unison.

The great-grandmother wiped away the tears from the corners of her eyes and, with emotion, urged the two children to rise quickly. She gently pulled them close to her side, took two red envelopes from her sleeve, and handed them to Kauko and the princess. With heartfelt words, she said, "If only your parents and grandparents could see you grown up and achieving such great things, how wonderful that would be."

Her gaze lingered tenderly on the princess, her face filled with deep affection and joy. She asked with concern, "My dear, I still don't know your name."

The princess smiled sweetly and replied, "Great-grandmother, I have no family name. Since I was young, people have called me Bamei."

Hearing this name, the great-grandmother's eyes sparkled with approval. "Bamei, what a lovely and endearing name," she said. Then she asked, "And where is your home?"

A flicker of hesitation passed through the princess's eyes. Just as she was about to speak, Kauko quickly interjected, "Great-grandmother, Bamei's home is beyond the Cang Mountains."

The great-grandmother nodded, her eyes showing concern. "And how are your parents?"

The princess lowered her head, her voice trembling slightly. "My mother passed away many years ago. My father is still alive, but I rarely see him."

The great-grandmother sighed deeply and said softly, "Bamei, don't mind my many questions. I truly adore you, child. Let me ask you this: since you've come with Kauko to pay respects to the Kau family, it must mean you and Kauko are deeply in love. Are you willing to marry Kauko?"

The princess's cheeks instantly flushed with a deep blush. Kauko, standing beside her, anxiously urged, "Bamei, say yes!"

The great-grandmother gently waved her hand and said kindly, "Child, there's no rush. This is a decision that will affect your entire life. Take your time to think it over." She glanced around, her gaze gentle yet firm, and then called out loudly, "Big Foot Sister-in-law!"

From the crowd, Big Foot Sister-in-law immediately stepped forward, smiling broadly as she approached. "Great-grandmother, are you calling for me?"

"Come here. Take Bamei to your home and care for her as if she were your own daughter," the great-grandmother instructed.

Big Foot Sister-in-law readily agreed, her face beaming with joy. "As you wish, Great-grandmother. It would be my pleasure to help ease your worries."

She then walked over and kindly took Bamei's hand, leading her toward the door. The great-grandmother watched their retreating figures with a smile, while Kauko stood still, his heart filled with complex emotions as he watched Bamei being led away. The great-grandmother gently tapped Kauko's head with her fan and chuckled, "I see your eyes haven't left Bamei for a moment. Impatient, are you? Go home first. This afternoon, I'll send a matchmaker to Big Foot Sister-in-law's house to propose the marriage. We'll have your wedding tomorrow."

Kauko's uncle took him to the new house on the west side of the village. Kauko, puzzled, said, "Bamei and I have already agreed. Why do we need a matchmaker?"

His uncle replied matter-of-factly, "Ah, it's the ancestors' tradition."

****

Just past noon, the sunlight bathed the small path on the east side of the village. The matchmaker walked with light steps, wearing a red coat and a fresh chrysanthemum in her hair, looking spirited and lively. She pushed open the door to Big Foot Sister-in-law's house, a professional smile on her face.

Big Foot Sister-in-law, sensing the matchmaker's arrival, quickly led Bamei to the inner room and whispered, "Stay quiet. I'll handle this."

The matchmaker got straight to the point as soon as she entered. "They're both willing. I'm just here to go through the formalities."

Big Foot Sister-in-law responded with dissatisfaction, "Even if it's just formalities, we must still observe proper etiquette. My adopted daughter is as beautiful as a fairy. I must discuss the bride price."

The matchmaker, knowing she was at a disadvantage, said, "Then speak. I'll relay your message."

Big Foot Sister-in-law raised her voice, "Two oxen and twenty sheep should suffice."

The matchmaker immediately frowned. "That's an outrageous demand. Do you think you're marrying off a princess? Which village girl dares to ask for so much? I hear Bamei doesn't even have a proper background."

"Have you seen my daughter's face, her figure? She's a rare beauty."

"Country women shouldn't talk about such frivolities."

The two women glared at each other, testing each other's patience.

Big Foot Sister-in-law eventually relented. She could see that Bamei and Kauko truly loved each other and didn't want to cause any unnecessary conflict over the bride price. "Fine, let's follow what Kau Fugui's daughter received when she married: one ox and ten sheep. That's the bottom line. Any less, and my daughter won't marry."

The matchmaker nodded and left Big Foot Sister-in-law's house.

Big Foot Sister-in-law went into the inner room and gave Bamei a triumphant smile. "Look at how much I've secured for you. It's comparable to what the most sought-after girl in the village received. Hee-hee."

Bamei, however, felt a mix of amusement and worry. She thought to herself, "Kauko only has a few coins that the great-grandmother gave him. How will he manage this? I have some scattered silver and jewelry. Could I lend it to him? But how would I get it to him?"

The matchmaker returned to report to Kauko's uncle. "That Big Foot Sister-in-law is usually so mild-mannered, but today, when it came to the bride price, she showed her true colors."

Kau Lame craned his neck and asked, "What did she ask for?"

"First, she demanded two oxen and twenty sheep! I talked her down, and after two hours, we settled on half that."

"Even half is too much. Kauko has nothing, and the bride is someone he brought back himself," Uncle Kau grumbled, frowning. He had hoped to quickly settle the marriage, but now this heavy bride price was a problem. Where would they get the money? Big Foot Sister-in-law was clearly trying to take advantage of them.

Kauko, however, remained calm under pressure. He gently patted his uncle's shoulder and said in a confident yet gentle voice, "Uncle, please help me find two oxen and twenty sheep. Don't worry about the cost. I'll take care of it after dark."

Although his uncle had great faith in Kauko's abilities, he couldn't help but show concern. "I know you're capable, nephew. But please, don't do anything reckless."

"Don't worry, Uncle. Actually, Bamei has some savings. I'll find a chance to quietly get some from her tonight," Kauko replied.

Songmao, eager to help, jumped in and said, "Kauko, I'm fast. Let me go get it for you. It'll save you the trouble."

But Uncle Kau waved his hand. "Songmao, you have your own tasks. Let Kauko and Bamei handle their own matters."

For the entire afternoon, Big Foot Sister-in-law and Bamei talked in the small room. Big Foot Sister-in-law carefully shared her experiences of married life, her words filled with care and expectation. She also patiently taught Bamei how to embroider a silk scarf, her movements skilled and elegant, each stitch revealing years of experience and craftsmanship.

As night fell, Big Foot Sister-in-law softly told Bamei, "Child, rest early tonight. Tomorrow is the most important day of your life—the happiest moment for a woman, but also the beginning of hard work."

Bamei lay alone in the dimly lit room, worrying about how Kauko would manage to buy the oxen and sheep.

Just then, a soft tapping sound interrupted her thoughts. She looked up in confusion and saw Kauko's figure moving outside the window at the back of the house. She quickly put on her clothes and went to the window.

Kauko whispered from outside, "What a beautiful moonlit night. Let's take a walk to the meadow behind the village."

The two of them quietly made their way to the open meadow, their hands tightly clasped, filled with affection. Bamei teased, "Tell me, why did you come to find me at this hour?"

Kauko, slightly embarrassed, lowered his head and said softly, "Actually, I came to borrow money." He paused, then looked up, his gaze meeting the princess's. "But why did you ask for such a high bride price?"

The princess blinked her eyes and smiled mischievously. "I was testing whether you truly love me. Understand?" As she spoke, she took out a small purse from her sleeve and handed it to Kauko.

Kauko excitedly took the purse, his face lighting up with joy. "Thank you, my wife. You are truly my savior."

The princess, however, reached out and pinched Kauko's ear, pretending to be stern. "Not so fast. You can only call me 'wife' after I see the bride price tomorrow."

Kauko gently held the princess's hand and looked at her with deep affection. "Bamei, with you by my side, I am the happiest man in the world. Do you know? Yesterday, when I saw you sitting in the wedding sedan, my heart broke. Can you tell me which deity sent you to me?"

The princess blinked her beautiful, watery eyes and smiled mysteriously. "That's a little secret."

***

On her final moments, Fire Rose leaned close to the princess and said in a weak but pleading voice, "Sister, I am leaving, but my spirit will reside in the rose tree in the Chinmi Garden, next to the violets. Please take care of it. In return, I will tell you Fire Maiden's secret—she fears strong light..."

After moving into the palace, the princess indeed went to Chinmi Garden to find Fire Rose's rose tree. She carefully transplanted it to her own backyard, meticulously removing pests from its roots and trimming away the withered branches. Every day, she watered it with great care, nurturing it with all her heart. In less than half a month, the rose tree regained its vitality, its branches lush and its flowers fragrant. At night, Fire Rose's translucent spirit would dance among the blossoms, like a celestial being.

Sometimes, the princess would sit beneath the tree and chat with Fire Rose. She gently asked, "My dear sister, if you had the chance to choose again, would you rather be a flower fairy forever or a princess?"

The rose tree gently swayed its branches and replied, "I don't want to be a princess. I'd rather be an unknown flower fairy, as long as I have your care, I am happy."

One day, Prince Qin came to visit the princess, and the two of them walked into the garden together.

Prince Qin's warm and magnetic laughter stirred Fire Rose's heart, making her unable to resist her feelings. While the princess was watering and pruning the tree, Fire Rose couldn't help but ask, "Sister, since you don't love Prince Qin, why are you marrying him?"

A trace of sadness flashed in the princess's eyes. "It's my father's command. I have no choice."

Fire Rose boldly said, "Then, sister, why don't you let me have Prince Qin? You already have Kauko."

The princess looked at her in astonishment and softly asked, "Do you really want to become a princess?"

"Who says I don't? I don't even understand myself."

The princess's heart stirred. "I would be willing, but how can I help you become a princess?"

"Just like before, give me a drop or two of your blood. We can help each other," Fire Rose said eagerly.

Without hesitation, the princess quickly took out a sharp pair of scissors and carefully pricked her finger. Drops of bright red blood fell onto Fire Rose's petals.

At that moment, a strange light flashed across the petals.

On the wedding night, Fire Rose transformed into the bride, dressed in a bright red wedding gown, sitting on the festive wedding bed, her head covered with a red veil. Prince Qin, having completed a series of elaborate rituals, walked into the bridal chamber with joy in his heart.

He gently lifted the veil and saw the beauty he had been longing for. A radiant smile spread across his face as he tenderly embraced her. "Fire Rose, my dear wife."

Fire Rose looked at him in shock, her eyes filled with disbelief. "How did you recognize that I'm not the princess?"

Prince Qin smiled and replied, "The princess is beautiful, but she is too cold and aloof. You, on the other hand, are a lively spirit, my true destined love. How could I not recognize you?"

Tears welled up in Fire Rose's eyes. "My Prince Qin, you must cherish me. I've waited two lifetimes for this day."

"I will cherish you, Fire Rose," Prince Qin said gently. "But from now on, I may only call you 'princess' and not 'Fire Rose.' I hope you don't mind."

At that moment, two souls finally found their destined home.

***

The next day, just as the sky was beginning to lighten, Big Foot Sister-in-law was awakened by the barking of a neighbor's dog. Before she could get out of bed, she heard a commotion in her backyard.

She quickly got up and went to the back door to see what was happening. It turned out that Kau Lame and Songmao had brought the bride price. Big Foot Sister-in-law went out to count: two oxen and twenty sheep.

She was shocked. Hadn't they agreed to half that amount? Why had they brought so much? Regardless, she wasn't about to refuse. Feeling pleased, she invited Kau Lame and Songmao inside to rest.

She cooked a bowl of noodles, added three eggs, ladled in two spoonfuls of last night's chicken broth, and sprinkled a handful of popcorn on top. When she brought it to Kau Lame, he was overwhelmed with gratitude and hurriedly stood up to take it, nearly tripping due to his limp.

As she watched him eat heartily, she listened to his constant praise. "Big Foot Sister-in-law, your cooking is amazing. I've traveled far and wide, but I've never tasted noodles this delicious."

The princess, having also gotten up, peeked out from the inner room, but Big Foot Sister-in-law signaled with her eyes for her to stay hidden. After all, she wasn't married yet and shouldn't be seen by the groom's family.

Big Foot Sister-in-law turned to Songmao and asked, "What would you like to eat?"

Songmao smiled and teased, "I thought you'd forgotten about me, only taking care of Uncle Kau. I have a letter here, and I almost didn't want to give it to you." He sat at the table, assuming a mysterious air, and handed her a small note.

Big Foot Sister-in-law took the note, opened it, and scanned the few lines written on it. Curious, she asked, "Who is this from?"

"From Kauko," Songmao replied.

Big Foot Sister-in-law was skeptical. "Are you sure it's not for Bamei?"

"It's for you," Songmao said firmly.

Big Foot Sister-in-law quickly walked into the inner room and handed the note to Bamei. "Help me read this. What does it say?"

Bamei glanced at it and couldn't help but laugh. She whispered to Big Foot Sister-in-law, "One ox and ten sheep are my bride price. The other half is a special gift from Uncle Kau to you. But he didn't say what it's for."

Big Foot Sister-in-law's cheeks flushed red. She tightly gripped the corner of her apron, her eyes sneaking a glance through the door crack at Kau Lame, but she was too embarrassed to go out.

Bamei smiled and nudged her, encouraging her. "Even if you haven't made up your mind yet, you should go out and thank him." She knew this had to be Kauko's doing.

After finishing his noodles, Kau Lame noticed that Big Foot Sister-in-law hadn't come out for a while, so he got up to leave. Only then did Big Foot Sister-in-law rush to the door and call out to his retreating figure, "Your legs aren't well, walk slowly!"

***

Sunlight quietly seeped through the gaps in the curtains, warmly illuminating a corner of the room. A gorgeous red wedding dress lay spread out on the bed, waiting for that important moment. The hem of the dress was embroidered with intricate and vivid floral patterns—peonies in full bloom, osmanthus flowers swaying gracefully, and chrysanthemums standing proudly. The colors were vibrant and lifelike, as if a gust of wind could make them dance.

The princess sat quietly at the dressing table, her hair meticulously combed until it was as smooth as silk, radiating a captivating sheen. She gently turned on the small stool in front of the dressing table, her gaze drifting to the vibrant world outside the window.

The green mountains rose in layers, embraced by clear waters, and the sunlight generously bathed every corner of the land, making the world appear so vivid and serene. Birds sang joyfully on the branches, and the scents of flowers and grass mingled in the air. The princess's heart seemed to float gently with the breeze outside the window, as she imagined herself and her beloved Kauko walking hand in hand through this landscape, spending their lives together. She had already merged her soul with these mountains and waters, with this small village filled with love and warmth.

In the soft glow, the godmother's hands lightly picked up a golden hairpin from a box and carefully adorned the princess's cascading hair with it. It sparkled like stars in the night sky.

The neighbor's eldest sister, not to be outdone, carefully drew a pair of elegant yet strong eyebrows for the princess, then picked up a bright vermilion rouge and gently applied it to the princess's lips, making them bloom like spring flowers, full of vitality and charm.

Next, the godmother and the eldest sister together took out a pair of silver earrings and carefully hung them on the princess's earlobes. The earrings touched her fair skin like a galaxy descending to the mortal world, stars embracing the moon, dazzlingly beautiful.

With the help of family members, the princess slowly put on the dreamlike red dress. The hem of the dress swayed gently, as if catching the rhythm of happiness. The godmother, with eyes full of boundless love, gently placed the large red veil over the bride's head, taking great care not to disturb the carefully arranged hairstyle.

The princess slowly stood up, her expression filled with shyness and anticipation, her eyes like those of a fairy in a painting, radiating happiness. She gently bowed to each of the relatives and neighbors present, her gratitude shining between her brows. The crowd around her erupted in sincere admiration and joyful laughter, genuinely happy for the new life she was about to embark on. At that moment, tears welled up in the godmother's eyes—tears of love for the princess's future happiness.

At that moment of anticipation, the sound of suona horns came from afar, breaking the tranquility of Kau Village and bringing with it a wave of overwhelming joy. The music rose like a rushing stream at times, and at other times fell like a gentle breeze, growing louder as it approached, until it suddenly arrived at the bride's courtyard.

Though covered by the large red veil, the princess's heart clearly felt everything outside the window. Through the hazy red gauze, she faintly saw Kauko, dressed in a bright red robe, each step exuding confidence and anticipation. Beside Kauko, the princess was delighted to see Monkey Three, Monkey Four, Monkey Shang, and Songmao. It turned out that after leaving the princess last night, Kauko had flown to Sien City and brought them back overnight.

The small red hat on his head was slightly tilted, giving him a playful look, and his drooping ears swayed gently with his steps, revealing his carefree nature.

Under the veil, the princess's lips curled into a happy and content smile, for she knew that the person who had captured her heart was waiting outside the window.

The godmother's eyes sparkled with worry and reluctance as she tightly held Bamei's hands, as if trying to convey all her advice and love to the girl about to step into a new chapter of her life.

"Bamei, the road ahead is full of bumps. Tell Kauko to be careful of puddles, mud pits, and rotten wooden bridges. You must hold onto his neck tightly, even if you break a bone, don't let go."

The godmother continued, "Bamei, beware of the scarecrows on the road. They might hide mountain bandits looking to kidnap brides. You must hold onto his neck tightly, even if it comes down to the last moment, don't let go."

Bamei tightly held the godmother's hands, her eyes shining with determination. "Godmother, Bamei remembers."

The godmother gently stroked Bamei's head. "Good. Bamei, the groom is waiting anxiously outside. After you go out, he will carry you all the way home. No matter what, don't let anyone else take you away! Now, I'm going to open the door. Think carefully! Once you step out of this door, you're no longer a member of this family."

At that moment, the suona band began to play a familiar and heartwarming melody—"Cangshan Sister." Each note tugged at the heartstrings, as if narrating her years of emotions. This melody had accompanied Bamei through countless lonely and quiet nights, and now, hearing it again, it felt like a soft thread pulling her through time, back to the beautiful moment when she first met Kauko.

Bamei remembered the warm conversations in the small attic, the figures chasing and playing in the wild, the sky dyed red by the setting sun, the crystal-clear streams, and those days filled with twists and turns.

Her tears could no longer be held back, not only as a reflection of the past but also as an anticipation and longing for the future.

Kauko stood quietly in front of the wooden door, a gentle smile in his eyes.

Behind him, the festive wedding procession was neatly arranged, drummers waving their drumsticks, the sound of gongs and drums joyful and rhythmic. Children ran happily among the procession, their laughter mixing with the dust kicked up by their feet, becoming an indispensable part of the celebration. The elderly leaned to the side, occasionally murmuring words of blessing or reminiscing. The neighboring wives gathered in a circle, discussing the bride and groom, their words filled with enthusiasm.

Yet for Kauko, the surrounding excitement seemed to belong to another world. His mind was focused solely on the door before him and the person behind it.

His hand trembled slightly as it touched the weathered wooden door, as if he could feel the heartbeat on the other side.

The door creaked open slowly, letting in dust and sunlight. In the hazy light and shadow of the door, the outline of the bride gradually became clear. Under the veil, her eyes held a faint smile, like the first ray of morning sunlight.

The bride slowly walked to the door, holding one end of a red silk ribbon in her hand. In her eyes, the glimmering light seemed to pierce through the red veil, reaching deep into his soul. She gracefully tossed the other end of the ribbon, which traced a beautiful arc in the air.

The thrown ribbon gently landed in Kauko's hand, carrying her warmth and presence. His fingers tightly wrapped around the ribbon, holding onto the hope and happiness of the future. They looked at each other, their gazes meeting, telling the story of a lifetime of love.

www.ingramcontent.com/pod-product-compliance
Lightning Source LLC
Chambersburg PA
CBHW070409310726
48977CB00003B/618